# Aqua

**R.S. O'Neal**

The Quest for the Aura series: Book Three

**Books in the Quest for the Aura series:**

- The Lightworker Trials

- Terra

- Aqua

- Caelus

- Incendium

Note to readers: The Quest for the Aura series is set in beautiful, sunny Australia, and all spelling and grammar is consistent with Australian English.

Aqua print edition ISBN: 978-0-9954473-4-9

*To Phelps and Edie*
*Who fought the Gothak and won*


*And the van Leeuwens, a second family*
*Ingrid, my very long-time friend*


"Trust your mind, and your conviction" – General Gel Lithium Silica

"Again, but better!" – The Unlit

"Keep your Light on" – Ranger Chrysanthe

"If your eyes are on the sun, you will not see the shadows" – Warrigal
Gundungurra

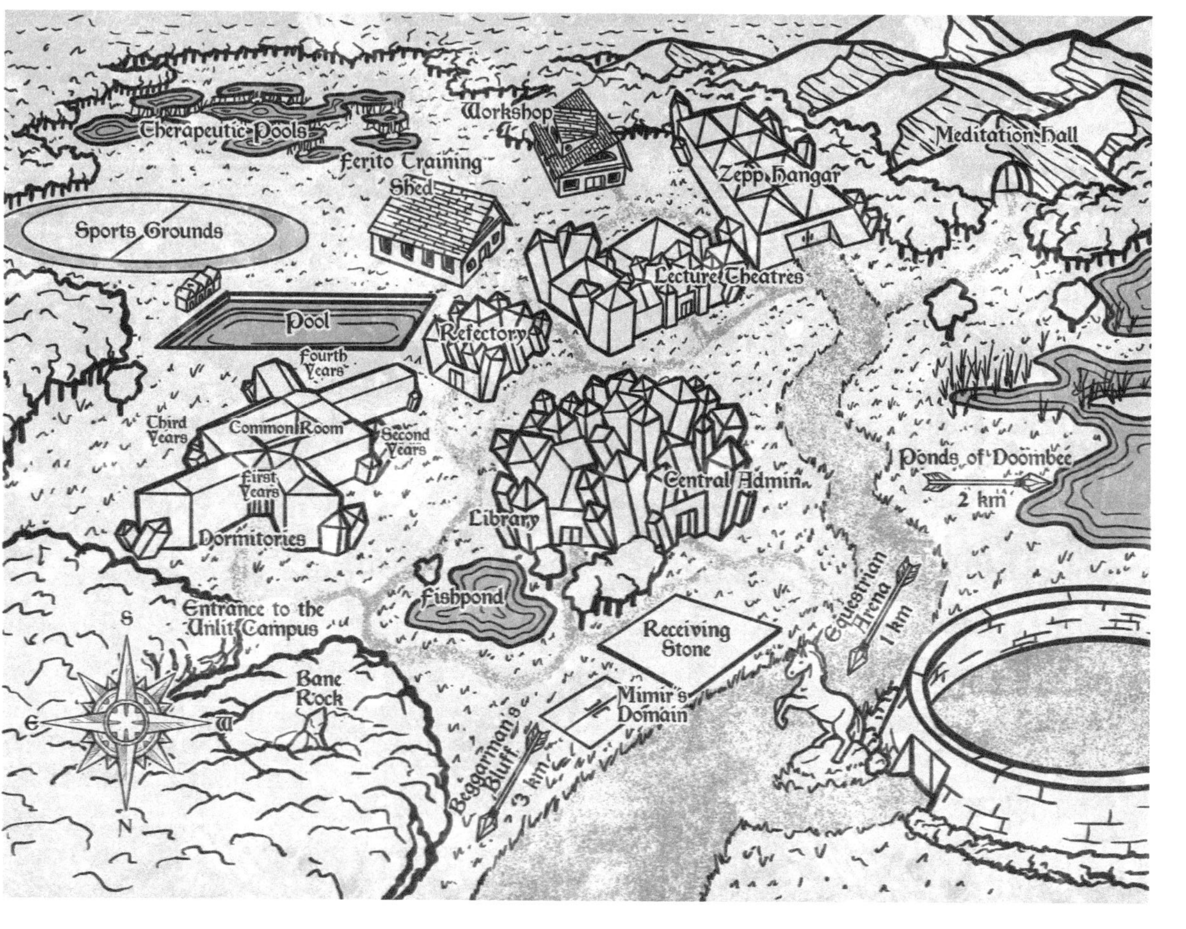

Therapeutic Pools
Workshop
Meditation Hall
Ferito Training Shed
Zepp Hangar
Sports Grounds
Lecture Theatres
Pool
Refectory
Fourth Years
Common Room
Second Years
Third Years
Central Admin
First Years
Ponds of Doombee
2 km
Dormitories
Library
Fishpond
Entrance to the Unlit Campus
Receiving Stone
Equestrian Arena
1 km
Bane Rock
Mimir's Domain
Beggarman's Bluff
3 km
S
E
W
N

# CHAPTER ONE

"ARGH! I'VE DONE IT again," Abby complained, rubbing her hand on her shorts. "That Bingi sap is so sticky, I can't stop it going everywhere."

Eyre nodded as she held the red crystal carefully and tried to drop it into the Bingi sap that filled the hole she'd made in her staff. Even with a steady hand it was hard to set the stone into the wood without it tilting and sitting crookedly and she'd had several goes at getting it right. Finally, after gentle nudging, she got it in place.

The uncut facets of the walnut-sized ruby were a deep crimson against the rainbow colours of her staff and she felt a pang as she remembered the TACI test in Terra last year, and where the stone had come from. Eyre and her friends had each found a stone on the desert sands of the Pyre of Va. In memory of their guide Shuvai, who had been killed by the Gothak, Eyre, Nick, Abby and Beatrice were setting their rubies into their staffs.

Eventually they each managed to get the crystals sitting straight and they looked at each other. After the past couple of months, and the hours of talking about that horrible day, there was nothing left to say about it, but they each now had a permanent reminder of the courage of the Nemoris guide who had saved their lives at the expense of her own.

After a long moment Beatrice sighed. "Let's leave them there to dry and go for a final walk in the bush. Whittaker Ray said he'd take us at two, when he gets back from the Echelon meeting."

Eyre and her friends carefully laid their staffs next to each other on the ground so that the rubies wouldn't move while the Bingi sap dried. Then they headed off towards the sandy track that led away from the campsite.

As they walked through the eucalypts, Eyre's thoughts were sombre. The weeks of the Christmas break had been dismal after the trauma of the events in Terra. Seeing the hundreds of dead Aether strewn across the battlefields was a sight none of them would ever forget, and knowing the dire consequences of that day made it even worse. All the Aether in the adult Lightworker population had been killed in one massive attack by the terrible creatures of the Underworld, the Gothak, which had decimated the Lightworkers' chances of reinstating the Aura for years.

Eyre's gloomy thoughts continued as she trudged along. Her friends had not realised it, but during the journey to Terra, Eyre had shown signs that she might be an Aether. However, after an intense fight with the Gothak and a huge scorpion-like creature called a Tuus, her powers had left her completely—even her normal Lightworking powers—and it seemed less and less likely as the weeks went on with no change, that they would ever come back.

Her friends had been sensitive about Eyre losing her Viq, and they had practised Ferito over the holidays, but there was none of the fun of the previous Christmas when they had only just received their Viq and the joy of levitating, telepathy and telekinesis was just new. This year, the days and weeks had just plodded on drearily, and Christmas came and went without the usual festive feel. The only bright spot in the weeks at the camp was that Ben Perrill hadn't turned up. Eyre had found out last year that his family owned the last cabin in the group at the campsite, but since Ben had attacked and nearly killed Eyre during the last Christmas holidays, he hadn't been back.

Eyre had spent some time in the basement of her cabin, studying the genealogy of her family line that was stored in her Wisdom. This time, there were no new messages from her parents, and the catastrophic words that had precipitated all the adult Aether of Entis to head to the Alterworlds, were now written permanently in the pages of her Wisdom: *The Isars can be seen by the Aether during the Leonid.* Every time Eyre saw those words she felt sick, wishing that she hadn't passed the message on to Whittaker Ray, an action that ultimately caused the destruction of all the Aether who had travelled to Terra and the other Alterworlds.

The sense of responsibility for that disaster weighed heavily on her, even though Whittaker Ray had tried to ease her pain. He'd found her one night sitting alone on the steps of her cabin, unable to sleep. Eyre suspected that Jengles had alerted him, because a flash of red beard disappeared behind Nick's cabin shortly after Whittaker Ray appeared at the front door. He came over to sit beside her on the step, wearing a striped dressing gown over his pyjamas and slippers. If her thoughts hadn't been so dark, she would have laughed; it was so out of character for the usually formally-dressed teacher.

"This would have happened regardless," he'd said after a long pause to Eyre during the conversation that followed. "As soon as the Aether headed to the Alterworlds, their fate was sealed. If anyone has to bear responsibility for that, it would be me rather than you—I didn't take the need for secrecy seriously enough, and that's my fault." He paused and shook his head before continuing softly. "I guess I just never expected a Lightworker to betray us all..." His face contorted with a cataclysm of guilt and pain. Then he looked back at Eyre and sighed.

"It was a terrible, horrible thing to happen, but the Aether knew it was dangerous and we must keep trying to fight the Gothak and find the key to reinstating the Aura. We must keep the faith that the Light will guide us. The Isars must be located, and perhaps you might be able to help with that, the Light willing." At that point he'd stopped and studied the night sky. The Leonid meteor shower had long passed, and there was no sign now of the streaking flashes of light across the black sky. "I guess we'll find out next November."

Later on, still unable to sleep, Eyre had looked out her window to see Whittaker Ray and Jengles deep in conversation beside the flickering flames of the silver matrix. However, she couldn't even guess what they'd been talking about.

As Eyre followed her friends up the uneven track, she thought about the coming year and her gloom deepened. She'd thought she had resigned herself to being part of the Unlit, but as the time drew nearer, it was harder and harder to think about. She wanted her Viq back desperately, and she didn't want to rejoin the school as a second-year in the Unlit student body. She felt she was such a disappointment, that she had somehow failed by losing her Viq. And trying to catch up to her peers at the Unlit Section— socially as well as academically—was a prospect she was not looking forward to. She had enjoyed her first year so much at the Academy, and she desperately wanted to go back as an Elevated student.

But being pragmatic, she knew she had to get used to the idea of her change in circumstances. This afternoon they were heading back to the Academy and beginning their second year at the school. It would be harder this time round, but Eyre had decided to make the best of it, despite her misgivings.

Finally, they arrived at the summit of the track, which overlooked a huge canyon. Up here, at the top of the mountain, the goal was to see the birds that circled in the updrafts looking for prey. Peregrine falcons and Wedge-tailed eagles in particular were territorial in the area, and spotting the spectacular creatures was worth the long journey up the hill. There was also lots of wildlife to see on the way, if you were quiet and had sharp eyes, and they all had made several trips up the track hoping to see kangaroos, koalas and dingoes.

Today there were a number of falcons and eagles in the air, and after watching the soaring birds for half an hour, they stood up to leave. But a strange clomping and humming from the undergrowth made them pause. Feeling a bit anxious, Eyre thought back to the many unfriendly encounters she'd had with creatures in the bush, and she strained to see what was making the noise.

In a moment her question was answered when a line of Mimir, the red-headed dwarfs who lived under the ground, stomped through the bushes into the clearing. They were carrying many branches, and their faces were red with the effort of the climb and hauling the wood. Jengles was at the front of the line, sweating and looking grumpier than ever.

"Here we go," Beatrice said in a resigned tone, looking at Eyre. "Get yourself ready, petal. Your cheer squad is here."

Eyre tried not to grimace. Every time the Mimir came near her, they seemed incapable of speech, and had a tendency to prostrate themselves in front of her, smile stupidly or look like they wanted to kiss her feet. It had been rather awkward over the past year, to say the least.

However, this time, Jengles muttered in annoyance when he saw them. He gave Abby, Beatrice and Nick his usual disparaging up and down look, and then when he turned to Eyre, he displayed none of the fluster she'd become accustomed to.

"Just gathering wood for the Mantle Basin," he said shortly. "We'll keep going."

Beatrice, Abby and Nick's mouths hung open as the group of Mimir marched past Eyre without even a second look. Even Eyre had to admit it was a surprise; she'd gotten so used to the usual uproar whenever they faced her. And then a feeling of disappointment came flooding through her. Even the Mimir knew she was a dud, that her powers were gone. The crushing feeling of failure flooded over her, and she was unusually quiet on the way down. Her friends could find nothing to say either as they trudged back after the astonishing event—they realised things had changed and Eyre could see they also thought it was because she had lost her Light.

Eventually they arrived back at the campsite and found that the Bingi sap had dried, shrinking tightly and holding the glowing red stones snugly in the shaft of their staffs. Eyre held her staff up so that the light shone through the crystal at the top—she'd found it in her dive at the grotto last year—a large pink diamond that flung rose-coloured hues out in all directions. Sourcing their crystal was usually a momentous occasion in a student's life, but for Eyre it had been a terrible event at the beginning of that first year, as she'd nearly drowned when an unknown creature trapped her at the bottom of the pool.

Eyre contemplated this as she studied her staff. She looked at the sparkling ruby and she felt a shard of sadness as she thought about Shuvai, and the sacrifice she'd made for the Lightworkers. But then she finally found a smile and twirled the rainbow- coloured wood, made from a branch of the Rainbow Eucalyptus, around her head in a parody of a martial arts she'd seen... way, way back in the times when she lived an obliviously normal life.

"Well to be honest, I never was actually able to use this stupid stick at all, so losing my Viq won't make much of a difference to me!"

Beatrice laughed and hugged her. "Your Light will come back, Eyre, give it time," she said fiercely. "Your body is still recovering. And you're not getting rid of us, regardless if it comes back or not! We're a team— BANE will continue, and no matter where you are, we'll come and find you!" She was referring to the signal they'd created last year. 'BANE' was an acronym for their names, and a coded message meaning that they needed to meet secretly. The designated meeting place was behind a sandstone rock in the bush that surrounded the Academy of Light campus.

Eyre felt comforted by Beatrice's words. It wasn't as if Eyre was losing her friends; it was just that she felt like damaged goods, embarrassed to go back to campus and admit to people that she still had no Lightworking powers. Everyone had assumed her Viq would return, but it hadn't. And after her trek with her friends to the top of the hill, the Mimir had probably just confirmed that this change was permanent.

Eyre's thoughts were interrupted by a bright flash as Whittaker Ray arrived, emerging by the Mantle Basin. He stood as the light faded and waited for them to pick up their bags. Apart from their clothing, they all had their staffs, and both Abby and Eyre had musical instruments: Eyre was bringing her guitar with the beautifully reconstructed neck that Jax had crafted from a piece of rainbow eucalyptus wood, and Abby had her theremin and her tortilis, the instruments she'd started to learn in first year. Nick had an armful of palum that they'd borrowed to practise their Clasis over the holidays, and Beatrice was wearing a large straw hat, her latest favourite, and carrying a blue and green potted plant, obviously something she had decided was an essential school item. And all of them had a precious lux in a string bag—all Academy students had been given one of the luxes from their TACI expedition to Terra last year. Whittaker Ray took in the ramshackle group and the odd assortment of belongings.

"I see you've thought of everything," he said, his blue eyes twinkling. "Come over here and we'll get going." They shuffled over and huddled together, holding on to each other.

A second later there was a flash of light and they all disappeared.

# CHAPTER TWO

THIS YEAR TERRIGAL FURNACE picked them up in the Zepp, along with Georgia Mahoney, Luke Jordan and a couple of new students. Unlike the Ranger, after giving them a quick greeting, Terrigal was silent as he drove the bouncing vehicle along the dusty road to the Academy. But the whirling hologram was there as usual, filling them in on any information that was new for the year. There were a couple of new students who craned their necks as the Zepp bounced along past the notable features of the campus.

Eyre was lost in thought as they approached the huge shards of crystal that made up the school's infrastructure, and a pang went through her as she saw the light gleaming from the planes of the magnificent quartz slabs. She was joining the Unlit, and they were not located in the main school campus. She wasn't sure where the Unlit students studied, but she knew she would be leaving this part of the campus behind.

Terrigal brought them to a halt in front of the Central Admin building. He turned around.

"You're to meet in the Common Room at 4pm," he said and Beatrice, Nick and Abby started to pick up their bags. Eyre wasn't sure whether she should get out, but Terrigal waved at her to go with them.

"All of you."

"That's wonderful, Eyre," Beatrice beamed as they got out of the Zepp. "We get to keep you for a while!"

They knew where they were going this year, and headed across campus to the second-year dormitory. The residential halls were built in the shape of an Inguz. Last year they had been in the northern arms of the complex; this year they would be in the western part of the central arms, which housed the second-year students. Nick left to go down the boys' arm of the wing, and Beatrice, Eyre and Abby walked down the hall looking at the names on the doors. Someone was approaching from the other direction and Eyre groaned softly when she saw who it was.

"I'm surprised to see you here, I heard you haven't got your Viq back," Pheria said with a small smirk as their paths intersected. "Sorry about that," she added after a pause that was a bit too long.

Eyre gave a tight smile. News obviously travelled fast around here. "Well apparently I'm to join everyone this afternoon. You're not rid of me yet."

Abby snickered at Pheria and pushed past her. The tall girl looked annoyed at being laughed at.

"I'm just heading off to find Jax," Pheria said pointedly. "We came together."

Eyre said nothing but looked irritated as Pheria left.

Beatrice rolled her eyes. "Ah, ignore her, she's just insecure," she laughed as they headed down the hall.

"Here it is!" Abby called from the far end of the corridor. "Eyre, you're with *us—again!* Yay!"

Eyre hurried down to the room and was elated to see her name on the door with Beatrice and Abby's. It looked like she wasn't going anywhere! And she liked the position of the room—right near the fire exit, so they could come and go without anyone knowing. For some reason, that made her feel secure.

They dumped their bags on their beds and Eyre put her staff in the special holder in the cupboard. As she clipped it in she ran her finger softly over the ruby that was now securely set into the rainbow wood. It would forever be a symbol to her of courage and self-sacrifice, and a memory of the darkness that was lurking out there. And it would always be there to prompt her into doing the best she possibly could, Lit or Unlit.

This year there was no difficulty with the lighting system in their room—Beatrice was a pro by now and filled the room with a soft pink glow.

"Calm before the storm," she said, plonking herself on the bed. "Here we go again!"

Abby shoved her theremin and tortilis under her bed. "I wonder who we'll have as a Dorm supervisor?" she said. "I'm a bit sad we won't have the Sergeant this year."

Eyre nodded as she unpacked her bags. The Sergeant was gruff, but she had a good heart and only wanted the best for the students. She'd been a major force in their lives for the time they'd been at the Academy and Eyre would miss her daily contact with the stern instructor.

No sooner had Abby uttered the words than there was a voice calling in dulcet tones down the hall.

"Girls? Girls? Please come out of your rooms." Beatrice and Abby looked intrigued, but Eyre, who recognized the voice, moved slower, trying not to guffaw. *This* was going to be interesting.

Doors opened up and down the corridor and girls edged out of their rooms and leaned against the walls. Jemima Periwinkle, resplendent in a bright yellow dress with eye-shattering purple stripes, beamed at them all.

"Welcome to second year!" she cooed. "I am your supervisor this year, and I am *so* looking forward to getting to know you!"

Eyre tried to smile, but felt herself grimacing instead. She'd suffered through Jemima Periwinkle's interminable genealogy lessons all last year, and she couldn't imagine what sort of mentor she was going to be. From Eyre's experience, the main skill of the large woman was boring people into slumber and an expertise at putting together a matching ensemble. As Eyre took in the purple shoes and co-ordinated scarf, she sighed. *By the Light!*

Jemima Periwinkle twinkled her fingers, which were also painted a fluorescent, sparkling purple. "Toodle-oo. Once you're sorted I'll see you over at the Common Room. Don't be late."

She walked away down the corridor, her voluminous dress swishing past the girls lined against the walls. Eyre watched her go. Trying to accept that she was the Sergeant's sister was like trying to decipher an illogical puzzle. About the only thing she shared with the Sergeant was her size—they were both very big women. Eyre was amazed that they were from the same family.

But her thoughts were cut short as Beatrice dragged them back inside the room. "Well then, let's make the most of the time before the meeting!"

Abby groaned as Beatrice pulled out Crystallography from her cupboard and tossed it on her bed with a huge grin.

Eyre laughed and jumped on the bed as Beatrice sorted out the crystals and dice. Eyre made room for Abby to sit beside her.

"Come on Abby, let's lose the game for the hundredth time!"

# CHAPTER THREE

THE NOISE IN THE Common Room was overpowering as Eyre and her three friends walked in. Groups of students were slouched on the stuffed chairs, leaning against the bookshelves, or sprawled on the ground, talking fast as they caught up from the holidays.

Eyre scanned the crowd, but she wasn't kidding herself. She noticed a lot of familiar faces, but she knew there was only one she was really looking for, and it didn't take her long to spot him. His black hair gleaming, Jax lounged against the wall as he talked with Rigmar. Jax laughed suddenly at something Rigmar said, and then as if sensing her gaze, his green eyes looked across at her. Eyre waved awkwardly, reflecting in annoyance that she always seemed to get caught out this way, but was relieved when Jax smiled a genuine smile at her. But to her disappointment, he made no move to come over. It seemed that the distance he'd put between them was firmly back in place this year.

Beatrice was talking to Robeson, and Abby was deep in discussion with Jensen, who now walked on his prosthetic leg without any hesitation at all. Eyre wandered over to join them as Dean Fraser and Whittaker Ray took the centre of the room. The Sergeant walked in beside them and her booming voice cut off all conversation.

"Silence!" she bellowed as she thumped her staff on the ground.

"Thank you Sergeant," Dean Fraser said. "I want to welcome you all to the Academy and I trust you have returned refreshed and rejoicing." A titter of laughter travelled the room as the older students acknowledged the traditional joke. The Dean paused a moment and surveyed the faces turned his way.

"We had a tragic end to our school year last year. It will never leave our memories, and for those of you who were there, I hope that you have had time to process the events that occurred during the TACI tests. If anyone is having difficulty this year because of that terrible occurrence, or indeed for any reason, please reach out to our staff. We have measures in place to help you, as we understand it may not be easy to come to terms with it.

"On a brighter note, we are looking forward to this year and meeting our new students. Please help them to settle in, and we hope you older students will be the role models we would expect of an Academy student. And we hope this year will be fulfilling and successful for all of you. Live with Courage and Light."

After polite clapping, the Sergeant spoke again. "Tomorrow you will pick up your uniforms from the uniform shop, and get the schedule for your assigned classes and extra-curricular activities. Let me know if there are any problems with this. You may return to your rooms; dinner is at the Refectory at 6pm."

A hubbub arose as students started to leave, but the Sergeant's voice cut above it. "Eyre, would you see me please."

A stone dropped in Eyre's stomach. She knew she wasn't going to be part of the normal school program this year, but accepting it was difficult. As she walked over to the Sergeant she saw a number of students looking at her curiously. Most of them had heard of the girl who had lost her Viq—it was big news, as it was such a rare occurrence; most of them didn't realise it could even happen. Eyre walked towards the Sergeant, trying to look nonchalant—she didn't want anyone to realise how much this mattered to her.

As she pushed through the crowd, the hairs on the back of Eyre's neck prickled and she turned around to see Professor Vela staring at her intently, a malevolent look on his face. She hadn't realised he was here, and when he turned away quickly she wondered if she'd imagined it. But knowing his style, she doubted that. And then, just to complete the hat-trick, she saw that Ben Perrill and one of his cronies, Tec Langford, were still in the room, sitting in the faded lounge chairs and laughing at her. She gritted her teeth. Ben Perrill would have been *ecstatic* to have heard the news about Eyre losing her powers. And it showed in his face, which was positively gleeful. Not wanting to give him the chance to come over and rub it in, she headed fast for the Sergeant.

"Hello Eyre," the Sergeant said, her face giving nothing away. "How are you doing?"

"I'm fine, thank you. I don't have my Viq back yet though." The Sergeant nodded.

"That is a shame, I'm sorry to hear it. You were making great progress," she said. "These things are unpredictable, and there is a chance you may regain your Light energy, but until that happens—if it does—you will be joining the Unlit for your education. Come and sit with me and I will let you know what has been decided."

By now most of the students had cleared out of the Common Room; only a last few stragglers were heading for the door. The big room was empty, and a breeze from the entrance ran across Eyre's shoulders as she sat in one of the reading chairs opposite the Sergeant.

"We are very sorry this has happened, Eyre," the Sergeant began. "You showed great courage last year, and we are extremely grateful that you are still with us. Because we are uncertain exactly what may happen with you this year, it has been decided that you will stay in the dormitory and eat morning and evening meals with your friends instead of joining the Unlit students in their barracks." The Sergeant smiled as she saw Eyre's eyes brighten. "However, instead of the Light skills training, you will join the Unlit in their curriculum, which I hope you will find interesting. Tomorrow morning I will have a second-year Unlit student come and collect you to take you down to the Unlit compound, and I would like you be here at 8.30am to meet them. Do you have any questions?"

Eyre thought for a moment. "What do I wear?"

"Just normal clothes; you will be provided with a uniform when you get to the Unlit compound."

When it was evident Eyre had no more questions, the Sergeant stood up. She took in the slump of Eyre's shoulders, and her stern eyes softened.

"Being part of the Unlit is an honour, Eyre," she began. "The Pinnae have a saying 'When the mighty sea rages, and the foul tempest blows, hold tight to the coral. Calm seas will always follow.'"

The Sergeant's eyes were kind as she continued. "The Pinnae know that tough times don't last forever, and your 'coral' is your support system: what you've learnt, and the people you can lean on. You see this as a failure, and a trial and I will agree that it won't be easy. But I am sure you will one day feel grateful that you are with the Unlit. You will realise that perhaps they are the 'calm seas', or the gift, that the Pinnae refer to. In any case, good luck and please feel free to come and see me if you need help at any time."

The Sergeant left the Common Room and Eyre headed back to her dormitory, feeling relieved that at least she wasn't going to completely lose touch with her friends this year, but definitely not feeling grateful about anything.

# CHAPTER FOUR

EYRE SHUT THE DOOR quietly to her room so she wouldn't disturb her friends. Abby was lying on her back, mouth open and snoring softly, and Beatrice was face-down in her pillow with her arms above her head, still sound asleep. Last night they couldn't help it—they'd talked late into the night and Eyre could feel the effects of the lack of sleep this morning. She yawned as she slipped outside into the crisp morning air and rubbed her eyes as she headed towards the Equestrian Centre.

She'd decided that she couldn't start the year without a visit to the grumpy old Lighthorse who had been assigned to her last year. Ischyros had shown a decided lack of enthusiasm about Eyre as a partner—indeed, it seemed his greatest joy was launching her off his back into the stratosphere. But she'd developed a soft spot for the old horse over the year despite his attitude, and she'd decided she would continue to visit him even though she was no longer part of the equestrian class.

She stretched her calf muscles for a few minutes, then took a deep breath and started to run through the campus at a fast pace. By the time she'd arrived at the stables, she was sweating and red-faced, but she was glad she was back into the routine she'd adopted all last year.

Before arriving at the Academy, Eyre had never been keen on sports. But over the months of training she had developed a love of running and the way that being fit made her feel. She intended to keep up the routine this year too. If she'd learnt nothing else, it was that events could change in an instant, and it was better to be strong and prepared when foul creatures were after you.

She walked past all the Lighthorses in the stables: proud, shining animals with brave hearts and acute intelligence. Their ears pricked as they watched her curiously and then returned to their oats. Not their Lightworker. Finally, Eyre arrived at the door to Ischyros's stable. He didn't like other horses, so he was housed away from them in an old stable at the end of the complex. He didn't really like Eyre either, she mused ruefully, but she was going to keep him well-groomed this year. Ever since the old horse had cried when she played him a song last year, she had felt a bond with him that she couldn't explain, despite his perpetual bad temper.

This morning was no exception. He looked up briefly as she entered and then went back to his breakfast.

"I thought I'd got rid of you," he said through a mouthful of oats. Eyre smiled.

"Nope. I'm back. I'm coming here anyway, so you may as well get used to it."

The old horse harrumphed and kept his head down, but he didn't protest as Eyre started to brush his coat. Over the break he had lost some of the condition he'd had last year, so she worked hard to get the mud out and untangle his mane. Finally she oiled his hooves until they shone and she straightened up with a satisfied smile.

"There you go," she said. "You look beautiful again." She put the grooming gear back in the bucket and let herself out of the stable. Ischyros still said nothing, but at least he wasn't being rude. That was a step forward, she thought.

By the time she got back to her room Beatrice and Abby were up and dressed, although moving slowly.

"Why did we stay up so late?" Abby moaned. "I'm so tired!"

"It's your fault," Beatrice said. "Couldn't shut you up!" Abby snorted and with a flick of her wrist, sent a beam of Light energy that launched her pillow into Beatrice's face.

"Child," Beatrice said as the pillow dropped to the bed. But there wasn't a repeat of the wild pillow fight they'd had last year and Eyre realised her friends were being sensitive to the fact that Eyre couldn't use her Viq any more. Sighing, she resigned herself to it. Inevitably there were going to be many such moments.

"Come on," she said, flinging a pillow into Abby's face. "Let's go and get breakfast, and then I'll find out what Viq-less purgatory I've been assigned to!"

# CHAPTER FIVE

AFTER BREAKFAST BEATRICE AND Abby headed back to the room and Eyre hung around in the Common Room, wondering who would come from the Unlit to get her. The clattering of feet outside the door and voices chattering softened in the hallway outside until finally silence reigned.

When the door opened, Eyre turned with a smile. But her smile faded as she saw who was entering the room with a mean smirk.

"Airhead!" Ben Perrill said. "Off to join the Losers' club? Rankins told me his family call them the Un-*Fit*." He snickered and a nasty gleam came in his eye.

"Unfit—so perfect. You're unfit for anything now, Lightward."

Eyre felt the familiar anger begin to build inside her, but this time it was tinged with uncertainty. She was not used to being without Light energy and she felt strangely defenceless. Ben moved towards her with barely restrained glee, his huge bulk seeming to fill the room. Despite herself, Eyre took a step backwards and her eyes darted around the room for an escape.

But then Ben seemed to get a glazed look in his eyes and Eyre felt a wave of dizziness pass over her. She shook her head and jumped in shock, because someone was standing in front of her. Where did he come from? Ben Perrill got a similar fright and shouted out loud.

"Geez! Sneaky little twerp!"

The slight boy in front of him smiled. "I've come to collect the fortunate student who is joining the Unlit. Eyre, would you come with me? Ben, I'm sure you won't mind getting out of our way?"

Ben made a sound like a dumpster clanging shut and reached with meat-hands towards the boy. But then Eyre felt another wave of dizziness and when her brain finally kicked back in gear, she was walking out the door behind the boy, leaving Ben standing in the middle of the room with a stupefied look on his face. Eyre rubbed her forehead, trying to clear her foggy brain.

"You have good timing," she said, looking back at Ben. "I think I just avoided becoming Ben's practise-dummy."

The boy laughed, his brown eyes twinkling. "Avoidance is something we do very well! I'm Christopher."

Eyre's befuddled brain finally kicked in. She'd thought he looked familiar. "Yes, I remember, Christopher Fingleton—you were in Water Lodge with me at the TEP training. So, you were accepted to the Academy after all!"

Christopher nodded, beaming. "It was a relief, and I have to say I've enjoyed the first year. Come on, we're heading down that path over there."

They walked along a rough track that meandered behind the Academy. It was largely surrounded by bush and the path itself was sandy and poorly-marked. Eyre was glad she hadn't had to find the way herself. Finally, they stopped in a small clearing. It was lovely in the peace and quiet, with the birds calling around them, but Eyre wondered where they were going.

"Here we are then, follow me," Christopher said and walked into the clearing and disappeared. Eyre stood a moment in shock and then hurried to follow. As she walked to the middle of the clearing there was a wave of cold tinged with an electric shock that she was familiar with. When she strode through she emerged into a compound that was wild with activity. People were rushing everywhere; there were falcons flying from the arms of students and arrows shooting through the air to thump into large targets. And the sound of weapons clanging was deafening as students dressed in brown uniforms fought each other in an arena as others sitting in the stadium cheered wildly. Eyre's mouth was agape as she looked around in shock. Where had all *this* come from?

"The compound is masked and warded," Christopher explained. "So that only those who are meant to be here can get through. You've been cleared, so you can come and go as you wish. That feeling as you come through is something you need to get used to though."

Eyre already knew the feeling of passing through a ward from her trips to the basement at her cabin, and she had walked through a mask at the Arant exhibit at the Sector Fair last year. But she didn't mention that as she followed Christopher through the surging mass of students towards a long rectangular building constructed out of rock.

"It's free time," Christopher explained as they walked along. "So students are able to spend the time how they like. Sometimes they practise and sometimes they chill out in the common room. I'll show you where that is later, but for the moment I'm to take you to see Whittaker Ray and UD1."

Eyre looked at him. "Whittaker Ray?"

Christopher laughed at her raised eyebrows. "Yes, Mr Ray is here quite often actually, he meets with UD1 and speaks to the students about what's happening in the Academy in general. But it's unusual for a student to meet with them—you must be *very* important." He laughed as he said it, but his eyes were slightly quizzical as he led Eyre into the large rock building.

It was carved from large sandstone blocks that were covered in runes and carvings, mystical scenes and the odd sparkling gemstone set into the rock. In many places the shape of an Inguz was apparent in the lines of angular symbols.

Christopher led her to a room in the building and then bid her farewell. Eyre walked in with a sense of trepidation; she had no idea what was ahead of her.

Inside the room was a large round table cut from what Eyre took to be polished obsidian. Whittaker Ray and UD1 were already there, deep in conversation but they both stopped talking and got up from their chairs as she entered. Eyre stood awkwardly as Whittaker Ray indicated a seat next to them.

"Come and sit down, Eyre, I know you will be keen to find out what is happening."

"Nice to see you again, Eyre," said UD1. The slight man was dressed as usual in brown clothing; nothing stood out about him at all. Brown clothes, brown hair, brown glasses—one could almost be fooled into thinking he was the most boring, mundane person one could meet. But then you looked into his autumn-brown eyes—kind, smart and all-knowing, and you realised you were dealing with someone quite unique. Eyre was happy to see him again; he had made a huge impression on her and her fellow classmates during the TEP examinations. And apparently, he had once won the National Ferito competition, something that was quite amazing for a Lightworker without Viq. But it seemed such a long time ago that she had taken his class. So much had happened since then.

Whittaker Ray waved for her to sit and they all sat down at the gleaming black table. Whittaker Ray got straight to the point.

"You're an enigma to us all, Eyre," he started. "First of all, your strange Inguz, your Viq that was sometimes incredibly powerful and yet sometimes almost non-existent. And always seemingly beyond your control."

"From various events that occurred, we felt early on that you had the signs of an Aether," UD1 continued in his soft voice. "And yet, no Aether has *ever* been born of an Aether, so we thought it was impossible. You have had us all confounded."

Whittaker Ray nodded. "Typically, Aether do not have an Inguz, although they have powers much stronger than normal Lightworkers. We wonder now that perhaps because you are an Aether from an Aether, it has accounted for your unusual Inguz; that somehow your Light powers have broken through the usual masking. That the Aether have no Inguz has been a benefit to the Lightworking community—they usually become part of the Unlit to keep them hidden. Until now this has protected the Aether from the Gothak."

Whittaker Ray hesitated, and then continued, his voice soft and regretful. He looked at Eyre and shook his head slightly. "Your parents obviously wanted to protect you, which is why they didn't tell anyone about your special power. The classes you took in self-control as a child should have alerted me—but to be honest," there was a pause before he continued, and there was pain in his voice, "it never crossed my mind that your parents would not have told me if they knew you were an Aether. When an Aether is born they have a blue Inguz on the crown of their head for two years until it fades. I remember now that your mother always made you and your brother wear a knitted cap or a sunhat—so I now assume he must have been an Aether also. But back then, I really had no idea—I never knew. Eric had red hair like you, and your mother would tell us the caps and hats were to protect your fair skin from the sun..." His voice caught on the last words and he looked down at the table. UD1's kind eyes looked at him and UD1 carried on the conversation when he realised Whittaker Ray couldn't.

"The Gothak have always targeted the Aether because of the prophesy Madame Overmantle foretold at a meeting of the Determinant Dozen many years ago: that an Aether would precipitate the end of the Gothak's rise to power. Unfortunately, that information was passed on by someone—*By the Light!*—to the Dark forces, and we cannot even fathom *who* would do that. But now that the Gothak know exactly what the Aether can do, they will be more intense in their efforts to track down every last one of them. They do not want the Isars to be found, because that is the way to reinstate the Aura."

A long silence ensued, and then Eyre spoke. "Well, I'm not sure I am an Aether any more," she said slowly. "At this point I don't have any Lightworking powers at all. I probably do belong in the Unlit, but not because I'm an Aether."

Whittaker Ray looked serious. "After the events of last year, Eyre, you must keep that possibility to yourself. No one is to know that you might be an Aether. We cannot trust anyone—recent events have proven that to us, and I will not make the same mistake twice. Your parents were right to keep it a secret, and now we must too. Only you, UD1 and I know this, and we must keep it this way until the expedition to Aqua."

UD1 patted her arm. "We are honoured to have you Eyre, and if you are no longer an Aether, it will be our gain. You will find we have a wonderful school here with very dedicated students. But until we find out exactly what is happening with you, it is safer to keep you in this division and out of the way of curious eyes."

Whittaker Ray picked up the conversation. "So, you will stay with your friends at the Academy campus, but come here for training in the ways of the Unlit. You will take two classes in common with the Lightworker students—the first of those is Underwater Training, because we will require you to go on the TACI expedition when the Leonid appears in November. If there is any chance you can still see the Isar in Aqua, we must take it. Unlit students normally take Aqua training with Lit students, so that will not seem out of the ordinary."

UD1 cleared his throat. "The other class you will undertake is equestrian training." Eyre mentally groaned, and then realised she must have done it out loud as she registered Whittaker Ray and UD1's sympathetic faces.

"I know you haven't had the most—er—*positive* start to your relationship with your Lighthorse," Whittaker Ray said regretfully, "but it is an integral part of all Lightworker skills. You must persevere, if only to keep your bond with your horse. Once you have a Lighthorse the only way to break the bond is death—either yours or that of your horse." As Eyre mulled that over, she reflected that they really didn't have a bond at all. And there were days she would quite cheerfully slay the horse in question herself. But a part of her felt happy that she would continue to be part of the riding program; in a way it made her feel that she was still a 'real' Lightworker. She hadn't made much—or any, really—progress with Ischyros to date, but she was nothing if not stubborn. Part of her was determined that one day she might be able to ride the cranky old beast without him chucking her into the middle of a cowpat in the paddock.

"Underwater skills and Equestrian training take place once a week straight after our meditation and Ferito sessions." UD1 said. As Eyre looked at him questioningly, he nodded. "Yes, we have that in common with the rest of the Academy. Every student begins their day with meditation and Ferito. These are essential skills for the Lightworker—whether Lit or Unlit. But Ferito for the Unlit takes all morning until lunchtime; the training is two hours, except for Tuesdays, when you start early at the Academy pool for Underwater Training. Equestrian Training is on Wednesdays. I have asked Christopher to give you a weekly class schedule to give you more information on the program when he sees you later this morning."

Whittaker Ray stood up. "Please feel free to come and see me with any concerns, Eyre. I know this must be difficult for you, but I'm sure things will work out well."

He left in a flash of light that filled the room. A moment later there was a knock at the door and Christopher entered again. UD1 smiled at him.

"Would you help Eyre find a uniform and show her the compound Christopher? And also explain the class schedule to her please. Eyre, like Mr Ray, I am here also if you have any questions, no matter how small."

Eyre felt a wave of vertigo and then realised UD1 was gone too. It was as if he disappeared into thin air. Eyre looked around her in bewilderment; then raised her eyebrows at Christopher.

"How...?" she began. "You don't have Viq or Light skills, so how does he do that?"

Christopher led the way out of the room. "Ah," he said. "There is much for you to learn, Eyre."

# CHAPTER SIX

THE FIRST PLACE CHRISTOPHER took Eyre was to the uniform shop. Unlike the Academy, where uniforms of the right size were folded and named ready for pick up, the Unlit uniform shop contained racks and racks of clothing of different shapes and sizes—all of which were brown. A matronly woman carrying a clipboard bustled over to them.

"Welcome, welcome!" she chirped. "So nice to have a new student! Let me see... yes, we'll sort your sizes out very quickly. You're in second-year?" She squinted at her clipboard. "Well, Eye-Ree, here you go, let's find you something."

Eyre sighed internally. No one ever got her name right. "It's actually pronounced 'Air'," she said and the woman laughed apologetically.

"Oh, I'm so sorry my dear. You must get sick of that. What a pretty name!" She fussed through the racks until she gave an exclamation of triumph, as if she'd just discovered a lost treasure, and pulled some drab clothing out. "These should fit you," the woman said with satisfaction. She passed Eyre a plain brown tunic with a lace-up tie at the top and brown leggings, and Eyre dressed quickly in the change room. A brown belt went around her waist with a scabbard she imagined was designed to put a sword in, and she received a pair of brown boots, also of a lace-up style. She was given a rough hessian backpack—empty apart from a bundle of rough paper tied together with a leather cover and laced with a leather thong, and a pencil. With a pang she folded her Academy clothing and put it and her black boots in the bag, underneath her journal and pencil.

Unlike the close-fitting clothing of the Academy, the Unlit 'uniform' (although it was hardly a uniform, as every piece of clothing seemed to be different) was rather shapeless. But she liked it anyway: because it was very comfortable and easy to move in. She slung the bag over her shoulder, thanked the uniform lady and headed off with Christopher to class.

The morning went by quickly. Meditation took place in a hall very similar to the one at the Academy campus, and Ferito occurred in a large training shed almost identical to the one she was used to. There were a lot of curious glances aimed her way when she walked in, but she tried to ignore them and focus on what she was meant to be doing. Next year they would all be receiving an arms endowment—both Lit and Unlit students were awarded their arms in their third year—and leaving the safer practise palums behind. She needed to be competent if she wanted to retain all her limbs.

One thing she did notice as she began was how accomplished all the second-year Unlit students were at Ferito. She'd managed to get quite good at it last year, compared to other students in first-year, purely by practising a lot, but she was no match for even the least capable of these students. Sweating, she moved through the Basic Clasis and practised her movements for Clasis for Single-Blade Weapon and Clasis for Two-Handed fighting. The instructor for the class was a fourth-year Unlit student who moved like a graceful jungle cat, his muscles well-defined and gleaming with sweat as he pushed himself and the class hard.

"Again!" he called as the students finished the three Clasis. "But better!"

"Again, but better! Again, but *better!*" shouted the students in response. And they'd all start again, not practising individually, but moving as one through all the positions. Eyre found it hard to keep up; they were so much more fluid at the movements than she was, and, she realised as the time went on excruciatingly, also *so* much stronger. She had been impressed with the athletic ability of the Unlit at the Sector Fair exhibit last year, and now she knew why they were in such good shape. Her own fitness had improved with the running she had done over the past year, but she was not like these students. Even their mental focus was sharper. No one looked anywhere but at the instructor, there were no comments or laughing; this was serious business, apparently. In here they were nothing like the lively rabble Eyre had walked through when she first arrived.

Eyre managed to struggle through the class, but she was exhausted by the time it finished, and quite dejected. She had never trained this hard before —two hours was such a long time for this level of intense exercise. She wondered how on Entis she was going to keep up with the class.

Christopher was kind though. "You did well," he encouraged. "We've been training all last year, and it's not easy. Your fitness will improve and you'll find it easier to keep up. Come with me and I'll introduce you to a few people over the lunch break."

At that point, all Eyre's tired mind could register was the delicious word: break! Thank the Light for that, she thought. *If I don't sit down they'll have to carry me off on a stretcher!* Christopher led the way to an outdoor area with tables and chairs and a sort of outside servery where a Jotnar was serving drinks and food to whoever queued up. A sign above the eatery said 'The Short Stop'.

"The Jotnar work here too?" Eyre asked as she took a cold drink and a sandwich back to their table.

"For this year, anyway," Christopher said through a mouthful. "They got the contract again. Apparently the Tumba from Incendium tendered too but didn't get it. I hear they weren't happy."

As Eyre mulled that over, a few students walked over to sit with them. A few of them she recognized from her time at the TEPs—Julia, whose last name she couldn't remember, but who had been number 53 in her lodge, and Eyre was happy to see Tina Pang arrive, and then Thomas Petersen, Rigmar's friend. Adam Bentley was there too—Eyre had spoken with him last year at the Sector Fair. But there were a couple of new faces—Gillian and Trenton, who had come from interstate. The five of them looked at her curiously as they sat down.

"So, what's your story?" Julia asked, her pale grey eyes studying Eyre. She was direct, but not rude and Eyre took no offence.

"I was at the Academy last year, but I lost my Viq," she said. "So I'm here scrambling to catch up with you guys. Not very successfully so far, unfortunately."

Thomas looked intrigued. "I didn't know it was possible to lose your Viq."

Eyre shrugged. "Me either, but I did it. The one thing I'm good at, apparently."

Tina laughed. "Well, I'm glad to see you again. It's great here—you're going to love it. Our next lecture is Breaking and Entering. Thomas is really good at it."

Eyre's jaw dropped. "You're not serious? They *teach* you that?"

Thomas's eyes gleamed. "Yep, exactly that, and it's great fun! Locks, decoding keypads, manipulating holograms, even climbing up buildings— it's really difficult and I want to specialize in it one day. If you need any help, just ask."

Christopher brought out a piece of paper from his backpack. "I guess now is a good time to give you this—it's the class schedule. No Felsics or flash gadgets here—just pen and paper. You need to learn to write well, and fast. Here's how the week is organised—apart from the joint classes we take with the Lit students, there's specialist classes in the morning, depending on your electives. I'm not sure how that will affect you, but I'm assuming you'll just join the majority for now. And our afternoon sessions are divided equally between the physical and mental training of Unlit skills. There's a map on the back showing you where the classes are."

Eyre looked at the schedule and noticed there were various subjects with intriguing names—most of which she had no idea about: Mazes, Shimmering, Decoding Ciphers, Communication, and Blending amongst them. But there were a couple she could work out, and she groaned when she saw Prohemium Training on the schedule. Given the success of her Terra prohemium last year, she knew this was going to be 'interesting'. Although she wasn't aware that anyone could do a prohemium without Viq, so that *was* something she would like to know about. She put the schedule in her backpack, resolving to study it more carefully later on.

The conversation went on from there to cover the school holidays and Christmas and Eyre sat silently as they filled each other in on what they'd been doing. Eyre didn't participate, deciding that she would just try to take things in and figure out who her new friends were. As she watched them, she suddenly realised that the group had one thing in common—not one of them stood out physically in any way. They were all average looking, of varying height and weight but no extremes; nothing striking or memorable about them in any way; even their voices were unremarkable. If you had to describe them in a line-up, it would be very hard to remember anything about them. As she considered her own fair skin and bright red hair, she wondered if she was going to have to do something about her appearance in order to fit in.

All too soon it was time to head to the first lecture. The break had only been half an hour, to Eyre's great disappointment. She would have been quite happy to sit all day: she was shattered from the hours of Ferito training, especially at the intensity they did it. It was dawning on her that her time with the Unlit was not going to be easy.

"I guess I see why they call it 'The Short Stop'," she said ruefully as she gathered up her stuff. "We haven't been here very long."

Christopher laughed. "Indeed! But there's actually another reason for the name—the short stop is one of the most demanding defensive positions in baseball. The eatery was named by a professor who loved the game—he thought it was a good description for the Unlit too."

He paused a moment and then a look of purpose crossed his face. He spoke softly, but his words were fierce. "We're all honoured to be part of this division. Someday, you will be too, Eyre."

# CHAPTER SEVEN

EYRE FOLLOWED THE CHATTING group into the great sandstone building she'd seen earlier, feeling quite out of place. Although the students were perfectly friendly to her, she was definitely the odd one out and she was missing her old friends desperately. It was still hard to believe that she wasn't going to be with them anymore and she had to confess, although she knew it was unworthy of her, that she felt the skills of the Unlit were barely more than recreations when compared to the Lit students' studies.

But as she entered the lecture hall, she was relieved to see that at least the setup was familiar to her—very much the same as the lecture halls at the Academy. She followed Christopher and Tina as they took a seat up the back of the room.

A figure strode in the door and the hubbub of voices instantly hushed. These students were a lot more disciplined than the Lit students, who could take a few minutes to even notice the lecturer was there, let alone stop talking. Eyre leaned forward to study her new lecturer.

A slightly-built woman stood quietly at the front of the hall, surveying the students. She wore a brown pantsuit and comfortable-looking shoes, and her brown hair was tied tightly back in a practical bun. After a moment her eyes rested on Eyre. Then to Eyre's immense shock, with a forward double pike, the woman had raced up to her, leaping from one desk to another until she reached Eyre, who was doing a great impression of a beached fish.

"Welcome, Eyre," the woman said, standing on Eyre's desk, and studying her with intense hazel eyes. "I am Professor Nithercott and I am very pleased to meet you. Class, please welcome our new student in the appropriate way!"

All the students in the hall leapt up onto their desks and did a complex routine that involved double pikes, backflips, hand gestures and thumping of feet, interspersed with a rhythmic chant. Eyre's hair almost stood on end as she watched the dramatic display. She would clearly have to adjust her assessment of the Unlit skills.

The Professor backflipped her way down to the auditorium stage, and the students leapt back into their seats. Professor Nithercott looked at Eyre.

"Gymnastic ability helps to move in tight or difficult spaces, and you will work on this too Eyre, not only for the 'Breaking and Entering' class. When working in the field for intelligence missions, these skills are invaluable.

"Now, our new student will be trying to catch up with our second-year classes, so I am assigning Thomas Petersen and Tina Pang to assist Eyre, as I was informed that they met her at the TEPs just over a year ago. Please give Eyre all the help she needs to get up to speed with our work."

Far from looking displeased at this extra work, Thomas and Tina slapped palms as if they had been given the greatest treat of all, and Eyre mentally shook her head. This was *most* confusing. Although she had liked some of her classes last year, these students seemed to revel in every aspect of their curriculum, no matter what was involved. She couldn't imagine anyone she knew being excited about having to help another student with extra work. Whittaker Ray had told her the Unlit were dedicated, but she hadn't expected quite this commitment. Christopher noticed her bemused expression and smiled.

"We see the opportunity for extra work as a chance to excel, to improve ourselves. In the Unlit the goal is unqualified excellence, and while we know that it might be impossible to achieve, we are striving to be the absolute best we can be. No one is unhappy about hard work in the Unlit; it's what we're here for. The defence of the Overworld is a privilege and a responsibility."

Eyre could say nothing to this, and a vague sense of shame registered as she recalled all the times last year she had grumbled about this class or that, or felt unenthusiastic about some of her training sessions. And also, to her regret, she remembered her preconceived idea of the Unlit. She obviously had a lot to learn about how the Lightworking world worked, but most especially, the amazing *attitude* here.

This lecture introduced Eyre to a variety of tools to do with accessing locks, and she was given a series of them to practise on. Thomas helped her to get the hang of it, and when she eventually got one to click open, he exclaimed in delight.

"Oh well done! Come on then, try this one!" And so she went from lock to lock, trying to get used to the pointed and bent instruments that would apparently help her to unlock even the most impenetrable of locks.

"We have this class again on Thursday, and we'll be doing keypads and digital fingerprints. That's a lot of fun," Thomas told her. Eyre tried to look enthusiastic, especially after the very kind help he had given her, but her head was going... By the Light... *BTL! How* was she going to catch up with all this?

Finally, the class finished and the students filed out of the auditorium, heading for the stadium Eyre had passed when she first arrived. The next class was 'Falconry', and she was trying to feel positive about it, since it obviously involved the sleek, beautiful birds, but her anticipation was tempered by her memories of her experiences in the equestrian arena, which hadn't *exactly* worked out well.

As the students entered the arena, they each found a heavy leather gauntlet from within their backpacks and pulled it onto their dominant arm.

Then the students formed a big circle around the inside of the stadium and held out their protected arm horizontally from their body. One by one every student let out a piercing whistle, each a different call, unique in sound. As each student called, a shining bird plummeted at unbelievable speed from the sky and landed on the gauntlet of the student who had called.

But as Eyre studied them more closely, she realised that they weren't like any falcons she had ever seen. For a start, they were much larger, with soft, grey feathers with black and purple spots along the wings. Their beaks were sharp and curved, and as she studied the profile of the bird next to her, which Tina had called, she could see that its eye was bright yellow. Some form of eagle? she wondered. But then the bird on Tina's arm turned to face her and Eyre jumped in surprise, because a third eye was situated in the middle of the bird's forehead, between the two others. Looking more closely at the circle of birds she realised they all had three eyes, so this was not any eagle she had ever seen; obviously not even from Entis.

Tina filled Eyre in as she whispered endearing words to the bird on her arm, and stroked its feathers. "They're called Venators, and they come from Caelus," she said softly. "Bred to fight, not only are they the fastest bird in the Overworld, they also have the best eyesight—they can even see in the *dark*—and they are one of the few creatures that can take down the Zyx. They are smart, brave and courageous, and they bond to their human for life."

Eyre leaned over cautiously to Tina's Venator and ran her fingers gently over the grey plumage of the spectacular bird. The feathers were soft and yet they hummed with the energy that was evident in every muscle of the creature, its watchful eyes, the tenseness of its strong legs and feet, as if ready at any moment to launch into the air. A warrior bird ready for action in an instant.

At that moment a gruff-looking older man entered the arena, holding a massive Venator on his arm. He gave Eyre a look as he passed her.

"Someone find that one a gauntlet," he said shortly as he headed to the centre of the arena. The bird on his arm screeched and turned its intense gaze towards Eyre, the three eyes unblinking. It was rather unsettling.

But she managed to catch the gauntlet flung her way and put it on her hand. It went all the way to her elbow, thick, tough leather that fit quite snugly over her arm.

The lecturer watched her put it on and shook his head in irritation. "Put it in your backpack and take a seat. You can observe this lesson."

Eyre flushed, feeling silly, and took the glove off her hand. She'd been imagining one of those glorious creatures might fly down and land on her arm—but obviously not. Feeling this was starting to go as well as her introduction to her Lighthorse, she took a seat in the stadium. They wouldn't have given her a gauntlet if she wasn't going to have contact with the birds, so perhaps someone was going to lend her their Venator to have a go. She brightened a bit at the thought—any interaction with one of those magnificent creatures would be enough for her.

"Don't worry about Rachis," Tina said. "His bark is usually worse than his bite." Eyre wasn't sure, but she sat back, content enough just to observe.

The training session began with the students whistling different calls to their Venators. Each whistle had its own meaning, because at one call the birds would fly way up high and circle above them. Another call caused them to form a triangular formation that shot fast across the sky as one unit. The birds would respond to calls to go left and right, and to plummet to the ground. And each Venator had a unique call to summon them back to their master. Eyre was riveted, watching the display, which was unlike anything she had ever seen.

After half an hour of this training, an older student appeared from the side rolling a large wooden machine that looked like a catapult into the arena. It had a thick rubber strap strung between two sturdy beams, and a box attached to its side which was filled with irregular black objects. The Venators were dancing in agitation on the students' arms. This was something they were familiar with, and were excited about.

"We will go in the usual order. Mylor, would you step up please, and Rook, start when he's ready." A boy took a couple of steps forward, stroking his Venator as they both watched the catapult intently.

Eyre wasn't sure what the usual order meant—alphabetical? The size of the bird? Its age? She couldn't see anything different about Mylor's bird, but she was amused to see how it hopped on his arm in excitement. Obviously something good was about to happen.

The older student, Rook, took one of the flat black objects from the box and held it against the broad rubber band. Then he pulled the band far back and released it, firing the black thing high into the air. With an ear-splitting shriek, Mylor's Venator shot from his arm straight into the air at such a speed Eyre could hardly see it—it was just a grey blur past her eyes. Half a second later the bird had seized the black shape in its sharp talons and screeched in victory before taking off into the distance.

Tina turned to Eyre awkwardly as her Venator was jumping around so much on her arm it was hard for her to keep her balance.

"Feeding time," she explained. "Those things are dried jerky, coloured with black molasses to resemble the Zyx. The Venators love it, and it's great training for them."

"How do they decide who goes first?" Eyre asked.

"It's the spots on the feathers," Tina explained. "For some reason, the purple spots are rare, and so in Caelus the ones with more purple spots are more dominant over the others. Of course it makes no difference to us, but for the birds it's important. Mylor's bird has the most purple spots, and so he is the leader of the flock and gets to eat first. You'll notice it's his bird that leads the V-formation—the Apex."

"But what if two birds have the same number of spots?" Eyre asked. "Surely that happens sometimes?"

"Then it's the speed of the bird—the faster is more dominant."

"They're not coming back," Eyre said as the birds caught the jerky and flew out of sight. "Where do they go?"

"Venators normally roost in a tree called a Ru-Ru in Caelus. There's a plantation of them by the compound here and they stay there until they're called. They have exceptional hearing as well as eyesight, so it doesn't matter where we are, they come on the whistle."

Tina noticed Eyre looking at the Venator wistfully. "It's not a good time now," Tina said, "they're all hungry and waiting for the jerky, and not easy to handle. But next time I'll let you hold my Venator if you like."

"Does it have a name?"

"Mine is Shu-Ne, which sounds exotic, but actually is just the Caelorian word for 12-1, meaning my bird has twelve purple spots and is the fastest of them. Actually," she laughed, "there's no other bird with twelve spots yet, but if someone came along with a bird who also had twelve spots but was faster, my bird's name might change to Shu-Fa, Fa meaning two, or second fastest in this context."

Tina smiled at Eyre's bewildered look. "I know it sounds complicated, but it's really just an identification process, a ranking. In Caelus, it matters. But I just call her Holly, because she came to me at Christmas. More important is the whistle you make to call your bird; that is the way you uniquely communicate with your bird. Birds call by sounds, not names. They don't care what number they are, they operate as a team, as we do. She's a beauty."

Rook fired a triangle of jerky into the air and Tina launched Shu-Ne from her arm.

Shu-Ne shot straight up into the air and within seconds had seized the black piece of jerky in her talons. Then, shrieking victoriously she followed the other Venators out of sight.

When the last Venator had flown, the students removed their leather gauntlets and headed out of the arena; no dawdling or time-wasting with this lot. Eyre started to follow Tina when Rachis called her back. The grizzled old lecturer had a very irritated look on his face.

"Where are you going? You can't leave yet."

Tina looked sympathetic. "I'll see you at the Shimmer lecture—look at your schedule on the map, it's in Theatre 2."

Eyre walked slowly up to the scowling man as the last of the second-year students left the stadium. Rook was wheeling the catapult across the deserted arena, its wooden wheels making an irregular thudding in the dry earth. Eyre wasn't sure if she was about to receive a dressing-down, but the old man said nothing as he followed the rumbling machine through some double doors at the side of the building.

Rachis led Eyre through to a small room that was heated, with ultraviolet lights running in lines across the ceiling, and banks of perspex boxes stacked neatly in rows across the room. It was hot and humid, and condensation droplets ran down the insides of the cubes. As Eyre peered inside she could see that each box contained a large purple, shimmering egg, looking ridiculously like a Cadbury's Easter Egg from Woolworths.

"Those ones are still being incubated," Rachis said shortly, walking past the boxes until he arrived at a long flat table. "But these ones are ready."

Dozens of the large purple eggs were crowded on the table, sitting in trays like egg cartons. The table had a raised edge, obviously for added security so that no eggs could roll off. Eyre looked at the eggs in admiration: their shells were a dazzling purple with flashes of rainbow colours through them.

"Well then," the old man said abruptly. "Pick one."

Eyre may have lost her Viq, but her temper was still firmly in place, and finally she had had enough of the man's rudeness. Indeed, he was a lecturer and entitled to her respect, but she had done nothing that she knew of to justify his bluntness towards her.

"Have I done something wrong, sir?" she asked as respectfully as she could.

The man turned sharp eyes towards her. "You are here against my wishes," he said. "You are not entitled to be in the second year, let alone the Unlit. Are you staying? What is your status? Our studies are of the utmost secrecy here, and we cannot have people just coming and going at will. I feel your presence jeopardises our very structure. And if you do fail and depart, then what will become of this special creature who bonds with their handler for life?"

Eyre said nothing for a moment, and then her sense of fairness brought a flush to her cheeks. "*I* did not choose to lose my Viq, *I* did not choose to be here and you can rest assured that it will not be I who lets any of your precious secrets out, if that ever should happen. And I would *never* desert any creature left in my care—not even a grumpy old warhorse. What I *do* feel is that you should give me a fair trial!"

There was a long silence as fierce eyebrows contemplated Eyre. "I've never been called a grumpy old warhorse before," he began. But before she could explain what she had really meant, his gaze softened a little.

"Well, you have the heart of the Unlit and perhaps you are right in saying I'm possibly being unfair. Let's see what you can do. I am the head Falconer here; my name is Rachis. I am not going easy on you though, there will be no allowances made, so you had better work hard to catch up or we are not going to get along."

Eyre mentally rolled her eyes but said nothing. He wasn't the first lecturer to take a dislike to her. Rachis pointed at the table.

"These eggs are inert at the moment, in a suspended state. You are to select one of them and keep it close to your body for the next two months. The warmth of your body and your energy of your chakras will cause the Venator to hatch, and once it has seen you, you are its partner for life. It will take three more weeks before the fledgling is old enough to join the flock in the forest, so you will have to be dedicated to enable it to survive. You will be feeding it around the clock until it is old enough to leave and live in the Ru-Ru forest. Just be happy it has a quick maturation cycle— normal birds spend a lot more time with their family group before they can leave. In Caelus, Venator chicks are prime prey for predators, so they have to grow up and become independent quickly."

Eyre studied the neat lines of purple eggs on the table, each one as big as an emu egg. She couldn't see any difference between them really, but decided that she would pick up the $88^{th}$ one—88 was her number in the TEP trials—so that seemed as good a way to pick the egg as any. It sparkled under the ultraviolet lights and seemed to pulse with energy as she held it in her hand and she gave a delighted grin. What a wonderful thing!

Rachis seemed slightly mollified by her obvious joy and he helped her to pack the large egg carefully into a padded, hard-shelled box which was put into a sling that hung over her shoulder.

"This is a warming cube," he said. "The energy from your body will help the process, but the warming cube keeps the egg at a stable 18 degrees Celsius, to simulate the final stages of the Venator egg's maturation. You can keep this sling on while you do your physical sports, but if you need to take it off, make sure you put it somewhere safe. However, it is imperative that the chick does not hatch on its own, so you must keep it near you at all time. Once we had a Venator bond with a rubbish bin and it was a real headache to sort that one out."

Eyre tried not to laugh as he let her out of the breeding house and shut the doors decisively behind her. The elation at receiving such a beautiful gift disappeared suddenly as Eyre realised she was going to be quite late for her next lecture. All she needed was another lecturer to be angry with her!

She studied the compound map intently and then hurried along the track to Theatre 2, trying not to skid in the door. Several eyes turned her way as she made a slightly dishevelled entrance, including those of the lecturer. But to Eyre's immense relief, the teacher regarded her with amused eyes.

"Welcome, Eyre," UD1 said. "So glad you could join us!"

# CHAPTER EIGHT

IT CAME AS NO surprise to Eyre that Shimmering was another subject she apparently had no skill at. She was philosophical about it—after all, she hadn't been here in first year so she really couldn't expect to be any good at it. She was realising she was in for a year of being extremely incompetent in *all* the subjects she undertook. But the positive thing about this class was that UD1 was teaching it—so not only would she have contact again with the enigmatic but admirable lecturer, she also knew he would help her, rather than judge her. That in itself was encouraging.

Shimmering turned out to be a form of mind control, or mesmerising, that fooled the brain into recalling events differently. This skill enabled the Unlit to change the memories of Lightworkers and other humans so that they were unable to recall what had really happened. Eyre remembered back to the lecture during the TEP trials when UD1 had somehow appeared in the centre of the lecture hall, and then later on had magically, it seemed, shackled Ben Perrill's leg to the lecture table. Somehow UD1 had mass-hypnotised the whole class into forgetting what had actually happened that day. Obviously, Christopher had employed the same skill when he'd saved Eyre from a thumping from Ben Perrill earlier this morning.

Eyre was intrigued by the idea of Shimmering, and determined to learn how to do it. But the mechanics of it eluded her—she had no idea what they meant by 'suggestive induction' and 'eye fixation' and 'focused intent'. Whilst several of her classmates—Christopher amongst them—were able to confuse Eyre's mind into dizzying but false memories several times during the class, Eyre herself was unable even to understand what she was meant to be doing. But Christopher was very willing to help, and didn't seem to mind when she looked completely blank at his explanations. Time after time he would adjust his spectacles, tap the page and try again to clarify things to Eyre. If nothing else, she was gaining an admiration for his tenacity and his kindness. She doubted any of her Lightworker colleagues would have been so patient with a newcomer.

The class passed without Eyre making any progress herself, but she had watched many of the other students Shimmer each other. She couldn't actually do it, but she understood what a great power it was and she was determined to practice until she *could* do it herself. Finally, it was time to go and UD1 congratulated everyone on their progress. Eyre looked sideways at Christopher and raised her eyebrow, but he patted her hand.

"You'll get it, Eyre, there's a moment when it works and you'll never look back. Each time you practise you get nearer to that moment."

"Well, I have many moments I'd rather forget in my life," Eyre said wryly, sighing as they walked down the steps of the lecture hall towards the door. "I've had a lot of failures, actually. But I hope I can learn from you, and understand the process of Shimmering—you all have such amazing talents that I had no idea about." As she gave a small laugh, Eyre was interrupted and called by UD1 to stay behind. Relieved, she thought it was a lot better than being called up by Rachis.

"How is your first day going, Eyre?" UD1 asked, his warm brown eyes looking at her kindly.

Eyre thought for a moment and then smiled. "You know, excellent, actually!" she replied. "This is a very cool place, although I'm not very good at anything."

UD1 nodded. "You will improve," he said. "And yes, it is indeed a very cool place. However, I must remind you that you are now part of the Unlit, and although you will be staying at the Academy campus, the ways and learnings of the Unlit are not to be shared with anyone outside our division. It is crucial to our effectiveness and the safety of the Lightworking community that the details of our training techniques remain within these walls, especially the information you will learn in future years. It is a discipline to be able to keep confidential information to yourself."

Eyre nodded, and felt a small glow that for a moment she was unable to identify. Then with a start of surprise she realised what it was—it was *pride*, pride at being part of this unusual group of people. She thought back to the TEPs and the disappointment felt by the students who had remained Unlit—the shame they experienced at being sent home. She knew, because she had almost been one of them. And yet—now she realised that there was no dishonour at all in being part of this unique section of Lightworkers. She had a lot to learn and she was looking forward to it.

But all she said was "I understand, sir," and UD1 nodded like he knew exactly what she meant.

# CHAPTER NINE

THE LAST LESSON FOR the day also took place in the arena where Eyre had been introduced to Falconry. Tina and Thomas were enthusiastic as they led her along the path back to the stadium.

"Unravelling codes and ciphers is my favourite class," Tina said as they walked past a row of round targets lined up on the left-hand side of the arena, "but archery comes a close second." Eyre smiled. There were no other students here yet, but Tina was walking fast—obviously she was keen to get started. The arena was about 100 metres long and at the end of it was an internal room that contained a block of lockers with carved wooden doors. Thomas nodded as he lifted the heavy brass latch on the locker doors and pulled them open.

"Me too," he said. "It's not the easiest skill, but it's definitely addictive!"

Inside the lockers were a range of bows and arrows stored carefully in tailor-made holders, as well as a hanging rack of leather braces that looked similar to the baldrics that Eyre had seen some of the staff wearing during her time at the TEP compound. Lightworking students received their baldrics in their third year, when they were presented with their arms endowment, and it looked like the Unlit used similar braces for their archery equipment.

Tina and Thomas strapped on their braces and slid a bow over their shoulder onto a hook at the back of the braces. The arrows went into a quiver that was attached to the side of the braces on the belt. Eyre watched them for a moment.

"Do you have your own bow? Or do I just take one? Do you get a bow as part of your Arms Endowment?"

"No, just grab one," Thomas answered as he adjusted his belt. "They're general equipment for all the years. Families often buy their student a bow when they graduate, it's part of our tradition. When you get your Arms

Endowment next year, it consists of an Acri dagger, a short sword called a Xiphos and a Flail."

Eyre selected a bow and then contemplated her sling with the precious Venator egg inside. She gestured to Tina.

"What about this?" Eyre asked. "I don't want to tell Rachis that I've somehow managed to fire it into a bullseye."

Tina laughed. "We were able to do it with the sling on," she said. "Just slide it to one side and you can put all the gear on. You get used to carrying the sling around and the warming cube is quite sturdy."

Eyre studied the line of bows and picked one that looked medium-size, similar to Tina's. It was made from a highly-polished wood with a leather strap wrapped around the centre and it felt light in her hands. She managed to get the braces on around the sling and she hung her bow on her back. Then she filled the quiver with arrows.

As they left the lockers a large group of chattering students walked in and began to get their gear on. But when Eyre entered the stadium, there were a couple of students in the centre of the arena who already had their archery equipment, and were shooting off arrows at a fast pace.

"They have their own bows already," Tina said, and after a pause she added, "usually because a family member has left it to them."

Eyre could tell from Tina's demeanour how the students had acquired their weapons—obviously someone had died. A bit like receiving her Wisdom, she mused. A beautiful gift received earlier than usual, but with a terrible price. The bows these students had were clearly something different than the ones from the locker—longer, with symbols and runes carved into the curved wood. And instead of leather around the centre, a band of hammered silver gleamed in the sunlight. The early students were practising hard, holding the silver band and nocking arrows into the taut string of the bows. The target bristled with arrows and Eyre realised they must have been practising for quite a while. She watched one girl she recognised, Julia, number 53 from her lodge during the TEP trials. Her face still with concentration, Julia sent an arrow slamming into the yellow bullseye, then she smoothly nocked another arrow before the one in the target had even stopped quivering.

Tina studied the girl, her eyes understanding. "The Gothak killed Julia's father last year and she's been practising every day since, sometimes for hours. She's a brilliant marksman. I think she singlehandedly wants to slaughter every last Gothak."

Eyre watched the short-haired girl send arrow after arrow into the target until the yellow centre could fit no more. Then Julia stalked over and wrenched them out and headed back to start again. Eyre could sympathise. She felt the same about the Gothak, so Julia was going to have company on her mission.

The instructor arrived at that moment, a taller girl who was obviously a student herself.

"Ok everyone, you know what to do. If you need a hand, give me a shout," she said, and the students moved over to queue up in front of the lines of targets. One by one they shot all their arrows at the target and then walked over to retrieve them and re-join the back of the queue. As Eyre waited in line, the instructor spotted her and walked over.

"Hi Eyre, I'm Silva—I'm a third-year student. Let me help you get started."

Silva showed Eyre how to hold her bow, and how to balance the arrow above her hand and nock it into the bowstring.

"Breathe in slowly and hold it; then let the arrow go when you're completely steady."

Eyre pulled the string back as far as she could and let the arrow fly. It streaked through the air and to Eyre's delight, hit the target in the white area on the outside of the target. But then she registered an intense pain in her arm after the string snapped hard against the inside of her elbow.

"*By the Light!*" she cried, flapping her arm. "It bit me!" Silva laughed hard and pulled another arrow out of Eyre's quiver. "You need to rotate your arm to avoid the string hitting you. I'll find you an arm guard for tomorrow, you really should have grabbed one when you got your bow. That wasn't a bad shot! Try again."

Eyre rubbed the inside of her arm until the sharp pain eased a little and nocked up another arrow. The last shot she'd made had ended up close to the outside right hand of the target, so she aimed slightly to the left and let the arrow go. But this time she made sure her elbow rotated up and around so the bowstring didn't whack her arm as it snapped back.

The arrow flew through the air and hit the blue area of the target and Silva applauded.

"Awesome, Eyre, you're doing great!" Eyre noticed Julia flick her eyes over to see what the fuss was about and then immediately turn away again. Clearly not interested in the average shots of a newbie; this girl was after perfection.

By the end of the class Eyre had managed to hit the blue section two more times, the black section once and completely miss the target the rest of the time. But she was overjoyed at how she had done—unlike trying to shoot Light energy from her staff, at least this weapon shot in the right direction! She was elated that she had made some progress and could see why Tina and Thomas liked it so much—archery was *awesome*!

Silva clapped her hands for attention to let everyone know the class had finished and it was time to pack their equipment away. Eyre headed for the locker with the other students, sad to put the bow away but already looking forward to the next session.

"See you tomorrow!" Tina said. "I hope you had a good day!"

"By the Light," Eyre said, "*Yes!*" And then she left at a run to find the clearing that led to the main campus of the Academy. "If you don't see me in the morning, send out a search party into the bush! I think I know where I'm going, but I'm not sure!"

Tina and Thomas both laughed and headed in the opposite direction.

# CHAPTER TEN

HOLDING THE SLING AGAINST her body, Eyre hurried back along the track to the clearing and stepped through the ward, feeling the familiar but unpleasant chill run down her skin. Her mind was full of astonishment at her day; at how unexpectedly wonderful it had been. She had imagined the Unlit to be dull and boring, like their drab uniforms. How wrong she had been! And this was only the first day—what else was she going to learn?

But she realised it was going to be difficult to keep the training details to herself. Her friends were going to want to know *something* about what she was doing each day. She decided that she would walk a fine line between the truth and her obligation to the Unlit and give an edited version that wouldn't give much away. Part of her felt guilty about keeping secrets from her friends, but she knew that it was not an option to reveal the reality of what went on at the Unlit compound.

So, it was no surprise when Beatrice and Abby seized her arms when she walked into her room and sat her down on the bed. Abby jumped beside her and Beatrice sat opposite on her own bed.

"*Well?*" Abby said. "What was it like?"

Beatrice laughed. "Did you fall asleep on the table? Come on, we want all the gory—or *bory* details!"

Eyre paused, her mind recalling some of the intriguing subjects listed on her class schedule: 'Night Vision Training', 'Surveillance Techniques', 'Navigation by Ley Lines', 'Alterworld Languages', 'Stalking and Tracking', not to mention her memories of the Shimmering class earlier that day.

"By the Light, yes," Eyre said after a minute, feeling uncomfortably disloyal to both her friends and the Unlit, "it was SO boring! First of all I was called 'Eye-Ree'." Beatrice and Abby cracked up. Eyre's struggles to get people to say her name right were becoming a regular joke for them all. Eyre rolled her eyes and continued, "Ferito for half the morning, then the most awful lecturer gave me a talking to about how he didn't want me there, and finally—the Light save me, an hour of getting in groups and *working* together. You've got no idea!"

"Working together?" Beatrice said. "What's that mean?"

"Teamwork, group discussions—argh, I was just about snoring!"

"Wow," Abby said sympathetically, "I know that's important, but to have a whole *year* of it? I'm so sorry for you!"

"Well, it gets worse," Eyre said sadly. "Apparently I'm to join you lot for equestrian lessons. I don't get out of that, unfortunately."

Abby laughed merrily and Beatrice snorted. "Won't Ischyros be pleased! I think he's been quite happy on his own down in his private stall. Looks like they're not going to let you give up on him! Still, I guess you don't need Viq for riding, so maybe he'll co-operate one of these days."

There was a silence and then all of them burst out laughing at this ridiculous concept. *As if!*

"What's in the bag?" Abby asked, indicating Eyre's sling. Eyre hesitated for a moment, not sure what to say. Then she realised that the Venator egg might hatch while she was at the Academy campus, and that probably everyone would eventually know about the Unlit and their raptors, so she figured this wasn't likely to be one of the secrets UD1 had talked about.

"It's my baby," she laughed, then explained. "The Unlit have a bird like a falcon that they train to fight with them. This is mine; it just hasn't arrived yet."

"It's an *egg?*" Abby cried, jumping over. "Can I see it?"

Eyre carefully opened the lid of the warming box and Abby and Beatrice oohed and aahhed over the sparkling purple egg, then Eyre packed it away before the temperature dropped.

"Well, that's one thing that's cool about the Unlit," Abby said. "I wouldn't mind one of those at all!" Eyre smiled, thinking there was a lot more that was 'cool' about the Unlit, but she just nodded.

"Well, come on then, let's get some dinner," Beatrice said. "Everyone's so keen to see you!"

When they arrived at the refectory quite a few people looked at Eyre, with curious faces. They all knew about the loss of her Viq, and being part of two campuses at the Academy was unheard of. Her sling caught the gaze of a few people too and there was a low buzz in the air as she made her way to her table. Eyre smiled at the people she knew and tried to look impassive as she sat down with her friends.

A movement behind her made her look up and instantly her muscles tensed. Before she could move, Ben Perrill had stuck a brown paper bag over her head.

"Whoa," he said in a stage whisper. "Look out, the Unlit is undercover! Looks good on you Airhead, a real improvement."

Eyre snatched the bag off her head, quivering in rage, wishing she could smash him into the ground. But the huge boy towered over her, and now there was not much she could do about it. Without her Viq she was powerless.

"Get stuffed Ben," Nick said and flicked the paper bag off the table in front of Eyre up into the air. With a gesture he sent a blast of Viq that screwed the bag up into a tight ball and smacked it hard into Ben's face.

Ben turned red in rage, but before the moment could escalate, the Sergeant's booming voice could be heard above the hubbub.

"Everyone take your places please, we have an announcement to make!"

Ben gave Nick a look that promised the incident was not over, but he slunk off to join his cronies. The Curtis twins snickered at Eyre and Wyatt Rankins pulled his arm across his face like a spy hiding behind his coat. Eyre gritted her teeth and ignored them, but felt her rage fuel a determination to master the skills those idiots knew nothing about. Just wait 'til she could Shimmer—payback was going to feel awfully good. She might not be the best at the skills taught by the Academy—Lit or Unlit— but she was certain she *was* the most stubborn person there. No one was going to make her give up, or get the better of her, she vowed silently to herself as she held her sling close to her body. The Sergeant cleared her throat.

"Tomorrow morning is the first lesson of the 'Alterworlds' class, where you will learn the underwater techniques you will require for Aqua later this year. Everyone is to meet at 6am at the school pool for training."

A soft groan ran around the room. No one liked the thought of an early start. Eyre sighed. If she was going to see Ischyros, that meant she would have to get up at 5, but she wasn't going to miss it. She was going to wear the old horse down if it took aeons.

"Silence!" The Sergeant looked at the dejected faces. "Self-discipline is part of your training here, and we do not want to interrupt the normal curriculum for your specialist training. Anyone who is late for underwater training will be doing it every morning for a week, so I suggest you arrive on time. Mentor Xiphias from the Pinnae will be instructing you once a week in these techniques and you are to extend every courtesy to him."

Then the Sergeant seemed to grind her teeth for a moment, before she spoke her next words. "Please look for Ms Periwinkle in the morning. She will introduce you to your instructor and give you instructions for the session. Are there any questions?"

No one had anything to ask so the Sergeant went to sit at the staff table and the hall filled with the familiar wash of voices. Eyre noticed that as usual the Sergeant sat at the opposite end of the table to Jemima Periwinkle, and yet again she wondered what the story was between them.

Her thoughts were interrupted when someone walked close behind her and thinking it was Ben Perrill back for round two, she jumped up with her fists clenched, ready to take a good hard swipe. Her jaw jutting, she pulled her chair back hard into the person standing there, almost knocking them over. But when she looked up, to her consternation she found herself gazing into two magical green eyes and she flushed to the roots of her hair. Jax stood there holding his tray, on his way to another table, and Eyre felt incredibly stupid, especially when she saw Pheria sitting with an empty seat beside her and *smirking*.

"Sorry," Jax said. "My fault," although it clearly wasn't. The two of them stood awkwardly and then Jax and Eyre both moved sideways, unintentionally stepping the same way as each tried to let the other past, like a ridiculous pas de deux step. Eyre sensed many pairs of eyes upon them, including, to her annoyance, some of the staff. Mandig Vela was watching them with a very mean little smile on his rat face, and Whittaker Ray also was looking their way, although his eyes were sympathetic. Somehow, news had got around that there was tension between Eyre and Jax—By the Light, news travelled fast! Exasperated and annoyed, Eyre exhaled hard.

"No problem," she said shortly, "I was just leaving anyway."

She let Jax manoeuvre past and she picked up her tray, ignoring the looks she was getting.

"See you back at the room," she said to Beatrice and Abby, not wanting them to think she was running for the hills again. But she quickly marched her tray to the servery window and left it there half full. Somehow, she'd lost her appetite anyway.

# CHAPTER ELEVEN

EYRE HOVERED OUTSIDE FOR a moment, undecided. She didn't really
want to go back to her room just yet, but she did want to get away from all
the curious looks and the mixed currents of emotion she had felt in the
refectory. She would never be anonymous from now on; everyone had heard
about her in some way and not everyone was on her side. She knew that
some students felt she shouldn't even be at the Academy anymore; that she
was taking a place a more worthy student could fill.

She started to walk along the path leading away from the Refectory, then
on a whim started to run towards the Equestrian Centre. No one would be
there now, and even Ischyros's bad temper would be an improvement on
the seething vibe she had felt at the Refectory. And it would save her a visit
out to the stables in the morning.

She reached the carved stone walls surrounding the centre and could hear
the ferocious roaring and screeching of the Strigis filling the air. Obviously
the Lighthorses were getting their daily recording of the terrifying creatures;
the goal being to desensitize the Lighthorses to the Strigis when they
headed into battle. Even though she knew it was just a soundtrack, it was a
fearsome sound and the hair on the back of Eyre's neck raised.

The bronze doors opened at her approach and she walked across the
arena towards the stables. In one of the storage rooms Lisa was filling some
feed buckets and she raised a hand in greeting as Eyre entered the long hall
of stables. Eyre was surprised, but glad to see her. She'd been a graduate
student last year and should have left, so obviously she'd decided to stay on.

The roaring continued as Eyre walked and her ears were hurting from the
sound, but the Lighthorses ignored it, calmly eating the grain and lucerne
that had been put in their feed bins.

All at once the screeching stopped and quiet reigned again. Eyre breathed
in a sigh of relief—the sound had been awful. She carried on down the long

hall and then realised she could hear someone talking in a very gentle voice and the irregular clatter of uncertain hooves.

"There, there my boy. Whoa, stay still for me. Thank you."

As Eyre walked towards the voice, she realised it was Colton, talking to his horse, a huge black thoroughbred that finally stood quietly as Colton mounted him. Eyre would have made herself known, but Colton started to walk off down the hallway and she figured she wouldn't interfere with his training session. She leant against the door of one of the stables and watched as he rode his horse out to the paddock.

Then a strange thing happened. A ginger cat trotted out from behind the stables and started to run towards Colton, then leapt high up on to the back of the horse. Far from being startled, the horse hardly broke stride and Colton ignored the cat completely. Eyre's jaw hung open as she watched Colton first trot, then canter his beautiful horse around the paddock, completely in sync with his mount as the ginger cat balanced perfectly on its rear.

Colton couldn't see Eyre as she stood in the shadows of the stables, and he was deep in concentration as he kicked his horse into a gallop. The shining black horse reacted instantly to his command and raced around the perimeter of the paddock, so fast it was just a blur, its feet flashing as it passed Eyre. And then, like the ride Eyre had had with Jax the year before, Colton's horse headed straight for the fence, towards the setting sun. With a massive leap it cleared the boundary easily, sending the ginger cat spinning up into the air. Eyre watched in complete amazement as the cat tumbled over and over in the air and suddenly morphed to become an enormous Wedge-tailed eagle, which soared upwards with a joyful flap of its wings.

And then, just after the black horse cleared the high fence, instead of landing on the other side it also headed up in the air, following the eagle's path. Before Eyre's disbelieving eyes, a pair of glorious black wings opened out from the horse's sides and with strong downwards beats, the beautiful creature and Colton spiralled quickly upwards.

Eyre nearly fell over in shock. Colton's horse could *fly*?

A soft voice at her shoulder caused her to jump and turn around. "You've obviously not seen this before," the Kikkuli Master said. Eyre could only shake her head dumbly, her eyes following the horse and the eagle as they headed up into the orange-coloured clouds.

"Colton has shown unusual aptitude, and an intense focus for riding," the Kikkuli Master said. Eyre wouldn't know—her time at the Equestrian Centre was usually spent avoiding Ischyros's teeth in his stable down the back, so she had no idea really how anyone was doing.

"Colton trains here a lot," the Kikkuli Master added.

"But—his horse—"Eyre stuttered, "it can fly?" The Master turned soft eyes to Eyre.

"All Lighthorses can fly, Eyre," he answered. "It just takes some of them a lot longer to learn. A huge measure of trust is necessary before the horse can become airborne, and students usually take a while for this to develop. Colton has a wonderful bond with his horse, but it's also because of the time he's spent here. Talent is one thing; putting in the hours is also necessary."

Eyre was taking in this startling revelation slowly, but she had another question. "The cat...?"

"I think you know about Warrigal," the Kikkuli Master answered. "He comes here to practise. He and Colton are great friends."

So many thoughts were crashing about Eyre's head, but that did make sense. "Therianthropy," she said. "So the cat was him? I thought he was meant to keep that to himself." Eyre had inadvertently seen Warrigal's ability to change into a dingo the year before, but she had never said a word to anyone.

"Some people know; the ones that can be trusted," the Master answered, and despite her mental confusion, Eyre felt a warmth travel through her.

The Kikkuli Master continued. "Warrigal's talent is a powerful force that the Gothak would like to eliminate; it's kept very secret here."

"Well, no one will hear it from me," Eyre said, searching the sky for the dark horse. But there was no sign of them returning.

After the Kikkuli Master left, Eyre walked slowly to Ischyros's stall, feeling slightly despondent. He was an old horse and not friendly, and she had accepted that it might take a long time for her to connect even in a minor way with the shambling, shabby creature—or maybe even never. After a year of dealing with the rude, grumpy horse she'd come to an understanding that this was her situation, and it wasn't going to change. But after seeing Colton rise upwards into the clouds, her heart was sore. She couldn't even sit on her horse and ride him, let alone take to the air like that. What a wonderful thing to be able to do!

But then, there was a slight movement in the sling around her neck and she felt a bit happier. Soon she would have another creature to care for, and perhaps this one might like her a bit better. In the meantime, she was going to go and see Ischyros, and check how he was doing.

She entered his stall and found him head down, with his nose deep in his feed trough.

"Hi Ischyros," she said. "Had a good day?"

"Was until you got here," Ischyros replied through a mouthful.

Sighing, Eyre got the grooming equipment out of the holder on the wall and began to brush the mud out of Ischyros's coat. Considering he didn't participate in the events in the arena, she wondered how he managed to get so much dirt all over himself every day. A bit sourly, she contemplated whether he did it on purpose, knowing it made more work for her.

However, after half an hour he was clean again and she felt glad that she'd done it. The steady rhythm of brushing and combing had taken her mind off the annoying incident in the refectory, and somehow, despite the fact Ischyros hadn't said another word to her, she was happy she'd come. She put the brushes and comb back in the holder and stroked him gently on the neck.

"I know you don't like me Ischyros," she said softly. "But you're my Lighthorse and that makes you special. One of these days you'll get used to me."

Cradling her Venator egg, she let herself out of the barn and headed out of the Equestrian Centre. Colton was still not back and the night was almost here. She wondered what he was up to, but one thing was for sure: if she ever got to fly on a horse, she wouldn't be back in a hurry either.

# CHAPTER TWELVE

THE NEXT MORNING EYRE, Beatrice and Abby headed over to the school pool. Nick had swimming lessons on a different day, so he headed off to practise Ferito with Colton and Warrigal. Professor Vela had announced at dinner last night that he was doing his annual cave tour this morning for anyone who wanted to go, but even the thought of missing out on early swimming was not enough to entice Eyre to join the tour. The prospect of listening to Professor Vela's droning voice for half a day was less than thrilling. She had to admit that it was a good idea—she really did want to be more familiar with the confusing network of tunnels under the ground and the various passages the Mimir used. But she wasn't up to it yet—just the thought of that dark place after her experience with Ben Perrill was enough to make her stomach roil. Maybe she'd do it next year.

The sun was barely up and Eyre was not feeling overly-enthusiastic about underwater training that morning as they trudged along the misty paths. But it was a good opportunity to fill her friends in on what she'd seen last night. Of course, she said nothing about Warrigal, but she did tell them about Colton, as she didn't think there were any secrets about Lighthorses—after all, she supposed they were all going to fly at some stage. And then with a wry internal smile she amended that thought. All of them except Ischyros, of course.

Abby's eyes were round as Eyre recounted seeing Colton soaring up to the clouds on his shining black horse.

"Colton is an amazing rider," Abby said. "He's been doing really well, but we haven't been told yet about *this*!"

Beatrice looked thoughtful. "Well, I guess the Kikkuli Master hasn't said anything because none of us are close to that happening. We've all been riding a year, but only a few of us can gallop well in our class. I knew

Colton was doing extra training, but I thought it was just because he loved riding. How extraordinary to think that one day we might fly!"

Once again Eyre felt a pang as she contemplated the fact that there was no way her horse was ever going to fly; she had enough trouble just being in the stable with him. But she felt happy for her friends and she couldn't wait for their horses to get wings—maybe they'd take her for a ride! The thought was delicious.

They arrived at the pool and joined the throng of students milling around. Not too many looked enthusiastic about the idea of getting in the water, especially at this hour.

"Alright students, please come forward and listen!" Jemima Periwinkle sashayed her way to the front of the crowd and motioned towards a creature who stood quietly at the side of the pool next to the equipment lockers.

"This is Mentor Xiphias, of the Pinnae. He will instruct you in underwater techniques and later on in the year there will be lectures about Aqua.

Many curious looks were directed towards Mentor Xiphias, including from Eyre and her friends, despite the fact that they had seen some of the Pinnae last year when they had secretly watched a meeting of the Determinant Dozen. The Pinnae were the race of creatures who inhabited Aqua, and as Eyre studied Mentor Xiphias she could see how they had the characteristics of a species adapted to living underwater. His human-like face was covered in iridescent scales and, despite the fact that he wore a wetsuit-like garment, the students could see he had flippers rather than feet, and very large hands with long, webbed fingers. Blue hair hung past his shoulders and he had large turquoise eyes, with heavy lids that closed for a second at intervals.

Xiphias stood quietly, as if understanding their curiosity. Then he held his hands together as if in prayer and bowed.

"Greetings from Aqua," he started. "It is my honour to instruct you in the ways of our world. We look forward to your visit later this year.

"The atmosphere of Entis is too dry for the Pinnae, so when I am here I wear this air suit," he said, indicating the tight-fitting clothing. "However, in our own environment, it is not necessary.

"Now, as to the instruction for the year. First, I will demonstrate on the side of the pool, then we will practise in the water. We will learn the techniques for movement underwater, and the prohemium for getting to Aqua."

"Do we get to go fishing? I'll take my rod!" a disrespectful voice hooted from the back, and Eyre was not surprised to see it was Wyatt Rankins, one of Ben's sidekicks. However, the Mentor was unfazed by Wyatt's rudeness, and he turned calm eyes towards the student.

"I suggest you focus only on what you are supposed to learn for your TACI exam," he replied. "Or perhaps it might be you who is the prey on your journey."

Wyatt flushed and looked away as other students snickered, and Xiphias continued.

"When you first arrive in Aqua, you will travel by Zepp. It is faster for you and less tiring to move through the water that way. However, you cannot travel the whole way in a Zepp, so you must learn techniques to breathe underwater for the final part of your TACI test. Today we will concentrate on movement and learning the 'current' technique. As you can see, my body has evolved for movement underwater and my hands and flippers mean I can swim extremely fast. What we do is search for the currents that flow strongly underwater and swim to them. The best way to swim with these currents is like this."

Xiphias performed a movement like a dolphin swimming underwater, with his hands out in front of him, one on top of the other. At intervals he pulled them backwards to his sides. After demonstrating this a couple of times he indicated the lockers beside him.

"Please get in the pool, forming lines behind the ten lanes. I would like you to dive in and swim down the pool practising this technique, then get out. When everyone has swum the lap, we will go back again, and repeat this for the next hour. If you need to take a breath, come to the surface, then continue underwater. With practise you will soon be able to swim the length comfortably without taking a breath."

The students chose their equipment from the lockers and lined up, some quietly sighing and grumbling. Obviously, swimming was not the sport of choice for them. Eyre liked the water, so she was quite looking forward to learning this, and the water felt cool as she dived in. But the technique Xiphias had described was not easy—it felt unnatural to arc her body up and down, and soon she needed to take a breath. The dolphin movement used up a lot of energy and she had to go to the surface to take breaths at frequent intervals until she finally got to the end and hauled herself out. It was going to take some practise indeed to improve at this. Most of the students were also struggling and gasping as they jumped out at the end. But then Eyre caught a flash of dark hair as someone swam the whole 100-metre length underwater. Jax pulled himself out of the pool easily, water dripping from the muscles on his fit body. *How could he do that?* Eyre watched him as she waited at the diving block for her turn to swim back again and then flushed as a voice came from the lane next to her.

"Looks pretty good, doesn't he," Pheria drawled. "Our families go to Bondi regularly—Jax was a surf lifesaver. We've spent a lot of time surfing together."

Eyre gritted her teeth and turned to Pheria. "I'll look forward to learning from you then."

They both dived in at the same time and Eyre swam as hard as she could. As she kicked awkwardly along she was desperate to breathe, but she was determined to keep going and she forced herself to kick harder. Out of the corner of her eye she could see the long form of Pheria beside her, inching ahead and then Eyre's stubbornness kicked in. There was *no way* that pain in the neck was going to reach the end before her! Eyre might not have any Viq now, but she was going to get there first! She took a breath about halfway, and then with a surge of energy she kicked harder than she had in her life and as she arced her body under the water, she suddenly found a rhythm that was new to her. She streaked ahead of Pheria in a swirl of water and touched the wall a body length ahead of the other girl. Eyre jumped out of the water and turned around as Pheria started to clamber out. Forcing herself to not breathe heavily, Eyre just looked at Pheria's furious eyes and raised an eyebrow. She didn't need to say anything.

A voice from the sidelines called out delightedly. "Oh well done, student! You got the current technique in that last third of the pool! Keep it up!"

Pheria's face darkened as she stalked to the end of the queue, and Eyre felt even more satisfaction when she noticed that Jax was watching her. Perfect!

As she waited to go again, she mulled over her recent successes in her head. First with archery, and now with this. It seemed strange that the moment she lost her Viq, she seemed to be doing better than she ever had. In the previous year she had struggled with most things at the Academy, but had managed to work them out through practise and sheer determination. It was unusual for her to learn so quickly. Mind over matter perhaps she wondered? Whatever, it was a nice feeling to be at the better end of the scale for a change.

The next hour passed quite quickly and by the end of it, Eyre felt exhausted. She had used so much energy in the race with Pheria that she was tired—she hadn't managed to get the current technique again and the time between the breaths she took became shorter and shorter. She wasn't alone—it seemed most people were having trouble spending so much time under the water. Everyone seemed relieved when it was time to go.

"Come on guys, let's get a shower," Abby groaned, "my muscles are aching."

They plodded along the path that led back to the dormitories. Eyre was walking slowly when she suddenly jerked back. Someone had grabbed hold of the Venator incubator that she'd slung over her shoulder, and pulled it off her arm. She turned angrily—that had *hurt*—and she shouted at the figure who held the bag up in the air, just of reach.

"BTL Ben, when will you *ever* let up? *What* is your problem?"

A muscle jerked in Ben's jaw and for a moment there was such a black look in his eyes that Eyre almost stepped back. But her friends moved quickly forward to her side. However, before they could do anything there was a voice from behind Ben.

"Give it back, Ben," Jax said softly. He walked around to stand beside Eyre and her friends.

"Ooh, lover boy is here to defend you again," Ben sneered. "Just as well, since you can't do it yourself anymore." Wyatt Rankins and the Curtis twins moved up menacingly by Ben's side and there was a tense silence as both groups stared at each other.

Beatrice's brows turned down. "Give it back, you moron!" She raised her fists as Jax took a step forward.

"Sure!" Ben hooted and flung the bag high up in the air. A collective gasp exploded from the group and Eyre cried out in fear. Her Venator egg! As the bag reached its apex in the air it slowed and then began to hurtle back towards the ground. But with reflexes like an AFL player going for the ball, Jax dived towards it and caught the bag just before it smashed onto the ground. Eyre ran forward and took it from him as he got up. Jax's eyes were flaming and he stalked towards Ben.

"Right. You've had this coming for a long time, mate," he said softly.

But suddenly Eyre felt a wave of dizziness and when it passed, Rachis was standing in front of them, his face a dark shade of purple and his jaw clenched. But it seemed he was so enraged he couldn't speak, because he said nothing. With an expression that looked like fire was going to shoot out of his eyes, he walked up to Ben, picked him up as if he weighed nothing and threw him on the ground, hard.

Ben jumped up furiously, but before he could react, Rachis had picked him up and thrown him on the ground again with even more force. Ben let out a loud grunt. Rachis stood over the boy menacingly.

"Stay there," he warned in a tight voice. "The third time will hurt." Eyre was pretty sure it had hurt the first two times, so the third time would be interesting, she thought.

However, despite the fact that Ben looked like he wanted to get up and fight the instructor, he wisely decided to remain on the ground.

"Who are you?" he shouted. "My father will hear of this!"

"Indeed he will," Rachis returned. "I report all attacks on Lightworkers to the Echelon, and anyone who threatens a Venator is a menace to our people. I'll be preparing a detailed account of this; you can be sure."

At the mention of the Echelon, Ben finally started to look unsure. A silence descended.

"Get out of here," Rachis said, with a look that caused Ben to scramble to his feet. He left sullenly, but fast, his cronies in tow. Even they could see Rachis was not one to be messed with. At least Rachis is targeting someone else this time, Eyre thought, but had to revise that opinion a second later.

"And you!" he shouted at Eyre, taking the bag from her. "Guarding your Venator egg is your *most* important task, one you have failed dismally!" He knelt down and opened the bag and took the box out. Carefully he opened the box and looked inside. His face relaxed slightly and he closed it again.

"Fortunately, the egg appears to be in good shape. If it had hit the ground, you would have killed your Venator."

"That's not fair—it wasn't Eyre's fault—" Abby began, but was interrupted by Rachis.

"It is the duty of the student to guard their egg, no matter what the circumstances are. No excuses—it is *your* responsibility!" He pointed a finger at Eyre and a disgusted look crossed his face.

"I knew this was a bad idea. Why you are in the Unlit is beyond my comprehension. One more chance, that's it." Another nauseating wave passed over Eyre, and when she opened her eyes, Rachis was gone. A blush rose up her cheeks—he was right, she realised. It would be her fault if anything happened to that egg. And it was embarrassing to be criticized so harshly in front of her friends.

"Jeez Eyre," Zanda said. "Are they all like that at the Unlit?"

Eyre sighed. "No, fortunately, but I do seem to have a gift for getting staff riled up—here *and* there. He doesn't like me very much. But at least my egg is okay, thank the Light for that." She looked over at Jax, who was now standing awkwardly, trying to find the right moment to leave, Eyre assumed. An instant of annoyance passed through her, and she thought—well *go* then, I'm not keeping you! But she swallowed the irritation.

"Thanks Jax, it might have been a different outcome if you hadn't caught the egg."

"No worries," he replied. It looked like he wanted to say something else, but after a pause he just raised his hand and headed off. A silence ensued as everyone looked at each other.

"I know Ben's a jerk," Beatrice said, "but even I'm starting to wonder why he dislikes you so much. It doesn't make sense really."

Eyre shrugged. She was tired of Ben Perrill, who had been targeting her from the moment they met. "Who cares? It's not worth worrying about. I'll just have to be more careful in future." She watched Jax's receding form with troubled eyes and Abby noticed.

"As for him," Abby said, nodding her head down the track. "Don't sweat that either!"

Eyre laughed and the group started back towards the dorms. "Good advice, as usual. Let's go get that shower!"

# CHAPTER THIRTEEN

EYRE WOKE WITH A start. A loud cacophony filled the dormitory as the sirens went off for the second time since Eyre started at the school. The sky was dark outside and she had no idea what time it was as she scrambled out of bed. Beatrice and Abby were throwing off their bedsheets as the deafening shriek pierced their ears.

"What's happening?" mumbled Beatrice as she rubbed her eyes. She squinted at the clock on her desk. "By the Light, it's 2am!"

A clomp, clomp, clomp could be heard out towards the Central Administration building, accompanied by a deep chanting that gradually increased until it formed a rhythmic background to the screaming siren. Suddenly the alarm stopped and a voice called from the corridor.

"Open your doors, girls." Jemima Periwinkle for once had lost her high-pitched voice and she sounded out of breath as she faced the heads appearing out of the doorways.

"Someone has tried to break into the Mimir's Domain," she said, as the stomping carried on outside. "The Mimir have prevented the attempt but we are unsure where the intruder may be as yet and the campus is being searched. Please stay in your rooms and keep your doors locked. There is no danger but you must stay there until morning."

Doors slammed up and down the corridor and Abby looked at Eyre and Beatrice with round eyes as she closed their door.

"Wow, I wonder what they were after?" she said. "There's an awful lot of gold down there."

"Maybe the weapons?" pondered Beatrice. "They'd be worth stealing I guess."

Eyre looked out the window into the darkness. "Well, anyone who would venture down into the dominion of the Mimir is either stupid or mad, I think. They'd never get past that ferocious horde."

An uneasy silence descended on all three as they listened to the feet marching in the distance, up and down the campus. Evidently the search was going to take a while, because even after a couple of hours the battalions carried on the hunt.

Suddenly a shout arose from somewhere across campus and the rhythmic clomping changed to a chaotic din of hard feet running fast.

"Here!" bellowed a loud voice. "Over this way!" The feet hammered the ground as the troops charged across campus and into the bush, gradually getting softer until silence hung across the school.

Eyre strained her eyes out the window, but the darkness was giving nothing away. The only thing visible was a dim light in the vicinity of the moldavite square. She turned from the window and sat on her bed.

"Well that was a bit of excitement."

Beatrice yawned. "I'm tired but I feel too wired to go to sleep."

"Me too," Abby said. "I could always practise my theremin I guess," she added, her expression deadpan.

Eyre and Beatrice struggled with their faces and Abby exploded into laughter. "No, let's talk about the History of Light. That's sure to send us to sleep!" Beatrice hooted.

"Or Nick's trip to the caves with Professor Vela! Nick said it was so boring, stumbling around in the dark while Professor Vela droned on and on. Nick reckoned it was *worse* than the History of Light!"

Everyone shook with mirth. Only Professor Vela could make an exciting trip to the caves monotonous. "Well, I'm going to try to sleep," Eyre said. "It's 4am already and I've got Rachis tomorrow. If I fall asleep in his class I'll be roasted."

She slid under her covers and her friends did the same. But despite the hour, it took a long time for sleep to come and dawn was streaking the sky by the time her eyes finally shut. She knew it was going to be a long day tomorrow.

# CHAPTER FOURTEEN

THE NEXT COUPLE OF months passed quickly. After the ruckus of the attempted break-in at the Mimir's Domain, there had been a noticeable increase in the number of Mimir on campus, especially around the moldavite square, but the days had quickly settled back to the usual routine. And unlike Eyre's previous experience with the Mimir, they ignored her when she encountered them on campus. Evidently, she was no longer a revered goddess, which she had to admit was actually a relief, despite making her feel like she'd failed somehow.

Eyre contemplated the last fortnight as she headed along the track towards the ward for the Unlit. She had been running back and forth between campuses, trying to fit in to both, but feeling that she didn't really belong to either. Although she was staying with her friends in the dorm, it was hard listening to their conversations about levitation and psychokinesis and the other skills that all required the Viq she didn't have. The year for them had obviously started well and Eyre felt a bit left out when they recounted stories from their time in class, although she tried not to show it.

It was also difficult to participate in equestrian training and watch the progress of all the other students while Ischyros remained the most recalcitrant animal she had ever met. He wouldn't let her on his back, and when she tried to lead him around the ring, he would buck and kick up a storm, dust flying everywhere as he snorted and whinnied loudly. If she kept trying to mount him, he would drop down to the ground and lie there, refusing to get up. The Kikkuli master would look sympathetic, and she knew that other students were trying not to laugh, and Eyre had to admit, Ischyros's behaviour did look rather ridiculous amongst the other gleaming, cantering Lighthorses. But her stubbornness had kicked in again. Despite the fact she had been given permission to work with Ischyros on her own, she'd decided to persevere with the group, no matter how much of a scene he created. At least that way she would learn what she *should* be doing by listening and watching, even if she couldn't do it herself. Her face impassive, she'd led the tantrumming animal around the arena time after time, showing no more concern than as if she were leading a gambolling fawn.

Underneath it all however, she felt a resounding regret that she was unable to connect with her Lighthorse. The other students were doing so well. A couple more horses had taken to the air with their riders, and the other students were well in to the techniques of proficient riding. Pragmatically though, she'd decided that since she now had no Viq, it was a bit silly to be complaining about not being able to ride a Lighthorse. She was there only in case her Viq came back, which was seeming less and less probable.

Her classes at the Unlit were progressing better. She was making good headway with locks and picks, and she'd started "Dialects"—which was learning the languages of the Alterworld. Using an intense, hypnotic way of studying, the students were able to memorise words at a very fast rate, and Eyre could already speak basic sentences in all four Alterworld languages. 'Communication' had proven interesting too. Because the Unlit didn't have telepathy, they communicated by Peragrc, or Light Paper. They were also issued a 'communicator set', which basically consisted of two metal rings and a wrist dial. The students wore the rings on the forefinger and thumb and communicated in morse code in a series of high-pitched pings. The wrist dial was used to tune the waves to the right frequency for the receiver of the message. Eyre loved tapping away in morse code, and felt very much like a spy as she worked hard to learn the dots and dashes.

Archery was a favourite subject for her, and although she hadn't progressed very far yet, she loved the feeling of nocking an arrow and letting it fly. Silva, the third-year instructor, had offered to give her extra tuition to help her catch up, and Eyre had stayed after class twice a week to try and improve her skills. Shimmering lessons continued, although not too successfully in her case, and she'd started Basic Faceting—the technique for shaping and cutting crystal shards. Crystals offered protection, healing and mental acuity if they were used and shaped correctly and Eyre had learned that it took years—even decades—to become proficient as a Master Faceter. Historically there were famous Master Faceters who were revered by the Lightworking community. Christopher was aiming to be a faceter, and he spent much of his time poring over books with intricate diagrams of geometric shapes, strange-looking tools and instruments, and coded geographical maps identifying the mineral deposits of the Overworld. Christopher had a photographic memory, which had to help with complex information like that. Although not in Christopher's league, Eyre loved faceting too and was enjoying learning to cut the crystal. She was fascinated with the uniqueness of each shard and how to cut it to bring the best out of it, to make it glow with light, or perform a critical function, such as transmit light or to become a robust part of a building's structure.

But most of all during her weeks with the Unlit, Eyre was learning about their dedication and strength of will. Every student here was focused and self-disciplined; they were a very cool bunch.

However, she didn't really fit in with them either. She'd missed the whole first year, and was trying to get to know people, but it was hard when there was little time to socialise. And although everyone was very friendly and helpful, Eyre felt a reticence from most of them. It was unknown whether she would stay in the division, and she hadn't really been accepted yet.

Still, Christopher, Tina and Thomas had made it their mission to help her improve her skills, and they were always happy to answer her questions. It hadn't taken long for her to familiarise herself with the compound and coursework, and she loved the subjects. She'd decided to accept her lot in life, and just get on with it.

She headed over to the lecture room for Shimmering, one of the subjects she'd found the hardest. It had been a completely new concept to her, and it was obviously going to take a while. As she entered the lecture theatre she scanned the room for Tina, and headed up to join her.

"Did you remember your assignment?" Tina asked, pulling her own immaculate pages from her bag. 'The Analysis and Deconstruction of the Shimmer' neatly typed on A4.

"Yep!" Eyre answered. She'd had difficulty with the assignment, but as usual, there had been people to help and she'd managed to complete it fairly well. In fact, going through the mechanics of Shimmering had helped her to understand it a bit better and she hoped that she would manage it someday.

UD1 walked in the room and there was instant silence. He was revered by the student body here and all eyes were upon him.

"Today we are going to concentrate on one student," UD1 began. "Eyre, would you come down here please?"

Eyre flushed with horror, remembering her time on stage with Dr Botolfe, when she made a complete fool of herself trying to make an object levitate. She hadn't been able to do it at all, and had been labelled a liar and an attention-seeker by the judgmental professor.

Here we go again, she thought as she got up out of her seat, aware that all eyes were upon her. But then to her surprise someone started to clap and everyone joined in. By the time she reached the stage, the applause rang loudly through the lecture theatre.

UD1 registered her confusion and as the clapping died down he explained.

"In this school we also celebrate the *lack* of knowledge. It is an opportunity to learn, for the vessel to be filled, and for us to grow as Lightworkers by giving the gift of assistance. We all know you are new here, and you have had trouble learning how to Shimmer. So today we are going to focus on you, and helping you to improve. Does anyone have any suggestions?"

"It helps me to close my eyes," called one student from the back.

"Maybe think of your mind as being connected by an electric wire," another suggested. "When I Shimmer, I send a pulse through the mental wire."

Many other suggestions were made, and although Eyre was grateful, she was beginning to feel the pressure. All these kind students were trying to help her—and she was sure she was going to waste their time. Still, she had to try, so she closed her eyes and tried to imagine the mental wire the second student had mentioned. All at once a calm came over her. If these students were willing to give their time to help her, the least she could do was try her hardest. Focusing intently, she pictured a wire travelling from her mind to Tina's, humming with energy. Then she sent a mental pulse down that wire, with as much of a push as she could. Keeping her eyes closed, she tried again and again, each time trying a bit harder until she almost had a migraine.

Feeling her head was going to explode, she opened her eyes in defeat. Obviously, this was not going to happen. But then she saw all the supportive eyes upon her, and knew she had to try again and with an inward sigh she shut her eyes. If nothing else, it was good that she didn't have to look at their expectant faces. Concentrating hard, she sent the mental wire out, stretching over the rows to Tina and *focused.* Again, but better! The slogan of the Unlit, and she *was* going to do it again, until she got it.

Suddenly Tina jumped up in her chair, checking her watch. "She did it! I've completely forgotten what happened since Eyre walked down to the stage! What *did* happen anyway?" Quiet laughter circled around the auditorium and Eyre opened her eyes. She looked doubtfully at UD1 but the smile on his face confirmed that indeed, she had finally done it! Eyre stood as UD1 indicated she should return to her seat and she spoke to the auditorium.

"Thank you for your help! I'll try not to use this on myself or I'll have to start again."

There was another round of laughter and more applause as Eyre returned to her chair.

"Thanks," she whispered to Tina as the lecture continued. Just then, Eyre felt a movement from the box under her arm. The egg! In the last two months, apart from being vigilant for any danger, Eyre had become so used to the bag being there that she didn't notice it any more.

"My egg's moving," she said softly.

"It will be starting to hatch then," Tina whispered back excitedly. "It takes about an hour. Yippee! You're allowed to leave lectures when your egg is hatching. Go and find a quiet place and open the top of the box while you wait. It's a wonderful experience."

Eyre stood up and UD1 smiled and held his palm to the door before continuing with the lecture, as if he knew what was happening.

Outside she looked around and then headed for an area on the outskirts of the compound that had shady trees and a patch of grass to sit on. She sat down and put the incubating box carefully beside her, then opened the lid.

Inside the purple egg was jumping and rolling around the box. Fascinated, Eyre watched it tumble until finally a small crack appeared and the tip of a black beak emerged. It tapped through the fissure until finally the whole beak was there, and then with a major crack, the sides of the egg split open and Eyre's Venator sat in the middle, soggy and mewling with its three eyes shut.

Eyre waited joyfully, loving the sight of this bedraggled little creature, which was only about the size of her fist. After a brief rest, the bird started to move again and then like a light going on, the three eyes opened at once, revealing the vibrant yellow colour that Eyre had seen in falconry lessons. The small bird looked at her fiercely, then crying out loudly, took a few wobbly steps in her direction.

"Come on little fella," Eyre said softly. "You can do it." She put her hand on the ground and the baby Venator staggered over to her, falling once on its face in the process. It clambered on to her palm and Eyre brought it gently in to her lap. With a tissue she wiped it clean and then put it back into the incubator box. She wasn't sure how to feed it, but from the demanding cries it was making, she was assuming it was very hungry. Those yellow eyes looked up at her very crossly, and Eyre realised that she had better get some help with this. Sighing, she reluctantly headed over to the falconry arena.

# CHAPTER FIFTEEN

THE ARENA WAS DESERTED as Eyre carefully carried her incubating box over to the double doors. She knocked hard on the door and waited. Eventually she heard footsteps and not long after, the door was opened. Rachis looked out at her, frowned, then waved her inside and without a word led the way to the incubation room.

Once there he turned on a bright light and motioned to Eyre to pass the box over.

"He's had a good look at you, has he?" Rachis muttered and as Eyre nodded, he picked up the dishevelled little creature. She noticed that it turned its head so that the eyes could keep sight of her as Rachis peered at its feathers.

"Hmmm," he said. "Well, it's not a he, it's a *she*, for a start," he said, looking carefully over the bird. "In good shape and... well, now..."

He sat back, then had another close look to make sure. "Lots of purple spots on this one," he said. "Unusual."

Eyre strained her eyes but couldn't see any spots at all. The little Venator was still wet from inside the egg, and to her eyes just looked black all over. Then Rachis gave the box back and left the room. The cries from the hungry little creature were getting louder but more pitiful, and Eyre picked it up and stroked its shining head.

"Won't be long sweetie," she whispered. "You'll be right."

The tone of her voice seemed to mesmerise the Venator and the cries became softer until the bird sat quietly in her hand.

Rachis did a double take as he reappeared with a box of something gross looking in his hand. He looked at the little bird nestling into Eyre's palm and then at Eyre. For a moment, did she see his face soften? Nope.

"Here's the food," he said in a definitely not-soft tone. "A teaspoon of the mashed-up stuff every hour for the first three days, and then for the next three weeks, feed alternate soft food with worms five times a day. Then just carry on with the worms and we'll add some insects in. Your Venator will grow very quickly, so you need to keep to the feeding regimen or its growth will be stunted."

He slid the box of feed over to Eyre. "Keep the sling and the box until the chick is too big. It will keep her safe and warm. You're going to be tired in the next few weeks, but you must attend all classes."

Then he threw a leather object at her. "Talon-guard," he said shortly. "Your Venator will learn quickly to sit on your arm—or shoulder—gently; they are very intelligent creatures. But for the first few months you need to wear that or you'll be visiting the infirmary on a regular basis."

Without another word, he left the incubation room. Eyre looked inside the feed box and saw the mush that Rachis had referred to, as well as a tangle of worms in a leaf-like material, and a teaspoon. Carefully she spooned out a small heap of the soft food and held it out. The baby Venator suddenly realised breakfast was coming and opened its beak wide, clamping on to the spoon as Eyre tipped the mush down her throat. The food seemed to satisfy the Venator, because an instant later its eyes lowered shut and it was asleep, its head nodding. Smiling, Eyre put the small bird carefully back into the box and the box into the sling.

As she headed back to campus, she mentally hugged herself. What a wonderful creature! *Hers*! She couldn't believe she was so lucky.

# CHAPTER SIXTEEN

EYRE YAWNED AND NOCKED an arrow into her bow. Having a newborn had proven hard work over the past couple of weeks. She'd been up all night, feeding her Venator, who she'd nicknamed Florence until the official name was given. Florence was a hungry little thing, and there was no way she could go longer than an hour without kicking up a real ruckus. It was exhausting, especially since she had to go to class as usual and complete all her tasks. However, Eyre had fallen in love with her now fluffy little chick, who ran around after her wherever she went. When the little creature tired, Eyre would nestle her in the box for a sleep, but she could see already that it wouldn't be long until Florence had outgrown it. Florence's spots had appeared, and as Rachis had said, there were lots of them, black and purple marks dotting the yellow down that covered her body. And here and there a few grey contour feathers were beginning to grow in, covering about a third of Florence's body. They would eventually form the permanent plumage, the spectacular glowing grey of the older Venators. But at the moment they just looked scraggly, almost like the new feathers were about to fall out of Florence's scrawny body. And she did nothing to contribute to the image of the mighty Venator as she scrambled behind Eyre with her pitiful bleating—it seemed she was always hungry.

Florence sat down on Eyre's foot, exhausted, and chirped up at her as she let the arrow fly. With a rush of air and a faint sigh, the arrow hurtled through the air and hammered into the bullseye of the target, to Eyre's immense satisfaction.

"Great shot!" called Silva. "You're doing well!"

Eyre smiled at her and grabbed another arrow. One good shot was not enough. As time went on, she was picking up the mental attitude of the Unlit: again, but *better*! Eyre was determined that she would do a great shot every time she nocked an arrow. Nothing less than that would be acceptable. Silva walked around the class as the students practised, occasionally correcting technique, offering suggestions or compliments when someone did well. But apart from Silva, there was only the whistle and sigh of the arrows, the rustle as another arrow was drawn, and the constant thud of arrowheads hitting the target boards as the students concentrated on their practise session. Eyre was silent too, her brow furrowed as she studied the target: archery was a skill she was determined to master.

A movement from behind her drew her attention and when she turned she was slightly unsettled to see Rachis there, examining her intently. His eyes dropped to study Florence, who by now was asleep on Eyre's foot, her feathers drooped over Eyre's shoe. After a moment Rachis seemed satisfied and left without saying anything. Eyre turned back to the target, feeling relieved that she had passed some kind of test.

An hour passed quickly when you were focused, Eyre realised with surprise as Silva called an end to the session. Eyre tucked Florence into the box and packed up her bow and arrows, and headed with the group towards their next class, 'Blending'. Now they were out of archery practise, everyone was very talkative, chatting loudly as they walked the pathways. Florence woke up and was complaining of starvation again, so Eyre fed her awkwardly as she tried to keep up with the other students.

Julia looked sideways at her. "You should enjoy this," she said. "They aren't with you for long. How long is it now since she hatched?"

Eyre thought a moment as she shovelled the mushy goo into Florence's wide mouth. "About two weeks, I think."

Julia nodded. "Yes, one more week then and she'll be leaving to join the flock in the Ru-Ru trees."

Eyre felt disappointment rise. She sighed. "I know. I'm going to miss her. I wish she was with me longer."

"Yeah," Julia said, "I was really sad when Ro-Ne left me. But it's important they join the flock so they can start learning the life of a raptor. And we see them just about every day."

Eyre stroked Florence's head. "Well," she said softly. "I'll make sure of that." Something about this little creature had seized her heart forever.

The students arrived at the lecture theatre and took their seats as their lecturer walked in. Ms Griz was a young woman, very toned and fit, with a calm demeanour and an eternal patience. She had large eyes that seemed to observe everything at a single glance. She had noticed Eyre immediately in Eyre's first lesson, and had taken time to help her with the information Eyre had missed in first year. 'Blending' had turned out to be the art of being inconspicuous by using a range of skills. How to dress, how to move, what to carry—all techniques that helped a person to be anonymous, invisible by being unnoticed or remembered. But ironically, as Eyre had discovered, being accomplished at blending required extreme skill in *noticing* things. The environment, who was around at the time, what was happening. With one look, a person had to sum up the entire situation and respond to it instantly; mentally and physically stepping back into the shadows. It was not easy—being unnoticed took some effort. And it didn't always mean being drab and dowdy—sometimes not being noticed meant dressing 'over the top' in order to just be one of the crowd. It was a complex subject.

Florence squawked loudly and several eyes turned towards Eyre, and soft laughter travelled around the class. It was certainly difficult to blend with Florence around, Eyre thought wryly as the little chick's grumblings filled the auditorium. She dropped a couple of wriggling worms into the chick's mouth and silence reigned as the class began.

An hour later Eyre trudged with the Unlit students along the pathway heading towards the ward. Their next class was another training session at the swimming pool, to practise further developing the 'current' technique. The class had been added to the week's schedule to help the Unlit improve their skills. All the students had been happy about it, including Eyre. She wanted to improve, and if another training session would help, she was keen to do it. *Again...* Eyre thought. *Better!*

She'd had erratic results since her first attempt, but last week she'd got it right for most of the 100 metres and she had liked the feel of rushing through the water. Although the rest of the session had been exhausting— it was obviously going to take some practise to maintain the technique for any length of time. As she walked along she thought about this year. For a change, she was not in the limelight at all. No one was overly interested in her, other than as a fellow student, which was a huge contrast to the previous year when she had either been doing things spectacularly wrong, been at the centre of some drama or other, or had the Mimir dropping in adoration at her feet every time they looked at her. For a change, she was actually doing quite well in some subjects. It was nice to be just one of the students.

Eyre put Florence in her box in the locker and changed into her swim gear. The year was moving on and it was getting colder outside, and several students put their towels around their shoulders as they walked out to the pool. Mentor Xiphias stood at the side of the pool quietly and waited for everyone to assemble. But before he could speak a coy voice called from the end of the pool. As heads turned, Jemima Periwinkle pirouetted in, twinkling her fingers and wearing a bright orange puffed-up dress and silver high-heeled shoes. Students looked sideways at each other, but no one was brave enough to comment. Jemima was just as big as her sister, Sergeant Tottingham, and probably not one to mess with, despite her sugary demeanour. And her hearing might be just as good too. She sailed up to Xiphias and took his arm.

"So nice to see you, Monsieur," she said as Xiphias stood awkwardly. "Class, please behave and listen carefully. I will be monitoring your progress." She tottered off to sit in the stadium and Eyre, who was standing at the outside lane near Xiphias was surprised to hear him muttering under his breath, which was most out of character for him. Jemima Periwinkle even had the ability to get under *his* skin, Eyre thought in amusement. But then Eyre's ears pricked up as she realised something. Xiphias's mutterings were suddenly making sense to her—Eyre's lessons in the dialects of the Alterworlds were enabling her to pick up some of what he was saying. What was that? Eyre caught a couple of words and thought hard. Double headed? No—*two* headed? Nope. Eyre's brow furrowed and then she snorted softly. Two faced... *two-faced.* Yes, that must be it. Mentor Xiphias was commenting on what he perceived was Jemima Periwinkle's... *insincerity.* Eyre kept her face straight as she realised this, but she certainly agreed; Jemima might be ridiculous, but she was also artificial and false. And an enigma, that was for sure.

Mentor Xiphias told the first swimmers to dive in and soon they were all in the pool, powering underwater and trying to get the current technique right. Eyre managed it a couple of times, her body arcing up and down like a dolphin, and when she did it properly the water seemed to stream smoothly over her body. She held her breath and tried to keep the movement going, her legs kicking strongly. It was impossible to keep it up for long though; it was exhausting. Eyre understood why it was going to take them all year to successfully learn this technique.

Eyre was on her third repeat journey at the bottom of the pool, when something at the corner of her eye made her turn her head towards the wall of the pool. The pool was made of quartz, so the earth could be clearly seen through the walls. Eyre had spent some time underwater studying the pool walls in the past year; it was a bit like an ant farm where you could see all sorts of fascinating creatures crawling through the earth, and she looked over, expecting to see a chubby worm or a colourful beetle making its way underground. But then, with a horrible shock, Eyre realised that she was looking into the red, menacing eyes of a foul and hideous creature. Slithering through the earth beside her and the other unaware students was a centipede as thick as a tree trunk, and almost as long as the length of the pool. It had grotesque pincers at the front and dark, mottled scales that rippled and grasped at the soil, propelling it forward, *following* her as she swam along. Eyre shot to the surface screaming.

"Strigis!"

Mentor Xiphias stood unmoving for a moment and then he felt the rumble at his feet.

"Run!" he shouted to the students at the sides of the pool and they took off without needing a second order. Life as Lightworkers had taught them that much.

"Out of the pool!" Xiphias screamed at those who had their heads above surface, and they leapt out, dragging each other up the sides. Eyre helped people out but there were many who were underwater, oblivious to the danger lurking beside them. Xiphias dove into the pool and after a second Eyre did too. There was no other way to warn the students. Xiphias swam to the closest students and Eyre went two lanes further, getting more students out. But three lanes remained, those students oblivious to the drama and unable to see the creature lurking at the other side.

Before either Xiphias or Eyre could get to the far lanes, the pool exploded as the Strigis smashed through its wall. Earth and chunks of quartz crystals flew up into the air and came crashing back into the water like artillery fire. A roiling sink hole of water dragged Eyre underwater into a mad, frothing whirlpool as the centipede crashed into the water, its sharp legs scrabbling on the slippery bottom of the pool. Desperate for air, Eyre forced her way up to take a breath, only to be dragged back in the swirling current towards the fearsome creature which reared out of the water. Its pincers snapped back and forth together, and it struck downwards, aiming for Eyre. Desperately she dived underwater and swam under the centipede, between its legs. But then the creature stood up on its long rear legs, ten metres above the water, and hurtled downwards with incredible speed, too fast to outrun.

Suddenly Eyre was flying upwards out of the water, way above its surface and away from the monstrous creature. Then, as she hurtled back down, the centipede twisted across and slammed into her. With a sickening thud she hit the back of the creature and slid down its rough scales, tearing the skin off her body as she splashed into the water. The centipede snapped its massive pincers down towards her, but once again she was in the air, soaring out of reach as it struck where she had just been. This time she landed out of the pool, sprawled on the piles of rocks and upturned earth. She stumbled as she stood up and swung around to face the horrible creature.

Crashing its way through the dirt, the huge centipede lurched towards her, swamping Eyre with waves of blinding mud. Mentor Xiphias leapt from the water to stand in front of Eyre as the monster reared high in the air above them. Eyre could see the last of the students scrambling out the end of the pool, some of them screaming in fear, and they stampeded across the campus towards an orange spot in the distance—Jemima Periwinkle, staying well out of the way.

With a terrifying roar, the centipede struck down with its pincers and Eyre ducked, already feeling the lethal bite which was inevitable. But to her surprise, the pincers smashed together over an invisible force, ineffectually chopping together as the terrible creature struggled to bite at them. Terrified, Eyre listened to the frustrated snapping of its jaws as she cowered on the ground.

Then, just as she thought the creature was going to force its way through the barrier, there was a huge flash of light and the head of the Strigis was completely blown away. The centipede's body hung in the air for a moment and then crashed to the ground in the upturned dirt, green goo oozing from the place where its head had been. A heavy silence hung over the area and for a moment Eyre was unable to move. Then she leaned over to Xiphias and hugged him, weeping.

"Thank you, Mentor," she gasped as tears streamed down her face. Xiphias patted her head as they sat on the ground.

"Was not me, Eyre," he said in his soft voice, his beautiful turquoise eyes looking at her in concern. Then they both turned as someone approached them. Large boots appeared and Eyre looked up to see Lord Clarembout towering over them, his face drawn with worry.

"Dealt with that foul creature," Lord Clarembout said, holding out a hand to help them up. "Are you alright?"

Eyre wiped her eyes as she struggled to her feet. Her skin was ripped off and bleeding in many places and she was bruised everywhere. But most of all, she felt an incredible tiredness that came from deep within her. Her legs gave way and as Lord Clarembout caught her, there was a flash of light and then blackness.

# CHAPTER SEVENTEEN

EYRE OPENED HER EYES. *Where? What?* Her head spun wildly as her scrambled thoughts crashed together, and then after a moment she realised she was in the Infirmary. She struggled as she tried to sit up, her whole body feeling pulverised and bruised. Sister Murphy, the Academy's nurse, walked over to her quickly.

"Wait there," she said soothingly, "let me help you. You've had a terrible experience."

With Sister Murphy's help, Eyre sat up gingerly as her muscles and wounds shrieked in pain.

"Is everyone okay?" Eyre whispered. Even her throat hurt; she had been screaming without realising it during the whole ordeal.

"Yes they are, thanks to you," said another voice, and Mentor Xiphias moved into view.

"He's been here since you arrived this morning," said Sister Murphy. "I'll leave you to talk."

"Florence?" Eyre asked, and then a tear of relief rolled down her face as Xiphias put the little chick on her lap.

"She quite likes me," Xiphias said, "but I think she's hungry."

Eyre stroked the squawking little creature. "Thank you for saving me, Mentor Xiphias," she said.

There was a long silence and then Xiphias spoke. "Well, it is I who needs to thank you, in actual fact."

Eyre looked up. "You pushed me up into the air. You shielded us from the centipede's pincers?"

Mentor Xiphias shook his head. "That was not me, Eyre. I do not have those powers."

Eyre looked confused. "Lord Clarembout?" Again Xiphias shook his head. "He only killed the creature. It took a while before any of the staff realised what was happening."

Eyre frowned. "Then Ms Periwinkle must have..." Her voice trailed off as she saw the look on the Mentor's face.

"She was 'protecting' the students, well away from the danger," was all he said drily.

Eyre shook her head. "But I have no Viq," she said. "So who...?"

Sister Murphy interrupted her musings, arriving with Sergeant Tottingham in tow. Xiphias looked at them for a moment and then patted Eyre gently on the arm.

"I will be seeing you soon, Eyre. I commend you for your courage. You gave us warning, and stayed to give enough time for everyone to escape. That was a fearsome creature, and the outcome could have been disastrous."

He left the room and the Sergeant sat down in his seat. She rubbed her brow as she studied Eyre.

"How do you feel?"

"I'm fine," Eyre replied, although she most definitely did not feel fine.

"Hmmm." The Sergeant shook her head and looked at her hands. "This goes no further I hope, but I would like to apologise for my sister."

Her voice was slow. Eyre recognised the taint of shame in it and hurried to reply.

"Someone needed to help the other students," she said quickly. "And it all turned out well anyway."

The Sergeant looked up. "You are very brave," she said in her gruff voice. "And kind." Then she stood up. "You will be here a few days to recover while we look into the incident. I hope you feel better soon."

Eyre slid slowly back down into the bed, trying to move as carefully as possible and exhausted even from that small exchange. Sister Murphy had applied some healing ointment to her wounds but Eyre's body felt like a train wreck and she wasn't looking forward to the next few days. She could hear Sister Murphy talking to someone in the corridor and then Beatrice, Abby and Nick burst in.

"By St Illuminado, Eyre," Abby cried. "We were so worried!" She sat down with a bounce on the side of the bed.

Beatrice rushed over and hugged Eyre then sat on the other side. "That *creature*, the Light save me!"

Nick hovered at the end of the bed, his eyes dark. "Twenty students were injured," he said. "But luckily no one has had to go home, although ten of them are here in the Infirmary—mostly broken bones. Georgia was one of them; she broke her arm." Eyre shook her head. Poor Georgia, *that* was going to interfere with studies.

Beatrice was stroking Florence, who had settled on the covers by Eyre's side. "Apparently they're starting the clean-up of the area this week. The locker room and facilities weren't hit, so it won't be as big a job as it might have been. And it was lucky for Florry."

There were footsteps down the corridor and Sister Murphy came bustling in. "I said a quick visit," she said firmly, standing at the doorway, her message clear. Abby smiled ruefully.

"Just when we were about to practise our Ferito—what a shame!"

Eyre waved at her friends as they left and studied the ceiling, trying to remember what had happened that morning. It all had been so quick. The burning red eyes of the centipede through quartz wall, the smashing of the pool and the screaming and panic. Being shot up into the air and then protected by a shield with Mentor Xiphias... it was all a blur really.

Someone cleared their throat, interrupting Eyre's musings.

"Can I come in?"

Jax hovered at the door, a bandage wrapped around his head. Despite the fact he had a black eye, his eyes glowed as green as ever and Eyre found to her annoyance that she was blushing—again. Would she ever be able to control that?

"Sure, no problem," she said. "What happened to you?"

Jax pointed at his forehead. "A lump of quartz. Five stitches."

He perched on the end of the bed and studied her carefully. "I'm glad you're okay," he said softly.

Eyre's blush deepened and she started talking, trying to cover the awkwardness. "Well, I've been trying to remember what happened, and it's really difficult. I mean, the whole thing happened so quickly..."

"I thought you were gone, Eyre," Jax said. "The way that creature came down..."

Eyre looked at him, realisation dawning. "You were there too?" she breathed. She thought back. "You lifted me up? Made the shield?"

Jax shook his head. "The shield yes, but I didn't lift you up. I got out of the water just as the thing tried to bite you. Thank the Light I was able to hold the force 'til Lord Clarembout got there." He moved up the bed and took Eyre's hand. "I never would have forgiven myself if something had happened to you."

Eyre was dumbstruck. Just when she was used to Jax ignoring her, irritating her or straight out running away from her, he turned around and said *that*? She opened her mouth in surprise, about to make an acerbic comment when Jax moved toward her swiftly and kissed her before she could say anything.

Eyre lost all capability of thinking as the wonderful feeling of his mouth on hers overcame her. It was like swirling through a sky full of stars—unfathomable, magical, it felt so *right*. And then the kiss ended. When Eyre slowly opened her eyes she saw Jax was still close to her, his own mesmerising eyes fixed on her.

"Don't give up on me Eyre," he whispered, and then left.

Eyre lay back and exhaled. OMG. Her skin tingled like it had been burnt, but in a wondrous, life-changing way—with just one light kiss, Jax had made her feel like she was levitating in a wondrous, sparkling spiral. She ran her fingers slowly over her mouth, savouring the memory. No matter what else happened, she was going to treasure this moment. Jax was indeed a mystery, but she had no doubt now how he felt about her.

Then she felt the inexorable tug of exhaustion, despite her exhilaration at the encounter with Jax and in a few moments her body had dragged her unwillingly into a deep sleep.

The next morning Eyre woke and felt much better than the day before. She had thought it would take days for her to recover, but in actual fact, her cuts and bruises were fading, and the terrible pain in her body had lessened to minor discomfort. Obviously the magical ointment had done the trick—or maybe, she thought wryly, it was Jax's magical care? Whatever the reason, she swung her feet onto the floor and stood up, realising that she was feeling quite good. Florence was causing all sorts of ruckus in the Infirmary, letting everyone know her complaints about starvation, so Eyre decided it might be a good idea to head back to her room. She was sure Sister Murphy had more than enough people to look after as it was. The harried Sister was surprised to see Eyre walking around so well, but agreed that if she was feeling okay, she could check out. After the Sister made a few notes on Eyre's chart, Eyre picked up Florence and her box and headed out of the building.

To Eyre's surprise, Florence wouldn't get back in her box, and insisted on running behind Eyre, occasionally flapping her wings as if to take off. She had more grey feathers appearing, so that now about two thirds of her body was covered. The new feathers were coloured dove grey, and the spots grew in with them, but they were now much more defined and iridescent. And most noticeably, there was a new light dawning in Florence's eyes, a focus that hadn't been there before. Eyre sighed as she realised that it would not be long until Florence took to the air and left to join the flock.

About half way back to her room Eyre hesitated, and then headed off in another direction, towards the stables. It had been a few days since she had seen Ischyros, and she decided she would spend a bit of time with him and groom him. Slowly she walked through the arena and down the laneway to Ischyros's stall. Florence jumped and ran behind her, her sharp yellow eyes taking in everything as she squawked and screeched. It was Florence's first visit to the stables—Eyre had been leaving Florence with her unofficial aunties when she went for her morning run. The little bird was chirping in excitement, scurrying along trying to keep up.

Ischyros turned his head as Eyre opened the door to his stall.

"What, By St Illuminado, is that ruckus?" he complained, tossing his head and staring down at Florence. "What an ugly creature! So unkempt!"

Eyre thought that that was a prize comment indeed, coming from the horse who usually looked like he'd emerged after three months in a windswept desert, but kept her thoughts to herself. She fetched the grooming kit and began with slow, gentle strokes of the brush. Ischyros said nothing, but that was a good thing really, Eyre thought, and Eyre herself found the grooming a calming task. She worked through Ischyros's mane, then tidied up his feet and was about to start his tail when with a hop and a shriek Florence took to the air and fluttered for a moment before landing on the ground again. If Eyre was surprised, Ischyros was apparently even more so, because with a snort he dropped to the ground, lying in the dust.

"Oh for goodness sake Ischyros, get up," Eyre said crossly. "I've just brushed you!"

Ischyros stayed stubbornly on the ground. "I can't be expected to stand still with that creature leaping around," he said in an ill-tempered tone. "Get rid of it. Send it off to the chef or something."

Eyre was suddenly overcome with an urge to giggle, but she controlled herself, knowing that this would not help. Ischyros was starting to kick his legs, creating a wild storm of straw and dust in the stall. So Eyre put Florence outside the door, steeling herself against the pathetic cries as Florence scrabbled at the stall door to get in. Eyre stuck her head over the door, looking down at Florence, who sat pitifully in the dust.

"Just a minute, sweetie. Be good." Then Eyre turned back to her mighty Lighthorse, who was now covered in dirt and straw and was still lying stubbornly on the ground.

"Come on, Ischyros, if you get up I'll brush all that off you." With a grumble Ischyros got back to his feet and Eyre started to brush him down again. After about half an hour she had finished, and he was looking quite good. Then there was a screech from outside and Florence flew up to land in a wobbly spiral on the stall door. That was it! With a loud whinny and a kick of his back legs, Ischyros flopped down again.

"Oh for the Light's sake, Ischyros, it's just a chick!" Eyre cried out in frustration.

"Well, what is it doing?" Ischyros snapped. "Appearing out of nowhere like that, all that fluttering and scrabbling – that's not flying! It's enough to give a horse a heart attack!"

In amongst this list of complaints a dawning suspicion was arising in Eyre. Was Ischyros *jealous*? Of this little creature? Surely not. But as the old horse carried on and on about the scrabbling and the hopping and the fluttering, she thought that maybe he was a bit put out that this 'unkempt' creature could fly when he couldn't. So she held her frustration and put a hand on his head.

"Come on Ischyros, get up," she said softly. "I'm sorry if Florence is upsetting you. Hop up and I'll get that dirt off you."

By the time she got the muck off Ischyros for the third time, it was getting towards lunch time. Third-year students were beginning to come in for their equestrian lesson, and Eyre decided to stay and watch. With surprise, as she stood with her scruffy horse and her scraggly bird, and her lack of Viq, she realised that for the first time she wasn't feeling envious of the other students with their beautifully groomed and shining mounts. She was quite happy with the silly old horse she had, and the flapping little bird.

She stayed in the stall with Ischyros, who by now had turned around and was nosing at Florence, occasionally shoving her off the door. Florence would happily flap back up to do it all over again. Eyre stroked Ischyros's head and played with his mane as they watched the exercises going on in the yard outside the stall. Many of the students were jumping obstacles and cantering with ease around the arena, and several horses took off into the sky—which caused Ischyros to knock Florence off the door again. But there was a peace seeing them all ride so beautifully, and Eyre was quite content to just rest and watch.

Eventually the class ended and Eyre packed up the grooming equipment. Ischyros, sensing she was leaving, shoved Florence off into the dust again.

"Bye Ischyros," Eyre said, as she picked up the little bird and closed the stall door.

"Glad you're taking that thing away," was all he said as he headed for his feed bucket.

Eyre smiled and tossed the grooming gear into the storage shed.

"Love you too," she called as they headed for the dorms, ignoring the loud explosion of wind from Ischyros's rear end that answered her.

# CHAPTER EIGHTEEN

THAT EVENING AT THE refectory there was a low hum in the air as students talked about the excitement of the past couple of days. They hadn't been told anything yet, so when Lord Clarembout strode to the front of the room there was an instant, expectant silence as all eyes turned towards him.

"Thank you," he said. "Please continue to eat while I talk. As you all are well aware, we had another breach on campus this week, which thankfully ended before more damage could be done. We all extend our best wishes to those who were injured and wish them a speedy recovery.

"The security at the Academy is of great concern to the Lightworking community, which is why Whittaker Ray has departed to speak to the Echelon and won't be back until next week.

"In his absence, and after talking to staff and students present at the time, I would like to fill you in on the facts. That creature, one of the Strigis, is called a Sublabor, as some of you might know. It is a deadly and ferocious creature, normally only found in the fiery depths of the earth. The fact that it has emerged on our grounds, and with such devastation, is of course, a very grave matter. Fortunately, Ms Periwinkle was able to keep the Sublabor at bay and she was able to help our students and Mentor Xiphias before it could kill or maim anyone."

After a moment an awkward round of applause smattered through the refectory. Despite this accomplishment, Jemima Periwinkle was hardly a popular teacher and the students' lack of enthusiasm reflected their opinion. But Eyre kept her hands determinedly in her lap. *What?* She was livid—*Jax* had made the shield that protected Eyre and the Mentor, not Jemima Periwinkle! She opened her mouth in outrage, about to cry out at this travesty, when she noticed Sergeant Tottingham staring down at the top of the staff dining table, her jaw gritted. Lord Clarembout might have been hoodwinked by Jemima Periwinkle, but the Sergeant obviously knew the truth. After a moment Eyre shut her mouth in frustration, unable to speak the words that would cause such embarrassment to the Sergeant.

But her stomach roiled as she saw Jemima Periwinkle waving a modest hand at the students. Not only a coward, but a *liar* as well, Eyre thought, and her dislike for the lecturer increased tenfold. She looked across at Jax, but he just caught her eye and shook his head. Evidently, he was quite okay with someone else taking the credit for his actions. Lord Clarembout continued, with only the muted scrape and clatter of cutlery on china in the background.

"I encourage you all to talk to each other, and we do have counsellors for those who might need a bit of extra help to process the incident. Please make use of the counsellors—there is no shame in seeking assistance; indeed, it is a smart thing to do," Lord Clarembout continued.

"Classes for second-year students will be as normal tomorrow, except for, of course, swimming classes. Instead, students are to go to Lecture Theatre 3 instead of the normal swimming lessons, and Mentor Xiphias will continue with the theory and introduction to Aqua, and the practise of the prohemium. Thank you, students, for your attention and if anyone has any questions, please see me after dinner."

Lord Clarembout left the room, his large boots clumping in the silence. But once he'd left, the buzz of many voices filled the air. Abby leaned over to Eyre.

"I thought you said Jax had created the shield?"

Eyre's eyes were furious, but she just shrugged. "Well, I guess it was rather confused—it was hard to tell what was going on really. I'm just glad that everyone is going to recover from it."

"More prohemium practise," Nick groaned, his head in his hands. "How's yours going, Eyre?"

Eyre rolled her eyes. "I wasn't any good at it last year, and I'm still no good at it. None of the Unlit have managed it—we're all struggling. It's so hard. I guess I should be happy for the extra practise time."

As everyone grumbled, Eyre smiled inwardly. The Unlit students would probably see it as a wonderful opportunity to learn and train, and would embrace the extra theory and practise with enthusiasm. Although Eyre was trying to adopt the "again, but better" slogan, she hadn't quite made it to that mindset yet. Oh well, she thought wryly: she was heading back to the Unlit in the morning so now she had the opportunity to work on improving her attitude.

Eyre looked back over at Jax, who was talking intently with Rigmar. As if he felt her eyes, he curved an edge of his mouth at her and winked, causing her stomach to backflip. *Stop* it, she chided herself. For goodness sake, be cool! She had told her friends that Jax had created the shield, but she hadn't told them about Jax's visit to the Infirmary, wanting to keep that magical moment to herself. She had to admit that a large part of it was her uncertainty that this... whatever it was... bond? between them would last, and not wanting to appear foolish if it didn't. So she just raised an eyebrow and smiled back, but subtly, so no one else noticed. Time would prove what this was; until then, she would be careful.

The next morning Eyre walked along the track towards the ward, with Florence scrambling along behind her. Florence was now fully covered in feathers, and was lifting off the ground every few steps as she got used to her wings. She still demanded grubs, but had turned her nose up at the soft food this morning—another thing her baby had outgrown, Eyre sighed.

Ferito was first up this morning, and despite the pain in her body, Eyre attacked her moves with gusto. After the frightening experience with the Sublabor, her determination to master the Aditus and Tego moves had risen again. The Unlit were incredibly good at Ferito, and Eyre was panting with effort as she battled Tina in the Clasis for Two-Handed fighting. By the end of the session she was dripping with sweat and she bowed in mock admiration to Tina.

"Thank you for the tutorial," she said. "If nothing else, I will be ready for my arms endowment next year!"

A commotion at her feet drew her attention. Florence was flapping her wings and hopping up in the air, squawking loudly with the effort. She rose a metre in the air and then crashed back down again onto the earth, gasping for breath. Two more times she did it, getting a little higher each time, but ultimately falling back down to sprawl awkwardly on the ground. Each time she landed in the dust her eyes seemed to glow crossly.

Tina watched her closely and exclaimed. "She's getting ready to leave, Eyre. That's early! She must be strong. Come on, let's help her!"

The whole class of the Unlit crowded around, clapping and encouraging the little bird as they watched her attempts to fly.

"Again, but better... again, but *better*..." they chanted in a rhythmic beat. In the background Thomas stepped up to rap on top of the beat.

*"My name is Florrie, I won't say sorry, I'll leave in a flurry and a great big hurry.*

*I'm headin' up there, takin' to the air, I guess that's fair cause my partner's Eyre!"*

Cheers and laughter followed Thomas's rendition and the little bird jumped harder and higher with each round of applause. Finally, with a loud screech Florence managed to fly above Eyre's head, circling awkwardly as she tried to maintain height. Then, faintly in the distance, there came the sound of a hundred Venators, their cries rising and falling in an orchestrated summons. Florence studied Eyre and tilted her head towards the sound.

"Bye, Florence," Eyre called softly. As if understanding that she'd been released, Florence flew even higher, catching an updraft until she was way above the ground. Then she lifted her grey wings and flapped unsteadily towards the sound of the birds until she was out of sight.

Eyre realised her eyes had filled with tears. Although she was happy her Venator could fly and was joining her flock, Eyre was going to miss the hopping little creature that had stuck to her heels for three weeks.

Thomas sighed theatrically. "Ah, they grow up so quickly nowadays," he said, clapping Eyre on the shoulder. "Come on Mum, let's get off to class."

# CHAPTER NINETEEN

BY THE END OF the week Eyre's aches and pains had virtually faded, and only the scabs remained to show what had happened at the pool. She passed the swimming complex as she, Christopher and Tina headed towards Lecture Room 3 for their Aqua lessons. The pool area was a busy construction site, with Mimir bustling around carrying huge chunks of quartz. Onsite, Master Faceters were shaping the new pool walls, and the Jotnar were digging and re-planting the gardens along the verges. In only three days a lot of work had been done already, and Eyre had heard that the school was aiming to have the complex re-opened in a couple of weeks.

Mentor Xiphias stood at the front of the lecture theatre, waiting patiently until all the students took their seats. Eyre went to sit with Abby, Beatrice and Nick. It was the only time she got to catch up with them in the day, so it had become her habit to do this for Aqua lessons.

"Where's Florence?" Beatrice whispered, looking around for the bouncing little creature.

Eyre sighed. "She hasn't come back yet. I guess it takes a couple of days."

Beatrice looked disappointed—she adored the little creature and loved picking her up for cuddles.

"Well, you have to bring her back to visit," she said, "her aunties miss her!"

Mentor Xiphias tapped the lectern for attention and silence fell in the auditorium.

"I would like to commend you on your behaviour earlier this week," he began. "The incident at the pool was a potentially life-threatening one, and you all acquitted yourselves well. It is good practise for your TACI test in November—you will encounter many difficult situations in Aqua.

"Today I would like to talk about the gazae you will harvest from Aqua." A low hum filled the air—this was something that had not been discussed yet.

"The gazae for the Aqua TACI test is a sea pearl found only in the Imum Clam, a giant bottom-dwelling shellfish. You will have to travel quite far to find the Imum shell beds, and you will also have to be quick, as they do not like giving up their treasure."

A coloured hologram appeared of an immense barnacle-encrusted clam, about the size of a small hatchback car. Inside the shell, the lips of the living mollusc were an electric neon orange and purple, with hundreds of small green circles dotting the tissue.

"The Imum has many photoreceptor cells in its body that respond to movement and act like eyes. So you will need to move fast to get the pearl out before it closes. We have had the occasional student get trapped inside the clam, and the only way out is to tickle the muscle at the base of the shell. It is not advisable to end up in this situation, however, as it can take up to an hour for the Imum to open again. Not dangerous while inside the shell, but definitely boring."

Laughter tripped around the room and Xiphias continued.

"The sea pearl is used for prophesy by those with the gift, and they are of inestimable value. Aqua allows only a limited number of these pearls to be harvested by the Alterworlds and Entis each year.

"You will require many skills to complete this TACI test. First and foremost of course, is your prohemium. You will also need to use the 'current' technique to move so that you use minimal energy, as well as to employ the skill of 'carousel breathing'—which you will learn next semester once you have mastered the current technique—to maximise the time you can stay under the water. The third skill you will need is 'water vision'. This requires you using your Viq to repel water in front of your eyes so you can see clearly. Employing all three skills will be the most difficult task you have yet learned—a complex skill called a 'tri-merit' skill; one that combines multiple skills. Until now, you have only performed uni-merit skills, and it will take you time and practise to achieve the tri-merit required to move through Aqua. Of course, Unlit students, you only need to learn the uni-merit skill of the 'current' technique, as you will use dive gear for this challenge.

"All of you will have an additional challenge in order to obtain your gazae. The Imum will close upon your approach, and in order for them to open again, you will have to talk to them. They are intelligent creatures, and shy. So you will have to communicate with them and find one who will allow you to take the sea pearl out. These pearls take years to form, so it may take you a while—the Imum do not give up their treasure easily.

"The language of Aqua is Thalassa, but you will not be fluent enough to use it during your TACI expedition. For that reason, you will need to work on your telepathy skills. Telepathy has no language, it is merely the conveyance of thoughts and meanings, and while you are travelling through Aqua it is how you will communicate with each other and any Aqua inhabitants. So, it is imperative that you practise this skill and become adept at it before the end of the year. Unlit students will take their communicator sets for this challenge."

Nick grimaced and looked at Abby. Telepathy was not his strong suit. "I'd better stick by you then," he whispered and Abby took his arm.

"Okay by me," she replied. Eyre's eyebrows rose minimally. Evidently some things had changed while Eyre had been spending time at the Unlit compound. Beatrice caught her eyes and gave a small smile. Yep.

"I would like you now to split into groups and practise your prohemium. Watch me as I demonstrate again—" Mentor Xiphias went through the now-familiar movements. Arms together, push up straight above the head, and then pull back down to the sides, almost like a breaststroke movement. The students stood and tried to copy his technique, but there were the odd giggles through the auditorium. It did feel a little silly to be standing doing movements like she was trying to fly up to the sky, Eyre thought, but pushed her arms up and tried again.

Suddenly there was a flash and a Seam appeared in front of Tina. Mentor Xiphias exclaimed in delight; no one had managed a Seam yet.

"Take a look," he said to Tina, smiling. Tina stepped through and the Seam closed behind her. There was a lengthy silence as everyone waited for her to reappear. Just when Eyre thought the Mentor might have to use the rainbow clip to retrieve Tina from wherever she might have gone, the Seam reappeared and Tina stepped through. She was soaked to the skin—and was that a piece of seaweed hanging from her hair? The seaweed was neon orange like a glow-stick and it looked quite ridiculous attached to her head. But Tina was elated, and Mentor Xiphias patted her on the back.

"Oh well done, student!" he encouraged. "Congratulations!"

Tina's success inspired everyone to try harder, and the lesson passed in a flurry of arm movements and deep breathing as students concentrated on getting the movements right. While the students practised, the Mentor showed holograms and talked about the various creatures they might encounter while travelling through Aqua—the dangerous Aqua Stickleback, a two metre long carnivorous fish with plates covering its body rather than scales; the swarms of poisonous Balloon Jellyfish that could kill a human with one touch; massive, twenty metre-long creatures called Nodolagem which looked like ancient dinosaurs with a long neck and three rows of razor-sharp teeth; and the mysterious and haunting underwater sirens called Scopuli that tried to lure humans to their deaths by singing. Xiphias also showed the fearsome Gigas Dragonfish, the ferocious sea serpent that Whittaker Ray had battled in his youth. Not the most friendly place to travel, Eyre thought, as she watched the array of lethal creatures appearing holographically above the podium.

When the lecture finished, Eyre headed down the aisles to congratulate Tina. She was patting her sodden friend on the back when she looked back to see her three friends watching her. Abby in particular had a strange, irritated look on her face—what did that mean? Jealous of her new friends? Eyre was completely taken aback. It wasn't her fault that she had joined the Unlit, and it was inevitable that she would meet new people. And although Eyre had not spent much time with her old friends this semester, really, it hadn't been possible.

Despite her justifications, Eyre felt troubled and unsettled as she headed back towards the Unlit compound.

# CHAPTER TWENTY

EYRE AND THE OTHER Unlit students headed to the falconry ring, where a stern-faced Rachis stood silently in the centre as they got their gear together. Rachis's eyes followed Eyre and she sighed. She was definitely not on the most-popular list with anyone today, it seemed. But she was hoping she might see Florence, who hadn't appeared since the morning she had flown away. Eyre was missing her.

When all the students arrived, Rachis motioned for silence.

"Today is a special day," he began and eyes looked at him curiously. "A count has been done and it has been determined that we have a new flock Apex." Rachis looked over at Eyre. "Our new Ne-Ne belongs to this student."

Surprised comments travelled through the crowd of students. They had all been well aware that Eyre had a new Venator, and that the chick was covered in spots. But to be proven the fastest as well, in such a short time was almost unheard of. Mylor, the owner of the previous Ne-Ne, smiled at Eyre, not concerned in the least that his bird had changed roles.

"I am happy for Fa-Fa to work with you and Ne-Ne," he said. Eyre's head spun. Ne-Ne, Fa-Fa, Shu-Fa... it was all very confusing and sounded a bit like something out of The Sound of Music—do, re, mi... ne-ne, fa-fa... Privately she decided that Florence would do very nicely. She remembered Tina explaining that Fa meant two, as in second, so Mylor's bird was now listed as having the second-greatest number of spots, as well as being the second-fastest in the flock. Florence had the most spots and was the fastest, which automatically made her 'one', or the leader. No wonder people whistled to communicate with their birds, Eyre thought. Who could remember where they fitted in the line-up? That was a matter for the Caelorian flock, with their piercing three eyes, to work out.

"Please summon your Venators," Rachis instructed, and the air was filled with high-pitched whistles. The calls were usually three notes in length, a short motif that was unique to each bird, and repeated at intervals until the Venator arrived. Within a minute the first birds could be spotted, flying high in the air on strong wings. But today there seemed to be a delay— and the students' expectant faces turned quizzical as they watched a few birds flying aimlessly above instead of coming in to land. As more birds joined the flock, it was obvious that there was a problem. First the birds shot sideways across the sky, then they spiralled high into the air. The bird at the Apex of the V formation suddenly broke away and glided in swoops like a rollercoaster heading down to earth, with an unruly clump of birds attempting to follow. Rachis's mouth was hanging open as he watched this display, and a line was beginning to form between his brows. Just when it seemed that the Venators had come down to land on the arm of their 'partner' (Venators are not *owned*, Rachis had told them acerbically) the first bird shot straight up into the air again, with the rest of the birds flailing behind, struggling to catch up. For the next thirty seconds the Venator (*Florence*, Eyre realised with growing dismay) did an aerial display worthy of a World War I biplane—loop-the-loops, zooming along horizontally upside-down, then swooping with large, soaring arcs that gave way to a plummeting drop. There was a joy in the flying that was palpable, and despite her consternation, Eyre was beginning to smile. The rest of the students were amused too, and the odd quiet laugh huffed from the crowd. But Rachis's face looked like thunder at the sight of this disorganised rabble. Birds all over the place flapping wings, trying to catch up to Florence; rocketing from the heavens and then stalling mid-flight; a couple even hit the ground, sprawling unceremoniously in the dust. It was hardly the impressive aerial force that the Caelus Venators were renowned for. The spectacle finally ceased when with a loud shriek Florence shot vertically downwards from a great height, pulling herself up at the very last moment to land gently on Eyre's outstretched arm. All around her other Venators were making ungainly landings as they attempted to keep up with their new Ne-Ne. By the time all the rather dishevelled-looking birds had made it to their handlers' arms, a volatile silence resounded through the stadium. Rachis's face was dark and his jaw worked.

"Hopefully a bit more practise and *team-work* will improve the efficiency of this new formation," he said tightly, his eyes looking hard at Eyre. Eyre was suddenly overcome by a terrible need to giggle, but she kept her eyes downcast and just nodded. Florence, for her part, seemed awfully proud of herself and she stood tall on Eyre's arm and strutted around, nailing the other birds with fierce eyes. Evidently she was taking her role as Apex very seriously.

"Student," Rachis continued, obviously unable to remember Eyre's name, she thought crossly. "You will work out your call with your bird now. Let her fly, then whistle to her. Once you have done it a few times, she will learn that it is her own call. Any problems, come and get me."

He turned and marched out, to the immense surprise of the students, who stood around uncertainly. A guilty look travelled around the group—it had been complete chaos and Rachis was certainly making his disapproval obvious. The birds were still panting, their eyes bright and hyped-up and it took some time before their handlers could settle them down.

Tina looked at Eyre, her eyes holding back laughter. "Well, we haven't had that happen before," she said. "Come along and I'll help you get started."

After trying a few combinations of notes, Eyre settled on a three-note motif based on a major tonic chord:

She thought it was a pure sounding melody, and strong, like Florence herself. Florence seemed to like it too: she responded to the call after only a couple of repetitions. It was like a game to her and her delight in flying up high and returning to the call made Eyre chuckle with happiness. What a beautiful creature she was!

After Florence had practised her dives a couple of times, Tina taught Eyre the other calls—flying sideways left and right, up, down, and assembling in a V formation. Eyre thought it was going to take some time to communicate those to Florence, but after watching the other students practising, Eyre realised that it was the flock who would teach Florence, rather than Eyre. Indeed, once the flock had formed the V a couple of times and run through the movements, Eyre could tell that Florence understood what the calls meant. Venators obviously had acute hearing as well as eyesight, because by the end of the training session Florence was performing the movements easily, at the Apex where she was meant to be. Eyre's heart filled with joy as she watched the birds flying through the sky with their strong wings and powerful bodies; it was a magnificent sight.

Rachis returned towards the end of the training and seemed slightly mollified as he watched the flock moving as a unit effortlessly across the sky.

Then as the session finished, Eyre and the other students whistled the farewell call, and the formation of Venators disappeared like an arrowhead into the distance.

# CHAPTER TWENTY-ONE

THAT NIGHT IN THEIR dorm room Eyre attempted to talk to her friends about the growing distance she sensed between them. Beatrice looked at her and shrugged.

"It's not your fault really Eyre," she said. "But you haven't actually spent much time with us in the past couple of months."

"We feel a bit like we've been dumped," added Abby, her cornflower eyes looking hurt.

Eyre struggled between a feeling of being unjustly accused, and distress that her friends were unhappy. She had been trying so hard to catch up and fit in with the Unlit, it hadn't left much time to do anything else. And with raising Florence and the furore of the Sublabor in the middle of it all, the days had passed quickly. But when she thought about it, and realised that when she did come back to the room, she was tired, and there hadn't been much conversation at nights like they normally did. Some of the problem was that while Abby and Beatrice could talk about their day and their training, Eyre was not permitted to talk about hers. So she hadn't raised the subject, finding it awkward. Part of her felt that her friends were being unfair: they had been supportive when she was not keen to go to the Unlit, but now that she was enjoying it, not so much. What was that about?

But most of all she just wanted things to go back to normal, so she swallowed her chagrin and did the only thing she could think of.

"Pillow fight!" she shouted, hefting her pillow into Abby's surprised face. After a moment, Abby's familiar grin returned and the battle was raging. By the end of it they were all gasping and laughing, and the tension was gone.

"We're just jealous," Beatrice chuckled, lying flat on her back. "We want a Venator!"

"And I want to be a spy," Abby added. "Those guys are so cool."

Eyre silently agreed. But out loud she said, truthfully, "They'll never replace you guys though. No matter what. I will be with the Unlit to finish my studies, but you both feel like my *family.*"

The girls hugged each other and Beatrice turned off the light. It took a while for Eyre to get to sleep, but she was relieved that for the moment things had been smoothed over.

✕✕

The next morning Eyre decided to visit Ischyros again, and to do some running. It had been a while since she'd done her early-morning exercise—the altercation with the Sublabor had interfered with her usual routine and she was missing it. So she left the dormitories quite early, enjoying the feeling of her muscles loosening up as she sprinted down the tracks in the cool post-dawn air. No doubt Ischyros will be happy that Florence isn't with me this morning, Eyre thought, smiling to herself. That horrible, fluttering creature.

She was so engrossed in her thoughts that she didn't notice someone was following her until he was right upon her. Thinking it was another student coming to work with their Lighthorse, Eyre swung around, smiling. But her smile disappeared when she saw who it was.

Ben Perrill grinned at her, but the tight smile was contradicted by the usual malevolence that lit his eyes.

"Thought you would have given up on that Pissy-Hoss by now."

Eyre clenched her jaw but didn't take the bait. She waved towards the track ahead of her. "After you."

But Ben just took a step towards her, and his eyes cast around furtively. Eyre suddenly felt very alone, and she took a step backwards. Then, with a blast of Viq, Ben hurled her into the bushes. Eyre landed hard on her back, winded, and she gasped for air as her head spun. Like one of the Strigis himself, Ben crashed into the undergrowth towards her and Eyre felt a streak of intense fear. Ben was a big guy and there was no one here but them. And he had Viq; she didn't.

She staggered to her feet before Ben got to her and took a deep breath to steady herself. Ben slowed as he got nearer, a malicious smile on his face. Then he raised his hand and sent a streak of Light energy towards Eyre. But the beam of energy hit the ground where she had been a moment ago—he had underestimated how fast she could move. Annoyed, Ben turned quickly and fired another blast at her, but again Eyre was gone, jumping up to a branch above her head and swinging out of reach. Desperately she swung herself in an arc past him, and then time seemed to slow down. She hovered a moment and then gave him a good clip around the ears as she passed. Holding his head, Ben cried out in rage and moved towards her with bared teeth.

"Right, I'm done playing," he said tightly, and pounded the ground hard, sending a wave of oscillating energy through the bush. Without thinking, Eyre slid up and down on the energy waves and then, concentrating hard, she *Shimmered* at Ben. Ben's mouth went slack and his eyes glazed over. Eyre dropped to the ground and in an instant was running as fast as she could towards the Equestrian centre. She had just gone through the doors when something hit her hard in the back and sent her sprawling in the dust. A heavy branch lay beside her and she rolled over to face the lumbering boy who had flung it from afar, using telekinesis. Eyre groaned, that had *hurt.*

"Your magic tricks don't do much," Ben leered. "Let me teach you about the true force of Light energy!" He rubbed his palms together fast and sparks started to fly outwards. After a moment he had created a circle of crackling lightning bolts, and Eyre scrambled backwards on her back, trying to get away. This was lethal force, and there was nothing she could do to combat it. Ben raised his hands, turning his palms towards her, when there was a commotion down the alleyway and the uneven clatter of hooves. Eyre looked towards the alley and her mouth dropped open as Ischyros emerged and charged across the arena. Even Ben was gobsmacked, and the lightning circle fizzed out as his attention was broken. Without stopping, Ischyros sideswiped Ben, sending him flying into the air across the ground until he slammed into the arena wall. Then Ischyros stood in front of Eyre as Ben stood up, his eyes wild, with a raging energy causing jags of lightning to spark from his hands.

"I'll kill you, you ugly old beast," he muttered, and took a step forward. Eyre leapt up, her blood boiling. The branch rose suddenly from the ground and flew like a missile towards Ben, but he dodged it easily and stood up with a sneer. The air was filled with a violent energy, but before anything could escalate, a soft voice came from behind Eyre.

"Ben, I think Whittaker Ray would like to talk to you," the Kikkuli Master said. Ben looked shocked and lowered his hands.

"We, we were just having a conversation," he said, his jutting jaw daring Eyre to say otherwise.

"I'm aware of what you were doing," the Kikkuli Master said. "And it's time for you to leave."

His calm demeanour caused Ben to slump and for a moment Eyre caught something else in his eyes. Desperation? She shook her head, confused and unsettled, and watched him go. The Kikkuli Master patted her on the shoulder and walked away, leaving her to lead Ischyros back to his stall. Halfway along Eyre flung her arms around the crusty old creature and buried her face in his ratty mane.

"Thank you," she whispered.

Ischyros snorted. "No one calls me a Pissy Hoss," was all he said.

Inevitably, Eyre herself was summoned to see Whittaker Ray, and she sat down in his office with hot eyes, feeling no small amount of resentment. Ben Perrill had targeted her since he had first laid eyes on her; vicious, even life-threatening assaults that were spiralling out of control and getting worse. How could the Academy allow it? If she were in Entis someone like Ben would be locked up. She sat in silence, furious, feeling this was a waste of time—nothing was ever going to be done about her tormentor.

As if reading her thoughts, Whittaker Ray looked at her apologetically, his blue eyes troubled.

"How are you, Eyre?"

Eyre shrugged. What could she say? And was he really interested? It seemed Ben would continue to be pardoned for his outrageous behaviour no matter what he did. Whittaker Ray nodded like he understood. He looked out the window for a moment, thinking, and then lifted a palm to Eyre.

"Affairs of the Echelon are not meant to be discussed outside the Chambers," he began. "Which has made it difficult for me. But in this instance, I am going to make an exception. You have been through too much and deserve an explanation."

Eyre looked at him in surprise. This was not what she had expected.

Whittaker Ray sighed and continued. "I am sorry for Ben's terrible behaviour, and that you have had to put up with it on several occasions. Ben's problem stems from many years ago, and the Echelon had decreed that he be supported because of it, in honour of Ben's father, who is a good man and who has sacrificed so much for the Lightworking community. But I fear we are at a point where alternate arrangements need to be made.

"Ben is infected by a mali, or demon, which is created by the Darkness. It was hoped that his attendance at the Academy might drive it out, but unfortunately, it only seems to be increasing in power. It is a tragedy—Ben was such a lovely kid."

Eyre sat back in her chair, hard. She'd never expected to hear the word "lovely" associated with Ben Perrill. But then, Abby *had* said Ben was okay once upon a time, way back. Then Eyre remembered back to the TEP trials before she joined the Academy, when Jengles had referred to Ben as a mali—obviously he knew all about this. At the time Eyre had just thought it was a reference to Ben's terrible behaviour, not an actual being. Thoughts spun through her mind.

"But how...?"

"When you were a baby, all your families—the Edmunsuns, the Wilsons, Richardsons, Perrills and your family—would spend a lot of time together at the cabins, most holidays, actually." Whittaker Ray shook his head sadly. "They were all such good friends. Or so we thought. Why, we will never know, but Ben's mother Deirdre went over to the Darkness, unbeknownst to anyone. It was she—heartbreakingly—who revealed to the Gothak that your mother, Alia, was an Aether, which brought the Gothak to the cabins. They tried to kill your mother when you were all having a picnic—the kids and mothers were sitting together under a tree while the fathers were barbequing by the Mantle Basin. They didn't kill your mother, but your brother Eric was killed in the chaos. Tragically, so were Nick's mother and Ben's older brother. But if it wasn't for the actions of Dr Perrill, many more would have died, possibly everyone. It was so unexpected, no one was prepared. Dr Perrill's quick reactions saved the others from certain death.

"No one realised at the time that it was Deidre who had betrayed them all—that wasn't discovered until many years later, when Ben was about ten. Deirdre had been feeding information to the Gothak for years, and her treachery was revealed when she assisted the Gothak in an attempt on the life of the Head of Aura Research."

It took Eyre a moment to register and then she gasped. "Oh no... that's terrible. Dr Perrill? Her *husband*? Is that why he limps?"

Whittaker Ray nodded, his blue eyes clouded. "When the attempt failed, Deirdre disappeared. But the close contact with the evil of the Gothak left Ben infected with the mali.

"It was a terrible, terrible day when your brother and the others were killed," he said slowly. "And it decimated Ben's father those years later when he realised that his wife was responsible for that, and for trying to kill him. I don't think he or the Lightworking community has ever recovered from that awful knowledge. After Ben's mother disappeared, the mali grew within Ben, filling him with hate and violence. Ben's father has struggled terribly with his loss. He has lost both his son and wife—in different ways, of course—but Dr Perrill's wife might just as well be dead. And Ben has never been the same since. It was like Dr Perrill's whole family was wiped out when Deidre disappeared. Dr Perrill left the cabins after that, and he and Ben didn't go back to them until recently. Dr Perrill remarried and does have a new wife now—who is not, as you have seen, very popular with his son—but Dr Perrill has never gotten over the terrible shock and betrayal. The Echelon has tried to help him, and to make allowances for Ben because of this tragedy, but I see now that this situation cannot continue.

"Ben blames your family for the death of his brother and the disappearance of his mother, and the mali exaggerates this rage and hatred, which unfortunately he has been directing at you. He has also focused his fury on Nick over the years, as he blames him too. Nick's father helped Ben's mother to escape after she tried to kill Dr Perrill."

Eyre tried to remember what she had heard. "Is that why he was made an Ex?" 'Ex' was short for 'Exile', and it referred to Lightworkers who had been stripped of their powers and banished from the community because of the terrible deeds they had done.

Whittaker Ray nodded slowly. "It's also why Ben blames Nick, and has targeted him over the years."

Eyre thought back to her time at the TEPs and tried to match the information she was receiving to what had been said before. She spoke slowly, frowning. "So, you knew who Nick was all along?"

Whittaker Ray eyes were troubled, and, unusually, he looked downwards. "I know this will be difficult for you, but I did. I couldn't tell him then, as it is information that should remain within the Echelon. And we did wonder at the time if he might be an Aether, so we needed to keep that possibility a secret. I really shouldn't be revealing all this to you now, but I feel now you deserve to know the truth, and it is probably better for your safety in general if you understand what has happened."

Eyre felt a violent fire arise within her. Her hands clenched as she looked at Whittaker Ray furiously. "How could you leave Nick there at the mercy of that monster of a father—and that beast Ben?"

Whittaker Ray rubbed his brow, as if in pain. "No one knew how badly Nick was being injured by his father and Ben. Nick took great pains to cover up his injuries, and he never said a word to anyone. When I arrived at the school I realised something was awry, and I was able to intervene. But it should have been done earlier, and it is something I regret immensely."

He sighed deeply. "I hope you can understand that the festering demon within Ben is what is prompting the attacks on you, and his generally vicious behaviour; this madness is beyond his control. However, although I am not sure how we will proceed from here, you can be assured that Ben will never lay a hand on you or attack you again. And I offer you the apologies of the Echelon for subjecting you to this danger. I had thought it might pass or improve; I know now I was wrong."

He sighed and looked out the window again. "These are dark times. The Gothak are rising, and it is evident in many ways, including this blackness festering in Ben's soul. We are fighting a potent enemy on many levels but please know that Ben's behaviour has been noted and will be controlled.

"I have kept you long enough," Whittaker Ray finished. "For a number of reasons, including the dictates of the Echelon, I am going to ask that you keep this information to yourself. Your friends do not know the truth about Ben's mother or the mali and we need to keep it that way. I hope you will understand."

Eyre grimaced. Yet another secret that she couldn't share with her friends. But she nodded. "That's okay, Mr Ray. It helps to understand why he's doing this, and I'll keep out of his way in future. Thank you for explaining it to me."

Whittaker Ray indicated she could go and he was still staring out the window as she left. An ominous feeling weighed Eyre down as she headed off to class. She was beginning to understand the secrecy her parents had operated under—it sounded like no one could be trusted. The Gothak were rising. And she needed to *focus*.

# CHAPTER TWENTY-TWO

THE AIR HAD A bite to it as Eyre and her classmates walked along the dirt track—autumn was nearly over and Eyre realised with surprise that she had spent half the school year with the Unlit. It had been a bit awkward with her old friends over the past months, trying to find time to be with them while still learning all she had to, and to catch up with the second-year Unlit students. But despite the difficulty of fitting it all in, Eyre did not regret one moment of it. She had learnt so much and her body felt fit and toned. Part of her motivation had been driven by the encounter with Ben Perrill—she had been seized with a determination to prepare herself as best as she could for any danger that might suddenly strike. The Gothak might be rising but she, for one, was going to give them a hell of a fight. To her surprise, Ben Perrill had backed right off from her in the past months; Whittaker Ray had been as good as his word.

This morning Eyre had undertaken Ferito training, followed by 'Tumbling'—a skill sort of like gymnastics that involved flips, tightrope skills and climbing to evade an aggressor. A parkour expert from Melbourne was part of the staff, showing students how to use the velocity of their body to launch themselves up seemingly impossible obstacles and balance precariously on difficult structures. And there was a mental component to the lectures as well—learning to focus and think, almost in slow motion. Initially Eyre had found the skill impossible, but over the past months she had improved greatly and found the adrenaline rush it caused was addictive. Just to prove her point, she did a somersault as she walked along. Tina looked sideways at her and, making no comment, upended to walk on her hands. Christopher, not to be outdone, ran up the wall of the archery stadium and flipped back over to land on his feet, then continued to calmly stroll along the path.

Laughing, they walked into the archery arena and retrieved their equipment from their lockers. By now Eyre's bow had been handled a lot, and the arrow rest above where she gripped the wooden 'limbs' of the weapon was worn with practise. Eyre had kept the bow she had originally been given, and she would regularly take it back to the dorm to polish it, but over time it was showing evidence of the hours she had put in trying to improve her technique. The students were on their own for the session this morning: Silva had left them to practise, telling them that they all knew by now what they should be doing—it was through spending enough time shooting that their shots became consistent. "One hundred and twenty arrows a day, ten quivers, if you want to get good at it," she'd advised, and Eyre had tried to do that over the past months.

Nocking yet another arrow, Eyre squinted at the distant target. Recently she had been practising with further distances and even the taciturn and dismissive Julia would pause occasionally to watch her shoot. Eyre's arrows always hit one of the blue, red or yellow central circles on the target board, and lately they were hitting the coveted X, or 10-point, inner circle quite often. She loved the training, feeling the bend and might of the polished wood as she pulled back the string and released an arrow; relishing the moment before it left in a blur, hurtling towards the target. It was a challenge and it was satisfying when the arrows landed with a loud *whump* into the target board. Today Eyre had a mental image of the Gothak at the centre of her target, and she was doing quite well at nailing the bullseye.

Eyre finished shooting a quiver of arrows and rested, watching her fellow students and trying to learn from them. After everyone had finished shooting, they would trudge down to the target and retrieve all the arrows before the next round of practise began again. However, suddenly she realised that something was about to go very wrong. As the last volley of arrows left their bowstrings, an emu appeared from behind the targets, picking up bits and pieces as it walked straight into the air space in front of the targets. It must have come from the bush, Eyre thought, panicking for the poor creature that was about to be nailed by a hail of lethal missiles. But then, a mini tornado of wind appeared in the arena and whirled across in front of the targets. Dust, sticks and the hail of arrows were sucked into the swirling air and then dumped with a clatter at the far side of the arena. The emu took fright at the ruckus, charging unhurt out the other side of the arena and there was an audible and collective sigh of relief—nobody would have liked to have harmed the silly bird. And as quickly as it had come, the whirlwind disappeared. The students also walked up to the fallen arrows in confusion. What had happened? A tornado? *Here?*

"Weird weather we're having," one commented.

"And where did that emu come from?" another asked.

"Very strange, but it *is* Entis," a third summed up.

There were no answers, so after all the arrows were collected from the ground and pulled from the targets, the students filled their quivers and began again. Much as the Unlit enjoyed a conundrum, their focus was too great to waste time when they could be practising.

Eyre studied the arena too, trying to work it out. Then at the far corner of the stadium, mostly hidden behind the targets, she noticed a familiar figure sitting quietly in the seating rows and she gave a wry smile. Whittaker Ray was here? Well, that explained it—although she couldn't explain why she hadn't noticed him before. Perhaps he had masked, or perhaps he could blend with the best of them. Whatever the reason, she nodded at him, glad the emu had been spared.

By the time Eyre had fired all her quiver of arrows—eight out of the twelve hitting one of the rings of the yellow central circles and three of those hitting the X circle—Whittaker Ray had disappeared. Checking up on her, Eyre mused, feeling happy that he cared. And she was pleased that she'd shot so well while he was watching. She may have lost her Viq, but at least she was making progress in the Unlit. Pleased with her success, she decided to take her bow and quiver of arrows with her after falconry, so she left them on the seat beside her. The bow needed a polish and a tune-up again and the arrows also needed some attention. There was never time during the day to do it, so she would work on them that evening.

She stayed seated in the arena as the other students returned their equipment to the lockers—the next session was falconry which was also in the arena. Eyre always looked forward to the class, despite the sour presence of Rachis, who had never warmed to what he considered an interloper within the ranks of the Unlit. Florence, after her initial tumultuous entry to the stadium, had improved weekly, and now she soared with ease at the front of the flock, her beautiful plumage fully grown in. Her yellow eyes could spot a lure from a great height, and she had learned to respond to the directional whistles as impeccably as a champion kelpie at a sheepdog trial. It was a sight to see the sleek bird shooting like a bullet at her call, and Eyre's heart swelled with pride as Florence—or Ne-Ne, if you used her official Caelus title, landed lightly on her arm. Florence's strong legs had sharp talons that curved dangerously, but her grip was gentle on the leather glove.

Venators also had to learn to respond to a hand gesture for silence; it was a critical factor in defence—not being detected was sometimes the best choice of strategy. As Rachis walked in, later than usual, the students all made the gesture and waited for instructions. But, obviously because he'd been held up, he bustled around without starting the lecture in the usual way. It was unusual to see him less than organised, and Eyre took advantage.

"Hello Florrie," she said softly so Rachis wouldn't hear. She scratched the top of Florence's head gently and the lids of Florence's three eyes drooped blissfully. She loved being tickled.

"Right," called Rachis eventually, his hair slightly awry. "I want everyone to launch their birds and then run them through the call sequence five times."

At his voice, Florence had lifted her head. She had learnt over the weeks that when Rachis spoke, the action happened, and she loved receiving the order to fly. So she hopped up and down in excitement on Eyre's leather gauntlet, until Eyre gave the whistle and released Florence into the air with a flick of her glove.

"Go, my beauty," she whispered as Florence soared upwards in the air. Within moments she was joined by the rest of the flock and the daily exercises commenced.

Halfway into the session, Eyre gave the routine call for Florence to dive, and she watched in awe as the flock followed, plummeting towards the ground. But then, something appeared in the corner of her eye and she turned to see what it was. So did Rachis, who seemed to have preternaturally sharp eyes; almost like a bird himself. As Eyre tried to figure out what the dark shape was that approached the birds at such a speed, horror bloomed on Rachis's face.

"Call your birds, CALL THEM IN!" he shouted, running towards the students, his arms waving. Pure panic thudded in Eyre's stomach at his tone, and when the dark shape neared she could see it was a black, vulture-like bird the size of a man. It had a wicked, sharp beak and monstrous talons, and its huge wings flapped as it soared beneath the Venators, cutting them off and interrupting their descent so that the V formation scattered in all directions. The Venators seemed terrified of the huge bird, and flew every way except the one to safety—downwards.

After a shocked silence, the students' distinctive calls to the birds filled the air. Eyre whistled wildly, her eyes fixed on Florence, who flew back up in a wide arc, trying to avoid the black bird as it swooped across the sky. Some of the Venators managed to flutter down to their partners' desperately outstretched arms. The distressed birds squawked with fear and turned terrified eyes upwards, following the menacing shape that flapped through the air. And then the terrible creature pursued one of the fleeing birds, catching up to it easily and snapping its body in two with its powerful beak. The pieces of the dead bird tumbled to the ground and landed with a 'whump' before the horrified students. Jogen, the Venator's handler, wailed in grief, a terrible sound as if he himself had been killed. He fell to his knees, and panic filled the stadium as the students watched the mayhem above; they realised that in a moment, they might also lose their beloved partner. Then, with horror, Eyre saw that the vulture had focused on Florence and was pursuing her at great speed, upwards, away from Eyre.

"FLORENCE!" she cried, and then whistled desperately, as loud as she could, over and over again. Finally, the call seemed to break through the terror that was driving Florence wildly through the sky, and she turned and plummeted straight downwards, too quickly for the huge bird to strike. It turned and followed her with great wing flaps, its lethal-looking beak wide open.

As she watched the foul predator hunting Florence, cold fury overcame Eyre, and a stillness rose within her. With one smooth motion she picked up her bow and notched an arrow, aiming it towards the sky.

"Come on, baby, come on!" she called to her panicking Venator, as Florence shot like a falling meteor towards her. Just as the dark shape seemed about to grasp Florence in its talons, Eyre released the arrow. It sliced through the air like a missile and buried itself up to the haft in the neck of the black vulture. The vulture shrieked in pain and hurtled towards the earth, landing with a great crash on the stadium seating.

The terrified flock was flying in all directions, and a moment later Eyre realised why, when more of the vultures appeared in the sky and circled below the Venators like hungry sharks. The panicking birds were scattered in all directions, unable to break through the dark menace that lurked below.

Eyre felt sick, but stroked Florence's head and lifted her arm. "Bring them down, my brave girl," she whispered, flicking her forearm, and then followed it with a soft whistle that was the "fly" call. Florence's bright eyes seemed to focus with understanding, and she streaked from Eyre's arm, straight up through the dark flock of vultures. The vultures followed, spiralling upwards towards the Venators with powerful flaps of their wings. Eyre wrung her hands as the evil-looking creatures approached the disorganised rabble. But then, like a beacon, Florence shot through the Venators, summoning them with a high-pitched cry. In a moment the flock had responded, forming the practised V with Florence at the Apex. Like an arrow, they turned and shot downwards, through the approaching vultures and towards the arena. But the vultures were quick too, and wheeled around to dive at great speed after them. Eyre's eyes burned and she fired several more arrows at the vultures. Another two fell out of the sky, but it seemed that the others were too close and as they stretched out their talons to seize the birds nearest them, fear rose like molten lava within Eyre.

But then, there was an ear-splitting *whoosh*, and a barrier of light suddenly speared through the air, stretching widely over the arena. The plunging vultures were unable to stop their trajectory and there were shrieks of agony, and the sizzling of flesh as they ran into the light. Several fell to the ground, roasted. There was a ragged cheer from the students as the barrier held; an impenetrable block of sparking energy that protected the Venators under it. The vultures that remained circled in frustration above the barricade of light for a few minutes, and then, screeching violently, disappeared into the distance.

Rachis had lost his normal taciturn demeanour and strode amongst the students. "Take them indoors!" he instructed. "Stress can kill a bird as easily as a predator, so calm them down, take them indoors and don't let them overheat. Anyone who has an injured Venator, please see me." His face was strained and he kept looking upwards, but for now it seemed the danger had gone.

Eyre's head was pounding as she tried to get quieten Florence. She shut her eyes and breathed deeply, and when she opened them again, the light barrier had disappeared. Hurrying, she followed the rest of the students into the stadium.

# CHAPTER TWENTY-THREE

HALF AN HOUR LATER, the birds were finally quietened down, and the students felt a bit calmer too. It had been an horrific experience, all the more-so because they had never before seen creatures like those evil black birds. Eyre stroked Florence, trying to soothe her with soft words. Florence couldn't see her as her eyes were shut, but the tone of Eyre's voice helped her to settle down.

"You valiant girl," Eyre whispered. "You saved them all."

Rachis was watching her with a strange look in his eyes. He seemed about to speak when the arrival of UD1 and Whittaker Ray distracted him.

"Please release your birds," Rachis called. "The danger has passed, and the flock needs to return to the forest to rest and recover. We will have them back tomorrow, so you needn't fret."

Reluctantly the students took the hoods off the Venators and launched their birds into the air. The birds seemed weary and subdued and disappeared out of the arena without their usual noisy departure. The students watched uneasily as they departed.

"They will be fine. I need to speak with UD1, but I will talk to you all tomorrow about this," Rachis said. As the students moved to leave, he added, "Eyre, please stay behind."

Eyre looked up in surprise, but also with trepidation, and then picked up her bow and quiver as the other students started filing out of the locker rooms.

"I'll see you a bit later," she said to Tina and Christopher, her eyes troubled.

Once the students had left, Rachis studied Eyre with his piercing gaze. Eyre felt very awkward with Whittaker Ray and UD1 there in the sidelines: the teachers she perhaps admired the most. But she waited for whatever was to come.

"You did well, Eyre," Rachis said, which nearly caused Eyre to fall over, because it was the first time he had given her a compliment, or for that matter, used her name. "Your archery skills were outstanding."

Almost speechless, Eyre finally asked, "What were those creatures, sir? Strigis?"

Rachis looked fierce. "No. Those were Vampire Vultures from Caelus. They hunt the Venator and feed on its blood and flesh. Very dangerous creatures, and normally a Venator does not survive an encounter with them." Gruffly he added, "We can thank you for that."

Eyre was surprised. "Well, I got a couple of them," she said. "And Florence brought the flock down. But it was Mr Ray's shield that protected them, really."

Whittaker Ray shook his head. "That was not me, Eyre. *You* did that."

Eyre was as shocked as if he'd told her she'd turned into a pineapple. "But... I have no Viq—and I didn't feel anything. That wasn't me."

"Come, we need to talk," Whittaker Ray said. "Rachis and UD1 have security issues to discuss, so I'll take you back to campus."

Eyre registered two things: firstly, that Mr Ray was talking about the Academy campus, not the Unlit campus, and secondly, that the school day was not over yet. Just as she was processing what that might mean, Rachis spoke.

"I owe you an apology, Eyre," he said in his sandpapery voice, "as I fear I have misjudged you. My own beliefs about what should constitute the makeup of the Unlit influenced my opinion of you, and I am sorry. You are the essence of the Unlit, and you proved yourself today. You had great courage and focus."

"I'm sorry you're not staying," UD1 said softly, as Eyre's bewilderment rose. She wasn't sure what was going on. It was if she had wandered into a conversation that was halfway over. Rachis registered her confusion and his face softened.

"Go with Whittaker Ray," he prompted. "Leave the bow. Come back and say farewell tomorrow."

Whittaker Ray touched Eyre's shoulder and with a white flash the locker room disappeared. A second after that she was standing in Whittaker Ray's office. As Eyre stood uncertainly in the middle of the room, Whittaker Ray waved her over to a chair and sat down himself. Eyre felt an echo of the last time she had been in this office, discussing Ben Perrill—a predator of a different sort, she thought, taking a seat.

"I can tell that you're a bit lost at the moment," Whittaker Ray began and Eyre nodded slowly.

"You are coming back to the Academy campus, Eyre," he continued, and Eyre was surprised at the jolt of disappointment she felt. How things had changed in a few months!

"But, I have no Viq," Eyre said. "How can I come back?" Whittaker Ray regarded her with steady eyes.

"We have thought for a while that you were showing signs of your Light energy returning," he said and Eyre shook her head, perplexed. *When?* As if she'd spoken the question out loud, Whittaker Ray continued.

"We didn't talk to you about it at the time, but it seemed evident that you escaped the Sublabor by levitating. All those nearby witnessed it, and none claimed to have helped you."

Eyre frowned. Jax had denied helping her to levitate, but she had decided that perhaps the momentum of the thrashing Sublabor had thrown her in the air. In actual fact she was surprised that Jemima Periwinkle hadn't claimed the credit. But she definitely couldn't remember any Viq of her own, that was for sure.

"So, we've been watching you, Eyre. You healed quicker than you should have, which was another sign your Viq might be returning. But really, it was safer for you to remain with the Unlit, so we left you there while we monitored your situation.

"Then the Kikkuli Master mentioned that you had used telekinesis at the equestrian arena with Ben Perrill. He said you threw a branch."

Dubious, Eyre thought back. At the time, she'd assumed the Kikkuli Master had hurled that stick, and in the chaos, she hadn't analysed it too much. But then she remembered skimming the pound, and hovering in the air as she passed Ben Perrill—both of which she'd put down to the normal momentum of tumbling skills. So, she wasn't convinced. How could she use Viq and not realise it? In the past she had always been aware when she was using Light energy.

"Then there was the telekinesis on the arrows today," Whittaker Ray continued.

"I thought that was you?" she said, and he shook his head. "Neither was the shield that formed against the vultures. The only person who could have done that was you."

Eyre shook her head, finding it hard to believe. But then, when she thought about it, she *had* felt a terrible anxiety about the emu that seemed to fill her whole body with energy; and the fear and rage that had been like a bushfire through her body when the vultures attacked had certainly left her with a massive headache. She looked at Whittaker Ray, a small bud of hope blossoming within her. Perhaps he was right? It scarcely seemed possible. But then a new worry entered her mind.

"What if I can't control it?" she asked. "That won't be any use at all."

"If your Viq is coming back, you will be able to control it," Whittaker Ray said. "It might just take some time. It is two weeks until the end of term, and you will have the semester break to practise. It's quite good timing really, because you will have the whole of second semester to prepare for the TACI expedition."

Eyre sat back in her chair, her head swirling. Her Viq was back? Really? She wanted to run out of the office and give it a go.

"But I thought that Aether stayed with the Unlit, to be hidden," she said slowly.

Whittaker Ray's eyes were sad. "Normally, that would be the case. But you are the only Aether left, and you must come back to the main campus. Unlike other Aether, you do have an Inguz, and it would draw attention to you if you were to stay with the Unlit." Eyre frowned, processing this. She supposed it didn't matter when she had no Viq; now it did. She sighed and got ready to leave.

But Whittaker Ray had more to say.

"Once again I will be asking you to keep certain facts relatively quiet," he said. "As Rachis mentioned, Vampire Vultures come from Caelus, which means that someone had to open the Seam and let them through. There is no evidence of the Gothak being involved, so we are again facing the probability that a Lightworker is working against us. I find it all very disheartening—an enemy we can't see. It's like acid, eating us away from the inside.

"We need to be careful and we need to investigate further to work out how that could have happened and to try and work out who it might be. Things are murky and it is hard to see the way forward."

Eyre could sense how depressed Whittaker Ray was, and she nodded her understanding. Then a sudden panic crossed her face.

"What about Florence?" she asked. Whittaker Ray was quick to reassure her. "She's yours," he said, "and you're hers. Venators bond with their handler for life; it's an unbreakable attachment, much as the Lighthorses have with Lightworkers. So Florence will remain living in the forest with her flock, but you will go to the Unlit once a week to practise falconry—it will be an elective subject for you while you are at the Academy."

Eyre sagged with relief. She couldn't imagine not seeing Florence again. Although comparing the bond of the Venator to that of the Lighthorse fell down somewhat when she thought about Ischyros. The only lifelong bond they seemed to have was to permanently butt heads.

"If you have any more questions, come and see me," Whittaker Ray finished. "You can join Beatrice and Abby for the last two weeks of class, and then next semester we will begin you on the Hese-based timetable. Welcome back!"

Eyre left the building, her mind churning, and feeling mixed emotions. She was glad Whittaker Ray thought her Viq might be coming back, but she didn't want to get overly excited until she knew it was true. She was elated at the idea that she might be going back to join her friends at the Academy, and that she might be using Light energy again. But then there was the fact she would be leaving the Unlit behind. She had come to love the classes and people there, and she would miss them greatly.

Then another memory struck her as she thought about the bow she had left behind. She was going to miss archery so much too, just when she was starting to get good at it. Who would have thought she would feel this way? But then she remembered Florence, and that she would be visiting the Unlit compound once a week, and she felt a bit better. At least she wouldn't be completely losing touch with them all. One thing was for sure —she couldn't have it both ways, so she had to make the best of whatever evolved.

# CHAPTER TWENTY-FOUR

IT WAS ALMOST LUNCHTIME, so Eyre headed towards the refectory, feeling strangely like the new kid on the block as she walked through the door. Lunch had been at the Short Stop all this semester, the eatery at the Unlit compound, so it felt a little strange as she looked for a table in the Lightworker's lunch room. Faces looked up in surprise as she walked through the large space. But voices were welcoming as she headed for the table where her friends usually sat for dinner. Eyre saw Georgia sitting with Pheria, and she was glad to see that Georgia's cast was off her arm.

"Are you back, Eyre?" called Rigmar. "I think this calls for a food fight!" He pegged a bread roll at her but with one swift movement she caught it in her hand. Life with the Unlit had left its mark.

Zanda leapt up and bowed to her, indicating the metal trolley by the buffet. "Ah, the entertainment has arrived!" He clapped his hands. "There is the food cart to trip over!"

"Well, if it's entertainment you're after... "Eyre pretended to stumble towards the trolley, then did a backflip right over the top of it, landing on her feet.

"That's my girl!" Zanda guffawed and he seized her in a hug. Luke Jordan waved at her and so did Robeson Paul, early for lunch as usual. Like Beatrice, he enjoyed his tucker. But there were other, less enthusiastic faces. Ben Perrill, of course, but he turned away without comment as she passed. His cronies hooted and hid behind their arms, dah--dah-dah--dah-da-hing the Mission Impossible theme. And Pheria looked at her with daggers in her eyes; Jax hadn't arrived yet, but she was guarding her turf. Eyre wondered what Pheria would think if she knew about the Infirmary, but chin up, Eyre ignored the other girl.

Eyre sat at the back and waited for her friends to turn up. Warrigal wandered up first and sat next to her, a wide smile on his face.

"Welcome! I thought you'd be back, after this morning."

As Eyre looked at him quizzically, he said under his breath. "The emu."

Understanding eventually dawned on Eyre's face. "That was *you*...?"

Warrigal nodded. "Whittaker Ray asked me to do it—he was sure you had Viq and wanted to test you out under pressure. I'm glad you *do* have Viq; I might have ended up looking like an echidna."

Eyre raised her eyebrows. "Well, I'm not sure it *was* me, actually, but you know Mr Ray would have saved you if I couldn't!" she said. "I must admit I did think it was a bit strange having an emu wander in—rather odd, to say the least! But you know, I just saw Whittaker Ray. He didn't mention you."

"He doesn't know that *you* know about my—er—ability. I didn't tell him that you know—since it's meant to be a secret."

*Another* secret, Eyre mused. She was a walking vault of them. But she just smiled at him. "You know it's safe with me, my friend."

At that moment the floodgates opened as the majority of students crowded in from their last classes. Beatrice spotted Eyre first and came running over, hooting with delight as she slid her tray onto the table.

"What are you doing here?"

"Apparently, I'm here for good now," Eyre replied, and Abby wrapped her arms around her.

"Thank goodness!" she cried. "We've missed you so much!"

Nick wandered in and sat next to Abby. He leaned over and punched Eyre gently on the shoulder. "About time you came back," he said.

"What happened?" Beatrice asked.

"Well, apparently my Viq is coming back," Eyre said. "I'm not all that sure about that though."

"We'll do it for you, if that's the case," Abby said wickedly and made Eyre's cup levitate into the air.

"I hope you're going to put that down for me too," Eyre smiled. "I'm not sure you should rely on my skills just yet."

Abby shook her head and lowered the cup. "Remember the Saevus?" she reminded Eyre. "You didn't think you'd done anything then either. Sometimes your body just does it for you. It never really did seem right that your Viq went away—soon you'll be back to normal!"

Privately Eyre wasn't sure, but she felt grateful to her kind friend. Even if Eyre had tossed the cup up in the air with her hand she felt that Abby would have applauded.

Her eyes were drawn to Pheria's table as Jax wandered in and sat down. He was brown and toned and Eyre wondered what he had been doing. Apart from dinners at the refectory, she hadn't seen much of him since the

Sublabor attacked. His muscles rippled as he walked across the floor and Eyre registered that she was not the only one whose eyes were following him. Abby saw her and chuckled.

"Jax has been having special tuition this term." Her eyes danced with mischief. "You'll never guess who with!"

Beatrice forked a mouthful of food and laughed. Eyre looked from one to the other of them. "Well, I have no idea of course—Terrigal Furnace?" When her friends shook their heads, their eyes merry, Eyre huffed in frustration.

"Well, come on, tell me. I'll never guess."

"*Jemima Periwinkle*!" Abby spluttered, and Eyre nearly fell off her chair. She looked over at Jax, and realised that her mouth was literally agape. Pheria turned and caught her looking at them like a blowfish, and Eyre snapped her jaw shut.

"What on Entis for?" she asked, incredulous. That ridiculous simpering creature who resembled nothing so much as an overpriced Christmas bonbon? What could *she* teach anyone? As far as Eyre knew, Jemima Periwinkle's skills didn't extend further than memorising the entire genealogical trees of the Petersuns versus the Rayburns. She shook her head in bemusement.

"Well, after the Sublabor attacked, Jax went to her and asked for special tuition about the Strigis and their dangers. He said she obviously had a lot of knowledge and that he'd 'value her tutelage'—*that* I heard from Zanda, direct quote. Apparently, Jax's learnt the whole list of the different Strigis— there's at least 100 of them—and he's been outdoors with Ms Periwinkle learning the defences that are best for each creature."

Eyre was speechless. Jemima Periwinkle had claimed credit for something Jax had done, and now *she* was giving *him* training? Eyre was still unable to speak when the person in question stood up and wandered over to their table, taking a seat next to Nick.

"Hello, Eyre," Jax said. "Welcome back!" His voice was mellow, like golden honey, or resin on a bow soaring across the strings of a well-loved cello, and Eyre shivered despite herself. But she turned bewildered eyes to him.

"I heard you were taking extra tuition," she said, the sentence like a question. Jax leaned back. His eyes crinkled.

"Yes I have," he said loudly. "And enjoying it immensely. I've learnt so much—I feel the next Strigis I encounter is definitely going to come off second-best! It's been good for my fitness too." He flexed a muscle and laughed as Eyre's eyes grew rounder. "In amongst it I've had some pretty solid genealogy lessons too."

That did it. Eyre looked at Nick. She looked at Beatrice. She looked at Abby. All their faces were echoing her own thoughts, he had gone completely mad. Jax continued.

"Did you know, about three generations ago, there was a branch of the Burnishes in my family? My mother's side, apparently, a distant cousin. Well, that's one for the Wisdom, isn't it?"

Eyre agreed feebly and Jax slapped the table.

"Well, I'll get back to my dinner. Just wanted to say hi." And with that, he headed back to his table, tipping his head at Jemima Periwinkle as he walked past the staff table. The older woman tittered and blushed as just about every other female did when faced with the Jackson charm.

Abby gave Eyre a look. "The poor lad has obviously been brain-damaged by that chunk of quartz," she said.

Beatrice shook her head. "Such a waste. It's obvious he's going to end up working with Mrs Abnett for the rest of his life in the archive section." Eyre suddenly saw the funny side of it—the mental image of Jax working alongside her old babysitter, the ancient librarian, was too much to bear. She burst out laughing, and so did everyone else. But as she finished her dinner she flicked a few glances at Jax. He was oblivious to her—didn't even once look her way as he entertained the table. Eyre felt confused and dismal —what on Entis? Maybe he *had* suffered a brain injury. Either that or he was having a massive joke at her expense. But why bother with that? Whatever the reason, she felt that the yawning chasm between them had re-opened, as truly as if the Sublabor had smashed it there itself.

# CHAPTER TWENTY-FIVE

THE NEXT DAY EYRE headed back to the Unlit compound for the final time. She had a few things to bring back to the dorm with her, and she had to return her uniform. She also wanted to say goodbye to the people she had met there. That was going to be difficult.

When she arrived she passed Ms Griz and Professor Nithercott, who were deep in conversation about what seemed to be the benefits of using a lock pick whilst hanging by one's feet upside down. They bowed and waved farewell as she walked by, then they carried on the discussion just as intently, gesticulating and nodding heads as they headed down the path. The students weren't the only focused ones on this campus.

In fact, everyone she passed called out a greeting or acknowledged her in some way—a cartwheel or a nod of the head. It was lovely, but was making the whole departure that much harder. Eyre emptied her locker and then headed to the uniform shop, her heart sore.

"Now don't you worry, my dear," the motherly woman in the store said, sensing her sadness. "A part of you will always be one of the Unlit. Once you've been here, it changes you. The lessons will stay in your heart forever!"

The woman put the rough uniform back on the hanging rack, and feeling tears threatening, Eyre quickly turned to go. But a rasping voice stopped her.

"A minute before you go," Rachis said, and beckoned her to follow.

Eyre followed, rubbing her eyes hard, completely nonplussed. She thought he'd said his goodbye yesterday. She hoped she wasn't in for a last reprimand.

Rachis took her down past the lockers and into his small office.

"I have something for you," he said, looking—for the first time that Eyre had ever seen—awkward. Silently he held out a bow, and a quiver full of arrows. The bow was made of ebony, and it had a beaten silver hand grip around the centre of the curving limbs. She opened her mouth, not sure what to say.

"It's for you," Rachis said hesitantly. "Anyone who handles the Apex should have a decent bow." Eyre was unable to move, she was so taken aback.

"Take it, you've earned it," he continued. "Your shooting yesterday was breathtaking. And I... er, well, I need to apologise for treating you the way I did this semester. My prejudices and opinions interfered with what I should have seen very early on: wherever you came from, you are worthy of the Unlit. I have no one to pass this bow on to, and I would like you to have it."

Now the tears did come, and Eyre took the bow reverently, feeling the lightness of it, but also its strength. The wood had been polished so smooth it gleamed like a mirror, and exotic runes were carved into the back of the limbs of the weapon. It was a most mysterious and spectacular thing.

"It came from Norway and was crafted after the Holmegaard design, which dates back 9000 years," Rachis said gruffly. "My family the Rachissuns lived there for many hundreds of years. I am the last of my line."

Eyre felt awkward. "But surely, Julia... or Silva...? There must be someone more worthy than me to give this to," she said softly.

Rachis turned to look at her fiercely, resembling one of the raptors he loved so much.

"I know who you are, Eyre," he said. "Make me glad I gave it to you."

At that, Eyre rushed over and hugged him, to his initial horror.

"I will!" she cried. "I will try so hard!"

After a moment Rachis put a rough-skinned hand on her back and patted her gently.

"I know you will," he said. "I have no doubt."

Eyre headed back towards the ward, her new bow held tightly in her hand. She looked at it in amazement, yet again. She still couldn't believe she had been given such a beautiful gift. In typical fashion, her Unlit friends had slapped her on the back when they saw it.

"Good for you!" Christopher said.

"You deserve it," Tina agreed. "You should call it the mighty VK, for 'Vulture Killer'. Don't people name their weapons?"

Eyre laughed, but thought it might indeed be a good name for the extraordinary bow.

"We're going to miss you," Thomas added. "If you don't come and see us, we'll be breaking and entering your dormitory!"

"I can come for Falconry," Eyre laughed, "and, I hope, archery. Surely Rachis wouldn't give me such a thing if I wasn't allowed to practise?"

Thomas had given her a high-five. "Well, you take care over there, but don't forget that you're also one of us now! Don't Shimmer away that information!"

Eyre took a long, last look at her wonderful friends and the Unlit compound that had been her home for so many months as she headed back through the ward.

Her eyes brimmed. "I could never forget this," she said softly.

# CHAPTER TWENTY-SIX

THE NEXT COUPLE OF weeks passed quickly as the semester drew to a close. Eyre sat in with Beatrice and Abby, picking various classes to attend while she waited to see if her Viq would come back completely. She sat through theremin and tortilis lessons (Abby), 'The Composition of the Aura and its Deconstruction' (Beatrice), 'Wielding the Flail with Efficacy' (Nick), 'Knot Theory—as Separate from Is Theory' (Beatrice), 'Pyrokinesis when a Fire Ban is in Place' (Nick) and finally, most memorably, 'Speaking with Rabbits' (Abby). Whilst appreciating being back at the Academy, Eyre felt rather glad she had not suffered through a whole semester of any of these subjects.

"Speaking with Rabbits is important," Abby protested, as they headed to their last lecture of the semester. "Rabbits are everywhere, they have their ears to the ground—they *know* what's going on!"

"Well, what is going on?" Eyre asked.

"Er... I haven't actually managed to communicate with one yet," Abby confessed. "But when I do, I'm sure it will be *fascinating!*" Her eyes danced. "Actually 'Speaking with Rabbits' is on the curriculum because they're one of the easiest animals to communicate with. They only have about three thoughts in their heads..." She burst into peals of laughter.

"Once I've mastered this class, I can move on to *important* animals—like wombats, or cane toads, or s-s-spiders..." Abby broke off, choking with merriment.

Eyre rolled her eyes, grinning. "No doubt! But I guess it would be cool to be able to do that. It sounds hard."

Abby wiped her eyes. "Yes it is; not many people can do it. In fact it's so rare those who can usually end up specialising in that field. But most of the time this term I've just sat staring at that cute fluffy animal, trying not to cuddle it."

"Well, just be thankful you're not in Virens," Eyre said drily. "You'd be sitting there all term looking at a pot plant."

Abby roared with laughter. "I've missed you Eyre, I'm so glad you're back!"

They entered the telepathy laboratory and headed to their places. The lab was set up as a series of comfortable chairs scattered around the room with a table in front of each. Then the door opened and a furry stampede entered the room: dozens of rabbits (a herd, Eyre had learnt) who scampered across and jumped up on to each table.

"Hello, Thumper," Abby said, scratching his ears.

Dr Botolfe strode in the door and fixed her eyes upon Abby. "No speaking in this class, as you know, Miss Wilson! Telepathy only!"

Abby gave Eyre a look. Obviously Dr Botolfe's demeanour had not changed. But Abby didn't say anything more, and started to concentrate on the rabbit, occasionally closing her eyes as she focused hard. The rabbit sat down, quite comfortable on the table. He groomed himself, sniffed the air, scratched an ear. Abby opened one eye then huffed in frustration.

"He either hasn't got a brain or I am completely hopeless at this."

"I suspect we know the answer to that," Dr Botolfe's voice echoed through Eyre's mind. "Did you not *hear* me about no speaking?" She moved over towards them and Eyre thought—here we go. Having been on the receiving end of Dr Botolfe's ire herself, she feared for her poor friend.

But then a strange thing happened. Thumper jumped into Eyre's lap. With a bound, the rabbit from the next table leapt on to Eyre also. Then it was pandemonium as all the rabbits in the lab hopped over and swarmed around Eyre, leaning their little forepaws on her knees, crowding around her feet and rubbing up against her legs.

Dr Botolfe's mouth hung open; then a look of fury crossed her face. Weighty silence hung over the room as the tall lecturer stared in disbelief at the crowding rabbits (also called a Fluffle in Canada, Abby told Eyre later in between her gasps of laughter). If telepathic thoughts were visible, Eyre thought there should have been a thunderstorm roiling around the room. But eventually Dr Botolfe gave up, her face suffused with a colour that was sort of a mix between raspberry and blueberry, and she telepathically ordered the students to "*take your rabbits outside*!" Laughing and falling over each other, the students rushed into the teeming animals, trying to sort out which one was theirs. Dr Botolfe finally lost it completely and roared out loud.

"By the Light, pick any damn one up and throw it out the door!"

The students each grabbed a squirming bundle of soft fur and let the rabbits out the door. The soft grey creatures loped off together towards the paddocks, obviously quite happy to be let out early.

"This class is over and you all get a FAIL! Dismissed!"

With that, Dr Botolfe turned on her heel and stalked out of the laboratory.

Abby was hiccupping with laughter as they left. "It was worth a fail to see that, Eyre, it was so funny! They absolutely loved you!"

Eyre looked bemused. "Well, maybe it was because I hadn't been there before."

But then Abby stopped, a delighted realisation dawning on her face. "No, no! I could hear them!" she said excitedly. "They were all saying 'love' 'love' 'love'! And then I could hear Dr Botolfe telling them to get back on the tables. They didn't listen to her, but they *did* love you!"

Eyre raised her eyebrows in bewilderment, but then thought back to that pile of soft, squirming creatures. She had loved them too. But she just slapped Abby on the back

"Well, good on *you* Abby! How incredible that you can hear them! That is so amazing—and now you can move on to wombats!"

That started them both laughing again and they were still chuckling when they entered their dorm room.

# CHAPTER TWENTY-SEVEN

EYRE AND HER FRIENDS bustled around, packing their bags for mid-year break. They were allowed to leave some of their possessions behind which was a relief, as they didn't have to pack everything up. Eyre had jammed mainly the basics into her backpack, but she'd made sure her guitar, her staff and her bow and quiver of arrows were amongst the things she had lined up to go back to the cabins with her. As her friends carried on deliberating about what to take and what to leave, Eyre strummed her guitar softly while she waited on her bed. The neck of her guitar was made from a piece of the beautiful rainbow eucalyptus, an ancient rainforest being. The tree had given a brilliantly coloured branch to Jax so that he could, unbeknownst to Eyre, repair her damaged guitar, which had been smashed by Ben Perrill. Just fixing the terribly broken instrument would have been a wonderful gift to Eyre; the fact that Jax had made such an effort to source the wood from the wondrous old tree made it all the more special. The new neck seemed to imbue the strings with a magical, haunting sound and the music rising from the guitar was melancholy, echoing Eyre's mood. Her thoughts were dark as she ran her fingers over the strings. Jax was such an enigma; she couldn't work him out.

Also contributing to her glumness was the fact that despite Whittaker Ray's pronouncements, she hadn't seen any evidence of her Light energy returning since she'd come back to the Academy campus. She knew people were watching her, and it was excruciating sitting through lectures that she couldn't contribute to: psionics, fulminology, and levitation had all proven dismal failures. And her third source of dejection was that her friends were going away for the break—their families were taking them snow skiing in Perisher for the three weeks of the Academy holidays. Eyre had been invited, of course, but she was so far behind everyone at the Academy, she had decided it would be better if she stayed at the cabins and tried to catch up.

Jengles would be there, so she wouldn't be completely alone. But she found it difficult to listen to the excitement as Beatrice and Abby talked about their upcoming holiday. Eyre hadn't been skiing or snowboarding, but she imagined a Lightworker would absolutely tear up the slopes. What fun it would be!

Finally, her friends were ready, with about twice as much luggage as was needed, in Eyre's opinion. Still, travelling by Light energy eliminated many of the hassles faced by the traditional tourist—one snap, and you were there! Imagine the faces of all those poor people lining up at airports if they knew that teleporting was an option! The thought made her smile as she zipped her guitar into its protective cover. Then she hefted her bags, with all the miscellaneous stuff crammed into them, and weapons on to her shoulder and headed out to the Central Admin building with her friends.

Peter Edmunsun was there, as usual, with his wonderful smile.

"Hello, my intrepid Lightworkers!" he cried, and Beatrice rolled her eyes.

"Yeah, dad," she said dryly. Abby tried not to, but she giggled.

"Hold hands then, let's get going—the Double Diamond slopes await!" Mr Edmunsun proclaimed.

Eyre grasped her friends' hands, trying to ignore the feeling of being left out.

"Tally ho then!" Peter Edmunsun shouted, and they all disappeared.

The wind howled through the canyon as Eyre sat on the squishy couch in her cabin. She had draped the hand-made rug Carly's mother had made her across her knees, and she nursed a cup of hot chocolate in her chilled hands. It was nice to settle in so warm and cosy, but she couldn't ignore the dismal feeling of being deserted. She was alone here in the little circle of cabins. But she didn't feel afraid. Jengles and his troops were very nearby if she needed help.

Abby, Nick and the Edmunsuns had left for Perisher not long after they had arrived back from the Academy. Abby's father was finishing up some work with his company and would join them at the ski fields later, and Whittaker Ray, as usual, was off somewhere solving the problems of the Lightworld.

Eyre smiled as she remembered Lachie running around in high excitement as he pulled a knitted beanie with a pompom onto his head.

"It's snowing up there!" he whooped and dragged his bag outside. He was ready fully half an hour before the others.

As Eyre looked out the window she could see leaves being blown in mini tornadoes by the cold wind. Winter was starting to bite. But despite the plummeting temperatures, it probably wouldn't snow down here, and even if it did, the Mantle would keep it out.

The peace in the cosy cabin was welcome after the wild weeks Eyre had had at the Unlit, and slowly her disappointment at staying behind lifted. Her body was relishing the stillness, and she sat for some time sipping her cocoa as she looked at the brilliant stained-glass in the windows, and her guitar glowing in the corner of the room beside the huge stack of books. She really felt like she was home now. If she was honest, she did wish she had gone with the others to the mountains, but it was lovely to relax and not do much at all, after the crazy months at the Academy. And she supposed, as Whittaker Ray had said, it was good timing for her to catch up and practise her Viq before the second semester began.

Eyre finished her hot chocolate and stretched and yawned. She stood up and decided to head for the basement. It was usually her first destination when she got back to the cabin—she always wanted to summon her Wisdom—it was almost like going back through a photo album. Even if there were no new messages there, it was enough to see the images of her family.

So, she wandered downstairs through the ward to the basement, shivering as she passed through the blast of chilled air in the doorway. She took out her Lightkeeper, the beautiful crystal box made of tanzanite and diamonds and traced her finger over the gold Inguz embedded in the lid. Her parents had designed this for her, to protect her Wisdom, and she now knew the importance of the secrets it guarded.

With a sigh she settled on the ground and opened up the box to release her Wisdom, and used her Tone Blow and the key on the chain around her neck to open it. She read through the words her parents had written to her previously, and she looked through the genealogical chart that hung as a hologram in front of her. She loved seeing the faces of her ancestors, and finding out how they lived. She was pleased to see a falconer way back in her lineage. She wondered if Sir Geoffrey Markett had had a falcon as fine as her own? Flipping over the last page she didn't really expect to see anything further, but to her surprise, there was a whole list of symbols written in lines, running across the hand-beaten paper from the top to the bottom of the page. This time there was no hologram from her parents to give her a clue to what it might mean; just this incomprehensible jumble of angular hieroglyphics and small black circles. She studied the characters intently, trying to remember the few weeks of coding she'd done with UD1 at the

TEPs, and her few lectures with the Unlit, but none of the symbols made sense, or were even vaguely familiar. Just a series of triangles, dots and spaces —by the Light, why not just write the message out? Eyre thought in frustration. But then she thought about the revelations of deception and treachery within the Lightworkers over the past few years, and she realised that, heartbreakingly, there had indeed been a need for great secrecy. Her parents had been betrayed by people they considered their closest friends, so it was no wonder they had taken the utmost precautions to protect their secrets. However, they obviously had a lot of faith in her—because at the moment she couldn't even imagine where to *start* with this confusing mass of lines and dots. It must be important. But what if she never worked it out?

Feeling suddenly tired, she decided to leave the code for another day—it was so complicated and was obviously going to take her quite some time to decode the message. She'd only just arrived at the camp and this was an awful lot to take in, so she thought she'd go for a walk to clear her head.

Outside the cabin, the cold wind whistling through the grounds was numbing but welcome. The crisp air cut through Eyre's muddled thoughts as she walked the perimeter of the Mantle, trying to work things out, and slowly her mind started to clear.

An approaching flash of red hair in the distance made her smile and soon Jengles met her, walking from the other direction. Jengles, more formally known as General Gel Lithium Silica, was looking rather casual today; more like the maintenance man Eyre had originally taken him for. He had armfuls of wood for the Mantle Basin and his plaited red beard had blown over his shoulder by the stiff breeze in a rather dishevelled manner. Despite this, he still carried himself like he was waiting for something to appear that he should throw lethal weapons at.

His words to Eyre were constrained, to her sadness, although she was glad he hadn't prostrated himself at her feet like he used to.

"You're on your own now? They've gone?"

"Yes," Eyre answered. "I really would have liked to have gone with them, but I have a lot to catch up on. And who would look after you, Jengles?"

A flash of light crossed Jengles' face but was so quickly gone that Eyre thought she'd imagined it. "Well, then," he said gruffly. "I'll be here, so come and get me if you need me."

He turned to go, and then Eyre had a sudden thought. "Actually," she said. "I could use your help with something."

Jengles turned back and waited for her to continue. "I want to write to a friend from the Academy," Eyre said. "But I don't know how to contact them. Can you help me? Is there a central record or something?"

Jengles looked at her for a long moment, then nodded. "Well, you'll be needing Light Paper then," he said. "Send a Peragro. Write your message and address it, and it'll get to 'em. Easy as that." He saw the dilemma showing on Eyre's face and continued. "Yea, Light Paper is precious, and hard to get hold of, but I can get you some—just one bit, mind, so you'd better write it properly the first time. Leave it with me. I'll go sort it out."

With that, he stomped past, picking up branches and muttering to himself as he examined each one, as if he were a red-headed madman, rather than one of the highest-ranking members of the Mimir.

Eyre's thoughts were troubled as she headed back to the cabin. During her stroll, she'd realised that she really needed to enlist outside help to try and crack the code her parents had left her. She knew there was no way she could work it out herself this side of the next twenty years, so she'd decided to contact Tina. Tina was obsessed with codes and deciphering cryptograms, anything complex—even the impossible steganography, where a secret message was hidden in an innocuous text. Tina loved the mental challenge; the harder the better. So, if anyone could figure this out, she could. And Eyre knew that Tina could be trusted beyond question to keep the message safe. But Eyre had no idea where Tina lived, or how to get in touch with her. Eyre hadn't been at the Unlit very long, and certainly hadn't exchanged contact details with anyone when she left. Jengles' suggestion of the magical Light Paper might be just the solution she needed. But she hoped this wouldn't break the secrecy her parents had warned her about.

Heading back to the cabin her spirits lifted and she decided to practise her archery and Ferito for a while. After her time with the Academy, she had realised how physical challenges could improve her mental outlook, so some practise would definitely help at the moment.

But her steps faltered as she neared her cabin. Something was sitting on the railing besides the steps and her first reaction was panic. But then pure joy took over and she raced towards the creature.

"Florence!" she cried, whistling her unique call, and the soft grey bird flew off the railing, up in the air in a tight arc and then landed on her shoulder, chirruping softly in her ear. Eyre's heart melted as she stroked the bird's head. "You're here," she whispered.

Heavy footsteps clomped from around the corner and Jengles appeared, clutching a silvery object in his hand.

"Approved by the Academy," he said, indicating the bird, as Eyre stroked the long flight feathers of the illustrious Ne-Ne. "Apparently they think you should have protection."

Eyre could only beam as she looked into the three golden eyes of her Venator. Suddenly she didn't feel alone at all.

"Here's the Light Paper," Jengles said gruffly, shoving the shining rectangle he'd been holding in his hand at her. "Also approved by the Academy. Write your message with anything you like, but don't make a mistake. You can't undo what you write."

In a moment he was gone, leaving Eyre with the mysterious, silvery paper and her beloved bird.

# CHAPTER TWENTY-EIGHT

EYRE SAT ON THE floor of her basement and stared at the symbols on the page of the Wisdom. Florence was upstairs, sitting on the railing again, seeming to prefer being outdoors. It made sense really, she was a wild creature and used to roosting with her flock in the forest.

Right now, Eyre could feel a headache coming on. Jengles had said that she had to write her message without making a mistake, and *this* was going to be quite a challenge. The symbols were so confusing and there were so many of them—they were going to fill up the whole A4-sized piece of Light Paper. But Eyre couldn't show her Wisdom to anyone, so this was the only way she could think of to get Tina to help her work it out.

The first line was obvious though—she had to tell Tina not to let go of the Peragro until she'd made a copy of the code to work with. As soon as she ceased to hold the Light Paper, it would disappear. Next, she *swore* Tina to secrecy. Then she had to reproduce those symbols *exactly* as they were in the Wisdom, and that was going to take quite some time. Sighing, she lay on her stomach and picked up her pen. It wasn't going to happen unless she got started.

It took her two hours and by the time she'd finished she definitely had that headache. But she had done it without errors, and had gone so slowly and carefully that it was a clear reproduction of what was in the Wisdom— whatever it meant.

She folded the paper carefully and addressed it: Tina Pang. Her hand hovered for a second and then she added 'Academy of Light student'. She felt a bit ridiculous, but that was as much as she knew about Tina. It seemed it was enough though, for with a blinding flash the Peragro disappeared, leaving Eyre with spots in front of her eyes. She definitely needed some fresh air, so she headed back outside with her bow and arrows, and her staff. She also took a weighted leather ball like a hacky sack—the lure used to train Venators.

Eyre practised her archery for some time, using one of the eucalypts to hang a makeshift target. Her archery skills were improving daily, and the bow that Rachis had given her was a thing of beauty. It was lightweight and sat perfectly balanced in her hand as she released her arrows, and she seldom missed the target now. Florence was excited by being out in the open and periodically took flight to survey the area.

Then Eyre packed up her bow and then spent some time throwing the lure for Florence, giving her the directional whistles as she did so. One thing she liked to do was to give the whistle for Florence to fly one way, and then throw the lure the other way. Like a flash of lightning, Florence would change direction and plummet to the lure before it hit the ground. Florence enjoyed the game as much as Eyre did, and she was getting very good at it.

Eyre also ran through her Ferito moves and pushed herself hard. She was sweating by the time she'd done each of the Clasis several times, but she was determined to keep up her fitness over the break.

Her final task was one she had deliberately left 'til last, and she dismally picked up her staff. Even when she had Viq she couldn't use it properly. And she hadn't had Light energy for quite some time, or not that she had realised, so she wasn't looking forward to practising and fumbling around.

It was such an exquisite object, with the rainbow-hued wood and the massive rose-coloured diamond set in the top. She'd polished the staff so finely it shone like glass, and the uncut ruby that she'd fixed in the wood to honour her Terra guide, Shuvai, glowed in the late-afternoon sun. That ruby made her grit her teeth and pick up her staff. Maybe she might never be able to use her staff properly, but she was going to make sure it wasn't for lack of trying.

It felt good to hold the staff again, and she realised that despite her lack of progress with it, she had missed the training lessons. A student's staff was an extension of themselves, chosen by a unique process that only happened once in a Lightworker's life. Even though it was an animate object, it was almost like a companion.

Florence had flown up to a branch on the eucalyptus tree where Eyre had hung the target, her three golden eyes fixed upon Eyre as she waved her staff around. Eyre could swear the bird was laughing at her as she strode confidently forward, wielding her staff and aiming it in a decisive manner at the target. Nothing happened. It was like she was rehearsing for a baton-twirling contest, she thought in frustration.

After half an hour of complete failure, Eyre sat on the ground and stroked her staff.

"Well, it's not your fault," she said finally, and as she did it sparked a memory from her first-year lessons. She'd realised back then that her lack of progress had been due to beating the staff with her mind, almost trying to force the energy out of it. She'd finally managed to get the staff to work when she had tried a gentler approach, letting the energy flow through her to the wood. She realised that indeed, her lack of success was probably her own fault, not the staff's, and she stood up to try again.

She thought of the staff as creating a circular force between her hands, the wood, the crystal and her mind. For ten minutes she approached the task almost like meditation, letting her mind open and feeling the surge of the power she had within her.

And then—to her immense delight, and Florence's squawking consternation—a beam of light speared from the diamond at the top of the staff and blasted into the ground at the bottom of the eucalyptus tree. Florence took off straight upwards at the speed of light, and Eyre laughed with delight. She'd *done* it! Not only had she produced energy from her staff, but, to her joy, this confirmed that indeed, her Viq *was* coming back. As before, her staff was not sending out the beam at all in the direction she'd intended, but it was such a wonderful moment, Eyre wouldn't have cared if it went backwards (which it had done in the past).

Florence came back down to earth with a reproachful look in her golden eyes. She did not appear too impressed with this new weapon.

Filled with a new motivation, Eyre spent the last half hour of daylight firing light beams in all directions. She didn't even try to aim it; just producing the Light energy was enough. Eventually she headed back to her little cabin, feeling elated. Florence sat on the railing and Eyre curled up on her sofa with the stained-glass lamps lit and cosy. All was right with the world.

# CHAPTER TWENTY-NINE

THE NEXT TWO WEEKS passed in pretty much the same way. Eyre would get up and study the notes she had missed the first half of the year. She discovered that the creature that had attacked her at the Crystal Grotto last year was one of the Strigis—something called a Latcher. Second-year students had studied many of the Strigis in detail and Eyre was glad she had time to catch up—there was a lot to learn. A Nahtaivel was a huge flying creature with spikes around its neck and scaled, leathery skin, and they were one of the apex Strigis. Something to look out for, she brooded. Along with the Characs she'd learnt about last year. So many terrible creatures from beneath the earth—how could they ever fight them all?

Eyre was also ploughing her way through History of Light, which had become no less boring than it had been in the first year. But at least she hadn't had to listen to Mandig Vela droning on in his monotonous voice. She'd learned the stories of St Illuminado and St Ria—who most of her friends probably already knew about. Eyre didn't—she'd just heard the often-used exclamations from the Mimir mostly, and occasionally other students. St Illuminado had been a warrior of great courage and integrity who had led the Light Wars in the 15$^{th}$ Century. And St Ria was an intrepid young woman who had saved the Mimir from the undead Draugr a thousand years ago. *No wonder they mention 'St Ria' so often,* Eyre thought. *They revere her.* She'd also been interested to read that there was an Overworld and an Underworld, which she already knew about. But there was also a Middleworld, which she hadn't heard before. However, no more information was given on that, so she thought she'd research that further another day.

Some of the subjects such as telepathy and psionics she would have to practise when her Light energy strengthened, but she worked through the theory of them all. It took some time and she skimmed through some of it—

it would be impossible to learn it all in a couple of weeks. But at least she would be familiar with all the courses she had missed in the first half of the year.

After lunch she would run with Florence flying above her, up the track to the pinnacle of the ridge and then she would send Florence out to soar with the peregrine falcons and the Wedge-tailed eagles. It was exhilarating watching the magnificent creatures spiral so high above the earth and then drop down with breathtaking speed. And Florence loved the exercise. Eyre was feeding her with a special mix prepared by Rachis which Jengles had dropped off, and Florence was reaching her full maturity and strength now.

Once they returned to the campground, Eyre worked through archery, Ferito and her staff skills for a couple of hours each day. She didn't mind the solitude as it allowed her to focus and she was happy that each day she could produce the beam of light from her staff quicker, and stronger.

She was concentrating so hard on her staff that afternoon that when Jengles spoke from behind her she levitated—literally—three metres into the air.

Jengles' eyes were amused. "Well done, Eyre. You just needed a bit of a prod."

Eyre came down and danced a jig, amazed she had finally levitated. "It's the first time I've felt it properly!"

"Felt what properly?" came a voice from behind Jengles and Eyre exclaimed in surprise. She ran over and hugged her friend.

"My Viq! Tina! By the Light, it's so good to see you—I reckon I could levitate with joy alone!"

"How about me then?" Christopher said, appearing from nowhere, and laughing, Eyre realised they had both just Shimmered her.

Jengles headed off and Eyre dragged her two friends into her cabin. "Can you stay the night?"

"Sure, that's the idea!" Tina said. "That conundrum you sent me was so incredibly complicated I need to show you how it works."

Eyre's eyes flickered to Christopher and Tina nodded. "He knows," she said. "I know you said it had to be a secret, but I needed Christopher's photographic memory to record that mess of hieroglyphics you sent me."

Christopher's eyes crinkled. "I converted it into a hologram so we could try and work on it together. And can I tell you—it took us a while to figure it out!"

Eyre clapped her hands. "You've *cracked* it? Oh, you absolute geniuses! I knew it was a good idea sending it to you, Tina!"

She bustled around and made cups of coffee and then they all sat on the sofa together. Christopher pulled out a crystal from his pocket and put it on the coffee table. When he rubbed it, a hologram hung in the air showing the symbols and code that Eyre had found in her Wisdom.

"It's very clever," Tina said, examining the shapes. "Whoever you got this from has made up their own code which looked incomprehensible."

"But then," Christopher continued, "we realised that it was constructed rather similar to a Rosicrucian cypher, more especially the Pigpen or Blue Lodge ciphers, which have angles and triangles as well as squares and lines."

"So then we had to work out what shape they used to create the code," Tina said. Christopher smiled.

"We worked out what 'a' was and then Tina figured out 'the'; which helped us sort out 'of' and 'for' and 'to'."

"Which basically led us to crack the code—and we worked out that it's based on the shape of an Inguz, like this " Christopher touched the crystal again, and an Inguz hung in the air, with letters of the alphabet in each section:

# THE WISDOM'S CODE

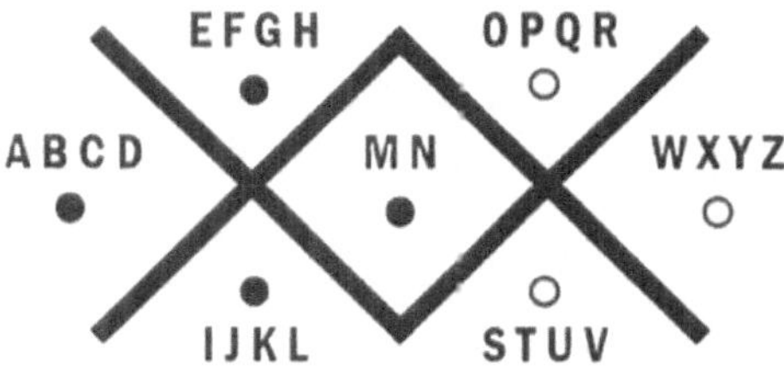


"The code uses solid dots and empty dots so that the whole alphabet can work within the Inguz. It's ingenious!" He pointed out how the solid dots and the hollow dots identified which letter the symbol represented.

Eyre could see how it worked. But she was too impatient to work out the symbols herself. "So what does the message say then?"

Christopher touched the crystal again and words appeared in the air.

*Search the bottom of the sea*
*To find the Seer and prophesy*
*Receive guidance to the light*
*By bearing a crystal of Angelite*

*But dry, and also Bloodstone*
*A gift for the all-seeing Sea Crone*
*Those who prove their worth*
*Will receive counsel for the Aura's rebirth*
*But only the stupid and only the brave*
*Would dare enter the Oracle's cave*

Eyre groaned. "Another puzzle." Tina and Christopher laughed softly, understanding that each step forward was yet another headache in a conundrum.

Eyre hugged them tightly. "Thank you so much for helping me with this. I am not permitted to tell you why it is important, and I still have to figure it out properly myself, but please believe me when I say that the safety of Lightworkers depends on you keeping this to yourselves."

Tina smiled. "Our life's mission as one of the Unlit is to protect Lightworkers at any cost; you didn't need to ask for our confidence."

"No one will ever know," Christopher added.

"But obviously your trip to Aqua needs to involve a visit with the Sea Crone, whoever that is," Tina said, unable to stop trying to solve a puzzle.

Eyre nodded. Another step forward. But more mysteries. Only her knowledge of the treachery that surrounded them helped her to understand why the secrecy was all so necessary.

# CHAPTER THIRTY

TINA AND CHRISTOPHER LEFT the next afternoon—by car, which seemed sort of ridiculous, really. It turned out that Tina's mother had dropped them off the day before, driving up from Canberra. Eyre had spent the time with her friends walking through the bush, and she took them to the Buyabarra Billabong and they swam in the strangely warm water, with their breath puffing in the cold air. Eyre had discovered over the past couple of years that the waters of the Buyabarra always seemed at a comfortable temperature; cool in the summer, warm in the winter. One of the mystical things about it, and Tina and Christopher had loved the experience of this secret place.

After her friends left, Eyre fell back into the same routine she'd adopted the first two weeks, so that by the time the end of the holidays approached, she had pretty much caught up on all that she could.

Trying to figure out the message from the Wisdom, Eyre had studied her Minerals and Crystals textbook. Angelite, she found out, was a crystal formed from dehydrating Gypsum. Further investigation revealed that if Angelite got wet, it would revert back to Gypsum. Then, looking through 'The Psychic's Guide to Crystal Properties' (written by the 'celebrated' and 'world-renowned' Madame Cheska Overmantle, as the cover proclaimed), she found that Angelite promoted psychic awareness and a connection to universal knowledge, but that those properties were lost if it changed back to Gypsum. So the "dry" part of the message made sense, although how Eyre was going to *keep* it dry was a bit of a mystery at the moment, when her destination for the next TACI test was deep down underwater. And unfortunately, Angelite was not found naturally in Australia, so that was another problem to solve.

Bloodstone on the other hand was relatively common, though she was a bit uncertain where she might get some. Bloodstone in ancient days was revered as a stone of courage and altruism, and of noble sacrifice. It was sometimes called a "Sun Stone" and it definitely sounded a worthy gift for a wise old Sea Crone.

The final study Eyre had to complete during the break was the last chapter of her History of Light textbook. As usual, she found it hard to keep her eyes open as she waded through the details of who had been in the Echelon through the years, the building of Lightworking infrastructure, the location of various government bodies and the complement of the Determinant Dozen, which by now was all very familiar information to most students. However, she became intrigued as the chapter touched upon a subject that was largely avoided in the Lightworking community.

The subject was 'The Proditio', or 'The Betrayal,' and it briefly detailed how the treachery of an important Lightworker had led to the Aura being destroyed. Apparently, this disloyal Lightworker had endeavoured to send the power of the Aura down to the Underworld. Part of this she already knew, but the next section was new information, because, apparently, it was only the intervention of a... *Thantos Nex?*... that had prevented the complete destruction of the world. The Thantos Nex had blown the Aura apart, killing the malign Lightworker in the process, and sending four sections of the Aura out of the Earth as inert Isars. One Isar had ended up in each of the Alterworlds, and the book proclaimed that once they were re-united, the Aura could be recreated. However, as the textbook stated, and as Eyre already knew, finding the Isars was the problem. *She* could add a bit of information to this chapter, Eyre mused, as she shut the book. *To be continued...* she thought.

She also wondered at the Thantos Nex, who had saved the world. She had thought the Thantos Nex were a race who observed, rather than participated, and she suddenly felt more warmth towards the cold, blue-robed beings she had seen while hiding with her friends at the meeting of the Determinant Dozen last year. Evidently, given enough reason, they would intervene, and it was lucky for the world that they had. Eyre felt a bit guilty for judging them so harshly last year; appearances could be deceptive. Eyre decided that this was something she should remember in future, and definitely a topic for the next BANE meeting.

She stood up and stretched and packed her textbooks away, planning to have some lunch and then go for her run as usual. But then a new thought struck her, one that for a second made chills run up and down her body. What if she went searching for Angelite and Bloodstone in the Transit? She knew what they looked like now, after studying her Crystal textbook, and she also knew that the Transit had formations of crystals not normally found in Australia. But to venture back there? Even thinking about it made her stomach churn.

Then her stubbornness kicked in. It was a truly magical cavern, and the only reason the last journey had been so disastrous was because of Ben Perrill. The cave itself was beautiful; it was only because Ben had tried to kill her that she felt dread rise within her when she thought of those tunnels. And she also realised now it was probably the mali within Ben that had sent the horrifying plague of flies after Eyre and her friends as they desperately tried to escape. Ben had not been back to the campsite since that day, so there was really no reason to fear the Transit itself, which was a hub for the Mimir as they moved under the earth. Last year repairs had been made to the Transit after something had caused terrible damage to the cavern, but after weeks of monitoring and patrolling by the Mimir, the Transit had been declared safe again.

Eyre considered asking Jengles to come with her, but she worried that he might not allow her to go, and now that the thought was in her head, she was determined, in her usual way, that she would. Then her eyes lit upon Florence, sitting patiently outside on the rail. Florence could come with her! That would be protection enough. Her powerful Venator had eyes that could see in the dark and she would be only too happy to dispatch a Zyx should they encounter one. That decided it! Eyre would go today.

Soon she had a backpack sorted with her lux, a rock hammer, some lunch and water packed inside it. She strapped a leather talon-guard on to her arm, then threw the backpack over her shoulder, grabbed her staff and whistled for Florence as she headed out the door. Florence, sensing something was different about today, flew in excited circles just above Eyre's head as she walked along the path towards the caves.

Eyre had a moment's hesitation as she faced the shadowed entrance to the tunnels, but she shook her head and scolded herself mentally. If she couldn't face a darkened passageway, she was certainly not up to facing the Gothak. So she rubbed her lux and sent it bobbing above her head with its gentle light, and whistled to Florence, who landed on her arm on the talon-guard. Then Eyre took a deep breath and headed into the tunnel.

Despite her bravado, for the first fifteen minutes her heart was beating hard and her breathing was shallow and fast as she walked down the winding passage. But as time passed, she became used to the darkness that lay beyond the lux's light. It was quiet in the tunnels and having her fierce Venator on her arm gave Eyre a growing confidence. In actual fact, it was quite peaceful down here, walking steadily downwards with only the sound of her footsteps echoing around her. And she was conscious that the Mimir were regulars down here; no doubt they were not far away.

She had walked for about an hour when she could sense that a greater space lay ahead. She couldn't see it, but there was a different feel to the air around her, and it grew colder, so she knew the Transit was near. After a few more turns in the passage, she stepped out of the tunnel into the cavern, and the lux rose higher, illuminating the magnificent crystal structures that lay all around. Despite the fact she had been here before, Eyre was still overawed by the many coloured geometrical structures that gleamed in the light of the lux. Some of them were huge—metres high, and others were scattered like gemstones around her feet. Eyre wandered around slowly, picking up a crystal here, running her hands over others, her eyes almost blinded by the beauty of the cave. Florence flew to sit on an outcrop of pyrites, but her eyes were watchful, scanning the shadows. Eyre sighed, rubbing her arm. She was glad to have a break from carrying the Venator: Florence was no lightweight and Eyre's forearm ached.

Eyre picked up a huge shard of emerald from the ground and looked at it in wonder. The flashes of green seemed to spear from the sharp edges of the hexagonal crystal. The colour was mesmerising. And what would be the value of this in Entis? But she put it back down. Material goods were not valued greatly in the Lightworking world: when you had access to the riches of the earth you realised there were things in the world that were far more valuable. While she walked through the huge cavern, admiring the colours and structures that thrust out of the earth, she scanned around for Angelite and Bloodstone. Angelite crystals were bluish and cloudy, in a rock-like form, and Bloodstone was dark green, often with seams of red running through it. But despite her efforts, she could not locate the rocks she was looking for, so after spending quite some time searching half the cavern, she decided to have a break. There were so many outcrops and layers of different minerals and crystals, it was hard to keep concentrating for very long, and she didn't want to miss either of the crystals she was searching for.

She sat in between a jutting shard of aquamarine and a turret of citrine and lay her staff beside her as she took out her lunch. Florence flew down to sit next to her on a low-set formation of quartz, her talons scrabbling slightly on the slippery facets. Patterns of light from the lux bobbing above them dappled the uneven crystal landscape, and suddenly Eyre's eyes caught on a smaller rock lying on the ground not far from her. It was an unusual shade of smoky-turquoise, about the size of her palm, with a feathery formation inside it that was made up of a riot of colours: pinks, greens, browns, blues—unexpected colours that mixed together like the residue of oils on an old artist's palette. Eyre picked it up curiously, studying the unusual inclusions in the rock, which had formed a fan-like design: elongated strands expanding downwards in branches and spirals of colour. It reminded Eyre of something. After a moment she turned the rock upside down and realisation dawned. The Crystal Grotto! It looked like the waters of the grotto with the crystal formations stretching upwards from the bottom of the pool, like magical plants reaching through the turquoise light. Eyre stroked the cool stone as memories of that day flooded back. That was when she had sourced the rare pink diamond for her staff, but if it hadn't been for Jax, she wouldn't have it today. She also wouldn't be alive. A thought dawned in her mind as she studied the beautiful stone, and she slid it into her backpack. Then she packed up her lunch and prepared to start searching again for the Angelite and Bloodstone.

But a sound from the side of the cavern made her freeze. Florence's yellow eyes opened wide and she turned her head in the direction of the sound. Eyre quickly made the gesture for silence and extinguished her lux, and they both sat motionless as footsteps approached from a nearby tunnel. A dim light from an approaching lux started to filter into the cavern and Eyre pulled herself even tighter into the crevasse between the aquamarine and citrine structures. Her heart was thumping but she hoped it was just the Mimir moving from one passage to another. When she heard the voice though, she knew it was not the Mimir who had arrived in the cavern.

"We have to be quick. The Mimir are not far away." Someone answered and Eyre was confused, because the voice was familiar, but she couldn't place it.

"I know," the man said. "The formation is just over here—take a look."

Panicking, Eyre thought for a moment that the footsteps were coming her way, but she realised that they were actually heading to the very far side of the cavern, where she hadn't searched yet. The echoes were making it hard to pick which direction the pair were moving.

The unknown person stopped. "Here, see—it's a big cluster, but hidden behind the quartz." Eyre could hear Professor Vela exclaim in triumph. "You are right! So rare, you've done well to find it. I have a container— careful, don't touch the crystals. Let me get some in."

There was the sound of scraping and then a jar screwing shut.

"Right," Professor Vela said. "I'm leaving. The attempt on the vault didn't work last time, but this might make the difference."

The other man made a sound of agreement. Weird, soft echoes jumped around the chamber as he replied. "In the meantime, inroads are being made. We've had the Menax in here increasing the tunnel space. You got the Latcher in the grotto, and we organised the Sublabor. We will wear them down; if the Academy is closed they will have to move the prize and we will have a greater chance of success. Those crystals will help."

As the man continued talking, Eyre felt a growing sense of horror. *It couldn't be.* Because she had realised that she recognised the voice, and it was someone she would *never* have thought would be part of this. It was *unthinkable*! Self-preservation had kept her sitting perfectly still, hardly breathing as the men finished their conversation. But she had to risk a look to confirm what she thought. She moved just slightly so she could see beyond the tower of citrine and get a clear look at the two. Then, feeling like she might be physically sick, she moved silently back out of sight.

She heard Professor Vela say farewell and then there was a flash in the cavern as he left. A moment later there was a second flash and Mr Wilson, Abby's dad, departed too.

# CHAPTER THIRTY-ONE

FOR A MOMENT EYRE sat rigidly, unable to move, feeling like she had been punched in the stomach. She was in total shock, and her mind could not fathom what she had just seen. And yet it was undeniable: Abby's dad was working with Professor Vela against the Lightworkers. A tear rolled down Eyre's face; it was so devastating that for a moment she felt like lying on the ground and sobbing.

But then a terrible thought arose. What if Mr Wilson got back to the campsite and found her gone? What if he saw her coming out of the tunnel? She *had* to get out of here, and fast, so he didn't realise she had overheard the conversation. But how quickly to leave? Was he going straight to the campsite? For a frantic, useless moment she wished desperately that she could teleport. But that was way beyond her.

Fortunately, her body took over where her mind was unable. She found herself standing with her backpack on and her staff in her hand. Without being called, Florence flew to her arm, as if understanding the urgency, and Eyre lit her lux to find the entrance to the tunnel that led home.

And then the running began. Uphill, it was hard work. But after a few minutes, she sent Florence off ahead of her, despite her fear of being alone. It was too difficult to move with the massive raptor, and she needed to run *fast*. Eyre was relieved as Florence flew like a bullet into the dank tunnel; Eyre wanted her to survive.

And Eyre wasn't sure if she herself would, after what she'd seen in the cavern. So she ran as if her life depended on it, and indeed it might. If Mr Wilson realised she had overheard his conversation, she was on her own at the campsite and there would be dire consequences.

Her breath was heaving and she felt sick to the stomach from the exertion, but she knew she had to get back quickly. Mr Wilson could possibly have gone elsewhere, but Eyre knew he was ultimately on his way to join Abby and the rest at the ski fields, so there was a good chance he would stop by the cabins before he left. Whatever he was doing, Eyre had to cover herself.

By the time Eyre emerged into the light her throat was swollen from the exertion of breathing so hard while trying to keep as silent as possible. Tears were streaming from her eyes as Eyre peered across at the campsite. She couldn't see any movement, but she couldn't risk crossing the open path to the cabins.

She ran silently around the edge of the huge cliffs, keeping behind boulders and jutting blades of rock to reduce the risk of being seen. Then at the end of the rockface, she ran into the bush until she found the trail that led from the campsite up to the top of the cliffs. She fell to the ground beneath a white gum, her chest heaving as the tears dried on her cheeks. Florence had been waiting for her, and she flew swiftly from across the campsite and fluttered up to sit on a branch in the white gum. Florence's three eyes had turned a dark amber colour. She knew something was up.

Leaning on her staff, Eyre finally allowed herself to cry properly. She wailed silently, her body shuddering as she thought of the terrible conversation she'd overheard. There was no ambiguity to it, no doubt at all. What were they up to? What were the crystals for? And *poor* Abby! By the Light, how would she cope when she found out?

Finally spent, Eyre sat back against the tree and looked upwards at her beautiful Venator, who waited patiently. Eyre wiped her eyes and sighed, a deep, mournful sound that signified the ending of something. Then she stood up and headed down the track to the campsite with Florence flying above her.

They emerged into the clearing to see three forms standing together by the metal basin where Jengles usually wove the Mantle. One was obviously Jengles, and, dread weighing down her steps, Eyre walked closer and confirmed that one was indeed George Wilson, a suitcase by his side. The other was Whittaker Ray, who must have returned from whatever important mission he had undertaken.

With more strength of will than she knew she possessed, Eyre forced a light-hearted smile onto her face and ran joyfully towards them.

"People!" she cried. "In my personal space! When did you get back? I've been up on the back face of the cliffs, letting Florence chase the Wedge-tailed Eagles!"

She focused on Whittaker Ray until she felt able to look at Abby's dad. But when she did, the look he returned was unsuspicious and with a huge relief she realised that he believed her ruse. Whittaker Ray smiled at her.

"She's a beautiful bird. The Apex, I believe?"

Eyre nodded and stroked Florence, glad for the excuse to look away from Mr Wilson.

"Yes, I've been training her every day. Her official name is Ne-Ne."

Jengles nodded—he knew she had been taking Florence out daily, so the confirmation helped Eyre's story. And Abby's dad was just looking at Florence, impressed. Having a Ne-Ne was unusual and special. No doubt he was wondering how many Zyx she could kill, Eyre thought, her mood suddenly violent. But she kept her face impassive.

"Are you off to Perisher then, Mr Wilson?"

Abby's dad smiled. "Yes, I just had to speak to Mr Ray for a moment— the Determinant Dozen are meeting again soon. But first, I'm off to carve some great turns!"

Eyre chuckled politely, but the rage was building within her. It was a relief to replace the heart-rending grief with a more survivable emotion.

"Are you staying here Mr Ray?"

Whittaker Ray nodded. "Just tonight, then I'm afraid I have to head off again. Are you managing alright Eyre?"

"Jengles has been looking after me," Eyre said, and she saw an intense, gratified expression appear on Jengle's face. But it was gone quickly. "I've actually enjoyed my two weeks," she added. "And I've caught up on a lot. So, I'm glad I decided to stay."

Mr Wilson picked up his bag. "Well, I'm off now. Enjoy your last couple of days Eyre—we'll be back the day before you head back to school."

Eyre just nodded, and then with a flash Abby's dad disappeared.

Eyre turned to Whittaker Ray.

"I *really* need to talk to you," she said.

# CHAPTER THIRTY-TWO

SOMETHING IN THE TONE of Eyre's voice must have registered, because Whittaker Ray and Jengles both gave her a probing look. Then Jengles bowed and left. He knew when to make an exit.

As Eyre led the way up the stairs to her cabin, a sudden thought gave her hope. Maybe Mr Wilson was working undercover? Sourcing information from the treacherous Professor Vela by acting as a double agent? Perhaps *that* was why he had been so deep in conversation with Jengles and Whittaker Ray? Even the slight possibility of that idea made her spirits lighten as she made a cup of tea for them both.

Sitting on the couch with the emerald-green pottery mug in her hands, she looked at Whittaker Ray's curious face and wondered how to begin. Then she decided that the information from the Wisdom was probably the best place.

"I received another message from Mum and Dad," she began. Whittaker Ray sat back in his chair and took a sip, but his eyes were focused.

"It was a code," she continued, "and I confess, I had help to work out what it meant. Anyway, here's the message."

She unzipped a tapestry cushion and passed over a sheet of paper that she had hidden in its cover. Whittaker Ray put his mug down and studied the translation.

"The Sea Crone has not been seen in a hundred years by a Lightworker," he said as he finished. "But if she has something that will help reinstate the Aura, then we must search for her, no matter how long it takes. Angelite and Bloodstone are obviously the key to finding her."

Eyre shifted in her seat, suddenly reluctant to make the admission. "I went looking for the stones," she said. "In the Transit."

Whittaker Ray looked stunned. "You went to the Transit? When?"

"Today," Eyre confessed. "I only just got back. I didn't find the crystals," she added.

Whittaker Ray's eyebrows were forming a distinct downward "V". Obviously, he was not happy. In a distracted tone he said, "Well, even if you found them in the Transit, they would not be of sufficient quality to appeal to the Sea Crone; we would need something quite unique for her. But what I am more concerned with, is *why* you would take such a risk on your own? After what Jengles and I saw down there the last time we went? Even though the Transit was cleared—why do this on your own? You knew we were concerned about the Strigis having been there! Why would you expose yourself like that to a potentially dangerous situation? Especially knowing how important you are to the Lightworking world? Are you looking for attention? It is only safe in a group down there!"

Eyre felt suddenly guilty, and all the reasons for her taking the hike to the Transit seemed insignificant and selfish. If she were honest, she had to admit that she *had* wanted to miraculously produce the crystals for Whittaker Ray and impress him with her initiative. And there was also an element of facing her own fears by returning to the place that had been so terrifying on her last visit. But Whittaker Ray's dismay made sense. At this point, she was possibly the only person in the world who could see the Isars —if she disappeared, there was no one else who might be able to locate them for many years. She realised she had made a very bad error of judgement.

"I, er, well, I'm really sorry, Mr Ray," she said feebly. "I had Florence with me, and I guess—well, I didn't really think it through properly. I thought if I found those crystals, maybe it would be another step forward. But it was a bad decision."

Whittaker Ray picked his emerald mug up again. His face worked for a moment as he stared into the contents. The mysteries of Earl Grey tea, Eyre thought, as she waited for a further blast from her mentor. But he was surprisingly circumspect, to her relief. He shook his head finally and took a breath.

"Well... okay, no harm done, as you are safely back now. But you must be more careful in the future—it is not an understatement to say that your safety is linked to the future of the world." He sighed, the lines on his face seeming more deeply etched than usual. "You know, historically, seeing the Sea Crone is not always an auspicious omen. But I guess we'll have to have faith that your parents put that message in your Wisdom for a reason." He rubbed his brow. "Anyhow, thank you for the new information. I guess we'll have to work on what that message means, and how we are going to find her."

"There's another thing though," Eyre said uncomfortably. Whittaker Ray raised his eyebrows.

"When I was in the Transit, there were other people there too. They didn't know I was there, but I overheard them."

Whittaker Ray put his mug down again, but didn't say anything.

"They were talking about the attempt on the vault at the Academy, and the Strigis that had come through the Transit tunnels, and the Sublabor, but as if they had *caused* those things to happen." Whittaker Ray's eyebrows shot up his face and he leaned forward, a question on his face.

"And they also harvested some crystals there—I don't know what for, but it didn't sound like they meant well."

"The *exact* reason you should not have been down there," Whittaker Ray said, exasperated but worried. "Imagine if you'd been discovered."

Eyre looked miserable. She knew that. And she really didn't want to say what she knew she had to say next.

"I know who they were," she said softly. Whittaker Ray looked amazed, but waited for her to continue. "One was Professor Vela. And the other was... Mr Wilson."

At that, Whittaker Ray looked shocked, and then, strangely, relieved. To Eyre's immense surprise, he chuckled. "Well, Professor Vela was with me all afternoon, so you must have been mistaken about that," he said, with a peculiarly light tone in his voice. "And George... well, I know you mean well, Eyre, but the idea is absolutely preposterous. George is amongst the most stalwart of the Echelon and has been with us for decades. It's possible you made an error there too. The Mimir didn't see them down there or they would have mentioned it." Eyre was completely taken aback that he would doubt what she had said, and a flush started to heat her face. *Yes, well the Mimir didn't see me either*, she thought.

"I know what I saw and heard, Mr Ray," she said, as respectfully as possible. "It was definitely them."

Understanding that she was upset, Whittaker Ray hesitated, his face thoughtful. After a while he raised his hands. "You know, natural gas is odourless, and if there was any trapped down there, you might have experienced a lack of oxygen. That can make you dizzy, and disoriented, even to the point of passing out."

Eyre was incredulous. He didn't *believe* her? Of all the possible reactions, that was the one she would least have expected. But as the awkward silence lengthened, doubt started to creep in. If Professor Vela had been with

Whittaker Ray all afternoon, then it actually *was* impossible for her to have seen him in the cavern, wasn't it? Had she imagined the whole thing? *Natural gas?* But then her conviction came back and she clenched her jaw. It *was* them. She didn't know how they had managed it, but she knew it was definitely Professor Vela and Mr Wilson at the Transit.

Whittaker Ray watched her, his blue eyes concerned. Eventually, calling on all the behavioural misdirection skills she had learnt at the Unlit, Eyre gave a wry smile and feigned unconcern.

"Natural gas, hey? Well, I suppose I must have been hallucinating. All the events lately have made me a bit paranoid, I guess." But then genuine apprehension filled her eyes. "You won't mention this to Abby, will you?"

Whittaker Ray studied her, and then shook his head. "No of course not. It's not worth mentioning to anyone. You should also keep it to yourself."

*Don't worry*, Eyre thought. If *you* don't believe me, then who else would?

# CHAPTER THIRTY-THREE

AFTER WHITTAKER RAY LEFT, Eyre sat on the couch clenching her mug. A feeling that was half rage, half despair consumed her and she didn't have the energy to get up. Mr Ray, completely off-track, had taken great pains to make her feel better—obviously he thought she was feeling silly now, and he tried to reassure her as he left.

"I'll get Jengles to check the Transit for gas, and he can also take a look where you thought the crystals were harvested. But don't worry if we don't find anything. The cave can be disorienting and many of us have imagined things down there that weren't actually true." *Like the Strigis?* Eyre thought cynically, but kept her face impassive. As if realising that Eyre wasn't exactly showing what she really thought, Whittaker Ray had touched her kindly on the shoulder.

"I'll check into what you said, discreetly, Eyre. I'm not completely dismissing you, be assured. But I know that you couldn't have seen what you thought you did."

*But I did, but I did, but I did!* Eyre thought fiercely, feeling like an argumentative child as she stared out the window. However, there was nothing she could do about the situation at the moment, so she started to unpack her backpack. As she slid her hand into the side pocket, she felt something cold, and with a smile, pulled it out. In all the rush and drama she had forgotten that she'd picked up that amazing stone in the cavern. She studied it again, admiring the unusual formations that flared from the bottom of the stone upwards. It was a truly unique find and she grabbed her Minerals and Crystals textbook from the bookcase. First, she would figure out what it was. Then, she had plans for this wonderful rock.

Eventually she found it under the Chalcedony section. The stone she had found was an agate, which was a type of chalcedony. But this was an extremely rare type of agate called a 'plume agate' because of the unusual inclusions within it that resembled a feather. Her blue-green coloured stone was more beautiful than even the ones in the photographs in the textbook, and Eyre was happy that the rock she had found and admired so much was actually so unique.

Next, she took Madame Overmantle's reference book from the shelf. She wanted to make sure that the properties of this remarkable stone were positive—no dark vibes associated with it. Imagine if she found out it was linked to avarice or slothfulness?

In a way that would be hilarious, because she'd decided that she was going to cut the stone into a pendant for Jax. After he'd gone to so much trouble to 'heal' her guitar (for that was how she felt about him fixing the poor, broken instrument), she had felt that she wanted to do something for him in return. She had learned how to choose the best cut for a stone during her Basic Faceting class with the Unlit—although obviously, becoming a master would take a lifetime of practise. But she felt she could find the best angle in this stone and make it something special.

When she found the metaphysical properties of agate, with delight she knew that this was the one.

Apparently, in ancient Babylonian times, agate was used to ward off evil, and the ancient Chinese civilizations prized the gem for its spiritual protection. Madame Overmantle had written that the aqua sage agate, which Eyre had found and which was one of the 'plume agates', was today used for psychic protection and filling one's aura with Light. It was also used to make warriors strong and victorious. Elated, Eyre thought that she had found the perfect gift for Jax.

It was good to take her mind off the recent discussion with Whittaker Ray, and especially the chilling incident in the Transit, so Eyre busied herself with getting her tools ready: the cutting 'lap'—a circular blade to cut the rock, the large 'dops'—stands of various sizes to hold the stone, and the Lightworker's loupe, a magnifying lens that helped to see the stone clearly, and to concentrate Light energy, which gave extra power to the cutting lap. Finally, she was ready and she carefully set the rock into a large dop with wax to hold it steady. Then she walked outside to get some air and light, and to clear her mind.

Florence regarded her with golden eyes, restless and always ready for action. Eyre walked over to her and stroked her head.

"If only you could talk," she said softly. "It would really help right now." Eyre was feeling a deep unhappiness, perhaps because it seemed that Whittaker Ray, of all people, had thought she was looking for attention, or at the very least, had been imagining things. After all the terrible things that had happened in the past few years, and all that Whittaker Ray knew about her, to be dismissed so lightly had hurt Eyre to the core.

But then she decided to look at it from Whittaker Ray's point of view, and she had to admit that what she had said to him might sound sketchy. Professor Vela was actually with Whittaker Ray at the time of the incident, (although Eyre knew he must have found a way around that) and George Wilson was a long-time, very close friend. No wonder Mr Ray found it hard to accept that they might be working with the Gothak. Even to Eyre it sounded completely unbelievable, and she had been there. So, if natural gas had been found in the Transit before, it was probably a much more plausible and palatable explanation for what Eyre had claimed to have seen.

However, Eyre knew she was right, and under normal circumstances, she would have enlisted her friends to sleuth the truth out. But how could she do that when George Wilson was Abby's dad? She sighed. It was way too difficult for her today.

Her mind in a turmoil, she walked back into the cabin, determined at least to do *this* right. She sat down in front of the plume agate, picked up the cutting lap and regarded the stone in front of her.

"Here we go, my beauty," she breathed. "I hope I do you justice."

# CHAPTER THIRTY-FOUR

TWO DAYS LATER, THE ski mob returned. They all had a raccoon mask suntanned around their eyes, and were full of stories about the snow and slopes with names that to Eyre's mind sounded like lethal madness. When they mentioned 'Olympic', she thought they were referring to their courage and bravery, but Lachie set her straight.

"We did one of the steepest runs in Australia!" he crowed. "I nearly killed myself, but Dad saved me."

Peter Edmunsun grimaced. "Lachie evidently didn't realise that getting down the slope on the snowfields is usually done on your feet. When he was in danger of causing a major avalanche from his face-forward technique, I intervened."

Beatrice roared with laughter. "You should have seen it! Lachie launched himself over the edge of Olympic, a *Double Diamond!* Ten points for air time—blimey, and *attitude*, but then there was a *major* fail on the landing! Some poor bloke had his ski broken in half as Lachie careered past on his board, sliding face down the rocks and moguls! It was brilliant!"

Everyone roared with laughter, Eyre included; it sounded so funny. She forced herself not to be envious of their holiday—there would be another time when she could join them. Her main concern was trying to stay nonchalant as she looked at Abby's dad. Like the rest of them, he was laughing at the story, but it made her blood boil. What a fraud. How could he be so light-hearted, while plotting the downfall of them all?

Abby was laughing as well, and Eyre's heart tightened. This wonderful, kind friend had no idea about her father. Well, Eyre could relate to finding surprises out about one's parents, and she knew that the truth was going to be a disaster for Abby. So, pretending to be happy amidst this catastrophe was actually causing Eyre physical pain.

Eventually, unable to cope with the hypocrisy any more, she said farewell and left, heading for her cabin. On her way back, she had a ridiculous fright when she bumped into Jengles, emerging from the shadows. She swore and then apologised.

"Sorry, Jengles," she said. "I'm a bit jumpy and my mind is playing tricks."

Jengles bowed. After a silence he said, "Trust your mind, and your conviction, Eyre. It is what your parents would have wanted you to do. And remember that Alexandrite is at the centre of everything."

Then he was gone, absorbed by the darkness of the night. Eyre initially was confused as she stared into the blackness. She hadn't understood his words, but she thought about it for a while in complete confusion until realisation dawned and she grimaced. With a horrible feeling, she felt that perhaps Jengles had been sending her a message; he had seen her envy, and was trying to help by reminding her of the big picture. Alexandrite was a special gemstone—she'd studied it last year in Minerals and Crystals 101. Amongst other things, its message and structure were aimed at loving others, and it was associated with regeneration, and changing one's world. Remembering her dark thoughts about Mr Wilson, she headed back to her cabin, feeling less than worthy.

Beatrice barrelled in through Eyre's front door. "We're all ready! How are you going?"

Eyre stuffed the last piece of clothing in her bag and picked up everything she was taking back to the Academy. As she turned to go, she suddenly remembered the translation of the piece from her Wisdom. She'd left it in the cushion! Beatrice hovered helpfully (unhelpfully, really) as Eyre dawdled.

"How about I meet you at the departure point?" Eyre said. "I've just got to grab a couple more things I remembered." Beatrice left and Eyre quickly unzipped the cushion and retrieved the piece of paper. She was standing with it in her hand when Beatrice suddenly stuck her head in the door. "Don't forget your..." she began, but then stopped when she saw the paper in Eyre's hand. Eyre was so surprised, she stuffed it into her bag with a most guilty look on her face. It was Eyre's expression more than the paper that aroused Beatrice's curiosity.

"What was that?" Beatrice asked. Not good at lying, Eyre blurted out the first thing that came to mind.

"Just some homework I was finishing off—Tina and Christopher were helping me with it."

Now Beatrice was really intrigued. "*Here?*" she asked. "Did they come here over the holidays?" Eyre could have kicked herself. She hadn't mentioned their visit, and she definitely hadn't mentioned the poem about the Sea Crone. She had been in such a spin about Abby's dad, she didn't know what to do—she definitely couldn't talk about the poem to Abby in case she mentioned it to her dad. And Eyre could hardly ask Abby to keep secrets from her dad without giving a reason. He was part of the Echelon, after all.

"Err, yes, they dropped in for a couple of days," Eyre said feebly. A hurt look crossed Beatrice's face—but whether it was because Eyre hadn't told them, or because she was jealous, Eyre couldn't tell. But Beatrice just said, "I just wanted to remind you to bring your orbuculum. First week back we start scrying lectures with Madame Overmantle." Then she disappeared down the front steps.

Eyre sighed as she went and got her crystal ball from her room. This was so awkward. She knew she had to go and talk to Whittaker Ray again, to convince him that what she had seen was true. Because each day she became more certain of what she had seen, and she knew that the Lightworkers were in danger because of it. She wanted to find proof somehow, and she desperately wanted to talk to her friends about it. But for the first time since she had met them nearly two years ago, she couldn't confide in them. She'd asked Jengles later what he had meant about the Alexandrite, but he had only looked at her and said enigmatically that he had no further information, but he'd been told that she would understand when the time was right, and would be drawn no further. It was a very lonely feeling trying to work it all out by herself. She looked at the crystal ball in her hand. Maybe her scrying lecture could help her divine what to do, she thought miserably as she packed the quartz ball carefully in her backpack.

After taking a final look around, Eyre left her little cabin and whistled for Florence. When she joined her friends at the departure point, they were looking at her quizzically, and Eyre realised that Beatrice had told them about her visitors over the break.

"You could have come and visited us, if you needed company," Abby said, half teasing, half wounded. "Whittaker Ray would have dropped you off."

"Yeah, I know," Eyre said lightly. "But I'm not sure I would have come back again! I probably would have been buried under a ton of snow. But anyway, I really needed to finish up some work."

"Must have been important," Beatrice said. She didn't miss a trick, and she knew something was not quite right about Eyre's story. But she didn't push any further.

Nick was looking from one of them to the other, sensing the mood. "Well, here comes your dad, Beatrice, time to go," he said, picking up his bags.

Peter Edmunsun was, as always, jovial as they all held hands. "Ahhh," he said. "What could be better than heading off to study and wear yourself out with lectures for eighteen weeks?" The resulting loud groans disappeared with them in the flash of light.

# CHAPTER THIRTY-FIVE

SEMESTER TWO BEGAN IN a flurry of activity. Eyre was not familiar with the timetable, or where some of the second-year lecture rooms were, so she had a bit of catching up to do. The first days passed in a blur, but despite missing her Unlit friends, she was desperately happy to be back at the Academy campus.

Beatrice had gotten over her initial chagrin about Tina and Christopher, and was back to her madcap self, already plotting midnight forays to the Common Room and antics to upset Jemima Periwinkle.

"She's been such a pain on campus!" Beatrice said with her mouth full, over breakfast that morning. "Always following us around quoting rules and regulations. Nick got a detention because his hair wasn't brushed the other day!"

Abby giggled. "Yes, it's about time we did something fun. I vote we have a BANE meeting and discuss! We need some more plans!"

Eyre was definitely keen on that idea, although what she was going to talk about remained a bit of a puzzle. She decided that she would visit Whittaker Ray that morning and try to make him believe her about what she'd seen at the Transit.

She also wanted to go and see Ischyros after the three-week break. It was funny how she missed the cantankerous old beast when she didn't see him. She guessed that she identified with feeling angry and different, and she no longer saw him as ugly and scruffy. He was rather cute with his black mark around his eye and his grey mane and shambling walk. It was only when you talked to him that you realised he was anything but sweet-natured and she seriously doubted that was ever going to change.

So, she headed off first to see the old horse. As usual, he was delighted to see her. "By the Light, I was hoping you wouldn't come back," he said. Eyre ignored him and gave him a good grooming.

"I'm hard to get rid of, Ischyros," Eyre said as she finished. Surely you know that by now."

"Yes, like a burr in the mane," Ischyros said rudely.

"Well, I'm looking forward to equestrian lessons this semester," Eyre said as she left. "We're doing it!"

Not surprisingly, there was no answer to that as she left.

Eyre decided that she would try to catch Whittaker Ray early, so she skipped meditation and headed straight for his office. But when she got there, someone was already inside, and despite herself, she moved closer to listen.

"I'm not sure what to do," Whittaker Ray said.

"She's a real problem," answered Professor Vela. "We need to act fast."

"You're right," Whittaker Ray said. "Leave it with me. I'll see you at the meeting of the Determinant Dozen at eleven eleven."

Eyre shrunk against the wall, aghast. Like a lightbulb going off in her head, an idea had exploded into her mind. Whittaker Ray had been so dismissive of her claims about Professor Vela—what if *he* were in league with him? Panicking, Eyre dashed from the building before either of the men could spot her, feeling like she was going to be sick. And as she leaned against the wall outside, a crashing sense of loneliness came down upon her. For the first time she truly understood how her parents had felt. *Not one* person could be trusted. How could she do anything when the ground constantly shifted under her—what was the truth of it all?

She stumbled away from the building and headed for her Ferito training. She had to act like she knew nothing, which meant sticking to the usual routine. But it was difficult to maintain any sort of normal façade as she went through the Clasis.

"You're particularly focused today," Sergeant Tottingham said approvingly, as Eyre performed her moves almost violently. "That energy will serve you well when you encounter the enemy."

But who *is* the enemy? Eyre thought despairingly. It was as if everyone was wearing a disguise. She shoved her arm forward in position 12, gritting her teeth. If she was alone in this fight, she had better get good at it. Her Viq was coming back a little more each day, and, combined with the intense sessions she'd had at the Unlit during first semester, it gave her the skill to make her a match for any of the Rufa students. The Sergeant continued to watch her as Eyre drove her body as hard as she could through the training session.

"Starting second semester with a bang," Nick commented, smiling, as they walked away. "You aiming for the Nationals?"

Eyre wiped her sweat off with a towel and forced a laugh. "Nope. Just want to take the bad guys down."

They headed for their first scrying lecture, which was held at the psionics lab. All students took Madame Overmantle's class in second-year, as it was a core subject in the curriculum. But Sappir and Tyros students would usually go on in future years to do more of it, as they were more likely to have the 'gift'. Eyre was anticipating she'd be as good at this as she'd been with any of the psionic classes: pretty useless. But she was interested in seeing how it worked.

In the psionics lab all the students took their orbuculums out of their bags. Eyre studied the crystal ball and stared into its clear depths as she set it on a stand on the lab bench. Scrying—or fortune telling using crystals—was a complex skill, and it was how Madame Overmantle had received the critical omens and prophecies over the years that had helped the Lightworkers. She was respected world-wide for her accurate readings.

Scrying consisted of focusing your mind into the crystal ball, and sending your Viq into it. If you were successful, a cloud of light would begin to swirl inside the globe, and those who were talented could see images and messages within it. Madame Overmantle suggested that the students focused their Viq in a similar manner to the way they used their staff, which was useful information to Eyre, as it gave her an understanding of how to achieve the skill. By using a gentle prod of Viq rather than a powerful blast. Not that it helped; her orbuculum remained as clear as glass all through the class.

Part of the problem might have been her focus—she kept checking the time. The Determinant Dozen at eleven eleven. She doubted the time was coincidental. Eleven was a master number regarded as having a high vibration, and 11:11 was considered an auspicious time of the day. Evidently the Determinant Dozen were having their Annual General Meeting today, and Eyre was determined to be at that meeting, as she had been a year ago. Last year the Determinant Dozen had convened quickly after the Gothak had attacked the school, and Eyre and her friends had managed to get in and listen to the meeting. But this time she was going alone. Too much was shrouded and unclear, and she wasn't sure who she could trust anymore.

So, with half an hour to go in the lecture, Eyre excused herself. Beatrice looked surprised, but Abby barely noticed. She was so intent on gazing into her orbuculum she just waved a brief farewell. Eyre walked out before she had to explain herself, and headed back towards the Central Admin building.

Once again there were Zepps and vehicles arriving and a crowd of people and beings from the Alterworlds entering the front door. It was a hubbub of activity, but this time Eyre masked before she neared the area. She didn't want any distant eyes noticing she was there.

Masking was difficult, but her Light energy was strong enough now that she could maintain it if she concentrated hard. She hovered at the side of the building as the strange array of beings arrived. She saw Rigmar's father, Chairman Essendon, arrive in a flash of light, as well as parents of other students she knew—including of course, Beatrice's parents, and Abby's dad. And amongst their arrivals were beings from all four Alterworlds: the Nemoris from Terra, the Pinnae from Aqua, the Caelites from Caelus, and of course the Armatura from Incendium.

Light footsteps made her heart leap, and, despite the fact she was invisible, Eyre leaned back hard against the wall. She looked up and Ranger Chrysanthe was walking towards her, looking almost as if he could see her. Surely not? Even Whittaker Ray hadn't been able to see her last year, and she was a lot stronger now. But it appeared that the Ranger did indeed know she was there. He propped himself beside her and whispered, "Come to join the party? I'll leave the door unlocked for you again."

Eyre was so surprised she couldn't speak and the Ranger started to leave. But there was a flash in front of them and before he could move, a group of the strange blue beings called the Thantos Nex materialised on the path. Their cold eyes looked the Ranger up and down and a sneer curled the corner of the tallest one's mouth.

"You are a disgrace," he said. "A clown performing at a carnival. We are well rid of you."

The Ranger's face was impassive. He yawned. "I think it's more a case of who is well rid of whom."

At that the group turned as one and left. The Ranger ran a hand through his green hair, and he looked wounded, despite his attempt at nonchalance. His bangles jangled as he gripped the stone that hung from his neck.

Eyre finally found her voice. "You were a Thantos Nex?" she whispered in disbelief.

After a moment, the Ranger nodded. "I did something once that was outside the code of my race and I've been excommunicated ever since. It's no secret." He turned to the invisible Eyre and his purple eyes were kind. "Sometimes courage is just making a stand, even if you do it alone. I don't regret the decision I took."

"They're horrible," Eyre spat, feeling defensive for the Ranger, who she could tell had been cut by the Thantos Nex's comments.

The Ranger's voice was soft. "No, just misguided, Eyre." He turned to her and added, "your path also will have many moments of solitude. Don't doubt yourself."

And with that, he left, following the throng of attendees into the building.

# CHAPTER THIRTY-SIX

EYRE WALKED INTO HER room, where Beatrice and Abby were packing
their books for their next lecture. Abby's face lit up when she saw Eyre, but
Beatrice's was more closed.

"Where did you go?" Abby cried. "You missed it! I managed to create a
light cloud in my orbuculum!"

Eyre smiled. "Well, good for you! I had a headache and I needed some
fresh air. I went to the stables," she improvised.

Beatrice gave her a searching look, but said nothing.

"Well, we're having a BANE meeting this afternoon!" Abby said. "It's
about time, so we'll see you there after the next lecture. I have news!"

Abby raced out the door and Beatrice followed more slowly.

"I looked for you at the stables, Eyre," was all she said as she left.

Eyre sat on her bed, feeling terrible. She hated deceiving her friends like
this. But she was so confused about which way to turn. The Determinant
Dozen's AGM had revealed nothing of note; it was just a routine meeting
and President Balthazar had sent his apologies—he was absent like he'd
been the previous year. Obviously he spent a lot of time travelling around.
Eyre thought she'd skip it too if she were him—the meeting just consisted
of a boring treasurer's report, droning statistics and egotistical opinions that
were written down industriously by Quillpro, the eight-armed octopus from
Aqua who was the Secretary of the Dozen. The Gothak were rising; there
were more and more incidents of breaches of Seams throughout the
Alterworld; and death and destruction had exploded from the Underworld,
but although terrible, this was nothing new. Eyre did note that Professor
Vela and Whittaker Ray sat beside one another, and the darkness she felt
intensified. *Who* had they been talking about this morning that had to be
'dealt with'? Obviously, Whittaker Ray and Professor Vela were actually
quite close, and Eyre had a horrible feeling that they may have been talking

about her. And she really regretted showing Whittaker Ray the prose about the Sea Crone. Could *he* have been 'the friend' Abby's dad had referred to in the cavern? It would have to be someone quite powerful to summon a Sublabor. But the very idea of Whittaker Ray being a traitor was *unthinkable*; if he was working with the Darkness, Eyre felt there was no hope at all.

Then there was the poor Ranger. Excommunicated by his own race. What could he have done? A thought dawned and she grabbed her HOL textbook, turning to the last chapter to re-read the section she'd gone over during the semester break. Yes, it was as she suspected. The paragraph didn't say *the* Thantos Nex, implying the race themselves had intervened to save the world, but rather, it was *a* Thantos Nex who had blown the Aura into pieces. Could that have been the Ranger? The kind, funny, but rather ridiculous-looking lecturer? If that had been the solitary decision he had mentioned to her, then no wonder the Thantox Nex were furious with him —it was a huge call to make, and it did go completely against their ethos of not interfering with the events of the Overworld. From the actions of those awful, cold beings she had witnessed this morning, the Ranger would never be forgiven for whatever transgression he had made. He was completely loathed by the Thantos Nex and something this big could certainly explain it. Definitely a topic for BANE, she thought—the Ranger had said what he'd done was no real secret, so she could share it with them and perhaps they could find out more.

A knock on her door interrupted her thoughts and she jumped up. When she saw who was there her stomach twisted, but she tried to look unconcerned.

"Come with me," Whittaker Ray said. "Bring your staff."

Eyre hovered, panicking and wishing she had told her friends some of her suspicions. If Whittaker Ray was working for the Dark side, she might never be seen again. But realising she could hardly take on the great man herself, she hesitantly picked up her staff and followed him out the door.

"I err... I'm really meant to be at my 'Tenets of Management' lecture," Eyre said feebly. "Do you think I should go?"

Whittaker Ray laughed. "No, I think the principles and guidelines of administration can wait this afternoon," he said drily. "I'll write you a note."

Miserably, Eyre followed him, feeling like she was doomed. Something of her mood seemed to strike Whittaker Ray, for he turned and looked at her, his bright blue eyes curious.

"Are you feeling okay, Eyre?" he asked.

"Oh, yes, it's just I'm so far behind, I though perhaps I should go to my lecture."

Whittaker Ray gave a puzzled frown but didn't say anything. Obviously, he had never met a student who wasn't happy to get out of the boring management class. They continued on, heading for the Central Admin building, and Eyre started to feel worried. Did he know she'd been there that morning? Was she about to get an earful? Still, she mused with black humour, that would be better than being blasted to smithereens.

Then another thought hit her to further her depression. She was going to miss the BANE meeting. What would they think of that? She could hardly send a telepathic message with Whittaker Ray a metre in front of her, so all she could do was trudge along behind him, her thoughts roiling.

They entered the admin building and headed for an elevator at the back of the main atrium. Madame Overmantle walked in the front door, arriving back from lunch, and Eyre turned and waved at her gaily. "Hi Madame Overmantle, how are you today?" she cried. Madame Overmantle looked confused and gave a slight wave. She'd just seen Eyre an hour ago, so Eyre's behaviour was a bit perplexing. Eyre didn't care if Madame Overmantle thought it was odd. She just wanted someone to remember that Whittaker Ray was the last person Eyre had been seen with.

Whittaker Ray flicked Eyre a look and pressed the down arrow on the elevator. Then, once they were inside, Eyre noticed there were many floors beneath ground level, going all the way to 66. He pushed the button for Floor -66. Great, the sign of the devil, thought Eyre. Down, down, down to the Underworld.

"Actually, it's an angel number," Whittaker Ray said mildly. "Of happiness and social connections. It's *666* that is sometimes referred to as the devil's number."

Eyre was horrified. Had he been aware of what she was thinking all along? Mortifying at the very least; probably her last hour at the worst.

The journey down was quick and the doors opened to reveal a rock-walled passageway. Whittaker Ray stepped out.

"Come along then," he said cheerily. Eyre had had enough.

"That's far enough!" she said, and held her staff up in front of her, not moving. Whittaker Ray's eyebrows rose.

"*Where* are we going?" Eyre said. "You need to explain."

"Put your staff down, Eyre," Whittaker Ray said. "We both know you're more likely to kill yourself with it at this point, especially in these narrow confines. *What* is going on?"

Eyre lowered her staff slightly. "Well, you tell me," she said fiercely. "You drag me out of my room without any explanation. What am I doing down here?"

Whittaker Ray looked baffled. "You know the need for secrecy, Eyre. I couldn't say anything up there, you never know who might overhear. But I'm sorry; I never thought you'd be worried by this." He took in Eyre's drawn face and her eyes bright with fear, and he suddenly looked appalled. "You're frightened of *me*?"

Eyre stayed inside the elevator, but was relieved at Whittaker Ray's question. He hardly looked like someone working for the murderous Dark side.

"I just don't know what's going on," she said. "We need Angelite and Bloodstone," Whittaker Ray said carefully, as if to a skittish animal. "I'm taking you to Aowx to get some." Aowx, Eyre thought, remembering the stories of the fierce dragon beneath the earth. Going for crystals or for a bbq—as in... me? Finally she decided to speak her mind. Either way it was going to clear this impasse, and show her what was really going on.

"You were with Professor Vela this morning," she said. "Talking about needing to take care of someone—a 'her'".

Whittaker Ray looked at her. He hesitated, but then replied after a moment. "You overheard that conversation? Well, we were actually talking about a student with family problems. How did you hear that?"

"I was coming to see you, and when I heard Professor Vela talking to you, I had to leave. He is a *bad* man, I have no doubt—allied with the Gothak. So why would you not believe me about that, unless you were working with him yourself?"

Eyre was ready to push the 'up' button after she spoke these words, but Whittaker Ray just looked horrified. "You think I'm working for the *Gothak*?" he spluttered, for once losing his usual aplomb.

"Well, why won't you listen to what I said about Professor Vela? And, apart from the Transit, I can tell you that I saw him give Ben Perrill answers for the TEPs exams. He is not an honest man."

After a pause, Whittaker Ray looked regretful and then spoke slowly. "We knew about Ben receiving answers," he confessed. "It was sanctioned by the Echelon when it became apparent Ben wouldn't get in under his own steam. We wanted to keep an eye on him here, and we also felt we owed it to Dr Perrill to allow him in. Professor Vela was very unhappy about allowing a student to—well—*cheat*. He, err... well, he also thought that *you* had been trying to cheat by eavesdropping."

Eyre was dumbfounded. "I thought he was going to *kill* me if he found me," she said indignantly. "And *someone* pushed me under the lake... and stuck my feet when the Armatura were coming... *and* knocked me off the Iridis during the TEPs!"

Whittaker Ray was apologetic. "We're trying to work that out and we're still not sure what happened. Unfortunately, it's not clear."

"But I *saw* Professor Vela in the cave with Abby's dad!" Eyre said in frustration. "Why won't you believe me?"

"It's because I know for a fact that Professor Vela was with me at the time," Whittaker Ray said. "It's impossible he was there. And Abby's dad is undertaking an important mission for the Echelon; in fact, he left last week. He is beyond suspicion—I have known him for many years. Hallucinations in a cave are not uncommon, you know. We've all experienced it at one time or another."

"Did you look for the crystals? The ones they were collecting?"

"Jengles looked, Eyre. There was nothing there."

Eyre gave up. Whittaker Ray was never going to believe what she had seen. But at least it was evident that he was not corrupt, which was a relief. If he'd wanted to get rid of her, he could have easily done it down here and the last Aether would be gone for many years. She relaxed a bit.

"Did the Ranger blow up the Aura?" she asked.

*That* gave Whittaker Ray a start. "How did you find out...? Well, no matter, it isn't a great secret, although it's not often discussed, at the Ranger's request. Yes, he did. He was once a great Thantos Nex, but when the Proditio occurred, *he* was the one who intervened and blasted the Aura as Isars to the four Alterworlds. Unfortunately, he lost both his memory of the event, and most of his power when this occurred, so great was the explosion. In Entis as you know, it was the most significant impact event the earth has seen in recorded history—referred to as the Tunguska Event.

"After the Proditio, the Ranger wandered around the Overworld for decades. The Thantos Nex wouldn't allow him back because of what he did," he said slowly. "And because he had lost most of his immense powers. But that is definitely our gain." He looked down, remembering. "He joined the Academy when the Sea Crone encountered him in Aqua. She gave him his second name, Chrysanthe. Leo, was the name he already had. He'd told the peasants who pulled him out of the river that much, although he couldn't remember anything else. Chrysanthe, ironically is Thalassa for 'nameless'. The Sea Crone sent him to the Academy because he wanted to try and help the Overworld recover from the dire effects of the Proditio, and he hoped he might piece together what happened that day. Unfortunately, his memory has never recovered."

A long silence ensued as they regarded each other and then Eyre lowered her staff. Her throat felt tight as she absorbed the enormity of the sacrifice the Ranger had made.

"So, we're off to see a dragon?" she eventually said. "Aowx tempers the blades the Mimir make?"

Whittaker Ray nodded. "He does, although in return for a significant payment of gold to bolster his coffers." He gave an amused snort and added, "He has quite a fondness for gold.

"Your offerings to the Sea Crone need to be of superb quality; the usual ones available locally will not be acceptable. Aowx sits upon the greatest hoard of crystals in the known Overworld. However, whether he gives us what we want or not remains to be seen." He hesitated a moment and then continued.

"Don't feel embarrassed that you questioned my loyalties, Eyre. It's a murky world we live in right now and things are not always obvious. You are wise to be alert."

Eyre blushed and then spoke in frustration. "It seems to me that the world of the so-called Lightworkers is darker than any of the others! How can Lightworkers be so false and treacherous? I'm relatively new to all this, but I thought we were the *guardians of the world*, the *protectors*—beyond reproach! The more I learn, the more I realise it's just a grubby quagmire of subterfuge. And no one really knows what's going on."

Whittaker Ray nodded, his face sad. "You are right, Eyre. Since the Aura was destroyed, our world has been out of balance, and evil is influencing us more than ever. It is a difficult war, a war of shadows and unseen enemies. But just because it's hard, it doesn't mean we shouldn't do it. We just have to learn to fight with our minds and souls, as well as our bodies, so that we see the true nature of the battle with perception rather than with our eyes. We ourselves are the weapons that will bring back Light to the world. I do know that we are closer than ever to restoring that balance, thanks to the efforts of your parents, Eyre. All we can do is continue on, and try as hard as we can. Now, let's go and look for those crystals. I have a feeling this is something you will never forget."

# CHAPTER THIRTY-SEVEN

EYRE FOLLOWED WHITTAKER RAY along the dim passageway. To be honest, despite Whittaker Ray's understanding words, she was feeling quite uncomfortable now about speaking out and letting him know that she had doubted him. The *Dean of Curriculum*? *And* a member of the Echelon, who had shown her only great kindness? She felt her cheeks flame again, and was thankful he couldn't see her as he strode on ahead.

She realised now why he had told her to bring her staff; not for protection, but to lean on and to help in walking up and down the very steep, uneven pathways. Some of the corners were dim and it was hard to see what was on the ground; without her staff she would have found it a lot harder to navigate.

They trudged for ten minutes through solid rock passages until they reached a massive set of bronze doors. Whittaker Ray knocked three times and the doors opened slowly to reveal a panting young Mimir with two braids and sweat rolling down his russet beard. A blast of heat came through the doorway, and Eyre realised why the short man was so red-faced. It was a furnace in there! She leaned on her staff, still breathing hard from the climb uphill, and tried to peer through the doors.

"Corporal Asscher, sir," the Mimir said to Whittaker Ray, saluting. "It's all ready." Then his eyes caught sight of Eyre behind the old man and he exclaimed, "Dimmog!" as he blushed violently. In this heat, could his face get any redder? Eyre thought, feeling extremely awkward. Not again, surely? She thought all that nonsense with the Mimir was behind her.

But Whittaker Ray fired a look at him, and after a moment Corporal Asscher gathered his wits and stood up straight.

"Honoured to meet you! Please come with me."

Eyre followed Whittaker Ray as he stepped through the doors into the blasting heat. Maybe we *have* arrived at the Underworld, she thought as the extreme temperature hit her like a physical blow. Her skin was burning from the hot air and her own boiling sweat. Not far ahead was a vehicle which looked like a Zepp, seemingly constructed from the same silvery material, but a much smaller version. On the side of the bus was its number: 66

Whittaker Ray walked quickly towards it and Eyre followed just as fast. She desperately wanted to get out of this awful heat. The doors of the Zepp opened and they clambered inside. Eyre slumped down with great relief; it was wonderfully cool inside and even a few minutes out there was exhausting. The walls of the Zepp were humming and semi-transparent and through them she could just make out the rockface of the passage outside.

"Welcome aboard!" a cheery voice called from the front of the bus. "Going down?"

Ranger Chrysanthe waved from the driver's seat, his purple eyes twinkling and the beetles circling busily around his green hair. Today his choice of fashion was a fuchsia-coloured velvet suit with an orange striped cravat. But Eyre just waved back, feeling she should really be bowing and kissing his feet, a la Mimir. She would never look at this man the same way again. Like a chameleon, he disguised the truth of himself.

"Belt up, here we go!" the Ranger called, and Eyre clicked in her harness.

Just as well she did.

What followed was one of the most stomach-churning, terrifying half-hours of her life. The Zepp first trundled into a circular chute and then dropped like a stone for fully five minutes. Then it went into a series of wild swoops and upside-down turns like the most extreme rollercoaster imaginable. It was an insane ride and Eyre felt her eyes were about to pop out of her head. Just when she thought she was going to lose her breakfast all through the cabin, the Zepp slowed and juddered to a halt. Eyre took a long breath and swallowed. Whittaker Ray seemed unconcerned, however, and unbuckled his harness.

"What a lovely ride, thank you Ranger," he said, without an ounce of irony in his voice. Eyre swallowed hard and undid her safety belt also. A lovely ride? *By the Light!*

Leaving the Ranger in the Zepp, they stepped out into another rock-walled passage, at the end of which was a beautiful, shimmering rainbow-coloured curtain that was made of falling water droplets. When they passed through it, Eyre realised the droplets were actually sparkling crystals that caught the light in every direction and fired out every colour of the spectrum. From their brilliance and shine, Eyre felt sure the crystals were diamonds. It was like walking through a shower of falling stars.

Inside, she couldn't help herself and she gasped, one hand to her mouth. A huge cavern lay before her, the size of a football field, and lit by massive flaming torches attached high up on the rock walls in bronze sconces. Treasures of all kinds stretched from one end to the other. Golden artefacts lay all around: goblets, candelabras, solid gold bars, and iron chests filled with piles of shining coins. There were towering piles of enormous raw crystals: rubies, emeralds and sapphires; and jewellery worthy of an Oscar nominee lay in tangled skeins throughout the heap of gold. Here and there, faceted gemstones of every hue were strewn around the glittering landscape, some of them as large as emu eggs. It made the Transit seem positively drab in comparison. Scores of artworks were hung erratically on the walls, some of them even upside down, shoved together with no regard for any of it. Eyre drew a breath as she walked past a canvas that she recognised from her art class textbook in high school. Her mouth hung open. *Surely not?* Raphael's lost masterpiece 'Portrait of a Young Man' had been missing since World War II, and *could that be it*—hung at an angle on Aowx's rock wall? If so, she pitied (almost) the Gestapo who had tried to hold onto it. Because, yes indeed, in amongst all this jaw-dropping display of spectacular beauty and inestimable riches, there were also scattered bones. Some may have been human, others were undoubtedly from other creatures, but all of them unwise enough to venture into Aowx's domain.

A deafening, horrifying roar filled the atrium and Eyre (ridiculously, she knew) raised her staff as her hair stood on end. The sound was more savage than the Strigis even; something primordial and terrible. From beneath the piles of gold coins and treasure, a massive triangular head rose, its huge mouth opening wide to the rocky ceiling as its roar thundered through the cavern, echoing in waves from the walls. Eyre dropped her staff and covered her ears, quaking. If this was what Saxon had encountered last year when he had attempted to steal some gold dust from the Armament stores, then no wonder he had been so terrified. He must have thought his bones were about to be added to the pile.

She dropped to her knees, cowering, as a monstrous creature rose from beneath the mound of treasure and crystals, gold coins dripping like sweat from its bronze-coloured skin. It was like the earth itself was being torn in two as the huge dragon emerged and crashed down the shining slopes towards them, its teeth gnashing and fire blasting from its nostrils. Aowx evidently didn't welcome visitors.

Whittaker Ray stood calmly before the onslaught, waiting. Just when the dragon seemed about to devour him with its massive, glistening fangs, it suddenly stopped. Eyre looked upwards in awe. The creature stood as high as a telephone pole, and just as long, its spiked, reptilian tail stretching up the slope behind it and its powerful wings extended in a fearsome display. Shimmering bronze scales covered every part of its body, and it had two curved horns emerging from the top of its head. Smoke drifted from flared nostrils as two slanted amber eyes studied the diminutive humans below it. Slowly, one huge leathery foot raised in the air and pointed a sharp talon at Eyre.

"Why have you brought that?" a deep, rasping, voice demanded.

Whittaker Ray stepped forward and bowed. "We come to ask a favour of immeasurable importance to the Overworld, Great One."

Aowx's eyes narrowed. Eyre noticed those fierce eyes had specks of emerald green stippled through the deep orange, and that the pupils were black, vertical slits. Mesmerising, but overwhelmingly terrifying.

"You know I care naught for the Overworld, nor the Underworld," the booming voice shouted. "Filled with boring creatures, every one of them. I care only for my own Middleworld. What is the favour you ask?" The huge cavern echoed as the dragon's words reverberated around the rock walls.

Whittaker Ray waited until the sound died away. "We need a gift for the Sea Crone. Two crystals: one of Angelite, and the other a Bloodstone, but both to be absolutely perfect of formation, worthy of the ancient Seer."

"And what is the importance of the Sea Crone?" pondered the huge dragon. "She hasn't shown herself in recent years."

"Wisdom. She has information that we need to further our quest to reconstruct the Aura. This girl," Whittaker Ray indicated Eyre, who would *really* rather that Aowx *didn't* look her way, "is to take them and receive the words from the Sage."

A metallic swishing and chinking ensued as the dragon shifted in the pile of gold, turning to look at Eyre. Rivers of coins ran down the hill from around his feet as he changed position.

"And why this girl?" he breathed. Sparks flicked from his nostrils and showered down over Eyre, but she forced herself to stay still. Taking a deep breath, she tilted her chin and spoke before Whittaker Ray could answer,

"I am continuing my parents' search for answers," she said proudly. "I am an Aether and I am tasked with finding the Isars."

Aowx was suddenly intrigued and he tilted his head, his orange eyes darkening as he mulled this over. "I met your parents once," he mused, "I helped them communicate with an old friend through my special orbuculum." Eyre noted that Whittaker Ray looked very surprised. This was something he hadn't known. But he evidently decided not to ask any questions, deciding that discretion might be the better part of valour at that moment. With dawning wonderment, Eyre realised that her parents had been cautious about sharing the knowledge they had searched the world for, *even* with the revered Whittaker Ray. It seemed that some people knew some things, and there was a chain of information that people could follow, but no one person knew it all. Only her Wisdom, it seemed, had the answers they were all looking for, and it also was reluctant to reveal its secrets too early. One step at a time, preventing the Gothak from understanding what the final solution was. Her parents were so *smart*, she realised with a great sense of pride, as the final piece of her understanding fell into place. She herself had found that no one could be trusted in this supposedly altruistic world, and her parents had also known it. No doubt the death of her brother Eric was the first step for them in this awful journey.

As Eyre thought more about it, she understood why they had dispensed the crucial information in pieces. If *no one* could be totally trusted, then as long as no individual knew the whole puzzle, then they couldn't give it away completely. Not even under duress. The final phase of her terrible grieving process finally blossomed in her heart: acceptance. She looked up at Aowx with something almost like gratitude, for the gift of closure he had unknowingly given her.

The dragon was stroking his face with one lethal talon, perplexed. "But how can it be that you are also an Aether? I believe your mother was one?" He tipped his giant, wedge-shaped head, thinking. "And I hear that all Aether of an age to possess Viq were dispatched by the Gothak last year. How did *you* survive?"

"Luck," Eyre said honestly. "And timing. There is nothing special about me."

Aowx regarded her for a long moment. "It happens that I have what you are looking for," he said. "But I'm not giving it away for free. What do you have for me in return?" The dragon's eyes glittered. A bit like some humans, Eyre mused, glad the dragon couldn't read her thoughts. Never satisfied and grasping for more, and as she surveyed the sheer magnitude of the dragon's hoard, Eyre felt a strange pity for the creature that thought it still needed something else for the heap. But this was important, and her face fell. By St Ria, what could one give a dragon who had all this?

"We have nothing worthy of your collection, which is unparalleled in the Overworld." Whittaker Ray said respectfully as he waved his hand at the glowing mountain of treasures. "Perhaps a favour in return?"

A calculating look crossed Aowx's face, and the dragon was silent, contemplating the suggestion. Then finally he spoke, his amber eyes swivelling back to Eyre. He bent his huge head down to examine Eyre's Inguz, and she could feel his hot breath blasting over her like a gust of wind across the Simpson Desert.

"Not very prepossessing," Aowx commented as he studied her strange-looking Inguz. All Eyre could do was shrug. He was correct, after all. The dragon studied her face and she gazed back at him impassively, hiding the trepidation she was feeling. After a moment, Aowx's eyes narrowed and he turned back to Whittaker Ray.

"Entertainment!" he rasped. "I am in need of distraction, and this one will provide it. An Aether from an Aether is something I have never met! I will pit my wits against her. Two challenges! One physical, one mental. Do you accept the offer?"

Whittaker Ray opened his mouth, looking concerned, but was beaten by Eyre.

"Of course," she replied. Whittaker Ray's white eyebrows moved up and down like a startled seagull.

"Ah—" he said but was interrupted by a booming voice.

"We begin!" shouted the dragon. "Get on my back, girl. Bring that thing," he added, indicating her staff with a huge curved talon.

"Now just a moment..." Whittaker Ray attempted again, but this time Eyre interrupted.

"It's fine, Mr Ray, I accept the challenge." Her voice was certain. If her parents could come here to try and save the Overworld, and ultimately give their lives for that goal, then she would also do whatever she had to.

And with that, she leapt onto the scaly rear leg of the dragon and climbed upwards, using the thick bronze scales as handholds until she reached the triangular spines that stuck up along the ridge of its back. If she sat astride the top of the dragon she could just fit between the hard plates. She wrapped her arms around one of the shimmering triangles and held on tight, with her legs stuck out almost horizontally, so broad was the dragon's back.

"Ok," she called down to the huge wedge-shaped head far below. Aowx's watchful eyes narrowed with satisfaction, and Eyre was struck by a feeling that she may have been tricked somehow. But there seemed no alternative. She hardly had a sack of gold and diamonds to give Aowx in exchange for the crystals. And at least she could say she had ridden a dragon! What would Ischyros think about *that*? Although, possibly the dragon would be an easier ride.

Moving slowly, the dragon crossed from one side of the cavern to the other, sniffing the pile of treasure as it went. Occasionally it would dig down deep, and as the muscles contracted and contorted underneath her, Eyre hung on tight to avoid being flung off, into the golden morass far below. After a great deal of scenting and excavating, Aowx exclaimed with satisfaction, a deep growl that rumbled through the cavern.

"Angelite!" he said and flung it at Whittaker Ray, who was now a miniature figure down the slope. The pale blue crystal turned over and over in the air, firing like a missile at the Dean of Curriculum. But with one untroubled hand gesture, Whittaker Ray stopped the trajectory of the object and it froze, suspended in the air.

"Now," muttered Aowx. "Where was that Bloodstone?"

Even greedy dragons had no idea of their inventory, Eyre decided, after another half hour of enduring what felt like a rodeo on a stegosaurus. Her legs and arms were aching as the dragon searched up and down the mountain of treasure, digging down at intervals to hunt for the elusive Bloodstone. Finally, after Aowx had stuck his head deep into the pile, he lurched upwards with a spherical polished green stone in his mouth, golden treasures and objet d'art tumbling down around him as he drew his head back.

"Success!" he mumbled around the stone, and spat it like a massive pip towards Whittaker Ray, who set the Bloodstone twirling in the air next to the Angelite.

"We have the trophies," Aowx declared. "Let the games begin!"

# CHAPTER THIRTY-EIGHT

"I WILL CHALLENGE YOU to one physical challenge and one mental challenge," the massive dragon declared, his voice booming in Eyre's ears as she hung on tightly. Aowx walked on his powerful legs up the steep slope to the top of the huge golden mountain of treasure. His wings were now tucked in to the side of his body and his long, spiked tail undulated behind him as he climbed, and his feet sank deep into the pile from the weight of his body. Whittaker Ray was a mere speck in the distance by the time they stopped, and Eyre realised there would be no help from him for the contest. Still, what did she have to lose? The dragon was obviously not going to challenge the brilliant mind and expert Lightworker skills of Whittaker Ray. Who could be a better opponent than *her*: with her feeble, unreliable Viq and possibly the worst Lightworker skills on record? Even her Inguz was indistinguishable. But, if this was the only way to get the precious crystals, she would try as hard as she could.

"First, a shooting match!" Aowx shouted. "Me with my breath, you with your sceptre! Down you get!"

Eyre stepped from the dragon's back into the air and lowered herself down, using her Viq for reverse levitation. She tried hard, but she noticed the dragon smirking as she wobbled amateurishly to the ground. When her feet touched the shining gold coins under her feet, she waited for further instructions. Aowx's voice reverberated throughout the chamber.

"There are twelve burning torches on the walls. We will have twelve attempts each and the winner is the one who extinguishes the most."

Eyre thought this was hardly fair, since the dragon had probably been practising shooting out the torches for hundreds of centuries. But she was realising that the dragon was cunning, and greedy, and Aowx was stacking the odds in his favour.

"Fine," she agreed. "Too easy."

Aowx's eyes narrowed. "After you," he purred.

Teeth clenched, Eyre turned and surveyed the burning torches, held in the bronze sconces far above her head. The nearer ones she might have a chance at, but the ones further down the chamber? Not a hope. Still, she had to try.

She took a deep breath and eyed the burning flames above her head. At least she had been practising during the semester break, but she hadn't improved much. She was glad she couldn't see Whittaker Ray clearly. He probably had his head in his hands.

But then she tilted her chin and raised her staff. She focused on the wood and let her Viq flow through her and into the weapon forged from a branch of the magical rainbow eucalyptus. She imagined a circle of energy, getting brighter and stronger, and then she fired the beam at the flame above her. She missed, of course, but to her surprise, not by much. A circular hole blasted into the rock face about a metre to the right of the torch. Aowx snorted with delight, smoke blasting from his large nostrils.

"Aha!" he cried. "Again!"

Eyre lifted her staff again and looked upwards, creating the energy flow within her staff again. Then she let the energy fire upwards, and once again she missed, this time about a metre to the left of the torch.

Aowx was so gleeful his tail swished back and forth with excitement, creating a large swathe through the glowing gold objects underneath him. "Again!"

Eyre gritted her teeth as she peered upwards. It was going to be embarrassing if she missed every one. But she looked at the holes in the wall on either side of the torch and felt a surge of pride. She hadn't missed by much. No shots going backwards, straight up in the air or blowing her foot off. She was improving! And although Aowx was impatient for her to continue, she took a moment and studied the holes, thinking hard. A memory came to her from last year when she was practising with her staff and the Ranger had given her some advice. He had said that her staff was like a gun with the sights off, and that she needed to make allowances for the problem—which was no doubt due to her pink diamond having a broken end. It made sense to her.

So, she looked up at the third flame and seared its location into her mind. Then she shut her eyes and concentrated on creating the energy beam, but this time keeping her eyes shut when she fired, and shooting with her mind to adjust the direction of the beam. There was an explosion, followed by a loud, annoyed curse from the huge dragon. Eyre opened her eyes to realise, to her great joy, that she had actually blown the torch out with her beam!

She was so surprised that her mouth hung open for a second. And the next thought was an exhilarating surge of amazement as she realised that finally, she *got* it! She could do this!

Eyre quickly fired another beam off and the fourth torch snuffed out. Then the fifth, sixth, seventh; rapidly all the way to the twelfth, with no hesitation or inaccuracy. Eyre was so delighted, she forgot it was a competition and fired fast, enjoying it as much as the days she had spent at archery practise. When she shot the last torch into darkness, she stood there, feeling a deep happiness flow through her. She could use her staff. *Finally!*

Aowx didn't share her joy, though. With an annoyed grunt, he fired a molten stream of fire at the torches and relit all twelve. Then, with a single blast of his fiery breath, he blew them all out at once.

"I win!" he said grumpily. Eyre was quite annoyed. So it *had* been a trick! He hadn't exactly cheated, but it wasn't really fair.

"The first round goes to me," Aowx bellowed. "We will now have a riddle contest. This time I go first!"

A *riddle*, for the Light's sake, Eyre thought despondently. All I know are dad jokes.

"What can be killed, but resurrected?" Aowx said pompously, adding quickly, "If you get this wrong, I win the competition!" For some reason, Eyre wasn't quite comfortable with the gleam that appeared in his eyes. She thought hard. She had to guess this or it was all over. At least she had spent some time with the Unlit and their cyphers and quizzes and codes, so perhaps she had some hope. At that thought, a spark went off in her brain and she concentrated, trying to tease out the meaning. Finally she realised what it was.

"The answer is 'hope'!" she said, attempting to sound confident. But then she straightened, sure of her answer: if anyone understood the concept of the reigniting of hope and faith after total devastation, she did.

And if a dragon could have a tantrum, Aowx did. Spurts of golden coins, like water arcing from the Trevi fountain, rained down the slopes as his feet stomped into the shining pile of treasure. As she tried to dodge the shower of flying coins, Eyre realised that she must have guessed right. She breathed deeply with relief; that meant the competition wasn't over yet.

"Your turn!" Aowx huffed, steam and sparks blasting from his nostrils. "A mere formality before I win this competition."

Eyre dismally considered her repertoire of jokes. "What do you call a hippie's wife? Mississippi." Brilliant. Or "Saw a slice of toast in the zoo yesterday. Heard it was bread in captivity." Hahaha...? Or the ultimate favourite her father always kidded her with: "I'll call you later. Don't call me later, call me Dad!" That last one nowadays always made her heart clench. But it wasn't going to save her today. The dragon's eyes glinted as she wracked her brain. Nothing from her time at the Unlit was going to help—they were more into deciphering than creating riddles while she'd been there. And then a sudden memory struck her; Beatrice, the ancient history buff, teasing Eyre about a Greek philosopher—Empedocles. Thinking hard, Eyre crossed her fingers mentally.

"What is my name?" She said confidently, her face completely impassive, masking her anxiety. "I am one of the four roots of Empedocles."

The dragon contemplated this and turned his gaze towards her. Her heart sank as she saw the triumph in his eyes. "Much more sophisticated than I would have imagined," he said in a soft tone, the green flecks in his amber eyes glowing. "But of course, I knew Empedocles, and I know his four roots are the elements Earth, Air, Fire, and Water." His lip curled with satisfaction, revealing very sharp looking fangs. "So naturally, you being from Entis, are 'Earth'."

Eyre realised she had been holding her breath, and then she exhaled in relief. She almost pumped her hand in the air as she realised *he was wrong!* But she restrained herself; game or no game, it didn't make sense to mock a dragon. "My name is Eyre," she said. "Air is the answer, not Earth. So, you are incorrect. And I believe that would make us one each in this competition. We are now tied."

The dragon stomped his foot in frustration, sending a blizzard of gold sovereigns over Eyre. His eyes narrowed. Steam drifted from his nostrils as he contemplated her with a look that made Eyre shift her feet nervously. She gripped her staff harder. Time to run? Her eyes flicked down the slope, looking for an escape route.

But then the dragon seemed to pull himself together.

"A decider, then," he said softly, a crafty look crossing his face.

He obviously hated losing, Eyre thought uneasily. What would happen if he *did* lose the competition, if he was this unhappy already? But she kept her face impassive.

"But of course," she replied. "What did you have in mind?"

The dragon responded by sinking his head into the pile of treasure and snuffling around underneath it, like a pig rooting for truffles. Then he walked along, still with his head under the golden mound, searching for something. A wave of surging gold followed his massive body as he moved from one side of the chamber to the other. Finally he stopped and flung his head up triumphantly. Treasures of all kinds tumbled around him as he emerged from the heap with his prize clutched firmly in his mouth. Eyre walked over to him unsteadily, finding it hard to stay on top of the pile. Her feet kept sinking unevenly, like she was walking on a soft sand dune. Except this was not sand, and her eyes were round as she walked across riches of unimaginable value.

When she got to Aowx she could see that he held a polished sphere about the size of a soccer ball, made of a transparent sea-green stone. The sphere was as clear as pristine water, and it shone with a magical glow.

Aowx put the sphere down. "An orbuculum made of beryl and used by the Druids in ancient days for scrying," he said smugly, boastful. "It is said to be the most powerful crystal ball in existence, and it is one of my most prized and valuable acquisitions. The last owner was the greatest seer in Lightworker history—the Sibyl of Kemet." His eyes took on a cunning glint. "I was very pleased to acquire the orb from her." Eyre felt more than a little uncomfortable about his happiness and wondered how he had acquired the priceless treasure. It didn't bear thinking about, really.

The dragon eyed Eyre. "So... our final challenge. Whoever locates this wins the competition. They win the Angelite and the Bloodstone, and I will throw the orbuculum in for good measure. Are you ready?"

Eyre was feeling more and more uncomfortable. Why would the dragon "throw in" one of his most prized possessions unless he was absolutely certain he would win? She'd accepted the challenge already, so there was no need to sweeten the deal. It made her feel like she was definitely being toyed with. But there was no going back now.

"Let the decider begin!" she cried, echoing what Aowx had said earlier. "I'm ready!"

The indecipherable gleam appeared in the dragon's eyes again, but Eyre was ready to get this over with, for better or worse, so she just waited for him to explain what they were to do.

Aowx picked up the crystal ball and tossed it high into the air. It arced to the middle of the cavern and dropped like a shotput towards the hoard, a blue-green meteor that disappeared into the depths of the pile. Then the huge dragon started to move his tail back and forth, burying it into the treasure mound until the mass of gold and gems started to move around the cavern like cake mix in a bowl. As the ground heaved beneath her, Eyre levitated three metres above it, staring in awe at the golden, unstoppable tsunami below. Treasure tumbled and moved from side to side like a molten flow of lava; a swollen river of gold—with objects flying in the air and then churning back into the surging heap. The whole room was a violent mass of moving gold, whirling around until the entire landscape had changed. New mounds had formed where previously there were canyons, and the stirring had uncovered new treasures and precious objects that had been hidden underneath. Others that had sat on the surface were nowhere to be seen. Finally the dragon stopped.

"Sometimes I like to mix it up a bit," he said. He'd obviously played this game before.

Eyre felt sick as she surveyed the wide expanse. *How* was she going to find that ball in the vastness of all this? She felt even more despairing when she saw the satisfied look in Aowx's eyes, and she knew she was going to lose the challenge.

"We begin," the dragon roared. "First one to find the orbuculum wins the competition!"

Immediately he stuck his head under the pile and started snorting and sniffing, moving his head from side to side. Eyre had to try, so she used her staff to move objects around her, looking without much hope for the shining orb. She couldn't even walk properly on the uneven ground, so her progress was slow, and as she saw Aowx mowing methodically through the pile from one side of the canyon to the other, she knew the competition was all but over.

But then a voice spoke in her head. "Divination. Use your staff. Concentrate on the orb," Whittaker Ray said. Eyre looked down the slope to the man who stood so far away, and he raised his hand. Eyre looked at her staff, and then lifted it up the way Whittaker Ray was indicating. She shut her eyes, and using all the force she could muster, focused on her memory of the light-green crystal ball. After a moment, she felt a flame of energy surge through her staff and she opened her eyes in surprise. Then she gasped: her pink diamond was glowing hot pink! As she walked tentatively forward she felt her staff moving in her hand, bending, pointing, tugging... *showing* her which way to go! And it was straight down the slope, away from Aowx, who was meticulously combing the chamber from side to side above her. Confident of his success, he didn't even pull his head out to see what Eyre was doing. In fact, as she watched, he completely submerged himself into the golden pool, with only the tip of his tail sticking out like a periscope as he scoured the depths below.

The realisation that she might have a chance after all galvanised Eyre into action. She stumbled down the slope on top of the shining treasures, slipping on crystals and tripping over priceless artefacts that stuck out of the pile. Then her foot got stuck tightly in something and looking down, she saw it was a large etched goblet. Feeling she had no time to spare, she clunked along with it awkwardly, like a strange shoe, until she realised she *had* to get rid of it and wasted precious moments as she kicked her leg hard a few times until it finally skidded off down the slope. She had only taken two steps after that when a sparkling ruby and diamond necklace looped around her feet like a malevolent snake, causing her to fall to her knees and roll down the slope until she finally crashed up against a massive golden statue of Pericles. Swearing, she untangled the necklace from her feet, flinging it away like a glittering quoit, and staggered to her feet in panic, frantically picking up her staff again. Feeling its power, she crashed on maniacally down the golden hill like a drunken sailor, following the pull of the energy. Her staff was hot in her hand and the pink diamond grew deeper in colour as she ran. She careered further down the strange terrain, trying to move fast, but she tripped over the lid of an old sea chest and smashed down face forward, landing with her chin on someone's long-lost gem-encrusted crown. She stood up painfully, winded by the fall, and she wiped blood away from her face with the back of her hand. Gasping for air in the stifling chamber, she turned her head to see what Aowx was doing. Her stomach clenched when she saw that the mountain of gold was surging upwards—he was coming up! If he looked down the slope, he would see her!

Lifting her staff high, Eyre staggered down the pile again, struggling for breath from her burning lungs. Her legs were weak from the difficulty of running, and her energy was flagging. She'd only recently acquired her Viq again and she didn't have much in reserve. She could see the diamond starting to dim, and pushed herself harder. She *had* to get to the orb first!

An ear-splitting roar of rage tore through the chamber. Aowx had evidently emerged and could see what she was up to, and he was *not* happy! Eyre didn't waste time looking backwards but she could hear the crash of his massive legs as he thundered down the slope towards her, and she pumped her legs harder, following the glowing pink diamond.

Her staff dipped downwards hard, jamming into the pile until the crystal tip was completely hidden. Eyre pulled the staff out and frantically threw treasure away, trying to find the crystal ball that she knew must be somewhere underneath. Missiles of goblets, silver jugs, and ornaments, and frisbees of golden plates went flying as she dug deep into this strange mountain. Aowx was almost upon her when she spotted the shine of the crystal ball. She flicked her eyes up to look at Aowx as she reached for the translucent sphere. And then, he reared high in the air and somehow, she just *knew* he was about to blast her with fire. And also, with a flash of clarity, she realised that he just couldn't *stand* to lose, never mind the prize. The sneaky, *cheating* old lizard! Suddenly Eyre's fear was gone as her temper started to smoulder. Pulling hard, she heaved the heavy orb out of the pile and sat on it.

"You might get *me*, Aowx," she shouted. "But you'll also blow your precious orb to smithereens. Your choice!"

There was a flash of light and Whittaker Ray stood by her side. Aowx screamed in fury and crashed back down to the ground. He gnashed his teeth and his eyes turned blood red, and fire blasted from his mouth, scorching the cave rocks black. It was as if a volcano had combined with a nuclear bomb within the body of a rampaging two-year-old—Eyre had never seen such a tantrum! Molten rock dropped from above and sulphurous smoke filled the chamber. Deafening screeches of rage rent the air for long minutes. Whittaker Ray stood calmly, but his body language was tense. Eyre remained sitting on the crystal ball, feeling that at any moment she might be scorched into a melted puddle. Dragons were rather temperamental, it seemed.

Finally the pyrotechnic display stopped. Aowx turned his furious eyes towards them, but at least he'd stopped spewing gouts of fire.

"It seems you have won the competition," Aowx said. "It also seems that I underestimated you, a mistake I will not make again. I don't suppose you'd consider double or nothing?"

After a long moment, the dragon gave a ghastly grin, a spine-tingling sight if ever there was one. "I suppose not then. Well, I will keep my word. Take your prizes, but I suggest *you*," he leaned down close to Eyre and sniffed at her, "don't darken my doorstep again. You won't like the welcome."

Eyre forced herself to keep still until the dragon straightened again and turned away from them.

"Begone!" he thundered as he headed back up the hill. Not needing further encouragement, Whittaker Ray snapped his fingers and they transported to the rock corridor, reappearing outside the spilling curtain of diamonds. Whittaker Ray held the Angelite and Bloodstone, and Eyre was still sitting on the crystal ball. Eyre stood weakly, looking down at the precious orbuculum.

"He doesn't like people taking his toys away, does he?"

"You did well," Whittaker Ray said softly. "It's not often that a dragon is bested." Then he added, in what Eyre considered to be the understatement of the year, "they don't like it."

She laughed and picked up the heavy ball, loving the feel of the smooth object in her arms which seemed warmed by some strange energy. "I'm glad I didn't come away empty handed!"

Whittaker Ray gave her a strange look as he headed up the corridor in front of her. "Well, you wouldn't have been empty handed," he said enigmatically.

Eyre trudged behind him. "What do you mean? Should I have stolen them?"

Whittaker Ray stopped and turned to look at her. "I mean," he said, "that you wouldn't have been here at all. Anyone who accepts a dragon's challenge and fails, gets eaten. A lesson, perhaps, in letting your elders handle the negotiations?"

Not surprisingly, Eyre couldn't think of a single response to that as they headed back to the Zepp.

# CHAPTER THIRTY-NINE

EYRE WALKED UP THE corridor of the dormitory, deep in thought. Whittaker Ray had assured her that of course he wouldn't really have let the dragon eat her, but she still felt chills when she thought of the staggering power of the huge creature, who definitely was not now her greatest fan. But how awesome was that experience? The memory of the incredible chamber would never leave her.

She opened the door and found her friends inside the room. They did not look at all happy when she walked in, and with a sinking feeling, Eyre remembered that she'd missed the BANE meeting. Abby was folding her washing, deliberately not looking at her, and Beatrice leant up against her desk, an unimpressed expression on her face.

"I'm so sorry," Eyre apologised as she shut the door.

"Where were you?" Beatrice asked. "We looked for you everywhere, including," she added meaningfully, "the stables."

Eyre opened her mouth and then looked at Abby. She couldn't tell them. A month ago she would have trusted them with her life, and she still did. But she didn't trust Abby's father, and she had no way of ensuring that Abby didn't mention this to him. Miserably, she gave an excuse.

"I was with Whittaker Ray," she said feebly. "I was asking for some help with catching up on classes I missed last semester, and I just forgot about the meeting. I'm *so* sorry."

Abby turned hurt eyes to Eyre and made an obvious show of looking at the staff Eyre held in her hand. Disbelief was written all over Abby's face. "What classes? I thought you'd done all that over the school holidays. Maybe you were back at the Unlit, since you seem so keen on them over there? And your chin is bleeding, by the way."

She flounced out of the room and Beatrice looked at Eyre with a serious expression. "We don't know what you're up to, Eyre. Or why you're keeping secrets from us. No one's happy about it. Even Nick's annoyed—he missed a Ferito tryout to come to the BANE meeting. I think you need to remember that we're your friends, and you don't treat friends like this."

She too walked out the door and Eyre sat on her bed, feeling awful. What could she do? But despite thinking hard about it, she couldn't come up with any answer at all, and she felt very alone.

✕✕

Finally, Eyre stood up reluctantly. She had better go and find Nick and apologise. But when she pulled the door open, her heart skipped a beat. Someone familiar was walking away from her room, down the corridor. He turned as the door opened and after a moment, walked back to her. Two brilliant green eyes looked into hers.

"How are you doing?" Jax asked, crossing his arms and leaning against the wall. His hair under the light shone like ebony and when he smiled, his perfect teeth contrasted against the tan of his skin. Evidently, he'd been spending some time outdoors. Eyre was stuck for words as she stared stupidly at him. Then she finally managed to blurt out an answer.

"I'm ah, great! Did you have a good break?"

"Yeah, we went to Canada. Dad wanted to check out some of the timber plantations over there. It was pretty cool. I have to head out again later this year."

"It's summer over there, hey? It must have been awesome." Eyre said.

Jax nodded. "Yeah, it was. The mountains and the wildlife, the lakes—it was really something." Then he looked up and down the corridor, as if searching for something. "Well, I'd better get—"

Eyre raised a finger. "Wait, I have something for you, just a sec." She hurried into her room and scrabbled through her desk until she found the little bag that she'd put the plume agate in. As she went to pick it up, she hesitated, feeling suddenly uncertain. What if he thought this was stupid? But it was too late now. Jax was waiting, propped against the wall like a gorgeous bookend.

Eyre handed him the bag, feeling suddenly shy. "I—ah, wanted to do something for you after you fixed my guitar. I cut it myself."

Jax drew the plume agate out of the bag and to Eyre's immense relief, she could see that he liked it. She had spent hours cutting the best slice out of the unusual rock, and then she'd buffed and polished the flat, oval disk until it shone like glass. The colours of the stone were enhanced from the time she'd worked on it, and the turquoise shade of the background was the hue of a Mediterranean sea. The tendrils of the inclusions in the rock stretched across in a multitude of colours, and it did indeed look like a magical underwater scene. Eyre had put a hole through the top of the stone and threaded a long, thin leather thong through it.

"You made this?" Jax said. "That is very cool."

"I thought it looked like the Crystal Grotto, and—you know—well, I wouldn't be here if you hadn't—"

Jax swooped in and silenced her stammering with a long, gentle kiss. His chest was against hers and Eyre put her arms up around his neck. When he released her, Eyre felt like she had just performed three hours of Ferito, her legs were so weak.

"Thank you, Eyre with the red hair," Jax whispered, tucking an unruly tendril of her russet hair behind her ear. "I love it."

Eyre traced his face with her fingers in wonderment. This day had been full of so many extremes—concealment and awful revelations; explosions of intense fear; the pummelling of overwhelming guilt, and now, whatever *this* was. But whatever it was, it was magical and she wanted more.

"It's a plume agate," she said softly. "It's for protection."

Jax hung the pendant over his neck. "I will never take it off."

Their eyes met again and slowly Jax pulled Eyre towards him. "You have the most beautiful eyes I have ever seen," he whispered. "Like the Richelieu sapphires." He lowered his head, his eyes upon hers, and his hands light on her shoulders as he pulled her near. But a caustic voice interrupted them, making them both jump.

"Eyre Lightward!" Jemima Periwinkle said primly. "You know the rules about boys in the dorm! That will be a detention for both of you. Friday afternoon—Miss Lightward on bathroom duty and you, Romeo, will report to Professor Vela for your duties. I will let him know you're coming!"

She waved her hands at Jax as if shooing off a pesky animal. "Off you go!"

Eyre's eyes lit up with mirth as a chastened Jax headed off. But the mocking look he threw back over his shoulder said it all, and Eyre had to race to her room before she exploded with laughter.

# CHAPTER FORTY

WHEN EYRE FELT ENOUGH time had passed she opened her door and checked the corridor. Jemima Periwinkle had disappeared, so she slipped out of the dorm in search of Nick.

She eventually found him deep in conversation with Warrigal at the side of Lecture Theatre 2B. Nick looked up at her and smiled, to Eyre's great relief. She didn't think she could stand another scolding today.

"Hi guys," Eyre said. "Am I interrupting?"

Warrigal flashed a grin at her. "Never! But I'm just about to leave. I'll catch you both later."

He headed away from the Lecture Theatre and Eyre looked at Nick curiously. "Warrigal's in Tyros—shouldn't he be heading to Astral Travel with you?"

Nick shook his head. "Warrigal's been having special classes with the Ranger. Warrigal's so knowledgeable about his country, (Eyre didn't need to be told *that*, she thought) so he's been studying orienteering and topographical maps as an elective. It's pretty cool; apparently he uses his mind and Viq to work out the compass direction."

Eyre nodded as if that made complete sense. But she suspected that the real reason Warrigal was training with the Ranger was to study therianthropy. Since she'd seen Warrigal turn into a dingo she'd realised he had the very rare talent, and no doubt the Ranger, who also had the gift, was helping him to expand those skills.

"Well, er, I came to apologise, Nick. I'm really sorry about the BANE meeting," Eyre said, leaping into the reason she'd come to find him. "I got caught up with Whittaker Ray and couldn't get away in time..." She trailed off at the calm expression on Nick's face, as she realised dismally that he was just waiting patiently for her to get her excuse over with; he didn't believe her either. She looked downwards, unable to meet his eyes. She wouldn't believe herself either, if she heard all this.

"Eyre," Nick said softly. "There is no need to explain. I know you have your reasons for whatever you're doing and I hope in time you'll share it with us. I'm okay with it. Living with my father taught me that sometimes there are things that need to be kept secret. Let's do the BANE meeting tomorrow afternoon. I'll talk to Abby and she can tell Beatrice."

Eyre was moved by his kindness. He had lived such a terrible life with his father and yet he had chosen to turn towards the Light rather than become bitter about it, or follow in the same brutal footsteps. She looked at him gratefully.

"Thanks Nick, for understanding."

He smiled and headed off for his Astral Travel lecture and Eyre decided to finish the day by practising her archery. Today she just didn't feel like she belonged on the Academy campus.

So she walked to the ward that led to the Unlit compound and stepped through the cold blast of air, feeling like she was heading home.

# CHAPTER FORTY-ONE

THE NEXT MORNING EYRE walked to class with Beatrice and Abby, who had thawed towards her. They were now on their way to a class they hadn't had before, run by the Sergeant and called 'The Summons'. Eyre was glad to be learning something different; all her classes so far had just been more of the same things she'd studied last year, and although she liked the feeling of improving in them, she was keen for something new. She'd been working hard on her tri-merit class for Aqua, and finally progressing in the multi-level skill.

Yesterday, Eyre had practised archery for hours, with Florence keeping her company as she fired quivers of arrows at the distant target on the Unlit campus. Her frustration, or perhaps it was her deep sadness, seemed to give her extra energy, and all her arrows hit the yellow central circle. Julia came up to her afterwards, her normally taciturn features curious.

"Nice bow," she commented. Eyre smiled but didn't explain where it had come from. "You're shooting well," Julia added. That was quite an accolade from the usually dismissive girl who had such expertise in archery.

"Thanks," Eyre said. "I want to shoot the eyes out of the Gothak."

Julia smiled fiercely. "Me too," she said darkly. "I'll be on your team."

Eyre had left that afternoon feeling lighter from being back amongst people she could completely relax with. She approached her room with something like trepidation, but when she got there, Abby had given her a big hug.

"We're doing the BANE meeting tomorrow afternoon," she said, and Eyre mentally thanked Nick.

"*If* you can fit us into your busy social schedule?" Beatrice added, but when Eyre looked at her, she realised with relief that Beatrice was joking.

"Thanks guys," Eyre had said softly. "I'll try to make it this time. *And* I have something to share." The surprise on Beatrice's face showed Eyre more than anything how aware her friends were of the secrets she had kept this year. She felt terrible as she realised just how much it had hurt them.

She thought about it as she walked with her friends to class. This year had been a difficult one; there had been a few instances of tension between them, and she was glad they had forgiven her for her subterfuge, even though they were still confused by it. Once again, she wracked her brain for an answer to her current dilemma, but if there was a solution, she couldn't figure it out.

'The Summons' class was evidently a mandatory course, because a large crowd of students from all the Sectors made their way into Lecture Theatre 1A, the largest auditorium on campus. Eyre noticed Jax walking up the front of the crowd with Rigmar, Robeson and Warrigal. Arant, Hese, Flava and Tyros Sectors were not usually scheduled together for a lecture; so this was going to be a big class. It was as if Jax could feel her gaze, because he suddenly turned and looked straight at her. He smiled and her heart tightened. The interchange was not lost on Abby, who raised her eyebrows at Beatrice, who then looked at Eyre. Eyre saw the question in their eyes and chuckled. "Guilty as charged," was all she said.

Eventually, when they were all seated, the Sergeant marched to the centre of the stage and motioned for silence.

"This will be a short lecture, and a long practical session," she announced. "Dr Botolfe will assist with the lecture part of the session." The sharp-featured lecturer appeared on stage beside the Sergeant. The Sergeant nodded at her and continued.

"It will have become clear to you that there are many weapons and tools associated with being a Lightworker; your Kulbeda and your Antaraks are your Arms Endowment, you all have a staff and some of you will also receive a Mnae in your fourth year. Then there are other weapons like the Flail that you will need at times. And of course, there is your Lighthorse."

The Sergeant snapped her fingers as she listed each of these weapons, and one by one they appeared on the stage, piling up in a heap. Then the class broke into laughter when she clicked her fingers and a spectacular grey Percheron materialised and stood quietly in the centre of the room.

"My Lighthorse, Audo," she said, and her voice held a gentleness Eyre had not heard before from the Sergeant. "In Latin, his name means 'the courage to take a risk'. Every Lighthorse puts their lives in the hands of their rider, so I think it's a very apt name." The massive creature nuzzled her arm, its placid temperament seemingly out of place in such a powerful creature.

"Advika Bhaduri, would you come up here for a demonstration, please?" the Sergeant called to the small girl who sat, as usual, in the front row of the auditorium. Advika's Sector was Flava, like Beatrice, and she was a particularly intellectual girl who aced all her classes. Advika looked surprised, but jumped to attention, of course.

She quickly walked on to the stage and stood by the Sergeant. "Okay," the large woman said. "I would like you to pick up all the weapons and climb onto Audo."

Advika made a valiant effort, but by the time she had the Flail draped over her shoulder, on top of the Antaraks and the Mnae, her knees were starting to buckle. She staggered slowly over to Audo and tried to levitate up to the gentle giant, who was twice as tall as her. Advika wobbled about a metre off the ground, and then dropped the Mnae, the Flail rattled off her shoulder and crashed onto the stage, and her staff fell from her hand as she tried to catch the slipping weapons. She ended up on her hands and knees, scrabbling to pick everything up. Audo tried to help by bending a knee to lower himself so she could climb on, but by now the whole auditorium was laughing uproariously as Advika bumbled around, including Advika herself. The Sergeant intervened.

"Thank you Advika, for your effort; you may leave the weapons and return to your chair. I think perhaps the point has been made: you cannot possibly carry all the weapons that are available to you at once. Or take your Lighthorse everywhere with you. So, 'The Summons' is a telepathic way of summoning the object—or creature—you require, when you need it. Similarly, the Reverse-Summons sends the thing back." Hence, Dr Botolfe being here, Eyre thought dolefully. The Head of Psionics was obviously going to teach them how to do it. Eyre just hoped she wouldn't be asked next to go up on the stage; it hadn't worked out so well with Dr Botolfe in her previous encounters.

Sure enough, "Dr Botolfe will now take over to demonstrate the technique of summoning the object you require," the Sergeant continued. "Practise is the key to developing this telepathic expertise, so I suggest you pay attention to Dr Botolfe so you understand how you are to achieve the Summons skills. It won't help you when you're battling a Gothak if you summon a daffodil instead of a Mnae." Once again, a ripple of laughter drifted around the room. However, when the severe Dr Botolfe stepped forward, silence fell like a wet fog. She stared critically around the auditorium. Several students looked down at their desks, and Eyre realised that she was not alone in her dislike of the self-absorbed lecturer. The professor's sharp eyes looked out at the class.

"The Summons is a form of telepathy mixed with telekinesis, where objects are materialised by drawing them to you with your Viq. And then pushed back again, when you no longer need them, using the same Viq. It is a particularly difficult task to master, because it is a combination of *two* psionic skills, and technically called a 'compound skill', which is why you begin to learn how to do it now. We hope by your third year you will be able to manage this ability to a degree, but it will take a great deal of practise." The professor held her arm horizontal, with her palm facing straight outwards, and as she concentrated, a deep, electronic vibe, accompanied by a high-pitched whistling, blasted the students' ears. Then, from nowhere, a sharp Antarak came spinning in and into Dr Botolfe's hand. She turned to the class with a satisfied look on her face. Eyre had to admit she was rather impressed that the weapon had ended up with the handle in Dr Botolfe's hand, rather than the blade. The lecturer continued, obviously well pleased with the spectacle she had created.

"The process is achieved by focusing hard on the object you desire, and then concentrating your Viq in a sharp blast, so that enough energy is created to transport the object from where it is, to you. This is a skill that Lightworkers must learn to manage, as it drains your Viq and can leave you vulnerable. Over the next two years you will build your strength in this area.

"To begin, I would like you to imagine a light force the *opposite* to creating a light beam with your hand. So instead of firing it out, you pull it back *towards* you. Telekinesis, obviously, but this force you create *within* your mind. Today I want you to concentrate on something soft and inanimate—a stuffed toy or a cushion, perhaps. Something you know well. No cats or guinea pigs please." A nervous titter scattered across the audience, but it was evident Dr Botolfe wasn't trying to be funny and it died off quickly. A sense of humour was obviously not in Dr Botolfe's repertoire, thought Eyre, grimacing. As if Dr Botolfe had heard her, the professor's piercing eyes whipped around to stare at her and Eyre groaned softly and cursed herself. Obviously, wisdom wasn't strong in her *own* repertoire. It really wasn't smart to think critical thoughts about someone who was an expert in telepathy. Yet another black mark on her record, she sighed.

For the next half hour the class sat in their chairs and concentrated in complete silence. Some people looked up, some at the floor, some shut their eyes; there were frowns and grimaces as the minutes ticked by, but no one managed to summon anything at all. Other than a massive headache, Eyre thought.

The Sergeant dismissed them when the lecture was over. "Don't expect success for some time. This is amongst the most difficult of Lightworking skills, much harder than the prohemiums. It is a compound technique of extreme difficulty." Several students groaned. Eyre saw Jax grinning at Rigmar, who had his head dramatically on the desk. The Sergeant continued. "So I suggest that you add this into your daily routine. Practise is the only way to acquire this skill, and it may save your life someday. That is all, you may now leave."

The students left in a hubbub of noise and self-deprecatory laughter. Most of them clearly felt rather inadequate at this point.

# CHAPTER FORTY-TWO

EYRE DECIDED SHE WOULD visit Ischyros during the lunch break. She wasn't exactly making great progress with him—he was still as rude as ever most of the time, but at least he wasn't throwing her across the arena anymore. Eyre had a routine now of walking him up and down the corridor, then grooming him in his stall before giving him a treat of molasses. She knew that it was probably only the molasses that kept him civil, but if it worked, she was happy with that.

She had just put Ischyros back in his stall when light footsteps headed towards her. A pair of soft leather boots appeared from around the corner. "Hello Eyre," the Kikkuli Master said. "You seem to be doing well with your Lighthorse." A loud harrumph snorted from the stall, slightly muffled by molasses, but the Kikkuli Master ignored it. Eyre found she had no response to his comment; it was so blatantly inaccurate.

"Walk with me," he said, to Eyre's surprise. She latched the gate of Ischyros's stall and followed the Kikkuli Master out into the paddocks, through all the fences until they reached the farthest one.

"It is important you learn to ride, and fly, before next year," the Kikkuli Master said. "As an Aether, it is essential you do the TACI test in Caelus, and it won't be acceptable if you can't fly when you are there." Eyre jerked her head around to look at him. He *knew* she was an Aether? The Kikkuli Master registered her surprise, his understanding showing with a sympathetic smile. "Yes, I might be out here in the stables, which, by the way, is a *privilege*, but I'm privy to what's going on in general. Whittaker Ray and I go back many years; we're great friends. I know that what you are is a carefully-guarded secret, and why it's essential it remains that way.

"Unfortunately, it seems that your Lighthorse, although you've calmed him down a lot," (*harrumph*! Eyre thought echoing Ischyros. *Calm?*) will not improve much in the foreseeable future. I had hoped that Ischyros might come around, but well, maybe perhaps he is too... *old* now to fly, and you have certainly tried long enough, I feel."

For a moment Eyre felt sad, and was relieved that they were in the far paddock. For some strange reason she was glad that Ischyros hadn't heard this conversation.

"Will he still be my Lighthorse?" she asked, a weird pain in her chest.

"Oh yes," the Kikkuli Master said, "that will never change. It can't, as long as either the Lighthorse or Lightworker is alive. But it has been decided that you will have special lessons in secret for the next year so that you will be prepared to travel in Caelus. In the meantime, we will try to find a temporary mount for you to ride for the TACI test next year.

"While we sort that out, Colton has agreed to teach you, with my help, so you will have your riding lessons in this paddock every Wednesday afternoon. The lessons must be kept confidential, because we don't want any questions to be asked, or anyone to look at you too closely. Which is why we have chosen this particular afternoon, because all other students are doing fulminology practise in the Training Shed—they will be far away while you are doing this. Your absence will be explained by you getting extra equestrian lessons, which is true, but it will be assumed you are working with Ischyros."

"Does *Colton* know I'm an Aether too?" Eyre asked, and looked appalled when the Kikkuli Master nodded. It was supposed to be such a secret, and yet now it seemed that every second person knew. Truth be told, she was also feeling a bit awkward that Colton was teaching her, after their most recent exchange.

But the Kikkuli Master didn't know about that, and he spoke to reassure her. "Colton's brother was a young Aether. He was drowned by the Gothak under a frozen lake, and Colton was there, tragically. It was a terribly traumatic event for him and his family. The reason Colton has trained and practised so hard on his Lighthorse has been driven by his—well I guess there's no other word for it—*rage*, really. He wants to go and fight against the Dark ones as soon as possible, no matter the cost. He has dedicated his life to the fight to reinstate the Aura and restore the balance of the world. And he wants retribution in a way I have rarely seen before. So he understands the importance of keeping this secret."

Eyre remembered the day she had practised aura reading with Colton during the TEPs. It seemed so long ago now. He had told her then that his brother had drowned, but he hadn't given her all the details until last year. So she knew about this already, but her heart still wrenched; she understood the permanent scars that grief could cause. And it certainly explained why he trained with such dedication. Eyre thought of Julia, and her similar desire for revenge. And she herself also identified with that deep, burning fire; she knew how they both felt, without a doubt.

At that moment, a massive Wedge-tailed eagle flapped its broad coppery wings and landed heavily with strong, taloned feet on the top of the fence surrounding the paddock. Dark brown, hooded eyes watched them carefully from above a strong, curved beak, then it turned its head upwards, searching the sky. Far up high, a black, winged shape spiralled down towards them. Colton came into sight on his Lighthorse, its wings spread wide as it soared into the paddock and landed gently on the winter-struck grass. The black wings folded in and disappeared and Colton jumped off the magnificent black thoroughbred.

"Eyre," he said, his crystal-blue eyes bright as he looked at her. "I hear we are to ride together." He seemed very at ease with the idea.

Eyre was conflicted. She wanted to learn to ride—and fly—more than anything. But she was once again feeling disloyal—it seemed to be her default mode this year. Firstly, to her friends, who she obviously couldn't mention this to, *the Light's sake!,* then to Ischyros (even though he didn't really want her to ride him, so she wasn't even sure why she felt like that), but probably most of all to Jax. What would he think if he knew about this? Because Eyre felt that Colton's gaze at her was... possibly, just that little bit too warm...? Which was okay... a few months ago perhaps, but now? This could potentially get difficult. Colton was such a good person, and, BTL... looked like a Greek god!

But then the Wedge-tailed eagle distracted her thoughts, as it writhed and struggled with its form, until eventually it morphed into Warrigal, who jumped off the fence and stood beside Colton.

"I'll be with you too," he said. "I need to practise my therianthropy, and I'm keeping an eye on things—looking out for Strigis and those other 'appealing' creatures that are not welcome around here." His face was fierce, a warrior with an unwavering purpose. Colton and Warrigal nodded to the Kikkuli Master as they walked away together, deep in conversation, out of the paddock. Eyre watched them go, realising that this meeting had probably been pre-arranged.

"Yes, Warrigal knows too," the Kikkuli Master said. "But who you are is known to a very few. Not the Echelon, just a very few key Lightworkers and the Determinant Dozen. We are concerned about the information getting out, so only those who truly *have* to know have been told."

Eyre could see that the Kikkuli Master had sensed her uncertainty about this revelation, because he smiled kindly, and tried to explain.

"Each week I will give you a riding lesson on Nox, while Colton and Warrigal work in the stables. Then Colton will take you up for a flight until you are able to handle it yourself. Warrigal will go with you for added protection." He waited a moment and then continued on to the major issue on Eyre's mind. "You will still be expected to continue to attend to Ischyros. These riding lessons are a temporary training arrangement that will cease once the Caelus TACI is complete."

Eyre took a breath, relieved in a way that the decision was made. Obviously, there was no choice here, and as she looked at the beautiful black horse, a sudden joy travelled through her. After being tossed in the dirt, flung up against fences, even dumped in horse excrement over the past eighteen months, the thought of actually having a proper ride seemed so exciting. She stepped up to Nox and stroked his silky mane.

"Hello, boy," she whispered. "I apologise in advance for my ineptitude."

The glossy creature turned his head and blew air out his nostrils and nuzzled her arm with his velvety-soft nose. Eyre felt strangely like she was about to cry.

And then her lesson began, one of the most wonderful days of her life. The Kikkuli Master explained to her how to mount properly, and she walked around the edge of the paddock on the tall horse, learning to hold the reins, how to set her legs without stirrups, and how not to pull too hard on the horse's mane when trying to direct him. Even walking felt a bit unbalanced, and Eyre knew she had a lot to learn. But she loved it so much! And Nox was quiet and patient. After an hour, the Kikkuli Master smiled in approval.

"You've done well, Eyre. I don't think it will take you long to catch up, if you work hard. Jump down now and I'll get Colton and Warrigal to come."

He obviously sent some kind of telepathic message to the boys, because not long after, they arrived back at the paddock. Both of them were red-faced and covered in wood shavings, so whatever they'd been up to must have involved hard physical work. Nox whinnied when he saw Colton, and pranced over to him, tossing his head. Their bond was evidently very strong, and Eyre felt a pang of envy.

"Okay, Colton, could you take Eyre up for a ten-minute flight, not too long for the first one. Do the route over Beggarman's Bluff, circle around to the Ponds of Doombee and back again."

Colton looked down at himself a bit self-consciously and quickly brushed the wood shavings off. Then he leapt onto Nox's back effortlessly, his hair shining like gold in the sunlight. He reached a muscular arm down to Eyre and pulled her easily up to sit behind him. After a moment, Eyre put her arms around his waist. She had better hang on or she wasn't going to get very far. Colton was strong and broad, and she could hardly reach around him, so she leaned her head on his back.

Then Warrigal started to shiver and groan, and his body contorted as a strange shimmering light wavered around him. He shrunk and changed, crying out as if in pain, until out of the flickering haze emerged the magnificent Wedge-tailed eagle Eyre had seen earlier. He gave a primordial screech and took to the air with one flap of his powerful wings.

"Hold on," Colton whispered to Eyre, and spurred Nox on towards the fence. This time—after her ride with Jax on Firestorm last year—Eyre knew what was coming. Nox galloped at full speed towards the fence and, just as he seemed about to crash into the wired barrier, he leapt high over it with his strong hind legs. But instead of landing on the other side, Nox kept rocketing upwards, as a mighty pair of shining black wings unfolded from his sides. They beat up and down unhurriedly, but with great power, as Nox soared upwards towards the clouds. Eyre held her breath, exhilarated. She watched the ground disappearing beneath her, and then they plunged into a cloud, emerging above it into blue sky and the mid-afternoon sun. Beneath them was a soft landscape of billowing clouds, and they soared above them until, through the gaps between the towering formations, Eyre could see Beggarman's Bluff way below, and the layout of the TEP compound. Colton pulled on Nox's mane and turned his incredible Lighthorse in a wide soaring arc. They sailed down through the clouds again, until they skimmed across the tops of the trees around the Ponds of Doombee. Then, with a last mighty flap of his wings, Nox cleared the top of the fence in the paddock and landed gently. His wings folded and disappeared, and Colton turned to gaze down at Eyre. Her legs and arms were trembling from the effort of holding on, but her eyes were exhilarated.

"Thank you," she breathed. "That was incredible."

With a screech, Warrigal landed on the ground beside Nox, and within a minute he had transformed back to his human form. He looked at Eyre with a calm certitude.

"We're on a mission," he said. "We'll help you, whatever it takes."

Colton jumped off Nox and helped Eyre down, his hands on her waist.

"I'll look forward to our next lesson," he said softly.

Eyre set off over the paddock, her mind swirling with so many emotions. Primarily elation, but also guilt, and an overwhelming frustration that so much of her life had to be kept secret from the people she really cared about.

But despite her weak legs, she took off at a run, because she realised that if she didn't hurry, she would be late for the BANE meeting. That would certainly ensure she would be excommunicated for life.

# CHAPTER FORTY-THREE

THEY WERE ALL THERE when she arrived out of breath from her manic run from the Equestrian Centre, the three of them waiting patiently for her at the sandstone rock. But to her relief, they believed her this time when she explained that she'd been at the stables.

"I know," Nick said. "Warrigal told me you were heading over there."

"Looks like Ischyros gave you a good workout," Abby said, chuckling. Eyre's hair was all over the place from the flight through the air, and it looked like she'd been dumped and rolled in the dirt a few times. Nothing out of the ordinary from her past experiences with Ischyros, and everyone cracked up laughing.

"I'm glad we're back together again," Eyre said, her words holding a deeper meaning. "What was the news you wanted to tell us, Abby?"

Abby took a deep breath. "Well, of course this completely remains within BANE, but I know I can trust you guys," she said in a happy voice. "My dad left last week on a *mission* to find out who the traitor in the Echelon is, and he said that they're pretty close to figuring it out. He's been talking to Whittaker Ray, and Dad's now gone to Coober Pedy—apparently they've got a good lead down there." Abby's eyes sparkled with pride and excitement and Eyre had a terrible sinking feeling. Something else was afoot, she was sure. And she was especially relieved that she hadn't said anything to her friends about what she had seen at the Transit.

"Fantastic!" Beatrice spat fiercely. "The treachery of that double-crossing snake has caused the death of so many Lightworkers. They need to pay for their actions."

"Occido," Nick agreed, iron in his voice. "The only justice for something like that."

Eyre was completely with them, but she just nodded her head, weeping inside for her friend.

"Well, I have found out about the gross creature you saw in Terra," Nick said. "Whittaker Ray told me. *That* is the creature called Rhabdor we read about in the Strigis manual, and he was once a Lightworker, and a member of the Echelon. The power went to his head and he turned to the Dark side." He shook his head. "The way he looks is what happens when a person forsakes their Lightness. He is the most powerful Underworld creature, and he *rules* the Gothak."

"You were lucky, Eyre," Abby said softly. "Thank goodness the Sergeant got you before that thing did."

"So, what did you have to tell us, Eyre? You asked us to come," Beatrice said curiously.

Eyre had so much to tell that she couldn't, and her heart constricted as she looked at her wonderful friends. But she also had amazing news she could reveal, and she spoke in a hushed tone. "Do you know, that the Ranger was once a Thantos Nex?"

A gasp of surprise came from everyone's mouth.

"But he doesn't look like them at all!" Abby said.

"His choice, I believe, because he's been excommunicated by the Thantos Nex. They can't stand him."

"*Really?*" Beatrice exclaimed. "Why?"

Eyre had deliberately kept the final bit of information until last. "The Ranger," she said, "was the one who saved the world when the Proditio occurred. It was *him* who blew the Aura into Isars and sent them to the Alterworlds."

A dumbstruck silence fell over the group. None of them had ever imagined the Ranger was anything more than a talented, but definitely wacky and eccentric, Lightworker.

"The explosion took most of his power away, as well as his memory of it. But worst of all, he was excommunicated, because the Thantos Nex are never supposed to interfere with the events of the world. Aren't they the most *despicable* creatures? How can you stand and watch when horrific things are happening in the world? They're worse than the Gothak, I think, or maybe just as bad." Eyre was furious as she related the history. She tossed her head in anger. "I think if you don't do anything, you may as well just join them! Anyway, the Ranger has been with the Lightworkers ever since."

"But that would make him... how old?" Abby frowned; the maths and the concept beyond her.

"I've got no idea," Eyre admitted. "*Very* old, I guess."

Beatrice was—amazingly—unable to say anything. She just shook her head, flabbergasted. Nick was processing, though. "They don't mention *that* in the textbooks," he commented. "How did you find it all out?"

"Well, Whittaker Ray told me—er, the other day when I was at his office," Eyre said hesitantly. "Apparently it's not a great secret in the Lightworking community, but the Ranger doesn't like people to talk about it."

She threw a stick ferociously into the bush. "He is such a... *hero*, and people laugh at him."

"Indeed, what an incredibly brave individual," Beatrice finally said, and a long silence followed.

"Well, speaking of incredible individuals," Abby said, changing the subject deliberately. "*What* is the news about *Jax*?"

Nick jumped like a snake had bitten him. He cleared his throat. "Well, I think this is the cue for me to make my exit," he said. "Warrigal's been out scouting the terrain; I'll see if I can bring any information from him to the next meeting. See you later."

He sauntered off, leaving the girls looking at each other.

"Well," Eyre said finally, continuing the previous thread, "I'm not sure that we're officially 'together', but we did have a 'moment' the other day."

Abby squealed. "You mean, like a *moment* 'moment'? *Really?*"

Eyre nodded. "It was quite something," she said softly and couldn't help her face showing how she felt. "By the Light, I think I've fallen hard."

"Come on girls, let's walk back," Beatrice declared. "This is official *Bae* business, not *BANE!* You can tell us more as we walk."

# CHAPTER FORTY-FOUR

THE NEXT MORNING THERE was a soft knock at the door. Beatrice opened it with a hairbrush in her hand, and then turned with round eyes to Eyre.

"Someone here for you, Eyre," she said, with a suggestive tone in her voice. At that, Abby stuck her head out of her cupboard to see, and a grin spread across her face before she quickly dived back in and busily fussed with her clothes.

Eyre wandered over and found Jax leaning in the doorframe.

"Hi," he said.

"Hi," she said back.

Beatrice headed across to the opposite side of the room and spent a lot of time fixing her hair in the mirror, with eyes that tried not to obviously look sideways at them.

"Are you keen to rack up another detention?" Eyre teased him.

"I would do anything for time with you," he said softly. "But unfortunately, I've come to tell you that I'm going away."

Eyre's heart fell, but she tried not to show it. "Oh," was all she could say.

"I'm leaving... *now*, Eyre," Jax said, his voice echoing Eyre's despondency. "My dad is very unwell, and I need to go and help my mother with the business. I'm not sure for how long. I'm sorry."

"Ohh, I see," Eyre said, crestfallen. "I hope your dad is okay."

Jax looked at her intensely, his green eyes filled with an indecipherable expression. "I'll be back as soon as I can." And then he leaned down and kissed her long, and deep, drawing her close to him, his hands moving slowly through her hair. Eyre was so caught up in the moment she barely heard Abby's gasp of delighted surprise from the background. And then Beatrice hissed a warning.

"Look out! *Incoming*! Periwinkle is just around the corner!"

Reluctantly Jax lifted his head, his eyes on Eyre's, and then he pulled her gently to him, embracing her with his tanned arms. Her head was resting against his chest, and Jax's chin settled on top of her red hair. She sighed.

"See you soon, Eyre with the red hair," Jax whispered, and kissed the top of her head. A physical pain tugged at Eyre's heart as he disappeared in the opposite direction to the inbound dorm supervisor.

The next few weeks passed quickly as the semester followed the normal routine: meditation, Ferito, early-morning trips to the pool where they had now embarked on learning the difficult water vision technique, the scheduled classes, archery and falconry practise with the Unlit, and visits to the stables to see both Ischyros and to practise riding with the Kikkuli Master and Colton.

Unfortunately, Ischyros hadn't been happy when he realised what Eyre was up to out in the far paddock, and his behaviour had become virtually uncontrollable again. He'd nipped her, kicked her and generally been extremely rude to her when she came to groom him, molasses or no molasses. But Eyre just gritted her teeth and kept up the tedious routine. She was not going to give up on him, and somewhat strangely, she felt he might be jealous—his behaviour was similar (but *worse*, she sighed) to when Florence had first arrived. So that had to be a good thing, *right*? It must mean he cared on some level? In any case, she wore her bruises and scrapes and the muck in her hair like a badge of honour, a merit award for not giving up.

The rides in the paddock, on the other hand, were something else entirely. Over the weeks she improved quickly, and she could now trot and canter around the ring comfortably. The Kikkuli Master was pleased with her progress and encouraged her every session. It was just unfortunate that she was not able to practise between lessons, as she would have if she'd had a horse she could actually ride, because she knew she would have picked it up even quicker.

"You are very fit," the Kikkuli Master said in approval. "That has helped your balance and strength, and it's why you are doing so well. Keep it up."

Then there were the flights with Colton, which gradually extended out to half an hour. It was miraculous and breathtaking, and she loved the feeling when the horse left the ground and soared upwards. After a few weeks she had travelled all over the area around the campus with Colton and Nox, and she was getting more and more familiar with the terrain. Warrigal always accompanied them, his sharp eyes scanning the landscape for potential threats.

However, it was becoming extremely awkward with Colton. She knew he liked her, especially after the dance, and if she were honest, she had to admit she wasn't completely immune to his charm either. When she flew with him she felt completely safe and cared for, and there was a magic in the air when they soared through the cool air, she with her arms looped tightly around him. She could feel his strength and his energy, which was pure and entrancing. So she thought that the sooner she started flying on her own, the better. All they did was fly together—with Warrigal nearby—and she realised her feelings were probably more associated with the flying than the rider in front of her, but Colton was undeniably magnetic, so she felt conflicted and disloyal to Jax. Fortunately, Colton was too much of a gentleman to make a move, but as Eyre trudged back across the paddock she decided to ask the Kikkuli Master when she could start going solo.

Her last lesson for the day was another class in the Summons. No one had summoned anything yet, so for her it was usually a very boring end to an exciting afternoon on Wednesdays. However, she did understand how important the class was, so she started running along the track to make sure she got there on time.

Everyone else trudged in, hot and sweating from fulminology training, and Eyre felt quite pleased that this was the class she was missing while she had her equestrian lesson. Of course, she'd have to make it up some time, but as she looked at all the red faces, she was quite glad that she'd been soaring through the clouds instead.

"How was Ischyros?" Abby asked as she plonked down next to Eyre, her fair complexion flushed and sweating. Eyre just grimaced at her. *That* was an accurate enough response; no need for further comment, and Abby looked sympathetic. Beatrice's lanky frame stretched out in the seat beside Abby, with Robeson on her other side. Nick ran up the stairs and slid in next to Robeson as Beatrice fanned herself with her Felsic.

"By the Light," she said, "if I don't ever need to use fulminology, I am going to be *seriously* annoyed! I might zap someone with a lightning bolt!"

Their laughter was interrupted as Dr Botolfe stalked in through the door.

"Well, there's a good target if I ever saw one," Nick muttered and started industriously studying his Felsic as Dr Botolfe nailed him with a look.

"We have had enough discussion about how to perform this task," Dr Botolfe began acidly, surveying the class, none of whom were meeting her eyes. "The Summons is the most important Lightworker skill you can learn. It is no good learning how to use your resources if you cannot make them available to you. So today I would like you to use the whole session to practise. It's not easy. It will take you a long time. I have no more wisdom to impart. You may start now."

Her voice was pragmatic and final; it was up to them.

Someone up the back yawned loudly, and Eyre was not surprised to see one of the Curtis twins pretending to snore on his desk. Dr Botolfe's eyes turned towards him and in an instant he sat up again, looking attentive. Even he knew that this was one lecturer you shouldn't mess with.

For at least twenty minutes there was complete silence in the auditorium, as students tried to conjure up a cushion or a soft toy. Even a cotton ball would be something for celebration, Eyre thought gloomily, picturing two more years ahead sitting in a silent lecture theatre for hours on end with an empty desk in front of her. She leaned back, looking at the ceiling, and her thoughts drifted off, as they often did recently, to Jax. No one had heard from him yet, including herself, and she wondered what he was doing, how he was. And most of all, when he was coming back.

Her reverie was suddenly interrupted by a commotion at the front of the auditorium, and gasps and screams rocketed across the seated audience. Students had stood up in front of Eyre and she couldn't see what was going on, so she jumped up on her seat. Then she gasped too, her hand on her mouth—what *was* that? Onstage was a massive, muscled wolf-like creature the size of a large wild boar. But it was no ordinary wolf. Its skin was bright red and hairless, and it had two horns on the top of its head. Its black muzzle bristled with spines and its lips drew back, baring vicious teeth. Dr Botolfe had stood up from her chair and was facing the fearsome creature, her face white.

"What is it?" Eyre cried. "One of the Strigis?"

"No, no, no… it's a *Devil Wolf*," Beatrice gasped. "It's from Incendium—how did it get here?" She turned to look at her friends, dread dawning on her face. "They're almost impossible to kill. Their skin is virtually impenetrable."

A horrified hush descended on the auditorium and a terrible snarling and growling filled the air. The creature moved slowly towards Dr Botolfe, *stalking* her, Eyre realised as she watched, horrified. The lecturer moved her hands frantically, as she backed away from the monstrous beast, and a Flail appeared in Dr Botolfe's hand. She swung it in circles above her head, although it appeared such an effort, and then she flung it at the creature. The wolf winced as the spiked object struck its side, but it kept coming. Dr Botolfe flung beams of Light energy at it, threw her Kulbeda straight at its head, and sent a whirling corona of sparking energy at the massive creature. She even hurled bolts of lightning at it, but the Devil Wolf's tough skin was impervious to all of them. And when an Antarak bounced off the body of the grotesque creature, Eyre knew Dr Botolfe was in serious trouble. She watched with growing panic, shocked as the powerful Dr Botolfe struggled to survive, with her last hope—a gleaming Mnae held out in front of her.

And then, as gently as a cashmere shawl, a calmness descended on Eyre. A vision suddenly came into her mind of her staff, and with a psychic comprehension that was inexplicable, she felt a power that came from somewhere outside herself and she *pulled* the staff to her. And like a baseball smacking into a mitt, the staff materialised from nowhere and *whacked* into her open hand. Beyond wondering, Eyre leapt over all the seats in one levitating surge, and raced down the stairs. The Devil Wolf sprang at that moment towards Dr Botolfe and a ferocious energy seared through Eyre, an intense anger and a feeling of righteous force that burned through her arm and up into her staff. The pink diamond glowed hot pink and as she crashed down the stairs, she blasted a light beam at the Devil Wolf. The blazing beam of energy hit the creature dead centre and the horrid thing fell mid-flight from the air, and thudded down and slid across the stage, a circular hole seared right through its body. It lay on its side with its teeth bared and red eyes open, but completely dead.

At that point, Whittaker Ray and the Sergeant arrived onstage in a flare of light.

"I called them," Abby stuttered in Eyre's mind, obviously upset and anxious. But then, Abby added wonderingly, "*How* did you do that? When did you learn to use your staff like that?"

All eyes were travelling back and forth from Dr Botolfe, to Eyre, to the creature that lay smouldering on the stage. There was a cavernous silence and the smell of burnt flesh hung in the air.

Whittaker Ray quickly took charge. It was obvious Dr Botolfe was in shock, so the Sergeant took her arm and disappeared with her in a flash of light. Eyre stood awkwardly to the side, leaning heavily on her staff, not sure what to do and feeling like a fleet of Zepps had run over her.

"Thank you for the demonstration, Eyre," Whittaker Ray said. "I feel perhaps you have figured out how to perform the Summons."

The irony in his voice broke the tension and the fear, and someone tittered. Then the whole auditorium erupted in laughter, and applause. All eyes were directed Eyre's way, especially from the Rufa students, and Eyre walked painfully back to her seat, feeling totally exhausted and extremely embarrassed by the attention. She did note however, that Ben Perrill and his cronies were sitting up the back scowling.

"Also, a great display of the power of your staff," Whittaker Ray said. "Now, I'm not exactly sure what has happened here. That was a Devil Wolf from Incendium, an extremely dangerous creature, and as you will have realised, it definitely wasn't planned as a teaching aid today."

Once again nervous laughter filled the auditorium and Eyre looked at Beatrice and raised an eyebrow. Beatrice had been correct when she identified the creature; she was obviously far ahead of everyone with her studies. Eyre had never even *heard* of a Devil Wolf.

Whittaker Ray snapped his fingers and the corpse of the massive creature disappeared. He continued. "However, we will get to the bottom of this, and you can rest assured it won't occur again." His voice was confident, but Eyre could see that he was worried. She was too. It was obvious that things were spiralling out of control in all directions.

It was a very subdued class that left the auditorium.

Beatrice looked at Eyre, deadpan. "If this is the result, I think I'll skip the ski trip next year and stay and practise with my staff too!"

Eyre laughed with them all, relieved that she 'sort of' had a cover story to explain what had just happened. But, in fact, she wasn't actually sure herself.

# CHAPTER FORTY-FIVE

THE NEXT DAY A very subdued mood hung over the campus. There wasn't even a special meeting called to reassure the students. What could the staff say? Already so many promises had been made, this year and last, and even during the TEPs, about campus security, that they hadn't been able to keep. Everyone carried on with classes as usual, but no one really knew what was happening.

Dr Botolfe had asked to see Eyre, and with some trepidation she went to the Infirmary, where the lecturer was recuperating. Sister Murphy took her through, and the disagreeable professor had looked at Eyre with her usual severe eyes. But her face was pale, and an uncharacteristic hesitancy was in her voice when she spoke.

"We live in a world of shadows," the lecturer began, after a pause. "Where nothing is as it seems, and where subterfuge, unfortunately, has become commonplace." Her sharp features looked at Eyre even more intensely.

"I misjudged you greatly," Dr Botolfe said, "and I apologise. I shamed you in the past in front of your classmates, and to my discredit, I know it was probably on purpose, because of my own preconceptions. It was wrong of me as an educator, but most of all, as a Lightworker." Her eyes were shrouded as she continued.

"I feel dishonoured because of that. But also because I should have been able to take down a Devil Wolf without too much trouble, although they are very vicious creatures. But it seems I was more confident of my abilities than I should have been."

A look of humiliation, mixed with confusion, shrouded her face. "I couldn't kill it. And I *should* have been able to. So it's made me wonder if I should be teaching at all, actually—I performed *so* inadequately. And if it wasn't for you..." She shook her head and fixed Eyre with her piercing eyes.

"Anyway, I need to thank you. And I apologise for humiliating you in the past. It is now my turn to wear the shame."

Eyre had been uncertain about coming, but as the professor spoke so humbly, which was *so* unlike her, she felt great empathy. Dr Botolfe was proud, and now she was undoubtedly going to have to explain why this debacle had occurred in her class—her fault or not. And from what the lecturer had been saying, it seemed that she felt she had underperformed; that she deemed herself unworthy. Eyre knew all about feeling less than adequate, and the judgements people could cast, so she understood what Dr Botolfe meant very well. Most of all, she felt admiration that the greatly respected professor could apologise like this to a student. To admit you were wrong took great strength of character.

So she took Dr Botolfe's hand and spoke honestly. "You were the epitome of courage. We all learned what it is to be a Lightworker by watching you. I've always admired you, and so has everyone else. We're all just terrified of you. Probably even more than a Devil Wolf."

Dr Botolfe laughed and squeezed Eyre's hand. "Dark times are upon us," she whispered. "But I know now we are fortunate you are here. Thank you for saving me."

Eyre was uncomfortable at hearing the acerbic professor so humbled. But she leaned over and hugged her. "We're all struggling to find the Light," Eyre said. "And the Light will prevail."

She left, feeling strangely troubled. If the best of them could be brought down, how was the world to survive?

# CHAPTER FORTY-SIX

AFTER THE FURORE, THE term continued on as usual. The drama with the Devil Wolf was talked about, and Eyre had her share of looks and comments, but most of them were positive. Beatrice and Abby were most impressed of all—when they'd last seen Eyre using her staff, she'd sent the beam shooting backwards to blast the top off the locker in the Training Shed. So this had been quite an improvement. Eyre explained it away— truthfully—by saying she'd figured out with practise that she had to adjust for the damaged crystal in her staff. But even she couldn't work out how she could suddenly generate so much power and accuracy.

Eyre had just spent a few hours practising archery and falconry at the Unlit campus, and had walked through the frigid ward to head back to her dorm room. As she emerged, an urgent message blossomed in her head: Bane, Bane, Bane...

Not being far from the track to the sandstone rock, and sensing the urgency in Abby's voice, she set off at a run, arriving out of breath and looking around for trouble. But she slowed to a walk when she saw her three friends sitting there; there was no danger it seemed. Eyre sat down and looked at them curiously.

"What's up?" she asked, looking from one impassive face to another. And then Abby spoke, and Eyre realised with a shock that the urgency she'd heard in the telepathic message hadn't been caused by panic, it was from *anger*. Rage streamed from Abby's eyes as she stood up and looked at Eyre accusingly.

"Did. . you. . accuse. . my *DAD* of being in league with the Gothak?" she said in a low, furious voice.

Eyre felt she had been punched in the stomach. How had Abby found out? Who would have told her?

Beatrice and Nick looked at Eyre too, wounded and disbelieving.

"Who told you?" Eyre asked, playing for time. But the question revealed too much; they all realised that it must be true.

"Ben Perrill told me!" Abby spat. "He was *laughing* at me. Tell me you didn't do that!"

All three of her friends looked completely shocked and betrayed, and Eyre couldn't lie to them. "Well, I only told Whittaker Ray," she said feebly. "I didn't think anyone would find out."

"Well, it seems they did." Abby said. "You're just jealous because I *have* a father, and you want to ruin it for me. You can't stand not being the centre of attention, as you have been *ever... since...* you got here! So you had to make something up—and something so *terrible*, after all we've done for you! You are NO LONGER my friend, and as far as I'm concerned, you shouldn't be part of this group any more. BAN only—*no* 'E', as in, you're *banned* from here in future. I never want to talk to you again!"

She ran off back down the track and disappeared as an accusing silence fell. Eyre could only look at her friends with pleading eyes. "Please hear me out," she began.

But a cool expression chilled Beatrice's face as she stood up. "I think there's been too many secrets and lies this year, Eyre," she said. "I've had enough of it too. I'm with Abby, we don't need you in this group." And she left too, crunching heavily away over the dry eucalyptus leaves.

Nick looked more regretful, but his eyes were curious. "Why would you do that, Eyre? How could you suspect Abby's Dad? "

Eyre opened her mouth to reply, but then closed it again miserably. Even Whittaker Ray hadn't believed her, so why would her friends? Why on Entis would they suspect Abby's Dad of anything? They *couldn't* believe her, and they were already so short of patience with her this year, she felt they wouldn't even listen in the first place.

"I wasn't going to say anything," Eyre said. "How Ben found out I've got no idea, but I guess as usual, he's trying to stir up trouble."

"Looks like he succeeded," Nick commented. And then he left too.

The next few weeks were the most dismal of Eyre's life. Beatrice and Abby completely ignored her in the dorm room, speaking about her in the third person, as if she wasn't there.

"If you see Eyre," Abby would say to Beatrice while Eyre was sitting on her bed, "Would you tell her that it's her turn to sweep the floors this week?"

And Beatrice and Abby would sit playing Crystallography without inviting Eyre to play, ignoring her as if she were invisible. They went to the Sector Fair without inviting her, and to be honest, Eyre didn't have the stomach to go on her own, so she sat alone in their room for the evening, missing out on one of the most fun nights of the year. Then Abby and Beatrice came back, talking to each other about all the wonderful things they'd seen. Robeson and Beatrice were also going well it seemed, but she was obviously not going to be included in *that* conversation.

Eyre was so miserable. She didn't know what to do, and it didn't seem fixable. But she suffered in silence, because she understood Abby's rage and hurt. Eyre would have reacted just the same way if anyone had accused her own father of such treachery.

But Nick eventually softened. As they walked to class one morning he told her he was sorry it had all fallen apart. And that he would do his best to help sort it out. Eyre was so grateful to him for his kindness—he was such a generous soul.

As a result of being ostracised by her friends, Eyre felt more comfortable eating at a different table. Everyone was curious about why the previously tight-knit group had fallen out, but it seemed that Ben, despite telling Abby about Eyre's accusations, hadn't spread the news any further. Eyre did wonder at that; normally he wouldn't miss a chance to cause mayhem. And she wracked her brain to try and fathom how he had found out. But she couldn't figure that out either.

So she sat with Carly and Advika and Lindi Jamieson some days at the refectory. Other days she'd head to the Short Stop at the Unlit compound to catch up with her friends there. But it was a very unsettling and lonely time. Her depression wasn't helped by the fact that Ischyros was misbehaving so badly that Eyre couldn't even get in the stall with him anymore. He was looking bedraggled and unkempt from his lack of grooming, and he kicked wildly at the stall door whenever she walked past. He'd only spoken to her once, bellowing about "liars and deceivers, fakes and betrayers, all of you!" Which didn't really make any sense. Perhaps the old fellow was going senile, and that made her sad too. But she persevered, standing at the stall door (carefully, no body parts hanging over the top) and talked to him, despite the fact that he, like Abby and Beatrice, was now completely ignoring her too. Once she'd talked to him for half an hour, Eyre would lob a sizeable piece of liquorice into his feed bin. It made her very sad. For a while she'd thought she was making progress with the motley old beast, but it was evident now that Ischyros didn't want a bar of her.

The only lightness in the week was her riding lessons with the Kikkuli Master. Eyre loved the feeling of cantering around the ring, and in the past couple of weeks she had finally learned to gallop. The Kikkuli Master watched her carefully this afternoon, calling out minor adjustments to her technique, but overall, looking very pleased with her. As she jumped down from Nox, he nodded his head in approval. "Next week you can have your first go at flying on your own," he said. "You gallop very well and your balance is now good enough to handle the flight. Nox is a gentle horse and patient with his rider. He will help you to learn."

Eyre was ecstatic. Although she had enjoyed her lessons with Colton (perhaps a little too much, if she were honest) she really wanted to fly on her own. And it would solve the problem of the increasing energy she felt between herself and Colton. It had been so many weeks since Jax was here, she wondered if he would even return this year. She'd remained completely faithful to Jax—on whatever level their 'relationship' might be, but she had to admit that she found Colton's strength magnetic. So it was good that their time together was going to end.

Colton walked across the paddock, his golden hair bright in the sunlight. His tanned face contrasted with the white of his teeth as he flashed a smile towards Eyre and the Kikkuli Master. Warrigal was walking with Colton and they were laughing at something Warrigal had said.

Snow had fallen across the top of the hills last night, and a crisp wind blew across the grass. Eyre wished she had thought to wear something a bit warmer—her light jacket was probably not going to be adequate up in the air with the change in weather. But it was too late now. Colton and Warrigal arrived to join them, and Colton looked down at Eyre with his aquamarine eyes. "Ready for your flight on Nox Air?" he asked. Eyre and the Kikkuli Master both laughed, and then the Kikkuli Master spoke.

"Eyre is ready to start flying solo, as of next week," he said, and Eyre registered the disappointment in Colton's eyes. But he covered it up quickly. "That's great," he said. "You've learnt quickly, Eyre."

"She has indeed," the Kikkuli Master said. "It is good of you to share your Lighthorse so she had the opportunity. Next week I'm sure she will do a good job solo."

"Well," Colton whispered to Eyre. "Let's make this last flight one to remember then." He pulled himself up on Nox, and helped Eyre up behind. As they turned towards the fence, Warrigal morphed into the Wedge-tailed eagle and soared into the air. Chasing him, they charged across the paddock and took to the sky in an exhilarating rush of frigid air. Far below, Eyre could see the Kikkuli Master heading back to the stables.

Colton had said he'd make it a flight to remember, and he was true to his word. They flew higher than they ever had before, way, way up, and then plunged down through the clouds in a breath-taking rush of speed. Then Nox spiralled up gently, playfully plunging into the clouds and out the other side. It was amazing, and one of the most memorable experiences of Eyre's life. But she realised that she was seriously underdressed for the occasion when her teeth started chattering. She held Colton tighter, trying to keep warm, and he suddenly registered from her shaking arms that she was in distress. He turned to look at her and saw her wind-chilled cheeks and blue lips as Nox soared across the top of the huge cloud formations, and he muttered something under his breath. Then, with a swift movement he took off his own jacket and passed it back to Eyre.

"Put this on," he said. "You'll get hypothermia if you don't keep warm." By now Eyre was trembling seriously from the cold, so she took the jacket gratefully, feeling like an idiot for not being better prepared. The coat was so huge on her, the arms hung way down over her hands, swamping her small frame and making her feel like a sumo wrestler. But the jacket was warm from Colton's body heat, and it smelt like him, and she wrapped it tightly around her as they finished the ride.

Nox flew low over the fence and landed gently in the icy field. Warrigal screeched loudly, then headed off towards campus, obviously deciding to take the quick route home.

Colton jumped lightly off Nox's back, but Eyre was so frozen, despite the coat, that she found it hard to move, and she slipped as she tried to jump from Nox's back. Colton caught her, his hands around her waist, and she looked into those crystal eyes and lost herself for a moment. A few seconds passed, and then the thought of Jax intervened, and she began to step back, forcing her eyes to look away from Colton's mesmerising gaze.

But it was if her thoughts of Jax had somehow miraculously caused him to materialise, because, with a horrified shock, and a feeling of guilt that was probably undeserved, she realised that... By the Light!... What?... *Jax* was there, leaning up against the fence with a very cynical look directed her way. He clapped his hands slowly.

"Nice landing," he said sarcastically, watching as Eyre very self-consciously returned Colton's coat to him. Jax's eyes were accusing and furious as he took in the scene, but his face was impassive. "Abby told me you were working with Ischyros, so I thought I'd head over.

"Looks like I'm interrupting," he added. "And I only stopped by as I'm heading off again this afternoon, so I guess I'll see you sometime." And then he strode ferociously out of the paddock without waiting for an answer. Colton, of course, was completely nonplussed, not understanding at all.

"That is one angry dude," he said, watching as Jax vaulted straight over a fence and kept going.

"He can't fly yet," Eyre said feebly, fumbling for an excuse, feeling terrible, for both Jax and Colton. She knew she should probably have been more upfront with Colton, but she hadn't anticipated this would happen and now it was too late. Still, she mused as she headed back to school, Jax had left rather suddenly six weeks ago when his father fell ill. But he could have written, or communicated in some way. And what did he mean by 'heading off again'? Where to? Clearly he wasn't coming back to campus yet, so why was he here? It was so frustrating to constantly be guessing at what was going on. Why wouldn't anyone *ever* be forthright with her?

She felt dismal. Nothing had happened with her and Colton, really. Although she had to be honest and admit that she guessed how Colton felt about her; she wasn't completely stupid. But she constantly felt on unstable ground with Jax—there had never really been anything official between her and him either—just those few, magical moments.

Thinking about those moments just made her feel worse, and as she passed Ischyros's stall a clod of mud came sailing over the gate at her, connecting quite accurately with the side of her head. She wiped her face despondently, and realised that she'd definitely made herself quite unpopular all over the place in the past few months. Ben Perrill could start a club with everyone who couldn't stand her now—two-legged *and* four-legged.

Sighing, she chucked Ischyros some liquorice (to be honest hoping that it would clip him around the ear, *smartly*) and headed off towards the purgatory that was her current existence.

# CHAPTER FORTY-SEVEN

EYRE WOKE EARLY THE next day and took a deep breath as she studied the ceiling. A crushing despair fell upon her as she recalled the previous day, and she felt like she might never get out of bed.

But Abby and Beatrice were still asleep and Eyre didn't fancy being there when they woke, so she dressed quietly and left for her early-morning run. This time she went further than usual. She didn't mind the solitude today, it was far preferable to the silent treatment from her friends, slaughtering looks from Ben and his cronies and the general pitying curiosity from the rest of the students. Her mood was so black she even decided to pass up Ischyros this morning; one mud pat in the face was enough this week.

Eventually, exhausted, she ended up at the sandstone rock where they'd held their BANE meetings. She sat down and leaned against the rock and sucked air in hard as she tried to catch her breath. Then, without warning, tears started to course down her cheeks and she began sobbing with her head on her arms, great wracking groans that seemed like they'd never stop. Everything was so awful and she had no one to turn to.

A crunch in the eucalyptus leaves made her swing her head up. She wiped her eyes and studied the undergrowth anxiously. Not a lot of good had come out of the bush lately. A second later, a healthy-looking dingo stepped into the clearing. Eyre leapt to her feet; dingos could be dangerous. But something about the calmness of this creature seemed reassuring, and she put her hands up in front of her.

"W-warrigal?" she asked. Sure enough, the dingo began to morph, the agonising-looking process now familiar to Eyre. But when it was finished, it was not Warrigal standing there, but the Ranger. He looked at her with his strange purple eyes and beetles whirring around his green hair, but with such kindness that Eyre couldn't help herself; tears coursed down her cheeks as if a tap had been turned on.

Trying to collect herself, she wiped an arm across her nose. "Sorry," she hiccupped. "Having a bit of a moment."

"Sit down for a second, Eyre," the Ranger said, and he did the same, sitting cross-legged in front of her.

"Breathe the air out here—it's beautiful. Look at the sun, the trees and the birds. This difficult time will pass for you. Shadows and secrets are causing you great pain, but you are standing strong in the face of a great onslaught. I am proud of you, it takes a special person to have the courage to stand by their convictions. You may feel like you are damaged and cracked at the moment, and struggling to cope. But think of the Japanese artform 'kintsugi': where the virtuosity and compassion of the brilliant artists of Japan fill the cracks of damaged ornaments with gold and precious metals— they consider the injured object all the more beautiful because of it. That philosophy has great meaning for you. Your cracks will be filled with mettle of another sort, and it will make you stronger too. Have faith, my girl."

"Are you a form of kintsugi too, then?" Eyre asked, sniffling, not really feeling much better, but realising he was just trying to help. "I know about the Aura, and the Thantos Nex."

The Ranger's strange purple eyes clouded for a second, and then he nodded, saying lightly. "I guess I am. Although I *really* would like to remember more about that day. Where I left my blue skin for a start."

That started Eyre laughing and she wiped her eyes. "I like you just the way you are, Ranger Chrysanthe," she whispered. "I will try to be strong like you."

The Ranger stood up and mock-bowed to her. "You already are, Eyre. Just keep your Light on."

And then he disappeared. Eyre sat for a moment and then stood up, looking around for him, but he was gone. She couldn't help thinking that if the Ranger had lost much of his power, he must have been a mighty being to start with.

After a moment, she sighed and decided she may as well go to the Refectory. Although she would have rather avoided it at all costs, she had to eat, so she headed to breakfast hoping that she might have missed everyone.

But the meal was still in full-swing when she arrived, and she moved to the back of the room awkwardly, trying not to look at her friends. As usual, they ignored her and their conversation became louder, hard and bright as if to prove once and for all that she would not be missed.

Eyre hovered uncertainly for a moment, not sure where to go. This was *excruciating!* She knew all eyes were on her; everyone was curious about the rift in this friendship. But a movement from the corner of her eye made her turn and with relief she saw that Carly was motioning her to come and sit down.

"It will pass," Carly said with her mouth full. "I've been through friendship dramas and they're never easy. But give it some time." Privately, Eyre doubted this friendship drama would pass in any amount of time. She also doubted that Carly had ever really had any friendship dramas either. But she was grateful; the big-hearted girl was trying to make it easier for her.

Eyre started eating her cereal. "How are your parents? And Aaron and Dean?" she asked. Aaron was four years older than Carly, a sandy-haired amiable giant who had Carly's sunny disposition. He'd made the State Ferito team that year, something that had overjoyed Carly's dad. Aaron visited Carly from time to time on campus, with a mob of young star-struck students trailing behind him.

Carly laughed. "Aaron's happy as a pig in mud. Loves the workouts and the life. Wants to be a coach one day. You know Mum and Dad, they've already got him lined up for the Internationals! Dean's going good too—he's doing a Masters in Faceting and seems to really like it." Dean was the oldest sibling, and Eyre had only met him briefly, but she remembered a quiet, serious sort of fellow who obviously adored his family. Once again, she felt a poignant sense of what-might-have-been when she heard about Carly's family. But she was happy for this generous girl, who seemed as strong as an ox in every sense of the word—physically and mentally.

"That's great Carly," she said, taking another bite. Then a strange absence struck her and she looked around the refectory. The head tables were virtually empty. "Where are all the staff?"

"Well, they're sick, I heard," Carly said. "The flu, apparently. Several classes have been cancelled today. It's just snowballed I think, started with a couple sick and now there are a whole lot."

Eyre raised her eyebrows. Staff seldom got sick at the Academy, and never so many at once. However, when she thought about it, Carly was right—in the past month it had not been unusual to have one or more staff missing. "Are any students sick?"

They studied the tables in the room, but there didn't seem to be any less than the normal number of students.

"I guess the staff caught it from each other," Carly mused, winking. "Staff meetings could be toxic, I imagine." Her eyes lingered on Jemima Periwinkle, one of the few staff present this morning. "But that one is too noxious to catch anything, I imagine." She put her spoon down and sighed. "Unfortunately, I've heard swimming is still on—let's walk together."

They took their trays up and headed out the door towards the swimming pool. Eyre wasn't keen this morning, there was a chill in the air and a bitter bite to the wind. August could be a capricious month, careering from sunny skies to bone-chilling sleet and the thought of getting in the water didn't appeal as the wind slapped her with icy fingers.

"Mentor Xiphias is teaching us carousel breathing today," Carly said. "That's going to be difficult. I might need a scuba tank, like the Unlit, in Aqua I think."

Eyre was distracted by the sight of people dressed in civilian clothes milling around the Central Admin building. She stopped and watched them.

"I wonder what's going on there?"

Carly grimaced. "Parents of students. Saskia's mum and dad are there— she told me there are a number of people most unhappy with the school at the moment and the parents are threatening to take their children out." She adopted 'a tone', "*Breaches* on campus, *Sublabors*, and now staff missing classes! It's just *not* what one would *expect* from a school of this quality. We certainly pay enough fees to expect better than *this*!" Carly and Eyre dissolved into laughter as they watched more parents arriving. There certainly were a few disgruntled faces in the crowd and Eyre felt sorry for Whittaker Ray—what a nightmare. She hoped he wasn't one of the sick staff members.

Mentor Xiphias waited patiently for the class to arrive and get in the pool. Eyre gasped as she jumped in—the pool was heated but it still felt chilled. Once everyone was in the water, the Mentor began.

"In Aqua there will be times when you will have to exit the Zepps and swim underwater. During this time, you will need to 'carousel breathe' while using your current technique to move. Carousel breathing is tiring, so you cannot do it for a long time. But it is imperative that you learn how before you leave for your TACI expedition to Aqua.

"It involves a technique of breathing out and in at the same time. The ancient custodians of your country have mastered a very similar skill to play the didgeridoo and as Lightworkers they often are amongst our most successful Aqua visitors. Below the surface, you will source oxygen from the water by using your Viq, which requires a lot of energy and should therefore be used only minimally. Think of sucking water through a sponge as you sit under water and it will give you an idea of what to aim for. Please go under and practise now. It will get easier once you have had some success."

Eyre groaned inwardly. After many months practising, most of the students were proficient in the current technique, at least enough to move reasonably well underwater. Both the Lit and Unlit students had learnt this fairly well, but now the Lit students had to learn to breathe down there using their Viq. And then eventually they had to learn the vision technique as well, also using Viq, and she wasn't sure how strong her Viq was to start with.

A tri-merit skill was particularly difficult, and it would take them weeks to learn. Sighing, she took a deep breath and put her head under the water. After a few moments of blowing and sucking beneath the surface, she threw her head back up, choking. She'd sucked in a huge noseful of water and it was burning all the way down the back of her throat. Spluttering, she laughed as Carly also exploded from below, coughing violently. Carly gasped in a huge breath of air.

"BTL, that is impossible!"

"The sponge, think of the sponge," Mentor Xiphias called encouragingly.

Eyre and Carly rolled their eyes at each other and tried again. But for the next twenty minutes, neither of them had any success, nor did anyone else in the pool. Eyre could see Abby, red-faced, her blonde curls darkened by the water and flattened forlornly against her head as she came up from under the water, choking. Beatrice was looking frustrated too—she hated not being able to do a required task. Eyre caught her eye and smiled tentatively, but Beatrice's mouth pursed and she turned her back. Eyre was not surprised. She knew it was unlikely she'd ever be forgiven by her friends. A feeling of desolation washed over her and she turned to Carly.

"I'm not feeling so good. I think I might call this one early."

Carly looked concerned as Eyre hauled herself out of the water. "I hope you're not getting the flu—maybe you should see Sister Murphy."

"Thanks Carly, I'll see how I go."

Eyre got her towel and quickly changed, exiting out the rear of the change block so curious eyes couldn't see her. The events of the year had taken their toll, and she was feeling totally exhausted. Losing her Viq, the intensity of training with the Unlit, the horrifying encounters with the Sublabor and the Vampire Vultures. And the debacle with Jax. It was all so hard, physically and mentally. But worst of all by far was finding out about Abby's father, and not being able to share the tragedy of that knowledge with anyone. She went back to her room and lay staring at the ceiling for a very long time.

# CHAPTER FORTY-EIGHT

EYRE WOKE THE NEXT morning feeling a bit better. Beatrice and Abby had already gone to breakfast and Eyre dressed quickly—she was going to be late if she didn't hurry. Although nothing was different from yesterday, Eyre's pragmatic side was surfacing, and she had decided that she couldn't change anything—she would just have to live with it. So she ran along the pathways, breathing in the cool air and enjoying the sunshine.

As she reached the Refectory she stopped in surprise. Students were milling around uncertainly outside and a low murmuring filled the air. Eyre pushed to the font of the crowd and saw that the Refectory was dark. The lights were out and the doors were locked, and the usual welcoming smell of bacon and eggs on a hot stove was missing.

Eyre turned to Robeson. "What's happening?"

Robeson shrugged and shook his head, looking as confused as Eyre was. He also looked very dismayed—he did like his tucker, something he and Beatrice definitely had in common. Eyre smiled sympathetically and headed for the one person who'd know, if anyone did, what was going on.

Zanda grinned at her. "Poor old Robeson. He's heartbroken—he's been first in line since we found the doors shut."

"So, what's happening?"

"The Jotnar," Zanda paused for dramatic effect, "are apparently on strike! The doors never opened this morning."

Eyre raised an eyebrow. "But why? What's going on?"

Zanda loved passing on information. "Well, at the meeting yesterday, Tec Langford's parents accused the staff of malingering, since none of the students were sick. Mrs Langford—Saskia told me—said it was *impossible* for just the staff to get the flu. So then, apparently, Georgia Mahoney's dad asked if there was the possibility of food poisoning, since only the staff table was affected. I guess Whittaker Ray decided to look into it—and I'd say the

Jotnar are not happy! I saw the Head Chef going into Central Admin this morning, looking like he was about to carve someone up for breakfast!"

He chuckled, loving the drama. "I think most chefs have some Jotnar in them," he added. Eyre looked around. "Well, there's no point staying here then. It's obvious breakfast is off! Are there any staff left to supervise us?"

"I think they're all sick. They're not here, anyway." Zanda looked gleeful. "A day off for us all!"

"Attention please, students, listen up!" A familiar voice called across the heads of the gossiping mass and the Ranger walked through the crowd, helping Whittaker Ray to the Refectory doors. Whittaker Ray was sweating and looked very pale, but his eyes were focused.

"Due to circumstances," he said, his voice strained and soft, "you will be not be required to attend classes today. The Ranger will transport you to Bathurst for breakfast; it's an interesting town, and you are free to spend the day as you see fit. We hope that by tomorrow the usual routine will be back in place. Please behave yourself in accordance with the Academy's expectations."

Even this short speech seemed to exhaust the Dean, because the Ranger took over. His eyes travelled upwards as a Zepp flew above them and circled down to land in front of the Central Admin building. The Zepp was a deep blue colour—the signature hue of the Echelon. The Ranger paused as he watched it taxi to a stop, then continued. "If you would meet me at the moldavite square in half an hour, I will send you in batches to Bathurst while we sort out this problem today. Please don't be late or you will miss out."

The Ranger's face showed none of his usual good spirits, and he held Whittaker Ray's arm to steady the other man. Whittaker Ray motioned for the students to leave and they moved quickly, as if afraid he might change his mind. A few cheered softly as they raced to their rooms—it was bad luck for the staff, but awesome news for them!

An hour later, the entire second-year student body was wandering through the streets of Bathurst. At this time of year, the temperature hovered around 10 degrees as the cool air from the Blue Mountains spilled over and down across the plains where the town lay. Compared to their visit to Lightning Ridge last year, another mining town sprung from the dust of the outback, this temperature was surprising. Lightning Ridge had been blazingly hot and uncomfortable.

Bathurst was the site of the first gold rush in Australia, and the oldest inland settlement, and it showed in the monuments and the heritage-listed sites. After breakfast, Eyre walked with Carly through the town, studying the historical buildings, but in truth, anxious to be back on campus. She was worried about Whittaker Ray—he had looked so unwell, and she felt strange being away from the school.

She noticed Nick, Beatrice and Abby, deep in conversation a block ahead of her, and felt a twinge. BAN it was now—she had indeed been banned from the group. As she watched them wistfully, a figure emerged from a shop behind them and Eyre's mouth opened. Surely not? Excusing herself to Carly, she hurried to follow, but kept in the shadows. The man was also trying to stay unnoticed, but he closed the distance between Eyre's friends and Eyre had to almost run to catch up. As she neared, she shook her head in astonishment. It *was*! Nick's dad was stalking them like a malevolent shark in the shallows! Confusion filled Eyre's head. He had been at Lightning Ridge too. She knew that Exes often kept to mining towns, with their deserted tunnels and darkened passageways that led deep into the ground. But this was too much of a coincidence. Why was he prowling around? Nick had made it obvious he didn't want anything to do with his father, so there must be some other motivation.

Eyre jumped as an arm shot out and dragged Nick's dad by the collar into a coffee shop. He gave a surprised grunt as he disappeared through the door. Breathing deeply, Eyre sidled into the doorway and peered through the window. Nick's dad was talking angrily and gesticulating at someone who had his back to her. And then Eyre's mouth dropped even wider as the man he was talking to turned slightly and she could see him properly. Professor Vela! What was he doing here—wasn't he sick? Rage filled her. He must have been pretending to be unwell, like the rest of the staff. And it was such an intense exchange—it was obvious that this was no random encounter. Professor Vela's eyes flicked sideways and Eyre lurched out of sight, flattening herself against the wall. What was Professor Vela doing, talking to an Ex? One thing was for sure, Eyre was certain that he wasn't supposed to be here. And she was also sure that he was up to no good.

A final shock was in store for her, because just then she noticed a shadowy form lurking behind a gift cabinet at the back of the store. Trying to appear casual, but definitely watching Nick's dad and Professor Vela. As he moved around, keeping out of sight of the arguing couple, Eyre nearly fell over. *Jax? BTL, what was going on?*

Carly caught up to Eyre and chuckled. "What *are* you doing, my friend? Lurking around like one of the Gothak!" Eyre smiled awkwardly and glanced in the door again. Vela and Nick's dad were now nowhere to be seen, and Jax had also disappeared. It had all been so quick she could almost have imagined it. Shaking her head, she started walking with Carly again. "Just someone I thought I knew. But he's not there now."

"Well, come on—we've got a couple of hours. Let's go pan for gold!"

They both laughed out loud at this—the idea of fossicking for flecks of gold was hilarious when they dined off solid gold tables.

Eyre shook her head slowly. "Do you mind? I'd really like to stay here."

Carly looked at Eyre, then at Beatrice, Abby and Nick up ahead and her face was thoughtful. There was a silence, and then she patted Eyre's shoulder.

"I don't know what's happened between you and your friends, Eyre, but I feel they are not seeing clearly, somehow. I know how much you care for them. I'm happy to stay here and stand guard—we can be like the Unlit, stealthing around. Come on, show me your skills!"

Eyre smiled gratefully. Uncomplicated Carly, with her wise, untroubled head. Her strong family had given her confidence and a faith in the best of people. No explanations necessary. So, they followed Nick, Abby and Beatrice for the rest of the time in Bathurst, unnoticed and vigilant. Carly made a game of it, enjoying the subterfuge and the fun of being undercover. But neither Nick's dad, nor Professor Vela reappeared, nor Jax for that matter. Eyre's feeling of doom intensified—she couldn't warn Nick, or talk of her concerns to her friends. They would just see it as another conspiracy theory, a bid for attention—and she knew they wouldn't listen. And indeed, what would she say? She had no explanation for any of it. Troubled, all she could do was watch and wait.

# CHAPTER FORTY-NINE

A COUPLE OF HOURS later the Ranger had deposited them back on the moldavite square, instructing them all to turn up for a sausage sizzle by the Ponds of Doombee at 6pm. It was getting late in the afternoon, and shadows were starting to stretch far across the campus. But as she walked to the dorms with Carly, Eyre noticed the blue Zepp still sat in front of the Central Admin block. Eyre hesitated and then bid Carly farewell.

"I'll see you at the sausage sizzle," she said. "I just want to have a word with the Ranger."

But instead of heading back to the moldavite square, after Carly left, Eyre walked through the gardens and around the edge of the Central Admin building. If the Echelon was here, she wanted to know what was going on.

She checked to see that no one was watching and edged behind the blue Zepp. Then, concentrating hard, she masked. When she was sure she could maintain it, she slipped in through the front doors of Central Admin and up the stairs.

Whether the Ranger had intentionally left the viewing room open for her, or whether it had been unlocked already, Eyre couldn't say. But the doors opened when she tried them, and she crept inside to the window after snicking them shut behind her.

Down below, the Echelon sat around the boardroom table, deep in discussion. The Head Chef of the Jotnar was at one end, frowning fiercely, and Whittaker Ray slumped at the other, pale and exhausted. Then the door at the side opened and the Ranger entered. All conversation stopped as he took his place.

Chairman Essendon spoke. "I trust all the second-years have had a good day and thank you for bringing them back, Ranger. In your absence we have finalised the main issues discussed this afternoon, which have been noted in the minutes. Chief amongst them is, firstly—our unreserved apology to the

Jotnar for any aspersions cast upon their catering." The sullen Jotnar nodded sharply but looked slightly mollified as the Chairman continued.

"Secondly, after our conclusive testing this afternoon, campus security will investigate how the Stibnite got into the staff cuisine." Eyre noticed the Ranger glance up at the window where she lurked in the shadows. So perhaps it wasn't just coincidence that the doors had been unlocked? And what was Stibnite? She had missed any reference to that, so she would have to research it later.

"Finally, reassurances are to be sent to parents of Academy students. We have only a few months left in the school year, so it is hoped that we can resolve any security issues before the start of the next year." The Chairman paused and looked at Whittaker Ray, who seemed unable to stand and talk. Chairman Essendon raised a hand to Mr Ray. "Our best wishes go out to the staff and we hope they are all back on deck as soon as possible. The school has had a difficult year, one which has tested all who have been here. These are troubled and dangerous times and we must unite to defeat the Darkness. Travel well, and *May the Light endure!*" A low murmur travelled around the room as the members repeated the last line. Then they pulled their chairs back and one by one headed out of the room. Shortly after, Eyre heard the rumble of the Zepp. She made it out of the Central Admin building in time to see the rotund blue shape disappear into the clouds.

It was dark down by the Ponds when the students assembled for the sausage sizzle that night, and Eyre shivered. The temperature had plummeted as the sun went down, and an eerie breeze was making the water jump and peak as if something was moving beneath the surface. Burning flames had been set up for light and warmth, but the halo of the fires barely cut the darkness. And though the Ranger was cheery as he barbequed the sausages, even his eyes were shrouded, scouring the blankness of the night intently. Eyre grabbed a piece of bread and the Ranger dumped some onion and a sausage on it. He looked at her carefully. "Good afternoon, Eyre?"

"Ah, yeah, thanks Ranger." She turned away and took a bite, almost scalding her mouth. It had actually been a very busy afternoon once she got back from the admin building. She'd scoured all her textbooks for any reference to Stibnite, but without luck. Eventually she'd ended up at the Library, where Mrs Abnett had helped her with the Dewey cataloguing system to find some sources. Once she was in the right area, there was a heap of information on Stibnite.

It turned out that Stibnite was a crystal, similar in structure to Arsenic and just as lethal. If ingested in enough quantity, it caused vomiting, diarrhoea, cramps and lethargy, and would ultimately kill the person. Eyre was horrified as she realised that someone on campus had *poisoned* the staff over the last month—the absences and illness of the staff members was now explained. Obviously, whoever had put the Stibnite in the staff's meals had done it in the Refectory where they could be specific about their target. Over time the staff had become increasingly ill until they were dangerously close to death. And with a rising fury, Eyre knew without a doubt *who* had done it. Someone who sat at the staff table. Someone with motive. Someone with the means. *Professor Vela*, sneaking around the Transit with Mr Wilson in tow, bottling up secret crystals, talking of bringing the Academy down. It didn't take a genius to work it out after what she'd seen and heard. A deep frustration filled her as she bit fiercely into her sausage. Would anyone believe her? Probably not. Whittaker Ray was so adamant that Professor Vela had been with him that day. Eyre wondered if Professor Vela was able to Shimmer. Perhaps that might explain how Whittaker Ray could be so certain and yet so wrong?

Eyre looked out at the dark water as the wind blew her hair into dancing strands of burnished copper. Sombre thoughts filled her head as she tried to work out what to do. At least the staff would recover. Eyre's research said that over time, and with medication, crystals and chelation therapy, the effects of the poison would wear off. But the threat of inside forces working against the Academy remained. And those forces would stop at nothing. She shivered, partly from the cold but mostly from the barrage of thoughts that roiled through her head. Something fell lightly across her shoulders and she nearly levitated in alarm. She turned in shock to find Jax standing calmly as he met her startled eyes. He indicated the coat he'd draped across her. "You looked cold."

"Oh, er, thanks," Eyre said, her mind even more crazy now. *What was he doing here?* They fell into an awkward silence, studying the irregular chop on the surface of the water. The burning torches threw orange streaks across the tips of the waves in the shallows of the Ponds, but further out it was only blackness. Eyre felt a weighty hopelessness that seemed synonymous with the life she was currently leading. The only light was at the edges—everything else was dark and confused.

"I wanted to apologise," Jax said eventually, his voice hesitant. Eyre waited. He turned and looked down at her, his hypnotic green eyes aflame and dancing with the reflected fires. "I was jealous when I saw you flying with Colton, and I'm sorry," he whispered, running his fingers gently down her cheek, and her skin burned where his fingertips passed. Jax's eyes locked onto hers, and Eyre felt a shiver of a different kind ripple down her body. She leaned towards him, falling towards an energy force she seemed unable to resist. *Jax*, her mind sighed. His arms pulled her closer and a magical breeze seemed to sing along Eyre's nerve endings. She closed her eyes, wanting desperately to give herself up to the feelings that ran so wildly within her and a there was a brief moment when she almost did. But then she opened her eyes and stepped back, her face uncertain. She ran her hands through her hair, feeling strangely close to weeping. The earth was constantly shifting under her. She didn't know the difference between the good guys and the bad guys anymore.

"You can't do that," she breathed, her eyes desperate. "You come to me, then you back off. You do *this*, then you ignore me. I don't ever know where I stand with you! And you disappear, all the time. What are you doing here? You said you were leaving, but you didn't go. I saw you, in Bathurst." Jax looked shocked, his green eyes widening as Eyre took another step backwards, out of his arms. "When you can be honest with me, maybe we'll have a chance at—I don't know, whatever *this* is. But I have too much going on to try and work it all out."

Then she flung his jacket at him, and turned and escaped into the darkness, fleeing to the sanctuary of her room.

# CHAPTER FIFTY

AFTER THE STIBNITE INCIDENT, campus life settled back into a routine. Everything was as it had been before, and yet so different. A strange focus had overtaken most of the students, as if knowledge of the encroaching darkness was seeping into their souls. They practised with a passion unseen before at the Academy: Ferito, psionic skills, the Summons and Reverse Summons especially. All the students learned how to perform the tri-merit, merging the current technique, carousel breathing and eventually even mastering water vision, so they could swim underwater endlessly up and down the 100-metre pool. And they performed the prohemiums over and over again until the Terra and Aqua hand gestures were second nature. By the end of third term, everyone could do them effortlessly. They improved greatly at their staff skills—anyone who had trouble was helped by the rest of the students. The lecturers, once they recovered and returned to classes, were impressed by the dedication of the second-year students. Something had gotten into them, and Eyre somehow felt that it was *her*. Somehow her own dread and desperation had infected all her classmates—a psychic panic underscored by rage. There was a graveness to them all, and much of the banter that normally coloured their conversations had disappeared.

Eyre had continued her flying lessons on Nox, and could gallop around the paddock and take off and land with ease. She had practised her archery and throwing the lure for Florence for hours, and she'd even suffered through Ischyros's cyclonic tantrums. She still couldn't get in the stall with him, but she ran to the stables every couple of days and talked to him over the top of the stall, resigning herself to his perpetual fury. And day after day she forced her body through the various disciplines, working for hours at her practise. It was fear that drove her on—something huge and malevolent was coming, she could sense it. She had to be ready.

Beatrice and Abby still ignored her, even when they were together in their dorm room, but she had gotten used to it. Eyre used her training as an excuse to escape and avoid interacting with them. Next year she would request a different room. But the pain of her friends' rejection had diminished as a dull acceptance set in. She'd never really had friends before, so the relatively short time she'd had such a closeness with Beatrice, Abby and Nick was just an anomaly. The weeks passed and she settled back in to her well-worn role of outsider with an equanimity that she knew only further irritated her roommates. Eyre's birthday fell on November 11th, ironically being 'Remembrance Day' for those who had fought in the war. This year her 16th birthday came and went, and no one noticed or said anything at all. Eyre was fighting a war of her own, she thought drily, but she still felt an overwhelming pain. She actually felt lonelier with Beatrice and Abby in the room than without them.

But there was nothing she could do about it, they were all at an impasse that seemed insurmountable. And Jax, of course, had deserted her again after that night at the Ponds. As confusing as always, he was back suddenly, and he hadn't even tried to explain this time. He and Pheria were often seen head-to-head in the Refectory, with Pheria throwing searing, triumphant glances at Eyre. Eyre ignored her. It seemed that she was weighed down by a dull indifference to anything but training nowadays. At least the fourth term was nearly over.

A few days after her birthday there was an unexpected knock on the dorm room door. The three girls looked at each other in surprise, but then, as usual, Beatrice and Abby's gaze skittered away from Eyre. She sighed as she opened the door.

"Good morning," the Sergeant said. "The three of you are to meet with Nick and Whittaker Ray at his office before meditation. You are not to mention this to anyone." The Sergeant was looking fit and muscular, back to herself after the sickness that had nearly claimed her life.

"Is Nick okay?" Beatrice said.

Eyre was confused. What did she mean? "What's wrong with Nick?" she asked and Beatrice turned hot eyes towards her.

"He had another migraine yesterday. He's had them all year," she said sharply. "If you were interested in anything other than yourself, you might have noticed he is often missing." Eyre flushed at the injustice. She hadn't even been here for half the year, and after the time at the sandstone rock, her friends had hardly welcomed her into their circle. But underneath her angst was a deep worry. Migraines? When had this started? She hadn't realised that Nick was prone to the devastating headaches, and despite herself she felt guilt scratch again within her. It seemed there was always some reason for her to feel she had done something wrong. Eyre certainly felt that Beatrice was right, she should have noticed that Nick was having problems.

"Nick has recovered well enough," the Sergeant replied. Her eyes travelled back and forth between the girls, all the staff had noted the change in their dynamics. But the Sergeant said nothing more and when she left, a dark silence descended in the room.

"Come on Beatrice," Abby said. "I'm ready—let's go." And they left the room without waiting for Eyre. Rather than trail along a few paces behind them, she let them go and sat on the bed. By the Light, she could hardly wait for the term to finish. Although there would be no escape—back to the cabins with the rest of them. She looked up at the ceiling and then gritted her teeth and jumped up. Best to get this over with.

Nick was already in Whittaker Ray's office when she got there. He looked pale and there were dark circles beneath his eyes, and he greeted them softly when they arrived, as if to talk too loudly would hurt. Whittaker Ray motioned for them all to sit down, and then leaned up against his desk, his eyes serious.

"Tomorrow you will be taking your TACI test, and you four will be once again assigned as teammates."

Abby scowled and Beatrice stuck her jaw out. "Wouldn't it make more sense for us to have different partners? You know we don't get along anymore."

Whittaker Ray's blue eyes studied her levelly. "For administrative reasons, you are to stay together until the end of this year. Next year we may be able to make some changes, but it is not possible at this time. I am expecting you to co-operate with each other and any attempts at subterfuge or sabotage will result in an automatic fail. I am holding you to this in good faith. Thank you, you may go. Eyre, I'd like you to stay behind."

Beatrice had hot red splotches staining her cheeks and Abby glowered darkly as they left in silence. Nick rolled his eyes, but he also said nothing. Eyre grimaced as she looked at Whittaker Ray.

"They won't forgive me," she said.

Whittaker Ray looked apologetic. "I don't know how Ben discovered what you said to me about Abby's father, and I'm sorry that he passed it on. It's inexcusable. But I can't change your group for the TACI expedition. The Gothak will have realised that somehow your group found the Isar last year, and they may be watching out for you. By keeping you together, they will not be able to figure out how the Isars are located. If we split you up, they will realise that it is an individual who makes a difference—you. If you stay together, even if they do realise an individual can see it, they won't know *who*. It will just be one of you, the same as last year."

He opened his desk drawer and pulled out two gleaming crystals that were familiar to Eyre: the pale blue Angelite and forest-green Bloodstone that they had acquired from Aowx.

"You will need to keep them dry. We have a waterproof bag for them, but you will have to perform Bullio to keep the Angelite dry under the water. The Angelite is a crystal of psychic connection, and that is how you will try to find the Sea Crone."

Eyre groaned. Bullio! Not her strongest skill at the best of times. If only she could let Nick in on the secret—he could manipulate the bubbles with his eyes shut. The magnitude of the task made her wince. "How do I use it? And where will she be?" Eyre asked.

"The Sea Crone," Whittaker Ray replied, spinning the shining Angelite on his polished desk, "is everywhere and nowhere at the same time. As Aowx said, she hasn't been seen for a long time, since before the Proditio, so it will be difficult for you to locate her—if at all. Still, it is essential that we get the information from her.

"When you get to Aqua, you will enter the water with the Angelite in Bullio. It is a crystal that you can connect with in a similar manner to scrying with a crystal ball. Focus on the Sea Crone and call to her, use your Viq and your psionic skills. If you do manage to make contact, you are to present the Bloodstone to her, and hopefully she will elect to help you—I am counting on the likelihood that she doesn't want the Gothak to succeed either. But please remember to be deferential, the old seer is wise, but apparently, she can be touchy. No small ego there. Do you have any questions?"

Eyre raised her eyebrows, but shook her head. The only questions she had would be answered once she got to Aqua. Whittaker Ray's sympathetic look showed he understood her silence completely—this was a desperate mission with a slim chance of success. But he continued on in a brisk voice.

"On this trip, Gegenees and Sir Philius Clarembout will be accompanying you. We don't want to draw attention to your group, but we need you to have back-up should anything go awry. For some reason, the Gothak have always been more active at this time of year—it's almost as if they are aware of the significance. But not of the process of finding the Isars. So, you will have to be alert—they will be around.

"Obviously, I don't need to tell you the level of secrecy this mission entails. You are carrying a huge burden in silence, Eyre. With courage and integrity, but no guarantee of success. Stay strong."

Eyre left Whittaker Ray's office reflecting that a large part of her burden was caused by him not believing her about Professor Vela and Mr Wilson. But that was a circular thought pattern that went nowhere, so she threw it out of her head. He was right about the 'no guarantee of success' part—her Viq seemed to be back, but could she still see an Isar? And how to find it anyway in such a huge place? It seemed impossible. But she was glad Gegenees and Lord Clarembout were coming—the thought gave Eyre a glow of confidence. She had encountered Gegenees at her TEP examination in the trials for a place at the Academy. The six-armed giant had been part of the testing, and at the time Eyre had thought her life was over. But Gegenees turned out to be good-humoured despite his fearsome looks, and all the students actually did make it out alive after their encounter with him. Eyre had seen how well he could fight, and she thought he was a good choice for this mission. And Sir Philius Clarembout, the Head of the Defence Department and Senior Lecturer in fulminology, was a formidable force. The pair of them could probably split the earth in two if they tried hard enough.

Her last port of call was the stables. She just could not leave without a final visit to her bad-tempered old mount. Despite his behaviour, she cared for him deeply, seeing in him a soul as wounded as her own. No matter how he behaved, she would not give up on him.

The bedraggled old horse opened a red eye at her approach. Never the best-looking horse, he now looked like a moth-eaten carpet bag. She hadn't been able to get in the stall to groom him for months, and his coat was patchy and full of burrs. His feet needed attention and his mane was a tangled mess of hair. He was a very sorry sight indeed. But there was nothing sorry about his attitude.

"What are you doing here, I was just sleeping," he snapped, turning his dusty rear to Eyre.

She sighed and gave a wry smile. "It's the TACI test tomorrow Ischyros, I just wanted to say farewell."

Ischyros snored loudly from the front of his stall, but Eyre was not deterred.

"I know you're not asleep, Ischyros. I just wanted to say that I'll miss you. I have enjoyed learning to ride on Nox—" Ischyros couldn't help himself, and kicked his feed bucket at Eyre's head. "—*but*," Eyre continued, ducking, "it's you that I love, Ischyros. You're my Lighthorse forever, and I hope one day we might ride together. In case I don't come back, I wanted to say goodbye. And to let you know that I'm glad you're my Lighthorse."

Did Ischyros turn a bit? Eyre waited for a while, staring. Maybe not, she eventually decided, but at least he didn't kick anything else at her. Sighing, she tossed a chunk of liquorice over the gate and turned to go.

"'Bye Ischyros," she said softly. A theatrical snore echoed from the front of the stall.

# CHAPTER FIFTY-ONE

THE MORNING OF THE TACI test dawned with pale streaks of cloud smudged across a washed-out sky. A weather change was in the air and a shrill wind whirled and shrieked through the crystal shards that towered at angles from the campus buildings. Everyone looked subdued and sleep-deprived as they talked quietly to each other by the moldavite square; Eyre suspected they'd had about as much sleep as she had the night before. Her eyes felt gritty as she waited for the Sergeant to dispatch them.

The Sergeant arrived with Whittaker Ray, who waved his hands for silence.

"Congratulations on making it to the end of your second year at the Academy. The expedition to Aqua will be the culmination of all the skills you have learnt this year, and we look forward to receiving the gazae you bring back with you. I won't speak any longer—you will be wanting to get started. May the Light be with you, and keep each other safe."

The Sergeant was standing in front of a pile of sharp golden blades that glistened despite the recalcitrant weather. When she was sure everyone was there, the Sergeant began a roll call, and the students stepped into their pre-arranged groups. As they sorted themselves out, a low rumbling grew, and the Academy's fleet of Zepps rolled out from the hangars at the back of the school buildings and pulled up on the edge of the bush that surrounded the campus.

"As discussed in class, you will travel the long distance underwater via Zepp with your Pinnae guide. Once you get to the Imum shell beds, you will disembark into the water for the rest of your test." The Sergeant indicated a shining pile in front of her. "Please pick up a Kulbeda and scabbard, and remember the weapon is sharp. Good luck to you all!"

The students moved forward and picked up their golden dagger and scabbard, and Eyre looped her scabbard over the uniform belt, setting the

Kulbeda in it snugly. As with their trip to Terra last year, students were given the Kulbeda for the duration of the TACI test only. Next year they would be issued their permanent Arms Endowment, which would include their own Kulbeda.

A flash of light blinded Eyre and she half-closed her eyes as a Seam appeared before them all. From within the light, many figures emerged, one after the other, until ten Pinnae, including Mentor Xiphias, stood lined up before them. All different shapes and sizes, but they each had the distinctive turquoise eyes and long blue hair, flippers for feet and elongated, webbed fingers on their hands. The Pinnae stood quietly as the Sergeant read the groups out loud and directed them to a Zepp. As each group boarded, one of the Pinnae jumped into the driver's seat. Most of the groups had 8-10 students in them; Eyre's group was the smallest, and the only one with four members. The Sergeant left this group until last, so that only they remained as the other Zepps disappeared into the Seam. Mentor Xiphias was the last Pinnae there—he was to be their guide, and Eyre was happy that he was coming with them. She had grown very fond of the courageous, calm lecturer over the year.

There was another flash of light and Lord Clarembout appeared, dressed most impractically for travel in his distinctive medieval-like clothing, and then in another flash Gegenees arrived, his six arms flexing.

Abby and Beatrice were craning their necks from one to the other, their eyes round. Even Nick's usual equanimity was shaken as the three of them looked at the new arrivals.

Mentor Xiphias climbed into the driver's seat of the last remaining Zepp. Beatrice's jaw dropped as Lord Clarembout and Gegenees strode forwards and climbed in too. She and Abby looked at each other, then at the Sergeant. *What?* The Sergeant remained impassive

"Come on you lot," Lord Clarembout roared, sticking his head out the door. "The Seam won't stay open forever!"

"In you go," the Sergeant said and finally Beatrice found her feet. She walked with Abby and Nick up the steps and into the Zepp. Eyre followed behind, but not before the Sergeant had clapped her on the shoulder.

"Walk Lightly," the Sergeant said gruffly. "Carry a big stick." Whittaker Ray just lifted a hand in farewell, his eyes shadowed.

The doors closed as Eyre took her seat and buckled herself in. Then, with a grumble, the Zepp rolled forward into the Seam.

Eyre's stomach dropped violently as the Zepp fell through the air in the blinding light, hurtling downwards like a torpedo until, with a juddering splash, it hit a body of water and plunged below the surface. The clear sides of the Zepp enabled Eyre to see that they were nose-diving deep into a vast expanse of turquoise water, a fathomless ocean that stretched endlessly into nothingness. Down, down, down they went until after quite some time Mentor Xiphias turned the vehicle so that it was horizontal again, pushing forwards through the water like a plump submarine.

Light shone in strange pink streaks in the water, and through the windows, the inhabitants of Aqua could be seen. Dancing leaves of neon seaweed curled and uncurled past the window. A swarm of Balloon Jellyfish floated past, their two-metre-long stingers twirling like festive streamers in the current—delicate but deadly. The creatures' bodies expanded and deflated as they propelled themselves through the water, the only sign that the silent organisms were actually alive. Further on, Beatrice gasped and pointed as a giant, armour-plated fish swam past the windows. Its black eyes swivelled, looking in at them, and Eyre was glad they hadn't reached the disembarking phase of the trip—the creature was an Aqua Stickleback, a meat-eating resident of Aqua who seemed quite interested in the contents of the Zepp. Lunch in a can, it no doubt thought!

A movement from beyond the window caught her eye and she turned to see what she thought was a posse of stingrays flitting out of sight into the murky depths. Craning her neck, she tried to remember what Mentor Xiphias had called a group of stingrays. Eventually she remembered. A fever! That was it—a fever of stingrays. But then the hairs on the back of her neck rose as the creatures glided back into view, and from the way that Mentor Xiphias jumped, she realised that he had seen them too. Because it wasn't stingrays that were swimming around down here with them. As the dark form swooped in and followed the Zepp, close by the window, Eyre shuddered. Those red eyes. The claws...

"Zyx!" shouted Abby from the other side of the Zepp, her eyes wide. From nowhere they were suddenly surrounded by a huge swarm of the creatures, which slid through the water and lay like leeches on the hull of the Zepp as they scraped at the metal with their sharp talons. The scritching sound made Eyre's heart race.

But Lord Clarembout wasn't having a bar of it. He stood up.

"Darned flying rats!" he boomed in a tetchy voice, eyeing the windows. "Keep away from the walls of the Zepp everyone, lean in and lift your feet."

When they had all done as directed, Lord Clarembout brought his massive hands together, moving them in a circular motion until a sparking, dense corona was formed. Then he hurled it upwards at the ceiling of the Zepp and as it connected, it exploded into rivulets of energy that travelled all around the shell of the Zepp, charging it with a lethal electrical force.

Outside in the water there was a boiling tumult as black forms blasted from the sides of the Zepp. Scorched remains drifted in pieces past the windows and the swarm of Zyx shot away from the submersible. High-pitched screeches could be heard through the hull as a foaming white wake signalled the predators had gone. Lord Clarembout clapped his hands and the zing of energy through the hull stopped. He leaned to the window and stared through the glass into the aquamarine water.

"That sorted 'em," he said with satisfaction. "You can put your feet down again."

Eyre continued to look out the window, but her awe at being in another Alterworld had given way to an uneasy watchfulness. Like picking up an unwelcome load again, she remembered that this wasn't a tourist jaunt, it was a mission that could bring death and disaster. Gone was her curiosity about this new world; her restless eyes searched the mysterious waters for only one thing—a vertical beam of light. Find the Isar and get back.

"We're about halfway to the Clam Beds," Mentor Xiphias informed them over his shoulder. "Have a look out your window—you'll see the Reefs of Gnil-Wor appearing. One of the natural wonders of our world."

The students peered out the windows and could dimly make out the uneven backbone of some kind of natural formation, too far away yet to see properly. Eyre sat back and waited for the Zepp to draw nearer.

But with a sudden jolt, the Zepp stopped dead, throwing its passengers out of their seats. Eyre ended up on her hands and knees in the middle of the floor, scrambling to stand up as the Zepp began to buck and heave, tipping as the thrust of the engines met an unmoveable force.

"Letalis Trapweed!" Mentor Xiphias shouted, struggling with the controls. "Hold on while I try to get us out." He pulled back on the throttle and shoved the gears, but even on full power the vehicle wouldn't budge. It was held in an unbreakable grip by the trapweed. Eyre knew from her classes with the Mentor that they were in trouble. The treacherous kelp grew from the bottom of the sea and it was carnivorous, like a Venus flytrap. It would grab its prey and hold it with its sharp thorns until it died —sometimes waiting for days—then drag it down to be eaten. Eyre doubted the sides of the Zepp could stand the onslaught of the thorns, even if they could survive for days in its clutches. They had to do something.

Lord Clarembout stood up. "Well, students, how do we handle this?"

"Buckle up, for a start," said Nick, raising an eyebrow and doing just that. His comment broke the tension and everyone laughed.

"It's your TACI test and you've learnt about this in class," Lord Clarembout continued, gesturing to the window. "Any suggestions?"

"We're too far away to swim yet," mused Beatrice.

"We should cut the weed away," Abby offered, but Beatrice shook her head. As usual, she'd read all about it. "No, if you cut it, it just grabs you with another tendril." She looked upwards, thinking, then clapped her hands. "Yes! I remember. You have to fool it. You stick something unpalatable in its mouth so it will let go!"

Mentor Xiphias was nodding, impressed. "Well done. Yes, that is correct. The difficulty is, of course, avoiding the tendrils while you swim down. If they get you, it's all over."

"What should we put in its mouth?" Eyre asked, and was taken aback when Abby shot her a look that suggested she had a very good idea of what —or who—she would like to put in its mouth. Eyre looked away, clenching her teeth. It *really* was time for Abby to get over it.

Nick had been thinking. "The metal box the life raft is in? We could shove it in the kelp's mouth?" All eyes turned to the container, which was tucked at one side at the rear of the Zepp. It was usually unnoticed, a permanent fixture in case of an emergency in the air or on top of the water —a situation that in reality no one ever thought would eventuate. A Seam could always get them out of here.

"Good idea," Lord Clarembout said. "So, who will take it."

Eyre was still burning at the look Abby had flashed her, and she jumped in. "I will." She stood up and stalked to the large metal box. But Lord Clarembout seemed to change his mind as he looked at her.

"I think for the sake of expediency, I will get Gegenees to take it down. We don't want to waste time, we need to keep pressing forwards. But I'd like everyone to help get the raft out. Quickly, the Zepp can't tolerate too much of this pressure."

As if groaning in agreement, there was a loud metallic clunk as something shifted in the infrastructure of the walls. It was a good motivator; all the students leapt to the back of the Zepp and in a few minutes had dragged the folded raft out of the box. Gegenees flexed his muscles and picked the box up with his six colossal arms.

Behind the podium that sat in the centre of the Zepp, the floor started to move and a hidden door slid back to reveal a plunge pool that led to the outside environment. Air pressure kept the water from entering, and waves lapped against the sides of the opening. Holding the box tightly, Gegenees stepped into the hole and disappeared into the dark water below.

As the hull of the Zepp creaked ominously around them, the group waited. It seemed to be taking a long time and Eyre peered anxiously out the window. What if he'd met a Stickleback—or the Zyx? But then there was a lurch and all the tendrils let go at once, leaving the Zepp bobbing back and forth in the water. Bubbles drifted upwards from somewhere below until a face appeared in front of Eyre, and she grinned as Gegenees knocked with all six of his hands on the window. A second later, he shot up out of the plunge hole and stood in a puddle of water, sucking in huge lungfuls of air. The door slid shut behind him, closing off the opening.

"Carousel breathing is not designed for someone my size," Gegenees complained.

Lord Clarembout, clapped the gigantic creature on the back. "You're just out of shape," he said, and then looked at the pilot. "Onwards, Sir Xiphias!"

Mentor Xiphias put the Zepp in gear and once more they moved through the water, nearing the Reefs of Gnil-Wor. As they got closer, Eyre realised that the reefs were formed from a combination of neon coral and shards of polished crystal. The crystal prisms jutted out of the brilliantly coloured coral formations like rock candy in a lolly shop; all sizes and colours of the faceted stones decorated the vast expanse of the celebrated Gnil-Wor wonder. Unlike the vast empty depths of the ocean they had already travelled through, here the area teemed with wildlife. There were spider-like creatures that propelled themselves through the water with a long swishing tail, schools of undulating centipede-like organisms about a foot long and many fish of different colours and shapes. Creatures of all sorts swam and crawled through the weed and coral that grew all over the iridescent reefs. They passed through a towering structure that glowed with myriad brilliant colours and Eyre mused that it was as if the Great Barrier Reef was hosting a disco. But nowhere could she see a bright light shooting upwards to reveal the whereabouts of the Isar. *How would she ever find it?* Eyre thought with a sudden despair. This world was so huge—it could be anywhere. And would she even be able to see it now? She certainly hadn't seen any sign of vertical light at all. Perhaps she would never be able to do it again—after all, there had been doubts about whether her Aether powers would even return. Her thoughts were dismal as she peered out the window, looking for any gleam at all.

Her friends, less troubled, were fascinated by the spectacular vista outside the window, and they called out in amazement as the Zepp manoeuvred through the canyons and monoliths of crystal and coral. Finally, a tiered structure appeared ahead of them. It was made of crystal, but formed in geometric shapes, too regular to be a natural outcrop. Mentor Xiphias motored towards it and piloted the Zepp into a gaping hole at the centre of the edifice. As they moved into the darkness, green lights powered on in the walls, and Eyre could see twisted, rope-like objects hanging from the sides. The Zepp slowed and finally stopped, bobbing fitfully as the backwash caught up with them. The plunge access opened and wavelets sploshed over the sides as the Zepp rocked back and forth.

Mentor Xiphias left the pilot's seat and walked to the opening in the floor, and then dived expertly into the water. A moment later he appeared outside the window, and floated motionlessly for a moment before he swam to one of the ropes, hauled it back and attached it to the side of the Zepp. Then he swung around and pulled back with his hands, in the manner of breaststroke, while kicking his feet together like a dolphin. Eyre watched in awe as the Mentor glided through the water—effortless and graceful with his flippered feet and long, webbed fingers. His blue hair streamed like a banner behind him and there was a joy in his movements—he was obviously happy to be home. Once he reached the other side of the hangar —for that was what it evidently was—he attached another rope to the other side of the Zepp.

The Mentor kicked and disappeared under the Zepp, then in an explosion of water, he flew out of the opening in its hull and landed beside Eyre. Xiphias's iridescent scales shimmered with a rainbow of colours as streams of water dripped from his skin. Somewhere on the journey he had shed the protective air suit he wore at the Academy—he was in his own environment now. His eyes gleamed.

"It is time for you to be truly introduced to Aqua," Xiphias said. "We have reached the Reefs of Gnil-Wor Depot, and the Imum Clam Beds are not far from here. Follow me closely, and good luck!"

Xiphias dived gracefully back into the water with a joyous arc that barely caused a splash inside the Zepp.

# CHAPTER FIFTY-TWO

BEATRICE, ABBY AND NICK jumped feet-first after him, and floated underneath the Zepp for a moment, before moving out of sight. As Eyre walked forward to take her turn, Lord Clarembout showed her a small, water-tight bag with a long handle.

"The crystals are in this bag. We will leave them here until you are ready to try and make contact with the Crone; Bullio will use up a lot of your Viq, so you should leave it 'til last. But first, go with the others and find your sea pearl. It is a good opportunity to look for the Isar. If you see any sign of it, let me know immediately and we will suspend the search for the gazae. Gegenees and I will remain on the Zepp with the crystals while you find your pearls."

Eyre followed the others into the water, and held her breath at the sudden chill. She hovered upright in the water and started breathing in the carousel method, using the rhythmic technique and her Viq to pull oxygen out of the water. It was much harder than breathing in air; as Xiphias had said, it was like trying to breathe through a sponge. There was also a mental component to the technique, as it was easy to panic and feel that you were drowning. Added to the difficulty was being unable to see properly at first through the water. Steadying herself, she concentrated on breathing and using her Viq to clear her eyes. After a moment, her vision cleared and her breathing became easier, and the initial nervousness she'd felt lessened as she relaxed in the water. She looked for the others and saw them waiting at the opening to the hangar, suspended in the azure water beside Xiphias.

When she reached them, the Mentor looked outwards, and after a moment, satisfied that all was clear, he led the way upwards to the shallower sections of the reef. They floated over brightly coloured sea plants, and tiny schools of darting fish. Only close examination showed they were different from home—some with one eye, some with odd-shaped bodies, others like a chimeric mixture of creatures she knew: a combination of a crab and a worm, or a prawn with long tusks. All of it fascinating and worth a second look, if only Eyre wasn't driven by a desperate feeling that she needed to *keep moving!* The Isar was out there somewhere and she had to find it. If she could actually see it. There was no knowing yet whether she still had the ability, and it added to her anxiety.

At the end of a long, uneven section of the reef, the formation dropped away to a deeper, sandy lagoon. At the bottom of the lagoon was a collage of wavy, neon shapes lined up in rows; the brightly-coloured lips of the Imum Clams. Mentor Xiphias smiled and hung in the water.

"Here we are then," he said in Eyre's head. "Remember what we talked about in class. The clams will shut when you get there, and you will have to coax them to open. Not all of them do, so find one that will. Then, get that pearl out of there quickly or you'll be stuck in there for an hour! If you do get trapped, let me know. And try to tickle the back of its throat, sometimes that will make it open so you can get out. I will wait up here until all of you have collected your gazae. Good luck!"

Eyre kicked her feet and headed down towards the brightly-coloured clams, pausing halfway to equalise the pressure in her ears. From a distance the lips of the clams looked small, but as she grew nearer she saw their true size—they were as big as a minivan. As she approached the lines of clams those closest to her slowly clamped shut, hiding their beautiful colours. Slowly Eyre spiralled down through the water and approached one of the massive shellfish. The shell itself was thick and heavily ridged, light blue in colour, with massive hinges that locked the two halves together. So, how to get it to open? Eyre mused.

She floated in the water before it, and used some of the Thalassa, the language of the Pinnae, that she had learnt during her time with the Unlit. Her introductory class in the dialects of the Alterworlds had taught her how to politely greet a native of the region.

"Ixan shallana jepo," she ventured, the words rolling awkwardly around in her mind as she tried to communicate telepathically. But obviously she hadn't got the pronunciation right, or else the clam wasn't interested, because it remained resolutely shut. Out of the corner of her eye, she could see that Beatrice, Abby and Nick were each floating in front of a clam, similarly engaged. As she watched, Abby's clam opened and she swam in quickly and emerged with a shining pearl the size of a soccer ball. It had taken her all of 30 seconds! Abby had a natural way of communicating with creatures, so Eyre grudgingly supposed it was to be expected. She turned back to the massive mollusc and pondered. Should she try another one? She looked down the lines of the giant shells, but decided to stay where she was. There was no way to know which of them would offer up their pearl, so she might as well persevere with this one. She was used to recalcitrant creatures, after all. The thought of Ischyros teased an idea out, as she remembered back to the day the old horse had cried. Music had broken through his crusty armour somehow, so perhaps a song might work? After a moment, she sang in her head the second verse of the song she had sung when the world of Lightworking was just new to her, when the Zyx had attacked and it all seemed so overwhelming. It seemed appropriate now too, with the responsibility and secrecy of her mission weighing her down. But she had to have hope, and she had to keep trying. Communicating with the clam was one small piece in the complex mosaic she was part of, and she wanted to succeed.

> *"So don't give up, and don't despair,*
> *though times ahead be troubled.*
> *The Light will guide us over there*
> *till we rebuild the rubble.*
> *Our spirit will soar high above*
> *whatever foul wind rises.*
> *And I will wait for you, my love,*
> *till the Aura once more guides us."*

The haunting melody of the well-loved song wove through her mind, and as she reached the last lines of the verse, the clam opened a fraction. Enough for the vibrant colours of its lips to be exposed, but not enough to reach inside. Stumped, she looked over at Beatrice and Nick. To her surprise, Nick had a pearl and was waiting with Abby, and Beatrice was disappearing inside a shell with neon purple and orange lips. Eyre was last again! Just once in these tests, could she ever be first? Or at least just not last! Especially *this* year, when she knew that Beatrice and Abby would be delighted to see her struggle. But she tamped down her frustration. It wasn't going to help. Studying the sky-blue lips of the clam, which were speckled with yellow spots, she decided to try something else.

She slowly swam downwards with her hand outstretched. The clam flinched and shut a bit, but to her relief, not all the way. Very gently she ran her hand along the soft muscular tissue, stroking the clam as she would a beloved pet.

"You are very beautiful," she said in her mind. "Thank you for trusting me. I trust you too, and I will show you that by putting my hand inside.

You are so strong, you can trap me if you decide to. But, if you let me, I will take the priceless jewel you have created, and I will treasure it for the rest of my life. If you don't want me to take your precious pearl, please shut now and I will try someone else."

She trailed her fingers delicately over the beautiful blue lips, expecting them to jam shut. When they didn't, she slid her hand into the clam and waited. After a moment, the water swirled around her and the heavy halves of the shell eased slowly open until the space was large enough to fit a person inside. Not wasting a moment, she kicked to the bottom of the clam, and picked up the pearl that nestled at its base. It was smooth and heavy, but she didn't linger. Careful not to knock the sides of the massive shellfish, she swam quickly back out. Holding the pearl carefully, she bowed to the clam.

"Shefama ali," she said in Thalassa. *Thank you for this honour.*

Swirling away from the giant creature, she kicked over to join her friends, as the feeling that she had resolutely kept out of her mind while she communicated with the clam—disappointment—blossomed. For the pearl she had plucked from the clam was not white, but almost black. It was a sort of dark green colour with the sheen of peacock feathers, the colour of an oil slick with the sun on it. Was it damaged, or rotten? Whatever the answer to that, she couldn't go and get another. This was it.

The others looked curiously at her pearl as they all kicked up towards Mentor Xiphias. But far from being dismayed, his eyes widened when he saw what Eyre held.

"A black Imum!" he exclaimed in Eyre's mind, running his hands down the sides of the huge pearl. "Very rare and much prized. You are very fortunate."

Beatrice rolled her eyes and Abby looked away, although after a moment Nick came over to have a quick look. Irritated, Eyre was glad they'd found the gazae. The sooner this expedition was over the better.

Just then, something massive moved by them, flashing through the shadowy water just out of sight. The Mentor snapped his head around and tilted it, as if listening. After a moment, his eyes darkened with dread and Eyre's head exploded as he shouted in their minds. "HIDE! Down in the shell beds! Hurry!"

With the thought of Strigis hammering in her memory, Eyre didn't need a second order. She kicked violently, flying through the water back down to the Imum clams. She had almost made it to the sand when something crashed into her and she was sent tumbling through the water. She lost her carousel breathing and took a deep breath of water. Panicking, unable to see as she choked violently, she desperately called out.

"What is it? *Where* is it?"

"A *Nodolagem*!" Nick shouted. "It's at the back of the beds. Get down! *Get down!*"

Eyre forced herself to breathe and opened her eyes. In horror, she saw a monstrous dark shape bearing down on her, and she froze.

But a flash of iridescence streaked through the water and crossed between her and the Nodolagem, stopping just out of reach. The huge dinosaur-like creature turned, diverted, to pursue the enticing lure.

"Mentor Xiphias!" Eyre called desperately as she realised the rainbow streak was her lecturer, leading the ferocious predator away from her.

"Get back to your clam!" he shouted. "Get inside and wait!"

The students needed no more instructions: they shot to the bottom of the sea and swam with panicky movements to the clam they had taken their pearl from. As if waiting for them, the clams were still open, and the huge molluscs let each student swim inside, still carrying their pearls. Then they snapped shut; an armoured fortress that even the power of the Nodolagem couldn't breach.

Inside, Eyre struggled to regain her breathing. Terror had blown her technique apart, and once she'd swallowed some water, it was difficult to regain the rhythm. But she was safe in the Imum clam, and after a moment she got herself back in control. The inside of the shellfish was adorned with the same pattern as the lips—sky-blue with yellow dots that glowed with a golden light, illuminating the inside. It was peaceful and Eyre calmed down, although she was still filled with fear for her lecturer. She just had to hope that he was okay.

"Thank you for protecting me," she said to the clam, in English, because for the moment all her Thalassa had deserted her.

"Ali Eem," a voice rumbled in her head. *Honour mine.*

"Can anyone see the Mentor?" Beatrice's voice.

"Should we go and help him?" Nick.

"I hope he's okay," Abby said.

And then, miraculously, the Mentor spoke. "It's gone for now, but we need to get back to the Zepp quickly. Ask your clam to open, and tickle the back of the muscle. Don't panic, but we need to *move!*"

"I need to go," Eyre said, stroking the tissue at the base of the shell. "Can you let me out?"

After a moment, the great shell opened by degrees, as if checking for danger. Indeed, the many photoreceptor eyes probably had a very good idea of whether it was safe or not—the shell was ready to slam shut at any movement. Eyre looked out tentatively, and when the clam was open wide enough she left its shelter, kicking wildly up towards Xiphias with the black pearl held tightly in her arms.

"Shr-Aka!" she called telepathically to the clam as she used the current technique to propel herself upwards. *Thank you!*

The others arrived at the same time as Eyre, and they all swam as hard as they could towards the Zepp. Mentor Xiphias followed behind, his eyes searching the water for any sign of the fearsome beast.

"*Quickly!*" An urgent hand movement from Xiphias made the fear thud inside Eyre again as she realised the creature was back.

They thrust desperately into the hangar opening just as the dark shape swooped around towards them. But it couldn't fit inside the opening, so it cruised past, one monstrous eye turned in to look at them. Following the others, Eyre blasted up into the Zepp so hard she nearly hit the ceiling, and landed with a bouncing thump on her rear end. Shaking, and with her teeth chattering, she decided that a sailor's life was definitely *not* for her.

# CHAPTER FIFTY-THREE

LORD CLAREMBOUT AND GEGENEES took the heavy pearls and carefully stowed the glowing treasures in the storage locker as the students dried themselves off with a blast of Viq. Then Sir Philius looked at Eyre and pulled out the bag containing the Angelite and Bloodstone.

"It's time," he said. Beatrice paused and stood up, her towel dangling from her hand.

"What's time?" she asked. Abby and Nick stopped too and all three looked curiously at Lord Clarembout as he pulled the Angelite from the bag. He replied after a short silence.

"Eyre has an additional task to perform, and we will be continuing our journey for a while. I ask that you not question this mission, but please be assured that it is critical to the Lightworkers—indeed—to the Overworld itself."

Completely baffled, all three students looked from Sir Philius to Eyre and then back again.

Beatrice shook her head slowly. "Yes, sir, but I don't get it."

Abby looked annoyed. "More secrets, Eyre? What a surprise," she snapped.

"Well, if anyone was talking to me, I might have been able to explain," Eyre retorted. She'd finally had enough.

Nick just went and sat down, looking a bit awkward. But no one said anything else and Eyre ignored them. She stood up furiously. Get this over with and get back home.

Handing the Angelite to Eyre, Lord Clarembout continued. "Mentor Xiphias will go with you. If the Light wills, you will make contact, and we will understand what is to be done next." He put a fatherly hand on Eyre's shoulder and his brown eyes were gentle. "Whatever you achieve Eyre, we know it will be your best."

Ignoring the others, Eyre focused her Viq hard and created a Bullio bubble in the air. When she was sure it was going to hold, she pushed the Angelite crystal into the centre of the bubble. Then, nodding to Xiphias, she jumped into the water with the Bullio trailing behind her. Mentor Xiphias dove in behind her and they both swam under the Zepp towards the hangar opening.

Mentor Xiphias spoke in Eyre's head. "You could try to contact the Sea Crone anywhere under the water," he said, "but there is a crystal grotto not far from here that is particularly sensitive to psychic waves. Follow me; we have to travel across to the reef and it's just around the corner."

Eyre swam as best as she could behind the Mentor, focusing hard to maintain her Bullio bubble. It was imperative the Angelite did not get wet, because all of its psychic properties would disappear if the crystal reverted to gypsum.

They swam from the hangar opening out into the open sea, and Eyre felt vulnerable as they headed towards the reef. This deep channel was very exposed, and predators of all sorts would be cruising around, including the terrible Nodolagem, which could still be lurking nearby. A jumpy feeling spiralled through her stomach and she kicked harder, trying to keep up as Mentor Xiphias glided effortlessly through the water. All the time she expected some awful creature to come hurtling from the shadows to grab her. The tri-merit technique and holding the Bullio formation was exhausting, and she could feel her mind beginning to quake.

But finally they reached the reef, and the shelter that the overhanging coral formations provided. Edging along under the jutting shelves, Eyre followed Xiphias closely until they eventually rounded the corner to see a gleaming crystal cave, formed entirely of Azurite, Amethyst and Iolite. The blue and purple hues of the three crystals blended together in a soft violet glow, and Eyre felt a wave of peace wash over her. Her mind calmed and she felt stronger as they entered the cave. The Mentor indicated for her to sit on a cluster of Amethyst and he waited patiently as Eyre floated down.

Settling herself, she tried to breathe calmly. She knew what she had to do, but she was very uncertain that she could achieve it. She shut her eyes and focused her Viq on the Angelite, trying to create a psychic flow between the stone and her mind. "Ancient One," she called, "would you talk with me?"

Over and over she breathed the words through her mind, as she softly focused, drawing in the energy of the violet crystals that surrounded her.

"Ancient One, speak to me... speak to me..."

Eyre's head was throbbing with the effort of her concentration, and she felt a stirring despair. Nothing was happening; perhaps this was the end of the road.

But then, the water in the cave, previously so still and clear, started to move around the edges of the cavern, until a small whirlpool swirled around them. A rolling whisper of voices echoed through her head like a roundelay, as a multitude of ghosts stepped through the open psychic door.

"I'm here..."

"Can you find me?"

"Help me. . !"

"Where am I?" they whispered in layers, trailing through her mind.

And then one voice spoke stronger, cutting above the cacophony with a sound like sandpaper. "Are you worthy?"

Eyre focused on that one voice. "No, I am not. But I come in good faith. Can you help me?"

The water moved faster, causing small eddies to appear amongst the crystals. A hovering form appeared before her, a vision of a bent old crone who seemed as ancient as the earth itself.

"*The illegitimate girl so high, high, not low,*" the old woman croaked. "You have come after these many decades. What do you ask of me?" *Illegitimate?* Eyre was shocked. What did she mean? But she carried on bravely.

"Wisdom and assistance, Great One."

The Old Crone looked crafty. "A gift for me?"

"We offer a small token, indeed," Eyre replied.

"I will grant you admittance," the bent dark form announced. "If you find the Oracle's cave."

The vision expanded so that Eyre could see the old woman was sitting on banks of white sand, in a large, shadowed cave. A pool of azure water lapped at her feet, and the walls were constructed from shining rainbows of shell. She searched desperately in the vision for a clue that might help her to identify the cave, but her mind was exhausted, and she could feel her Viq start to wobble. Then, like a scaffold collapsing, her control shattered and the Bullio bubble broke. The Angelite was engulfed in water and the vision snapped out.

Eyre slumped against the amethyst crystals, totally exhausted, and with an overwhelming feeling that she had failed. She could barely open her eyes as the Mentor spoke.

"Did you see anything?" he asked.

"I did," Eyre answered, her eyes downcast, "but I'm not sure that it will be helpful."

"Well, let's get back to the Zepp," Xiphias said. "We'll work it out there."

Leaving the Angelite to fully turn to gypsum on the bottom of the cave, they headed out into the deep water and back to the Zepp.

# CHAPTER FIFTY-FOUR

LORD CLAREMBOUT LISTENED CAREFULLY as Eyre recounted her vision.

"So, we need to find the Oracle's cave," she finished, "but the Sea Crone didn't give me any directions. I couldn't hold the vision long enough to ask her where it is—I'm sorry, I just wasn't strong enough." She left out the reference to the illegitimate girl; she was sure that Abby would *love* that bit.

As for the other students, Beatrice, Abby and Nick were trying not to look intrigued, but Eyre knew they were paying close attention.

Mentor Xiphias was focused too. "Can you describe it?"

Eyre shook her head in frustration. "It was just a cave—a big one, with a sand bank, and not flooded with water—well, there was actually a grotto there, with bright blue water."

The Mentor concentrated hard, musing. "An underwater cave then, close to the surface. Only a tunnel would access that sort of formation. Was there anything else you saw? Any detail?"

The memory came back to Eyre. "Oh yes—the walls," she added thoughtfully, "they were made from sheets of an unusual shimmering shell, sort of like a peacock's tail."

The Mentor's expression cleared. "Reef Paua!" he said. "I know where it must be! We are most fortunate—there is only one such area of shell in Aqua, at the end of the Reefs of Gnil-Wor."

Eyre noticed the flood of relief on Lord Clarembout's face and she realised that he had been as worried as she was. They weren't done yet—another clue, another step forward.

Mentor Xiphias didn't need to discuss anything. He dived into the water and quickly unhitched the ropes attaching the Zepp to the wall. A few minutes later he was back in the pilot's seat and reversing out, as everyone took their seats and buckled up.

Xiphias turned the Zepp around and headed forwards, propelling the submersible through the deep channel to the edge of the reef. Then, he hung tight to the perimeter and skirted around the shelves of coral.

They travelled in silence. Obviously all three of her ex-friends had taken Abby's comment about secrets to heart—none of them would look at Eyre. They were angry and hurt because she hadn't confided in them. Eyre's heart was sore, but she looked stubbornly out of the window, determined not to show it. Last year she'd had a sound lesson in keeping faith when times were tough, but she had to admit she was finding it a bit hard to maintain that attitude after the events of this year. She sighed silently and shut her eyes. Only the chug of the Zepp's motor sounded through the cabin as each occupant sat deep in thought.

Finally, the Zepp slowed as the Mentor changed gears and brought the craft to a stop beside a large outcrop of vermillion coral speared by emerald shards of crystal. As the Zepp rocked in the water, Xiphias came back to talk with them.

"This is as close as I can estimate. Around here, the Reef Paua grows in huge beds, so I am guessing that the cave will be nearby." His eyes clouded. "If you cannot find it here, then I am afraid I do not have any other idea where it could be."

Lord Clarembout stood. "So you think we need to search the reef for a cave entrance?"

"Yes," Xiphias replied. "Around here there are many caves and tunnels, and I hope that the Oracle has chosen one of them. I will search with you, once I tether the Zepp." He disappeared into the water, and Gegenees stood up. Obviously he was coming too.

"Right, everyone," Lord Clarembout began, then stopped to wait as Xiphias returned. "We will enter the water and search for the tunnel. In pairs please: Beatrice and Abby; Nick and Eyre." At least she wasn't with Beatrice or Abby, Eyre thought, but she felt dismal at Nick's resigned face. Were these people *ever* actually her friends? Their continual rejection felt like death by a thousand cuts.

"Mentor Xiphias will assist us in trying to locate the cave. If we are fortunate enough to find it, my good friend Xiphias will then pilot the Zepp back home, as we will have no further use for it. He will also ensure that the gazae gets safely back. Should we need to travel, I will teleport you, and we will use the prohemium to return to the Academy when we are ready. Any questions?" Sir Philius looked around at the wooden faces. "Okay, well, get your gear on and when everyone is ready, we will depart."

A few minutes later they were ready, and one by one they jumped into the warmer water by the reef. The Mentor, who was so much faster than the rest of them, headed off at a blinding speed, searching the edge of the coral banks, and he soon disappeared out of sight.

Eyre took a cautious breath and relaxed when she realised her carousel breathing was working. The reef stretched out either side of the Zepp, and below, on the sandy verges at the bottom of the incline, Eyre could see clumps and nests of black shining shells the size of tennis racquets. Neon-blue weed clung to the sides of the shells and in the ones that were open, she could just see a gleam of the rainbow lustre she had seen on the walls of the Oracle's cave. The Mentor had been correct about that—so at least they were on the right track.

Breaking off, they started searching up and down the steep faces of the reef, Beatrice, Abby and Gegenees going left of the Zepp, and Lord Clarembout, Eyre and Nick going right.

Eyre quickly found a person-sized tunnel that seemed promising and she drifted into it to investigate. But a massive, sharp-toothed, cross-faced creature that filled the entire passage emerged from the gloom and made her back-pedal furiously. As she lurched backwards a second head appeared, striking towards her in displeasure. *A Javani Eel*! Patterned in neon-blue and orange stripes, with two large and angry heads, it was an aggressive denizen of the coral reefs, and neither head seemed happy to meet her! Not venomous, but it could inflict a nasty bite, so she reversed out as fast as she could.

Once she got out, she noticed Nick not far from her, struggling madly with his head down a hole. She swam over quickly, and saw that he was stuck—a branch of coral had hooked his uniform and he couldn't reverse out. Eyre unhooked his shirt and released him.

"Thanks, Eyre," he said shortly. They looked at each other for a moment and then began searching the reef again.

Eyre was moving beneath a flat, fan-like formation of crystals and coral, when a strange, haunting melody started to coil through her mind. Poignant and heartbreaking, she heard voices rising mournfully in song. She looked over at Nick and saw that he could hear it too. There was a strange intimacy in the song, an urgency that filled Eyre with a sense that she had to *do* something. That she had to find the source of the melancholy calls. Drifting from the reef-face, she headed out to deeper water, with Nick not far behind. Her mind was blank, but filled with the sound of desolate voices that drew her further outwards and down. Beatrice was floating just behind them, and Lord Clarembout was frozen in place, battling some unseen force. Ahead of her she saw Gegenees, spiralling deeper into the murky depths, drawn by the mysterious singing.

Then a voice shattered the music inside her head. "NO!" cried Abby, shooting past them towards Gegenees, kicking her feet hard until she reached him. "Wake up Gegenees!" The gigantic creature stopped and hung motionless in the water for a moment. Eyre shook her head, ridding it of the cottonwool that seemed to have clogged her rational thought a moment ago. She looked down at the fathomless sea below her and was horrified. The Scopuli! If Abby hadn't resisted the call of the music, they would all have been lured down to their deaths. Despite herself, Eyre felt grateful for Abby's strength of mind. Something had held tight in her and saved them all.

They moved back to the face of the rocks and continued searching with increased determination. Already an hour had passed with no luck, and they were reaching the edges of the Reef Paua beds. If they didn't find the tunnel here, they would have to give up.

And then Mentor Xiphias appeared, shooting through the water towards them in a graceful swirl. "I've found it!" he called. "Come with me!"

Regrouping, they followed the Mentor far along the edge of the reef until the Reef Paua beds had diminished to just a few shells. At the bottom of the face of the reef, a dark hole gaped, revealing a tunnel a metre and a half high that curled upwards and out of sight.

"I've been through it and had a look," Mentor Xiphias said. "The walls inside are lined with Reef Paua. I'm sure this is it!"

Lord Clarembout examined the aperture, his feet floating above him in the water as his robes twirled around like ribbon dancers. Holding on to the entrance with one large hand, he spoke to them all.

"I think we must assume this is our destination," he said. "If it is not here, we must return home and try again some other time. Thank you Mentor Xiphias for being our guide, and for helping us to locate the cave. I think it is time for you to take the Zepp back with the gazae, and we will carry on from here. Students, please thank the Mentor for his care and assistance."

The four of them called out their gratitude and goodbyes to Mentor Xiphias as he headed back to the Zepp and he raised a hand in farewell.

"The Light be with you," he said as he disappeared out of sight.

# CHAPTER FIFTY-FIVE

LORD CLAREMBOUT LED THE way and Gegenees brought up the rear while the students straggled in between. The tunnel was dark and as Eyre's shoulders brushed up against the sides of the coral she felt her breath catch. Imagine being trapped down here! She shuddered and pushed forward, anxious to get out of this tight space.

Eventually the twisting shaft broadened a little and light started to filter through, gradually turning the blackness ahead into a cerulean blue. With a sigh of relief, Eyre left the confines of the passage and kicked hard through the water to the crystal-clear shallows. Finally, she broke the surface and sat beside Beatrice on the bone-white sand, breathing the air in deeply as Nick and Abby surfaced behind her.

The cave was filled with a kaleidoscope of light from the paua shell that lined the walls, a moving glow that painted the shadows with colour. It was serene and yet eerie, a silent dance of rainbows.

As Gegenees walked out of the water, the last out, a rasping voice spoke to them.

"You are to remain there. The girl comes alone."

Eyre could feel Beatrice, Abby and Nick's eyes boring into her back as she took the waterproof bag from Lord Clarembout and moved cautiously towards something that sat hidden behind a rocky outcrop.

A shapeless form sat hunched on a rock as if in pain, its face shrouded by a black cloak. As Eyre approached, the hood fell back to reveal a lined face the colour and texture of the bark of a redwood tree; burned and craggy, a contoured landscape of creases. But most disturbing was the single eye in the middle of the ancient woman's forehead. Its colour changed in beautiful and mesmerising whorls of green and blue, but Eyre felt extremely unsettled as it regarded her in an unblinking stare. The old crone shifted her humped back awkwardly and lifted her arm.

"You venture to the Oracle's cave," she rasped, holding out a clawed hand to Eyre. The nails were long and discoloured and Eyre had to repress a shudder. "What bring you for me?"

Eyre hurried to open the bag and pulled out the gleaming Bloodstone. Kneeling, she held it out.

"Bloodstone, Great One," she whispered. Her voice echoed around the cave. *Great One... Great One... Great One...*

The crone examined the stone minutely, holding it up to her single eye. Finally, she seemed satisfied.

"Bloodstone. Heliotrope, the Sun Stone. With the gift of healing and noble sacrifice. I wonder whether you will make the ultimate sacrifice. How far will you go?"

Her eye spiralled as she looked outwards, contemplating this question as if the answer were written in the walls of the cave. Then she turned her craggy face to Eyre. "How got you the old lizard to part with this?" she croaked. "He is not one to give away his treasures."

"A challenge, my sage," Eyre replied.

The old woman studied Eyre and cackled shrilly and slapped her leg. "You bested the Wurm? That is fine to hear. How he would have hated that!"

Eyre nodded, thinking, *that's* an understatement, but she said nothing more and waited.

"You require my assistance, like your mother and father before you," said the crone, watching Eyre carefully. Eyre kept her face impassive. So, her parents had been here too! Or *were* they her parents? The Sea Crone's declaration about Eyre being an illegitimate girl had rattled her to her very core. But she just nodded again. There was a long silence as the crone stared at her, deciding. Eyre was aware that everyone else in the canyon was staring too; she could feel the tension in the background.

"Well, I am not fond of the other worlds," the Oracle said, as if she had something nasty in her mouth, "but I am even less impressed by the Gothak. So, I will help you. What do you need?"

Eyre realised she had been holding her breath, waiting for the crone's judgement, and she exhaled softly in relief.

"It is said that you have information about restoring the Aura," she said deferentially, "and we are searching for the Isar."

The eye in the crone's forehead grew stormy. "That would be *two* favours," she croaked. "I'd be needing two gifts then!"

Eyre was trying to be respectful, but her nerves were on edge. Why wouldn't the acerbic old witch just help them? Eyre was tired, cold and sick of it. *Another* gift? Remembering her time with Aowx made her clench her teeth. She wasn't about to go back for another prized stone.

"Technically," she snapped, before she could help herself, "it's just one, since finding the Isar is part of restoring the Aura."

There was a screech of rage and the hunched figure jumped up, pointing at Eyre with a quivering, gnarled finger.

"Do not speak back to me!" the old woman snarled. "You are but a speckle of light on my foot!" From the corner of her eye Eyre could see Lord Clarembout lurching forwards, but he was not quick enough. A bolt of light zagged out from the bony finger and a deafening clap of thunder reverberated through the cave. But Eyre felt her Viq rising, and a calmness descend. She raised her hands and formed a shield without thinking, and the lightning ricocheted into the ceiling.

Screeching in rage, the Sea Crone hurled bolt after sizzling bolt at Eyre, but her shield held. She was aware of the others ducking for cover as the burning missiles bounced all around the cavern, but she held the gaze of the infuriated creature, determined to show no fear, until finally the old crone lowered her hand.

Eyre bent her head. "I apologise for my discourteous speech," she said. "Sometimes I need to bite my tongue." Lord Clarembout uneasily moved back again as the Sea Crone stared at Eyre, her twirling eye blinking fast. Finally, she huffed a scratchy laugh.

"Well, courage, you have," she said. "And quick to move. This you'll needing for the trials ahead. I see a terrible darkness surrounding you, but will you triumph?" Closing her fearsome eye, she seemed to fall into a trance, chanting words that Eyre couldn't understand. They echoed through the chamber in a spine-tingling incantation, and the water in the grotto leapt and boiled. Then the crone opened her eye suddenly and threw the Bloodstone in. Immediately the water turned blood-red and a blinding golden light filled the cavern.

The old crone looked outwards, seeming to be elsewhere, unseeing in this world as she looked deep into another. Words croaked out from her cracked lips.

*When all seems forsaken*
*And the darkness awakens*
*To dispel chaos and peril*
*Find the Golden Beryl*
*And at 7.17*
*When the colour is green*

*Free the last treasure of Pandora*
*From the diapaused Aura*

She fell silent again, and then seemed to focus once more on Eyre. The golden light subsided and Eyre was left feeling frustrated and annoyed. More puzzles? What did that mean? Why couldn't the old crone just speak so she understood? And there was no clue to where the Isar was in that jumble of words.

But she'd learned her lesson, so she lowered her head again. "Thank you for the wisdom in your words, Great Oracle," she said. "We are grateful for this gift."

With a shrill cackle and explosion of smoke, the Sea Crone disappeared. Eyre was still feeling deflated, so it took a moment for her to register what she was seeing. *The Isar!* It had been hidden under a rock behind the Sea Crone the whole time and now she could see it, glowing a brilliant silver from the crevice.

She turned to Lord Clarembout, so excited she could hardly get the words out. "Sir Philius! The Isar!" Beatrice, Abby and Nick looked confused, scanning the cave for any sight of the shining bar, but of course they couldn't see it. It wasn't until Eyre raced forward to pick it up that the light from the mystical bar shone brightly for them to see. As Eyre walked towards them, she thought that if Beatrice's mouth hung open any further, it would touch the sand.

"What... *how...?*" Abby stuttered, staring at the gleaming treasure that Eyre held.

But before Eyre could respond, there was a flash of light and someone stood beside her.

"Dad!" Abby cried in surprise, but her father ignored her, his eyes focused on Eyre and the shining Isar.

"You're an Aether?" he breathed. "But how...? That doesn't make sense—your mother..."

At that moment, Lord Clarembout stepped out from the side of the cave, nonplussed and rubbing his beard. "George? What are you doing here? This is supposed to be a secret mission!"

Using the distraction, Eyre moved the Isar tightly under her arm and performed the prohemium for Terra. The Seam appeared and she dived into it, shutting her eyes at the brightness that surrounded her. She landed in the forest of Terra, deep amongst the aromatic trees. But then a Seam appeared beside a towering Eeb tree and Mr Wilson emerged, his face a mask.

"Eyre," he said softly as he walked towards her, "give me the Isar. You can't outrun me."

But Eyre flipped her hand and performed the prohemium to return to Entis. In a flash she was gone, landing by the moldavite square. But Abby's dad was fast, and he appeared seconds after her, lunging for the Isar. Desperately, Eyre moved her wrists in the prohemium for Aqua, and she was back in the depths of the subterranean cave. Beatrice, Abby and Nick were still frozen in place, their faces shocked and uncomprehending as Mr Wilson materialised beside Eyre. He lurched towards Eyre, but Gegenees put a large hand on Mr Wilson's shoulder.

"It's alright," Gegenees boomed. "We'll take it from here." But before Gegenees could move, Mr Wilson turned and blasted his arm off with a beam of light. Gegenees' eyes glazed and he fell to his knees as blood poured from his destroyed shoulder, then he landed face-down on the sandy verge.

Abby screamed and wailed in a voice filled with pain, "*Dad?!*" She raced over to Gegenees and skidded down beside him, her hands trying to hold back the blood as she looked up at her father with tortured eyes. But then Gegenees moaned and she focused only on him, searing his bloody shoulder shut with a flash of Viq. Speechless, she sprawled back and watched her father with horror.

Mr Wilson punched Eyre in the face and tore the Isar from her hand as she fell backwards on the sand. Eyre gasped in pain, as blood ran down her face, but struggled to her feet, her fists raised as a violent fire rose within her.

Then there was a roar of rage as Lord Clarembout charged in from the side, his Mnae held high.

At the same time, the water in the cave started roiling, and with a dawning horror, Eyre realised that the Zyx had found them. Their black forms cut through the water like rabid stingrays and they exploded upwards in a huge tsunami of water. The cave was filled with the foul creatures as Mr Wilson's Mnae appeared in his hand, summoned to do battle of the worst kind. He faced Lord Clarembout with the Isar in his other hand, his eyes filled with a dead menace.

"Bring it on then, Philius," he said in a low voice, circling around the huge warrior.

Then, from the darkness of the cave, a Gothak emerged, and another, creeping towards them. George Wilson threw the Isar to one of the Gothak and the sinister creature disappeared in a flash.

"Noooo!" cried Eyre in despair, running towards the other Gothak in the cave. A terrible commotion ensued as Lord Clarembout clashed his shining weapon against Mr Wilson's blade, a deafening sound as sparks flew from the lethal edges of the weapons.

The Gothak seized Eyre, his hands burning her flesh like acid.

"Good," it breathed, "I will enjoy this." But Eyre's friends finally reacted and there was a blinding light as Beatrice summoned her staff.

She stepped forward and sent a searing flame from the emerald glowing at the top of the long, polished branch. Beatrice had become quite accomplished at the skill in recent months and she didn't miss—the Gothak holding Eyre disappeared in a black roil of soot. Eyre staggered to the side of the cave, keeping her back to the wall, and focused her Viq hard as the Zyx circled above them. In a second Florence appeared, and in another, her hand held her beloved Vulture Killer, the bow that Rachis had given her. Florence screeched in fury, as, without any hesitation, she did what she was trained for: diving and swooping to attack the hideous dark shapes with her razor-sharp beak and claws. And Eyre nocked arrow after arrow, sending them seamlessly into the pulsating mass of Strigis. The creatures screamed in pain as Florence's strong talons pierced their leathery skin and Eyre's unerring arrows seared through them, and the bodies thudded to the ground. But a movement from the shadows signalled that more Gothak had arrived, the dead-eyed and pallid-skinned army pouring in from the darkness. They were accompanied by innumerable grotesque Characs, their scaly, lamprey-like mouths dripping drool from filthy teeth. The Gothak approached with their eerie sideways-forwards, joint-cracking movements as the horrible Characs lumbered towards the hopelessly outnumbered Lightworkers like they were tonight's dinner.

Abby scrambled to her feet and there was a faint *whack* as her staff appeared in her hand. She scrubbed at her eyes as she ran over to join Beatrice, and then Nick stepped up too. The yellow sapphire at the top of Abby's staff glowed a brilliant gold, and Nick's ruby burned like fire as they stood shoulder to shoulder with Beatrice and blasted the Gothak and Characs that streamed from the bowels of the cave, ducking to dodge the burning atra that the Gothak hurled towards them. The three friends cut down dozens of the evil creatures as they lurched out of the darkness, but the Dark forces were relentless, and slowly the students were forced to retreat to the edge of the water. The air was filled with smoke and fire from the molten atra, and the heat was unbearable.

Despite the valiant efforts of the Lightworkers, they were vastly outnumbered and it seemed it would only be a matter of time before the swarm overwhelmed them. Eyre nocked another arrow desperately and sent it flying, sweat pouring off her as she backed towards the waterline. The heat in the cave was unbearable as the group battled the grotesque creatures, and it seemed their fight would soon be lost. A Gothak broke through and leapt towards Eyre, its black eyes triumphant as it lunged for her neck.

But suddenly the water behind them began to swirl violently in huge waves and a fearsome wind howled around the cavern. Just as the Gothak's long fingers wrapped around Eyre's throat, a Javani eel exploded from the water and one of its ferocious heads sliced through the Gothak's neck. The Gothak's body slumped to the ground and disappeared in an oily black stench. Eyre turned in shock, to see creatures of all kinds streaming from the boiling water as an enraged voice filled the cavern. The rasping tones of the Sea Crone reverberated from the paua shell walls.

"You dare to bring your fight to my domain?" she hissed in a voice that shredded Eyre's ears. "Well, you shall pay the price!" There was a clap of thunder and at once, the creatures of the sea lurched from the water and began to attack the Gothak and the Strigis. Their unearthly screams set Eyre's hair on end as she returned to the fight. Eerie Scopuli lifted themselves from the water and grabbed onto the Gothak, then dragged them into the water and disappeared. Huge crab-like creatures lifted their six snapping claws to chop the Zyx in half, and the dead bodies rained down around them. Any Gothak or Charac that ventured too close to the water was cut in two by the sharp teeth of Razor fish the size of a man. The fight was more even now, and Eyre and her friends regained some lost ground. But she was tiring, and there seemed to be an endless vortex of foul creatures streaming into the cavern. A Zyx slashed her arm deeply and she fell to her knees, her arm dangling and dripping blood. She sent Vulture Killer back and seized the Kulbeda from her belt.

Then she staggered to her feet, her eyes on fire. "COME ON, THEN!" she howled as blood dripped from her nose and her arm. With eyes like a mad creature, she stepped into the fray and swung the lethal blade around her. The white sand became red with the blood of creatures of all kinds and the air was rent by screeches and the smell of smoke.

Then there was a loud scream and Mr Wilson dropped his Mnae. He held his stomach as a river of blood cascaded onto the sand, and he looked down in surprise. But his eyes were already losing focus. Lord Clarembout, sweating and distressed, roared in pain and rage.

"WHY, George? How could you do this?" He looked like he had been mortally wounded himself as he dropped his hand with the Mnae and fell on his knees beside Mr Wilson, ignoring the seething creatures around him.

But it was almost over, and the only words Mr Wilson spoke were to Abby. His eyes begged forgiveness as she slid on her knees to hold him, her face slashed with hot tears.

"DAD?"

A strange gurgling choked up from Mr Wilson's throat as he looked at her.

"Sorry, my girl," he said as he fell backwards.

The Gothak took advantage of the lull and surged forward as Beatrice, Nick and Eyre fought back furiously. More sea creatures emerged from the water, and the cavern became the bowels of hell: searingly hot, the foul stench of blood and entrails in the air and the deafening screeches of multitudes of unholy creatures. All the while the water seethed and roiled, and flashes of searing light clashed with burning atra and rebounded from the walls. It was hard to breathe through the black smoke and Eyre felt her strength failing. Spots swam before her eyes as she gasped for breath and struck at another Strigis.

"The prohemium!" thundered Lord Clarembout. "By the Light, get out of here!" He waved his hands in the air, then grabbed Gegenees in a bear hug.

With a blinding flash the Seam appeared and the group flung themselves through, Florence firing like a bullet behind them. A moment later they landed in a tangle on the moldavite square. Staggering to their feet, silenced by distress, they could only look at each other. Eyre was in agony—she was black with soot, and her arms were striped with wounds from the clawed fingers of the Gothak. The tops of her shoulders were burnt where the Gothak had grabbed her, and her left arm was deeply cut by the talons of the Zyx. But most of all, a terrible feeling of failure seared her soul. She had lost the Isar!

Lord Clarembout stood to the side in silence, smoke coiling up from his clothes. Beatrice, Abby—covered in her father's blood—and Nick looked at Eyre, then slowly wrapped her in a tight knot of grief. All of them cried desperately as the wind soughed mournfully across the tops of the trees.

# CHAPTER FIFTY-SIX

EYRE, BEATRICE AND NICK trudged towards the Central Administration building. It was two days since they'd returned from Aqua, and Whittaker Ray had asked to meet with them now that they'd had time to rest a little. When they returned, they had gone straight to the Infirmary, where Sister Murphy had quickly administered the anti-venom for the Zyx. Although exhausted and traumatised, none of them were badly wounded, and they had recovered within a day. Indeed, as usual, Eyre had healed almost overnight and the wound from the Zyx was gone. But Abby was still at the Infirmary, too grief-stricken to do anything but sleep and cry. She lay in a room next to the one that Gegenees occupied; he was still unconscious from his terrible injury but was expected to recover.

Gloom followed Eyre like a black lux, bouncing in time with her footsteps and tethered by her overwhelming sense of guilt. Fail-ure! Fail-ure! Fail-ure! The horror of that final day in Aqua would not leave her.

Beatrice and Nick had been greatly apologetic and said they were abjectly sorry for how they had treated her. Eyre had told them that she understood, and she did—no one would ever have believed that of Mr Wilson. But part of her held back, still extremely hurt by their behaviour towards her over the past months. She felt that it might take some time for that wound to heal.

Whittaker Ray stood up as they entered and then waved for them to sit. He pulled up a chair himself and offered them a cup of tea, pouring the steaming cups himself from a bone china teapot. Finally, he sat back and looked at them with troubled blue eyes. His white eyebrows dipped slightly and he put his cup down.

"You have had a shocking time," he said. "I am very sorry. Poor Abby will struggle to make sense of it all, and I know you will help her with that." Nick nodded, and Eyre knew that of all people, he would understand the shame and the pain of having a parent turn to the Dark side. And Mr Wilson was gone, which was going to make it all the harder for Abby to work through.

"Beatrice and Nick, I asked Eyre to keep many secrets this year which were critical for the good of the Lightworkers, and the Overworld. Now, I am going to ask you to do the same. You will have realised that Eyre is an Aether—and you understand now that only an Aether can see the Isars. Eyre is the only Aether left who is old enough to search for the Isars, which is why it is imperative that no one finds out about her, as she would then become a target for the Gothak. Fortunately, this time, the potential for the Dark side to find out about Eyre died with George Wilson—none of the Gothak saw Eyre locate the Isar. We must keep that knowledge to ourselves until we find the Isars in Caelus and Incendium. Next November we will be better prepared—the Gothak had inside information this time and knew where you would be. We will not make the same mistake twice."

*Unless someone else passes on information,* Eyre thought, but said nothing.

"After school finished last year," Whittaker Ray continued, "and after the disaster in Terra, I asked the Mimir to tone down their behaviour towards you, Eyre. Somehow—before any of us—they had already identified you as someone unique. Certainly, you have some inexplicable skills that I can only attribute to you being an Aether born of an Aether. Erratic those skills may be at the moment," Eyre rolled her eyes in agreement, "but certainly powerful, and well—the staff really haven't known what to make of it all." Whittaker Ray shook his head and after a moment continued. "We have all agreed to wait and see—no doubt those skills will evolve as they're meant to.

"The Mimir are protective of you, Eyre, but I didn't want them to call attention to you with the Gothak lurking about, and the Mimir's behaviour was certainly causing problems." Beatrice gave an ironic snort. *That* was an understatement. Prostrate forms, idolising looks and battalions forming in defence—not exactly conduct that would pass under the radar. But this time Eyre didn't find Beatrice's chagrin quite as amusing as she had in the past; she'd had enough attitude from Beatrice in the past year. Eyre just lifted her eyebrows and nodded.

"I would like you to fill me in on what happened at the cave," Whittaker Ray said. "I have had a report from Lord Clarembout, but I would like to hear what you saw, particularly you, Eyre. Perhaps you could start, and if there's anything you'd like to add, I'll hear from you after that." He nodded his head at Beatrice and Nick.

Eyre began to speak, recounting her meeting with the Sea Crone. She hesitated a moment and then sighed inwardly. "The Sea Crone said to me I was 'the illegitimate girl so high, high, not low'. I'm sure my parents were married, so I don't understand that." She desperately hoped there was not some horrible family secret about to emerge. But, she supposed, she wouldn't be greatly surprised, given all the mysteries of the past two years.

Whittaker Ray looked thoughtful, then stood and walked to his bookcase where racks of leather-bound, gold stamped hardcovers stood along the shelves. He studied the spines and selected a narrow dark blue book, opening it and reading.

"It sounds familiar," he mused, running his finger down the lines and flipping the pages. "One of the later quatrains, I think..."

"Ah, yes, here it is. Nostradamus, Century X: 84

*The illegitimate girl so high, high, not low,*
*The late return will make the grieved ones contended:*
*The Reconciled One will not be without debates,*
*In employing and losing all his time.*

"But what does it mean?" Eyre asked, her brain hurting from all these puzzles and rhymes.

"Well, 'illegitimate' has more than one meaning and does not only refer to birth out of wedlock. One of them is: 'something that's not in accordance with accepted standards or rules'. It could be said that you, Eyre, born an Aether of an Aether, is not the standard or norm by any means. And 'high, high' indeed you are, with the unusual skills you have demonstrated. So yes, perhaps Nostradamus *was* referring to you in his quatrain.

"As for the rest of it," he looked at it pensively. "I cannot yet decipher the prophesy. No doubt it is important, but the truth can only be revealed by time." He closed the book and returned it to the shelves. "Please carry on, Eyre."

Eyre returned to the story, but when she came to the Sea Crone's prophesy, she stumbled, apologetic. "I, er... ah I'm so sorry... I did try to remember the exact words, but I can't. It was something like—'when all seems lost and darkness, ah... falls?'" she broke off, looking upwards as she tried to remember. It had all been so chaotic. A voice spoke up.

*"When all seems forsaken*
*And the Darkness awakens*
*To dispel chaos and peril*

*Find the Golden Beryl*
*And at 7.17*
*When the colour is green*
*Free the last treasure of Pandora*
*From the diapaused Aura"*

Beatrice recited. At their startled looks she said, "I heard the old crone, and I memorised it."

"Well done, Beatrice," Whittaker Ray said. "This is why you make a formidable team." Beatrice, Nick and Eyre cast awkward looks at each other but said nothing. Whittaker Ray handed a piece of paper and a pen to Beatrice. "I would appreciate if you could write that down before you leave." Beatrice, of course, started to write immediately.

"And then the Strigis arrived," continued Eyre, picking up the story and relating what had happened until they arrived back on campus.

"So, the Gothak have an Isar," Whittaker Ray said softly. "But that doesn't mean we can't get it back. The Mimir are in conference as we speak, discussing strategy. I will confer later with General Gel Lithium Silica and find his recommendation for the best way forward. Thank you, Eyre, for your careful recollection of events. Was there anything else?" Whittaker Ray asked.

Eyre looked thoughtful. "No, but I do have a question. I would like to know what the Gothak are going to do with the Isars if they get them. How does that work?"

Whittaker Ray's face was sombre. "The Isars individually are inert, which is what I believe 'diapaused' refers to in the Sea Crone's prophesy. 'The term means to have been suspended in development, and as Lightworkers believe that the Aura was a living entity, that would actually fit. But although singularly the Isars are powerless, together they contain the greatest force in the Overworld. If the Gothak can get all four Isars to the Underworld, we know that they intend to capture the power by using the Egeo Blackstone."

At their enquiring looks, he continued. "The Egeo Blackstone is a stone of great Dark power and is only used for evil purposes. A Blackstone is found only in the heart of the most malign being of the Underworld, and it is dug out of the heart after that foul creature dies. Our spies tell us that the one they have now came from the heart of a terrible traitor from decades ago."

*The Betrayer*, Eyre thought, but didn't say it aloud. Whittaker Ray sighed as if he could hear her thoughts.

"The Egeo Blackstone sucks the light out of any object that nears it, and once the Isars have been reunited, the Gothak will use the Blackstone to trap the Aura's energy for their own terrible purposes. It would put the whole Overworld at risk if that ever happened."

"I have another question," Nick said, after they had all considered that sobering information. Whittaker Ray nodded.

"Why did you send us in such a small group to Aqua?" Nick asked. "We were sitting ducks for the Gothak."

Whittaker Ray sighed. "We thought that it would be safer, and draw less attention to you, if you travelled as a normal TACI group. If we'd brought in troops, and more guardians, our reasoning was that it would alert the Gothak that something important was happening. At the time we thought the Gothak were unaware of the importance of the Leonids in the Alterworlds. And we still had three Isars to find," he added. "The problem is that only one can be retrieved a year, now that only Eyre can see them—and that's if we're lucky, so we were trying to keep everything very secret."

He shook his head slowly. "We did not realise that George Wilson had informed the Gothak that something was afoot. He was suspicious when Gegenees and Sir Philius accompanied you, but fortunately he did not know Eyre was an Aether, so he has not passed that on. Next year, we will have more protection in place, as your group will now be a focus for the Gothak. They will have figured out we are after the Isars now, that the Leonids are important, and that somehow you are involved. There is no doubt that they will try to get them from us again."

As silence descended in the room, Whittaker Ray turned his cup slowly on its saucer. "I have one more thing to say."

He looked at Eyre. "We owe you an apology for not listening to you when you warned us about George—Mr Wilson. Why he went over to the Dark side, we will probably never know." He hesitated and a line of worry creased his brow a little as he added, "or for how long."

He looked out the window, and watched as a kookaburra swooped down to land on the grass to peck at a grub. "I should have given your words more weight, Eyre and I'm very sorry for what that has brought upon us, and for what you've been through." Eyre nodded and Whittaker Ray stood up.

"You will be leaving tomorrow for the cabins and I will see you back there in due course. Thank you for your bravery and skill—you are all shining examples of what a Lightworker should be."

The students filed out of the room, each with their own thoughts. Whittaker Ray's words had not got rid of her black lux, Eyre noted as they walked back to their rooms. It still swirled above her drearily like a soggy pinata. Professor Vela was still out there, so many puzzles and questions remained, and the task of re-uniting all the Isars seemed further away than ever.

# CHAPTER FIFTY-SEVEN

THAT AFTERNOON, EYRE WALKED with Beatrice and Nick to the Infirmary to visit Abby. She sat up as they entered, her face wan and puffy from tears.

Beatrice raced over to embrace her. "My poor, poor friend!"

Eyre could hear Abby snuffling into Beatrice's shoulder and she was overwhelmed with pity. She knew the pain of losing a parent and although it got easier to live with, it never went away.

Finally, the sobs stopped and Beatrice sat down in a chair by the bed. They all waited as Abby struggled and finally composed herself.

"Thank you for coming," she said in a small voice. Then she looked at Eyre and her mouth drooped. "I was so, so horrible to you Eyre. Will you ever forgive me?" The cornflower eyes were brimming with tears, and at that moment the stone in Eyre's stomach that she had been carrying for months, evaporated as if it were never there. She raced over and gave Abby a big bear hug.

"Don't speak of it again," she said softly. "I have already forgotten."

Abby held her tight. "Thank you, Eyre."

Heavy footsteps sounded from the hallway, and all four students looked up warily. Anything that sounded large was potentially lethal in the world they now occupied, and Nick jumped to his feet.

But the face was familiar as he clomped through the door.

"Gegenees!" Abby cried. "You're okay!" And then she dissolved in tears.

"I'm so sorry!" she wailed as she hid her face in her hand, unable to look at him as her shoulders lowered beneath an intolerable weight.

The massive creature spun around. "I'm minus an appendage, but good as gold," he said, flexing five arms. Then he dropped to one knee and presented Abby with a shining golden medallion. "From the ship of the Argonauts," he said, his warm, brown eyes serious. "The Argonauts in

Ancient Greece were heroic and courageous fighters, as you are. I am only alive because of you; indeed, you saved my life twice, and I am forever indebted to you."

Abby took the medallion and her mouth trembled. And then she completely lost it again as she saw the eagle stamped on the front of the pendant, the age-old symbol of courage. Everyone waited for a few minutes until she finally drew a breath.

"I will try to live up to this," she whispered, "and honour my ancestors."

Gegenees' face softened as he regarded the crumpled, defeated girl, and he rose to his feet, taking her hand in his.

"You need not wear your father's coat," he said slowly. "How you dress in this life is entirely up to you."

Then he bowed deeply and kissed her hand, before leaving the room. Eyre watched the huge form recede down the hall, his wide shoulders almost touching the sides of the corridor. He might have one arm missing now, but he was still as imposing as ever.

Sounds from outside the window drew their attention, and they saw the Zepps rolling through campus along the verge of the bush, dripping weed and water along the track. The other students were back! Sure enough, a chattering, bedraggled mob of students flooded from the moldavite square, heading in straggles for the dormitories. From the energy and laughter in the group, it sounded like their TACI tests had been successful, and Eyre felt a flood of envy wash over her. If only the gazae was all she had to worry about on the expedition! To visit the Alterworlds with only that one task to accomplish!

She turned away from the window. She'd seen Jax, walking easily with Pheria and Zanda and laughing at some story Zanda was telling, and her heart was sore. A feeling of finality struck her: it was definitely time to go back to the cabins.

Beatrice stood up. "We'll let you rest, Abby. I'll pack up your stuff and we'll see you tomorrow."

Nick gave Abby a gentle kiss. "Warrigal has a great saying," he whispered. "'If your eyes are on the sun, you will not see the shadows.' Stay in the sun, Abby, I'll take care of your shadows." He ran his fingers through her golden curls and she managed a wobbly smile.

They bid farewell and left the forlorn, broken girl alone in the room with her brooding thoughts.

The next day was a stampede of departures as the dorms cleared out quickly after breakfast. Flashes of light, Zepps heading to the departure site, suitcases, bags, backpacks, students running around looking for misplaced musical instruments and sporting equipment... the usual pandemonium at the end of the school year.

Eyre folded her last bit of clothing and shoved everything in her bag. She felt none of the excitement that most of the other students had at this time of the year. For them it was the holidays, Christmas, family fun and an endless summer to hang out with friends. This time of the year was always hard for Eyre, as she felt the absence of her parents achingly. And this year there was the added sadness from the death of Abby's dad, and Eyre's own self-reproach at losing the Isar. Struggling to close the zip on her stuffed bag, Eyre felt a very un-holiday-like gloom settle on her shoulders.

She could see that Beatrice was not feeling very jolly either. She'd packed her own gear and was now sorting through Abby's, with none of her usual banter. When the theremin went in without any sort of comment, Eyre realised that Beatrice was also very down in the dumps. It wasn't a good way to start the festive season.

They piled their bags against the wall outside the dormitory and waited for Beatrice's dad to arrive. He'd been delayed by emergency talks with the Determinant Dozen and the Echelon, and they knew that he might be some time yet, so they sat in the shade and waited.

"I'm definitely feeling a bit flat," Eyre said eventually.

Beatrice agreed. "Not much Christmas cheer this season. The summer's going to be a bit of a drag."

"We'll have to help Abby. It's going to be awful for her."

Beatrice nodded and they both stared glumly as another Zepp trundled off the campus.

Then a jovial voice called from above their heads and they looked up in surprise.

"Care to join us?" the Ranger asked. He wore outsized purple aviator glasses and was sitting on his faded black and orange striped carpet, with Nick perched at the rear. Nick had a huge grin on his face as the rug rose up and down in the breeze.

The Ranger snapped his fingers and the girls' luggage disappeared. A delighted smile appeared on Beatrice's face, and with a pang, Eyre realised that the cheeky grin had been missing from her friend's face for many months. Eyre had been so wrapped up in her own troubles, she hadn't seen the pain that her friends were also in.

Needing no more encouragement, Beatrice jumped to her feet and levitated up to the carpet. She clambered on to the threadbare rug and leaned back over the edge. "Come on Eyre, get up here!"

Eyre felt a sudden lightness blossom within her, and she did an impromptu somersault that would make the Unlit proud as she followed Beatrice up to the old carpet. As she flopped onto the striped rug, the Ranger let out a whoop. "Tally ho! To the Infirmary!"

As if Ranger Chrysanthe had pulled on invisible reins, the carpet wheeled around, nearly tossing the three of them off. It was like trying to balance on a floating yoga mat. But Eyre bolted herself to the black and orange stripes with a zap of Viq and she screamed with laughter as the hovering rug shot forward at great speed. Sailing over the dormitories, the carpet transported them in an undulating blur, gliding around corners and through archways, even shooting straight through the Library, to Mrs Abnett's horror. It seemed a long way to go to get to the Infirmary, which was just the next block over from their dorm. But Eyre suspected there was method to the Ranger's madness.

By the time they sailed through the Infirmary window and hovered above Abby's bed, Eyre's hair had turned into a Crone-like tangle. Her cheeks were flushed and her eyes streamed with tears of laughter. Beatrice was in a similar state and she gasped as she leaned over to talk to Abby.

"BTL girl, get yourself up here! You *have* to have a go at this!" Abby's blue eyes were huge in her pale face and Beatrice patted the carpet beside her. "Come on, we can't go without you!"

Abby reached up to the Ranger, who clasped her small hand in his large one. Then he swung her up over the side of the carpet so that she landed in the middle of them all. Beatrice, Abby, Nick and Eyre looked at each other with unexpected glee. They settled in and held on.

"Buckle up, babies!" the Ranger shouted, "The Bumblebee Bus is leaving the station!"

And then, streaking out through the Infirmary window, swerving past buildings and zooming along the wind currents, the Ranger started their riotous journey for home.

**The planet's defenses remain in shards. But will her growing powers be enough to prevent a deadly betrayal?**

The Blue Mountains, Australia. Eyre Lightwood's return to the Academy is stained by trauma. Although she's reconciled with her friends, nothing can erase the tragic finish to the last school year. But even as the third year begins, the young Lightworkers' efforts to restore Earth's protective shield falls under threat with the prophecy of a powerful darkness hiding in plain sight...

With the annual Lighthorse race fast approaching, Eyre and her buddies barely have time to collect themselves when she discovers she's been cruelly entered along with her ancient mount. And knowing the event will only make a fool of them, the plucky girl suspects a traitor among them is plotting her downfall.

Can Eyre comeback with a vengeance and turn the tables on a malicious foe?

Follow the link or the QR code below to grab your copy.

https://thequestfortheaura.com/caelus

# About the Quest for the Aura

Discover more exciting facts about the Quest for the Aura and download a free glossary from R.S. O'Neal's website here:

https://thequestfortheaura.com/

9 780099 544734